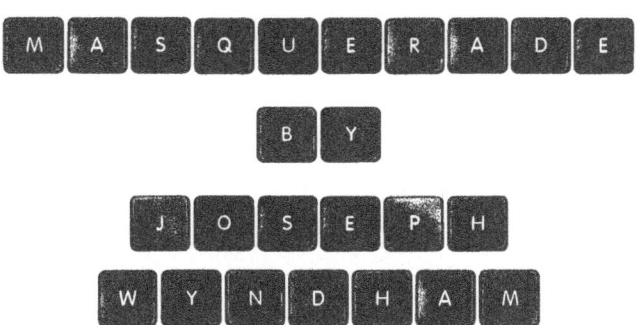

Masquerade

ISBN 9798487976666

© Copyright 2021 Christopher Thomas

Second Edition

All rights reserved. No part of this publication may be reproduced, stored in or introduced into a retrieval system, or transmitted, in any form, or by any means (electronic, mechanical, photocopying, recording or otherwise) without the prior written permission of the publisher. Any person who does any unauthorised act in relation to this publication may be liable to criminal prosecution and civil claims for damages.

This is a work of fiction. All the names, characters, businesses, places, events and incidents in this book are either the product of the author's imagination or used in a fictitious manner. Any resemblance to actual persons, living or dead, or actual events is purely coincidental.

To order more copies of this book or

for information about other books available, please visit:

www.lamplightpress.net

Table of Contents

Chapter 1: A Tentacle Twitched

Chapter 2: Deceptive Disguise

Chapter 3: Greasing the Wheels

Chapter 4: Dark Deeds

Chapter 5: No Little Break

Chapter 6: Puppet Propaganda

Chapter 7: Taking Stock

Chapter 8: Minor Reprisal

Chapter 9: Trojan Horse

Chapter 10: Chameleon

Chapter 11: Kalyptra Genesis

Chapter 12: Recount

Chapter 13: Circularity

Chapter 14: Wages of Sin

Chapter 15: Business and Fratricide

Chapter 16: Spectre of a Thief

Chapter 17: Shadow Stalker

Chapter 18: Network Exposé

Chapter 19: The Trappist

Chapter 20: Chasing Shadows

Chapter 21: Prima Facie

Chapter 22: Divided Loyalty

Chapter 23: Gittins Responds

Chapter 24: Resilience

Chapter 25: The Brief

Chapter 26: Choppy Waters

Chapter 27: Road to Redemption

Chapter 28: New Ally

Chapter 29: Rural Retreat

Chapter 30: Nascent Rebel

Chapter 31: Dark Dilemma

Chapter 32: Alta Heist

Chapter 33: Rendition

Chapter 34: Key Node

Chapter 35: Suspicion

Chapter 36: Special Delivery

Chapter 37: Cold Calling

Chapter 38: Riot

Chapter 39: Express Delivery

Chapter 40: Setup

Chapter 41: Kidnap

Chapter 42: Bad Blood

Chapter 43: Revelation

Chapter 44: De Facto Foe

Chapter 45: Blood Ties

Chapter 46: Breakthrough

Chapter 47: Rescue

Chapter 48: Hedging Bets

Chapter 49: Ensnared

Chapter 50: Extraction

Chapter 51: Improbable Allies

Chapter 52: Inside Information

Chapter 53: Antidote

Chapter 54: Volte-Face

Chapter 55: Pursuit

Chapter 56: Rat Run

Chapter 57: Cordillera de la Ramada

Chapter 58: Justitia

Chapter 59: Tribulation

Chapter 60: Reformation

Masquerade

Chapter 1: A Tentacle Twitched

They say knowledge is power; in Julian Dark's case, knowledge instilled a feeling of terror. He had been caught red-handed, and he knew it. Dark had been prying into classified state documents, and he had just discovered the most outrageous secret. He clattered up the archive's concrete stairs in a state of panic as the terrible repercussions of his discovery began to sink in. His mind was a tumult of conflicting emotions as he fled outside into Whitehall. He had verified his suspicion that the Home Secretary was personally involved in a long-running corruption scandal ensuring substantial Government contracts were awarded to associates. Upon learning the associate's names, he now feared for his life. The list named powerful men – including organised crime bosses, heads of black ops security companies, and brutal third-world dictators. But his overriding emotion was terror; this illicit knowledge made him a target.

The chill of a grey April afternoon brought Dark up short. For the first time in an hour, his brain began to function logically. Whatever happened, he had to pass the photocopied documents in his briefcase, proving the Home Secretary's corruption, to his associate, Heinz Gombricht. He began to stride down Whitehall, oblivious to his surroundings. Dark worked as a Senior Economist in the Foreign and Commonwealth Service. Gombricht worked for the Austrian Diplomatic service. They were close friends and colleagues. They had long-held suspicions that a secret cabal of Multi-National Companies was bribing Government Officials for contracts.

Dark's terror was not unfounded. As soon as he signed the chit to visit the Home Office section of the Archive, the Clerk followed a Standing Instruction to notify MI5 immediately. Unbeknownst to Dark, that moment had placed him in grave danger. As he left the building, he was marked and followed by a group of undercover agents, whose orders were to retrieve Dark's briefcase and at all costs prevent him from contacting or passing the briefcase to anyone.

Dark was well aware his whistle-blowing not only flouted the Official Secrets Act, but the authorities would brand him a traitor. That was indeed frightening, but corruption had become so blatant and commonplace in political circles, he felt it his patriotic duty to expose those responsible.

Dark knew full well that within hours of him passing the photocopies to his colleague Heinz Gombricht for publication, a firestorm of indignation would force the Government to face a vote of no confidence in the House, and more pertinently, would cause outrage in Establishment circles about their nefarious secrets becoming public knowledge. The very same thoughts were causing considerable alarm in the Home Secretary's inner sanctum. The Right Honourable Reginald Crowthorne had just been informed of the theft by Dick Pargetter, the Head of MI5. Crowthorne's cultured voice grew shrill as he fluctuated between fury and blind panic at the news of this treachery. Recent scandals about questions for cash in the House had exposed the growing rift developing between the public and their political masters. Crowthorne didn't precisely know what had been stolen, but whatever it was, the fallout would be catastrophic.

"Now listen here, Pargetter; this is a direct order. You are to ensure that briefcase is in my possession within the hour, do you hear? This is a matter of National Security; use any and all means to retrieve that briefcase."

Pargetter was accustomed to such orders, but he wanted absolute confirmation. "Minister, are you sanctioning a kill?"

Crowthorne barked, "Indeed. In fact, I demand it."

"Yes, Minister. But I must have that in writing."

"Of course, dear boy. Now get on with it. And no loose ends!"

Crowthorne's hands shook as he lit a cheroot and began pacing his opulent office. He had no intention whatsoever of committing such an order to print; after all, he needed plausible deniability.

Back at Whitehall, a group of MI5 agents were stalking their mark like a pack of wolves. They formed a loose semi-circle behind Dark; now they had orders to terminate, they made no effort to conceal themselves; on the contrary, they wanted Dark to see them and panic - it would make their job easier. In front of Dark, another pack of wolves waited, sat astride powerful motorbikes - MI5 operatives disguised as Hells Angels.

As Dark hurried down Whitehall, he gradually became aware that people were staring intently at him; he looked around, puzzled and saw the reason. A gang of six hard men shoved people out of their way as they closed in on him. Instinctively he broke into a stumbling trot.

"Oh my God! They know already!"

The Establishment made it their job to know; their spies and informers were everywhere, reporting unacceptable behaviour on friends and family alike. They knew everything about everyone.

Masquerade

The wolves closed in on Dark, herding him into Great Charles Street. Desperately, Dark looked for an escape, but at every turn, another wolf made him veer away, sending him inexorably toward the bikers. By now blind panic paralysed Dark's thinking, he stumbled down the road, suddenly he found himself amid a group of American tourists. They called loudly to each other as they posed before an old-fashioned red phone box. Instinctively, Dark pushed the milling tourists out of his way and dived into the phone box, ignoring cries of indignation.

He ducked down and checked for his pursuers; there none to be seen. Satisfied he had bought some time, his only thought now was to alert Heinz that he had the evidence they so desperately needed and that he, Dark, was in grave danger. His hands trembled violently as he dialled Heinz; he cursed nonstop while he waited for the ring tone. Eventually, there was a distant click.

"Hello? Heinz, is that you?"

Heinz's voice sounded metallic, "Julian? What's wrong?"

Dark cut him short, "Quiet! Listen. I've photocopied the diary; it's as we thought. It proves Crowthorne and his cronies are receiving huge bribes for giving contracts to the Corporatists."

"Bloody hell! We've got the bastards!"

"Not quite; they know I've been to the archive, and there is a gang chasing me. They're determined to stop us."

"Damn! Where are you?"

"I'm leaving the photocopied diaries folded in the directory in a phone box in Great Charles Street off Whitehall. Get here as fast as you can to pick them up. You might just make it before they discover I don't have them. But you must hurry!"

"Julian, wait!"

Too late, Dark dropped the call and hastily shoved the photocopies inside the directory, then pushed it back into its cubby hole.

Just then, the door yanked open; petrified, Dark spun around, dreading seeing his tormentors. Instead, an irate elderly American clad entirely in beige berated him.

"Is that the way you limeys treat people nowadays?"

Dark stammered, "Sorry, emergency." Then he pushed his way past the fuming American. Crouching low, he scrambled through the crowd and turned into Horse Guards. As he cleared the tourists, Dark was relieved not to see anyone suspicious. But they were there in the shadows formed up in a horseshoe, gradually shepherding him toward their trap. As he made his way along Horse Guards, it was apparent he had been outflanked; the only route with no visible threat was St. James Park. Turning, Dark stumbled badly, once again gripped by icy panic; he abandoned any effort to hide and ran across the grass toward another group of tourists.

One of the MI5 agents radioed the bikers to intercept the mark. They had been lounging on the grass near the lake, now they stood nonchalantly, and after catcalling three teenage girls, casually wandered in Dark's direction.

A thoroughly unfit Dark lurched and stumbled across the grass. Burning breath came in staccato bursts, his legs felt like jelly, he was rapidly nearing collapse. Only a primal survival instinct kept him going. After another twenty yards, his legs gave up. He collided with one of the bikers and collapsed. He lay prone on the grass, chest heaving, the biker leaned over.

"Hey! You just barged into me!"

Dark saw only a shadow and heard only a vague noise.

"Look where you're going, man!"

No response.

The biker prodded Dark with his boot. He yelled.

"Hey! I'm talking to you!"

The biker raised his voice for the benefit of passers-by, "You should look where you're going. You could've hurt someone."

His companions encircled Dark; two of them grabbed him and hauled him to his feet.

Dark mumbled, "Ss... sorry, didn't …."

"Sorry, don't cut it, mate! You nearly tore my jacket."

Dark gasped, "Accident."

"Accident or not, you're gonna pay!"

Frantically Dark looked around, "No … No money."

Masquerade

The biker grinned maliciously, "No worries, I'll beat it out of you. Suits me either way." And with that, he aimed a vicious blow into Dark's solar plexus. Dark doubled up; every breath of air sucked out of his lungs. Another biker brought a baseball bat down on his shoulders with a resounding thud. Dark was pinioned by two, while the other six beat and kicked him in a practised and methodical action. It only took a few moments; they let Dark fall to the ground like a discarded doll, mercifully unconscious. They carried on kicking his head - the surest way to kill. Suddenly, as one they rested, pausing for breath. They stood panting heavily, impassively watching their victim's lifeblood pour from his mouth and ears. A large red pool gathered around his head.

Then, business-like, the leader snapped, "Get the briefcase. Let's go!"

Like a well-drilled squad of troops, they turned outward with expressions that challenged any of the shocked onlookers to intervene. One of the bikers collected the case, and they ran laughing and joking to the far end of the park.

In the shadow of a tree, a man spoke into a radio, "Control... Mission complete. Briefcase secured."

Masquerade

Chapter 2: Deceptive Disguise

Ten years after his father Julian's murder, George Dark sat before a large, illuminated mirror applying makeup. He lived in a converted warehouse in East London, although this was only one of many haunts. As someone who was wanted by most Western Governments, he lived off-grid, never staying in one place for long lest his habits became predictable. In the years since his father had been killed in a Government sanctioned assassination, Dark had learned the art of disguise from his actress Mother, Felicity. He had also gained a wide knowledge of the languages and cultures of Europe and Asia, and as a child of the nascent digital age, he had become an expert hacker. His skills and knowledge made him invisible to Government systems, allowing him to move around the world freely, without leaving a trail.

Dark suddenly remembered his mother's reproof, "Not like that, George, darling. Less is better.'

Behind Dark, his handler, Heinz, watched the TV news, "Lord! Can you believe this nonsense? How do these people have the nerve to call themselves journalists; they just regurgitate Government propaganda, without challenge."

In the TV Studio, two attractive newsreaders smiled condescendingly at the camera while the programme's theme tune faded. The woman studied her notes then, "Good evening, this is Rankah Jervis and Richard Brise with tonight's headlines."

Brise adopted a sincere expression, "The Home Secretary has approved plans for widespread deployment of CCTV cameras equipped with Facial Recognition in the fight against terrorism."

Rankah added, "A spokesperson for Libertas criticised the plan, saying it was another nail in the coffin of personal freedom; Britain is now a Police State."

"Thank you Rankah, in other news, retail spending was up for the third consecutive quarter. The Prime Minister says Britain's business is booming."

Now it was Rankah's turn to project empathy, "In America, the White House confirmed a Syrian rebel base was destroyed by a drone strike last night. Reports of civilian casualties were strenuously denied. The Secretary of Defence stated that the rebels always used the local population as a shield; however, the United States would not be deterred from attacking rebels wherever they hid."

Dark muttered, "No mention of Yemen, then? Who gives a shit about a humanitarian crisis when there's no profit in it? A Government has to get its priorities right!"

Heinz snorted, "They only tell us what they want us to know; the awkward stuff is left out. Who knows what the truth is anymore?"

Back in the darkened TV studio control room, a huge bank of monitors cast a ghostly glow over a row of technicians controlling the cameras while three people sat on a raised dais directing the newscasters. The Studio Manager barked out, "Camera two, focus on Rankah. Stand by Camera five, close-up on Richard."

He turned to his assistant, "Did the engineering job loss story get cut?"

"Yeah, Bullmore sent over a revised schedule of stories he wanted to broadcast."

The Studio Manager snorted in disgust, "Dear God! What have we come to? I remember a time when editors decided the headlines. Now they are micro-managed by some bloody Government lackey!"

Masquerade

Chapter 3: Greasing the Wheels

The Right Honourable Giles Stryckland was hosting a business lunch in an exclusive restaurant in central London. He had invited six of his most powerful backers, all of them CEOs of multi-national corporations based in the UK.

Stryckland cleared his throat, "Gentlemen, welcome, please be seated."

Geoffrey Lewis, a large bluff character and CEO of SupaFoods PLC - a huge food processing company, piped up first, "Giles. It's been a long time. We're looking forward to your speech at the Mansion House. SupaFoods is expecting the Government to co-operate more fully with its business goals this term."

"Geoffrey, to the point as ever. I can safely say you won't be disappointed." Stryckland waved at an aide, "Hugo here has been burning the midnight oil incorporating your recommendation into the bill."

Lewis was dubious, "You made a similar promise last time we met; how do I know you'll keep your word this time?"

Stryckland mentally counted to ten before answering. "Because the Government has to! If it wants to retain your financial backing, it has to honour its promises. It's that simple."

Rupert Blandford, an Investment Banker, interrupted, "And I trust the damned residency legislation is being revised. The Bank is concerned, Giles! If there is no progress soon, we will have to reconsider your funding."

"Rupert, please. Parliament has a busy schedule. The issue would have been resolved by now if it wasn't for the fuss about large corporate's shady tax deals!"

Stryckland was under fire; these people were part of the corporate clique who ruled the West. They funded Government policies and expected results. They didn't accept failure; non-compliance was almost always career-ending or worse for the person concerned. The problem was Stryckland didn't have complete control of Government MPs. The Prime Minister presided over a split party, MPs loyal to him accounted for just over half the whip, whilst Stryckland controlled the rest. Stryckland was having a great deal of trouble integrating his corporatist friendly agenda of business and tax-friendly legislation into law. MP's loyal to the PM had thwarted him every time he tried. As far as the Corporatists were concerned, the current situation was untenable. Their goal was to do away with elected Governments altogether, and the UK was the prototype for a strategy that would see every country in Europe ruled with an 'iron fist' by the Corporatists.

Masquerade

Chapter 4: Dark Deeds

Dark was a thief, a stealer of secrets. The Corporatists had labelled him a terrorist and put a five-million-dollar price tag on his head. The Corporatists controlled the major Multi-Nationals and Western Governments and were desperate to stop Dark exposing their activities. They had many corrupt secrets which they were determined to keep hidden. Dark's activities risked exposing those wicked deeds.

Consequently, George Dark was a fugitive, hunted in every country in the West. The only thing preventing Dark's capture was his genius at disguise.

To stay alive, Dark lived outside the boundaries of normal society, beyond the reach of the databases and surveillance systems used to scrutinize and control ordinary people. He was invisible to these systems. The sheer mass of humanity in modern cities masked his presence to the all-seeing cyber systems. In the twentieth century, information technology was fast reducing people to mere codes, alphanumeric characters in hegemonic databases. People had been stripped of their personalities, humanity and idiosyncrasies. For his part, Dark refused to be labelled and categorised by an insentient box of microchips and wires. Every fibre of his being rebelled at the suffocating and systematic attempts by these impersonal databanks to de-humanise him.

To fight the persistent encroachment of Government control systems, Dark used his expertise for disguise and acting. As a loner, he could assume a new identity as easily as someone putting on an overcoat as they walked out of their front door. He could adapt his posture, change his accent, and with skilfully faked identity documents, he immediately became a different person – all the easier to confuse the cyber systems.

Security Forces such as MI6 or the CIA monitored non-compliance amongst the public. Governments were determined to silence anyone who dared speak out against their ominous activities. Governments violated National, International laws and human rights treaties without a second thought in their frantic attempts to mask the truth. The Oligarchs, alarmed that the public might listen to the brave individuals who questioned their activities, called them *'terrorists'*. If there was one thing that kept the Corporatists awake at night, it was the fear that their control of the ironically named 'Free World' would be exposed. Dark was determined to shatter this illusion and show people they were being cynically manipulated. The

Corporatists were aware that their grip on power would be destroyed instantly if the public turned against them.

In the beginning, Dark fought against the system's impersonalised brutality and manipulation. He soon realised the real agenda was to control society, to make it subservient to the Corporatists. So he concentrated his efforts on helping people regain their individual liberties. He dedicated his life to tear down the carefully constructed mask of secrecy and to shine a spotlight into the dark, avaricious machinations of Corporatism.

As far as the Corporatists were concerned, Dark and his contemporaries were treacherous terrorists, not freedom fighters, hell-bent on destroying a carefully constructed network of alliances that had taken decades to build. Their response was predictable and brutal. They sent national security services to covertly stalk the terrorists and eliminate them.

Tonight, Dark had to steal more secrets. His Swiss associate Heinz wanted evidence to link a Senior British Government Minister with a Security firm they suspected of operating a private army inside the UK. They wanted to know its business associates, owners, directors, and suppliers. They knew Albion Security was a company that worked exclusively for European Governments. The sixty-four-thousand-dollar question was: were they ordinary suppliers, or was there something nefarious to hide? It was public knowledge that Albion provided low-level security guards for Government buildings, courts and prisoner transfers, but recently a radical newspaper, The 'Enquirer', had discovered a series of payments to the Company from an unusual source. One of the analysts at Heinz's Hacker Network had connected this snippet of information with reports of increased street-level surveillance upon anti Government activists. There had been fights at opposition group meetings, intimidation of high-profile activists. The analysts at The Hacker Network drew the obvious historical parallel with paramilitary units used to intimidate political opponents in 1930s Spain, Italy, Russia and Germany. Surveillance, harassment and assaults were the usual *modus operandi*. Normally carried out in such a way that the Corporatists could plausibly deny any connection to the violence. The question vexing Dark was this: firstly, could he prove beyond doubt that Albion Security was responsible for the unrest? Secondly, prove Albion Security were following explicit directions from someone close to the Corporatists, i.e. the British Government.

Masquerade

Dark slumped back in his chair and rubbed his temples. He had a thumping headache after staring at the computer and drinking too much. The sound of heavy rain spitting against the window caught his attention, and he walked over to look outside. In the distance, a solitary street lamp tinged the rain a grubby orange, while a gusting wind snatched plastic bags along the street. Dark thought it was a depressing scene. Damn, he would have to go out in this later. He checked the time; he would need to get a move on if he wasn't going to be late for the shift.

He walked over to a workbench in the corner of the room. The laminating machine hummed as he powered it up. Taking a small plastic sleeve from a shelf, he carefully slid a head and shoulders photo inside. It was one of his stock disguises. Unkempt moustache, tousled, greasy wig. Four day's growth on his face. A pair of cheap thick-rimmed glasses completed the disguise.

Plastic crackled as the edges sealed. Dark inspected the badge closely; the photo sat squarely in the sleeve, and his alias was printed neatly below the agency logo. It would easily pass the cursory inspection normally afforded when clocking on to the night shift. He placed the ID card on the worktop and went into the bathroom to transform himself into the person in the photo.

Three days previously, he had found the employment agency that recruited Albion Security's cleaning staff. Their website was an off the shelf product and easily hacked. He found a list of their operatives and added his new fake persona. The Cleaning Operatives were made up of the usual rabble of itinerant workers; they were a transient underclass invisible, yet indispensable, to society. It would be easy to blend in as such people appeared and then disappeared regularly. Greedy recruitment agencies didn't bother checking the apprehensive individuals who came looking for work and didn't ask awkward questions. If someone failed to turn up for work, a call to a gangmaster would see a dozen desperate new faces at the door.

Nine o'clock. Dark regarded his image in the bathroom mirror; he studied it carefully, checking his new disguise. He took a great deal of effort when creating his impersonations. The mask would have to be comfortable to wear and pass close scrutiny by co-workers for many hours, no matter how hot or cold he became. Eventually, satisfied with the results, he switched off the light and slammed the front door behind him.

Masquerade

Albion's offices were located in an anonymous inner city business park, surrounded by drab boxlike housing. At ten o'clock precisely, Dark shambled through the underground entrance leading to the Supervisor's desk. All of the agencies used the same cleaning uniform, so Dark's clothing fitted in with the other cleaners. It was grubby, patched up in places, worn at the knees; he looked unremarkable, as intended. The Supervisor glanced at Dark and barely looked at his name tag. He was in, simple.

Dark yawned as he pushed his cleaning trolley along the dimly lit subterranean tunnel. He thought about a chilled beer and a film when he got home. But first, there was work to do. Tonight's job would take place on the tenth floor. He pushed his trolley through the fire doors into the service area in the basement. He pressed a button and waited for a lift to arrive. Mentally, he ran through the sequence of events needed to break into a Briggs & Jewels digital time lock. Unconsciously his hand reached around to the small of his back, checking the leather pouch containing his tools. Satisfied, he dipped his hand into the cold, dirty water of his mop bucket to make sure the combination breaker was still submerged in its waterproof case. The lift arrived with a ping, the doors opened and disgorged two cleaners and a supervisor. They ignored Dark and brushed past, noisily chattering and gesticulating about tonight's big game on the radio.

The supervisor, a short, rotund Thai with a cherubic face that belied a domineering attitude, turned back. "You're the new temp? Got your job sheet? You know which floor you are going to?"

Dark played the fool. He looked at the floor shuffling from one foot to the other, eager to please. "Yes, boss. I'm good, I'm good. I'll be done quick like. You can rely on me."

The supervisor regarded him with distaste, "Fine! Don't take all night! We've got homes to go to. Understand?"

Dark kept up the pretence, "Yes, yes. It's OK. Very OK, soon be done. Boss."

He stepped into the lift alone and leaned against its cool bare aluminium. 'That should keep him out of my hair.'

The doors opened on the eighth floor. He pushed his trolley into the foyer and checked his job sheet. He had the whole floor to clean.

Masquerade

The corridors were dark and deserted; the office staff had long gone. The only people around were security. After years of undercover work, Dark knew that many security staff became lax when they had been on the job for a while. They got into a routine, and they, like most of the cleaning staff, were illegals, so they kept their heads down and minded their own business for fear of being asked awkward questions.

He decided to clean for a while before going up to the tenth floor to look for evidence. He found an office in a corridor close to the lift and began vacuuming. He calculated that he would have thirty minutes to get into the office, make the search and get out again undetected.

Eventually, Dark pushed the trolley around to the lifts. Thankfully the lift arrived empty. He took a card-key from his tool bag.

In today's climate of paranoia, Albion protected sensitive areas of its business with multiple layers of sophisticated security systems. In this case, staff involved in sensitive work were located on the tenth, eleventh and twelfth floors. These floors could only be accessed by lift and an encrypted card-key. Only thirty of these cards had been issued. Dark had made the thirty first, a copy of the Financial Officer's card.

The tenth floor was deserted. Without hesitation, Dark turned right; he had memorised the layout of the offices. Getting past the state-of-the-art security protecting the office doors would be tricky but feasible. The whole suite comprised a cube constructed of sapphire and titanium bulletproof windows with titanium and carbon-composite walls. The carbon-ceramic armour-clad outer doors were protected by a 'Briggs & Jewels' digital time lock, meaning the doors could only be opened during normal office hours and only then with the correct code. Modern electronic safes employ multiple key combinations to secure the door. A standard code just unlocked the door; a distress code unlocked the door but sent a silent alarm to security and the police. The consensus of expert opinion was that this manufacturer's clock and codes, with two hundred and fifty-six bit encryption, were impossible to crack. Dark had broken numerous two hundred- and fifty-six bit encryption codes and knew better.

Dark retrieved a waterproof bag from the bucket of dirty water, carefully opened the protective wrapper, then pulled out a slim box of electronic gadgetry. Outwardly there was no indication of where the lock itself might be located; only a handle was visible. Dark stooped and placed the device six inches from the floor, close to the edge of the door. Then he pulled the trolley close to the door and, using it as a ladder, stretched up to place a duplicate device at the top of the door. Climbing down, he attached several leads from the box around the door handle. He pressed the power button and watched as the device came to life. One by one, a line of LEDs started flickering on a small display. He waited as the LEDs gradually turned from red to amber and, finally, flickering to a constant green as the device found the combination. A display panel showed the current time 02:19 hours. Satisfied the device had identified all available connections, Dark pressed another button, and the device began to advance the lock's internal clock to 08:00 hours. A few minutes, and he would be in. Dark waited, one minute, then two. He tugged at the door, nothing; it was unyielding. "Bloody thing! Hurry up!" It must have a time delay fitted. The building plans didn't mention that. Eventually, after what seemed like an eternity, a heavy metallic click announced the door was ready to open.

Just then, Dark heard distant voices. "Bloody Hell!" He jumped up on the trolley and grabbed the top terminal of the lock cracker, then gingerly jumped down again, grabbing the other device as he landed. Throwing the gadget onto the trolley, he heaved the heavy door open, pulling the trolley inside with him. Hurriedly he closed the door and dropped the lock so it wouldn't open if the guards decided to check the door.

Breathing heavily, he slumped to the floor. Sweat trickled down his back as he listened intently for the guard's approach. He heard distant footsteps on the marble floor outside the entrance. They had stopped after all. There was an interminable silence. *'What were they doing?'* Then he heard a burst of static on the radio as a message came through; the footsteps moved away.

Chapter 5: No Little Break

Dark walked into a small reception area. He pushed open a door at the far end and entered a hallway flanked by a suite of six offices, all with glass partitions.

He knew from the building plans there were no alarms to worry about now that he was inside the time lock door. So he set about searching for the documents he needed. Dark walked into a large modern office with minimalist décor. Huge oil paintings depicting British military prowess at Balaclava, Rourke's Drift and Waterloo hung on three walls. Incongruously a large Regency walnut bookcase filled the remaining wall. Opposite the entrance, a large chrome and wood desk was located. Arranged in the centre of the room were meeting a table and chairs, with two large burgundy leather sofas against the far wall. Dark sat at the desk. He inspected the arrangement. Computer screens, keyboard, telephone, blotter, remote control, no clutter. Nothing amiss. One lock secured all three drawers; he took out his key pick, and seconds later, the drawers were open.

Dark was about to begin searching the desk's contents when he saw the silhouettes of two security guards through the opaque wall of the office. "Christ! What were they doing back so soon?" The silhouettes paused briefly to listen to a radio message, then sauntered off. Dark heard muted sounds along the corridor; they must be checking doors. Silence. He wondered if they could see through the opaque glass. He decided to wait a few minutes and see what happened. The two shadows returned and stopped, seemingly unsure of what to do. He crouched down behind the desk. The faint sound of a two-way radio burst into life. His mind raced; had he been discovered? One of the guards responded, cutting the static. Dark strained to hear but could not make out anything. The radio burst into life again, sounding inordinately loud. A guard clicked the radio off. Dark could hear their mumbled conversation as they marched onwards, passing the time-lock door. Dark remembered there was a maintenance area there.

He turned his attention once more to the contents of the desk drawers. It revealed nothing more than office paraphernalia: a jotting pad and assorted biros and pencils. The second drawer contained correspondence. The third, deeper drawer, contained suspense files, expenses claims, meeting agendas. He sat back and cast an eye over the desk once more. It

Masquerade

was then he noticed a slim panel under the main lip of the desk. He tugged it, but it didn't move. There were no obvious means of unlocking it. However, in the course of prodding and pushing, he felt it give, then spring smoothly open. Inside the drawer was a small dictating machine, a cheque book and a few sheets of A5 paper filled with small densely packed handwritten notes.

He picked up the dictating machine, selected the most recent track and listened. He smiled grimly, rewound the recording further back and listened once more. Satisfied he now had evidence to link Albion to a senior Government Minister, and by implication to the murder, he copied the recording onto his MP3 player and photographed the notes.

Satisfied the desk had given up its secrets, Dark wandered over to the antique bookcase and inspected it closely. It was huge and filled the whole wall. It contained scores of volumes of leather-bound books and atlases. Most books had a military theme. There were biographies of Alexander, Caesar, Bonaparte, Wellington, Rommel, Zhukov, Vo Nguyen Giap, a large tome of British Regimental War Diaries, and several books on military campaigns of the eighteenth and nineteenth centuries. Dark wandered over to the far left side of the bookcase, nothing unusual there. The bindings seemed genuine. The book spines looked faded, well-worn and studied frequently. He moved slowly to his right, letting his eye wander randomly over the covers. He had nearly reached the end when he retraced a few steps. Something had caught his eye. He retraced his steps and waited patiently for the answer to come to him as he scanned the covers. Three volumes of "The Grand Tour." Now, what would a student of military history need with an eighteenth-century travel guide to Europe? He carefully opened the bookcase door and took down the three heavy volumes one by one. They seemed at first glance to be perfectly ordinary books; there were no handwritten annotations, no marked pages, no missing pages. He could find no fault with them, but something nagged at him. He was missing something obvious. What the hell was it? Then it dawned on him. He flicked the pages over to the front cover. There was a symbol, one he had seen before: a Tanburg Eagle.

Chapter 6: Puppet Propaganda

The faint hum of distant London traffic drifted in through an open window as Eric Johnson tapped his pencil impatiently on a leather blotter. The Minister was late again. He made a show of checking his watch and then looked around the table at his colleagues, rolling his eyes in exasperation. They displayed their solidarity with a chorus of well-practised sighs. Such was the lot of mid-ranking Civil Servants.

Johnson examined his surroundings in an attempt to alleviate his boredom. The grand salon was richly decorated. Its lofty ceilings twenty feet high were decorated with ornate gilded cornices and architraves. Huge oil paintings portrayed a succession of Permanent Secretaries from the eighteenth and nineteenth centuries, their stern expressions calculated to imbue the current occupants of the room with the same sense of awe as their forebears.

Eventually, the heavy silence was punctuated by the approaching sound of two contrasting accents arguing vociferously. The voices grew louder until the heated exchange paused briefly outside the door before bursting in. The Home Secretary and the Prime Minister's Press Secretary strode to the head of the table.

"We'll finish this later, Graham, in my office." The Home Secretary glared at his antagonist as he took his seat.

Sir Miles Lansdowne, Permanent Secretary to the Minister for the Home Office, steeped in the traditions and etiquette of Westminster and Whitehall, softly followed the quarrel into the meeting room. His distaste at the vulgar display of dissent was all too apparent. Graham Bullmore was a recent addition to the Prime Minister's inner clique of sofa 'consiglieres'; his boorish behaviour and expletive-laden tirades making him the most reviled member of the PM's cabal. So great was his influence over the PM that he was untouchable by his numerous critics. His opinionated outbursts carried more weight than Ministers with years of experience. A word from Bullmore and even the most loyal politician was exiled. All except Stryckland, he was too powerful even for Bullmore.

The Right Honourable Giles Stryckland, Home Secretary, assumed control of the meeting. He made a show of arranging his pad and pens on the table, reasserting his authority.

Masquerade

Then, "Good Morning, Gentlemen. There will be a change to the published agenda. So let's get the routine matters out of the way." He turned to Lansdowne, "Miles, are this week's news stories ready for distribution to the Print and TV editors?"

"Yes, Minister."

"What topics are you covering?"

"We're concentrating on the EU Grants negotiated by the Prime Minister. They're due to be awarded next month. There are follow up newspaper articles scheduled which repeat the message several times every week right up to the award ceremony at the EU Finance Minister's Conference in Brussels. The message should get through to the masses."

Stryckland nodded his approval. "What about the timings? Does it clash or cover?" Bullmore looked smug; he had helped plan the strategy.

"Cover. The National Statistics Office are due to release the Employment and Economic Performance data for Q2 later this week. I'll make sure the editors get their priorities right. The EU story will fill the headlines; the statistics stuff will be buried somewhere. It will take the wind out of the Shadow Chancellor's sails."

Stryckland was put out; he had asked Lansdowne the question, not Bullmore. "Very well."

He turned back to Lansdowne, "Did you speak to the News Editor at Channel TV as I asked? That dammed Food Industry documentary! The Chairman of the Foodstuffs Association called me after the programme, complaining about the coverage. He wants something done about the journalist; he called the programme a pack of lies."

Lansdowne looked pained, "Yes, Minister. I spoke to the Controller and the Producer. They were both adamant the facts were correct and had been verified before the programme was broadcast. They claim the company is well known in the trade for lax hygiene and for breaching guidelines on banned ingredients ... 'E' numbers and so on."

Stryckland dismissed the excuse with a snort of derision, "The truth of the programme maker's claims is irrelevant. What matters is that the Foodstuffs Association is paying us to look after their interests which doesn't include being dragged through the media. Make sure the Controller issues a statement apologising for the story. Blame the journalists. By close of business tomorrow. Understood?"

Bullmore interrupted, "Tell the bastards if they don't comply, I'll freeze them out of future news briefings. If they don't get *on-message* quick, they'll be reassessed as untrustworthy and scratched from the preferred media list." He turned to Stryckland and gloated, "They always toe the line after that. A news channel with no news is bloody useless."

Stryckland scowled, Bullmore's constant interruptions irritated him beyond belief. "Very well. Now for the new item on the agenda. I want to address the issue of fake news media and their sources. You will all be aware of the recent spate of leaked confidential information from Government offices and those of several of its major corporate partners. This has caused the Government a great deal of embarrassment. Four extremely damaging articles have been published in the last six months — many of them by the 'Enquirer' and several websites which use their newsfeed. The journalists responsible have been identified in the weekly office circular – Media section. By the close of business today, I want a plan to root out the source of the leaks. Then, I want a strategy to shut down these damned activist journalists once and for all. Time is of the essence, Gentlemen." He left the thought hanging.

Before anyone else could comment, his Permanent Secretary, Lansdowne, spoke. "Look. Number Ten is extremely concerned with these leaks. They make us look like complete fools. Recent cyber-attacks on Government computer systems have reached epidemic proportions. But they are not entirely unexpected, and we have strategies in place to combat that threat. Now we're in the digital age, we are unprepared for physical thievery; it's an old fashioned concept. That is the cabinet's greatest fear. It's not only us; similar occurrences are being reported by our associate Corporations, and yet none by companies not on the Government preferred supplier list. Gentlemen, we are engaged in a war; I'm serious. We cannot see the enemy and cannot trace them, but they are causing irreparable damage to our image of trustworthiness. It is imperative you use every and any means to find these people before they destroy our systems. Fifty years of careful implementation of *The Plan* will have been in vain if we fail."

Although the majority of Civil Servants were reticent about discussing politics, Eric Bullmore had no such hesitation.

Masquerade

"Bloody disgrace! Treacherous bastards! Everyone working for the Government has signed the Official Secrets Act, you know. If this is an inside job, there will be severe consequences. Which Departments are involved? I'd sack the bloody lot if I were you, Stryckland. Get some new blood!" He slumped back in his chair, muttering expletives.

Wearily, Stryckland put his face in his hands and ignored the interruption. Bullmore was behaving like a bellicose oik, as usual. "Miles, which Departments have had leaks?"

Sir Miles was a time-served member of the British Establishment, experienced in the arcane ways of the organisation. "So far, Minister: The Department of Health; The Office for National Statistics; The Audit Office; The Ministry of Defence; and The Department for Overseas Aid." He kept his reply brief. Understanding knowledge confers power, he meted out nuggets of information parsimoniously.

Stryckland checked, "Have these been reported in the press?"

Lansdowne carefully lifted a corner of his file and glanced at a page, "Yes, all of them. Three leaks have been published in the 'Enquirer', one on the 'Corruption-Expose' website and one was picked up by a subscription channel on a video website."

The Home Secretary drummed his fingers on the table, exasperated. "I take it we have taken steps to ensure this doesn't happen again?"

Lansdowne laconically shuffled his papers, "Well, Minister, we have shut down the 'Corruption-Expose' website. It was run by a solitary, deluded conspiracy theorist with no training as a journalist. He was tried *in camera* last week and has been sentenced to twenty years in a maximum-security prison."

Stryckland jotted notes on a pad. His pen poised mid-air at the pause. He looked at Lansdowne. "Well? Is that it? What about the damned 'Enquirer'? What have you done about that nest of vipers?"

Sensing an opportunity for kudos, Eric Johnson eased Lansdowne's evident discomfort with a small but significant interruption. "Sir, I believe Deputy Commissioner Rawlings sent a delegation to the magazine a few days ago, Sir. We don't seem to have the report yet, but I'm sure the Deputy Commissioner has made a suitable impression on the paper's editor. After all, the Editor of the 'Republic's' trial only finished last month, and he got twenty years for publishing material which may be useful to a terrorist organisation."

Stryckland affected surprise that a junior member of the meeting would dare address him directly. "I was speaking to Sir Miles!"

Johnson took the rebuke on the chin, satisfied Sir Miles would reward him in due course. He noted the corner of Lansdowne's file lift once more.

Bullmore barged in, snarling, "The Prime Minister asked me specifically to repeat to every one of you the necessity of catching these bastards. You need to be 'on-message'. If the public realises what we're doing, there'll be a bloody revolution. Other Governments in the International Community are openly ridiculing our inability to close this down."

Stryckland considered the dimwits seated around the table; only he and Lansdowne were members of the 'Establishment' inner circle. And only he was a member of Kalyptra. Only he was aware of Kalyptra's Plot, which would soon bring lasting power to a select cabal who considered themselves the only people capable of ruling Britain and Europe. If the plot remained secret, Kalyptra would achieve its goal. Otherwise, the country would be doomed to destruction by self-absorbed pressure groups and liberal do-gooders.

Bullmore droned on, "The PM is insistent we put out a press release within the next few days to the effect we are managing a spike in terrorist activity. That's the excuse for the increased surveillance. Even the broadsheets are asking us awkward questions. They need something shocking to put on the front page to frighten their readers. Nick Ashford from 'The Guardian' is asking why they are toeing the establishment line when mavericks like the 'Enquirer' are publishing sensational exposes. It makes them look out of touch. As an ex-editor, I can tell you it would make my blood boil to be short-changed like that. Gentlemen, it took us a decade to get the newspapers compliant enough to do as they are told; we would be bloody stupid to piss them off now. Don't forget if they turn against us, it will be the end of the gravy train."

Stryckland, "Very well! I want a plan of action and a press release on my desk by midday tomorrow! "

He turned to Lansdowne, "Miles, have you run background checks on the staff at the departments involved?"

Masquerade

Lansdowne was back on firm ground once more, "Yes. I've instructed the Under Secretaries to run the checks. They will report anything unusual."

Stryckland nodded, "What are you searching for?"

Lansdowne, "People who have started work recently and those who have left in the same time frame. Unusual political affiliations... religious tendencies. It seems prudent to check the obvious avenues first."

Stryckland concurred, "Quite so, quite so. I don't suppose anything has come to light yet?"

Lansdowne, "No. Nothing. Although I've taken the liberty of asking GCHQ to pull up mobile call records for the last twelve months. We can ask the American NSA for British emails. We should have those results in the next twenty-four hours."

Stryckland was impressed. "Very good. By the way, I seem to remember our friends at Debden Oil & Gas and Gentis Pesticides both suspected they suffered security breaches. Those may well be connected with these leaks. Get the Met onto it, will you?" He stood to leave. "Speak to DCI Gittins; he will be able to help you."

Lansdowne made notes in his file, "Of course, Minister."

Stryckland turned back, "One other thing, Miles. Ask the Met Commissioner to meet me tomorrow, urgently. He's to cancel his meetings for the day. I want to see him at 10:30 sharp — my office. Tell him I want anything he has on the European Network hackers we heard about last year. I want a summary of the salient facts on my desk in time for the meeting."

"Yes, Minister."

"Let me know the moment you find anything from your database search. Gentlemen, that concludes the meeting."

The Meeting broke in a sombre mood – a complacent Establishment was feeling distinctly nervous. Later that afternoon, Stryckland was sitting at his desk when his secretary knocked, "DCI Gittins, Sir."

Stryckland beckoned without looking up from his papers. Gittins marched breezily into the room and waited for Stryckland to finish.

"So, Gittins, what can I do for you?"

"Just the usual, Sir."

"Ahh, yes. My word... it soon comes around, doesn't it?"

Stryckland reached into a drawer then pushed an envelope across the desk.

Gittins, "Sir," then turned to leave.

Stryckland waited for a second, "Gittins! A word to the wise. I have put into place the means to shut down the most dangerous elements of the activist press. However, it's a complete waste of time if you don't do your job and identify their informants. I want results. Quickly, understand? Now get out and find them."

Gittins stormed out of the office, slamming the door behind him, "Bastard!"

Chapter 7: Taking Stock

Susie Esterhazy leaned on the balcony rail, gazing out at the Mediterranean. Boats in the marina swayed in unison with the ebb and flow of the current. In the distance, superyachts carved their way across the bay, making for a berth in Monaco's harbour. Weak evening sunshine dappled the quayside in front of her hotel. Rows of forlorn palm trees cast feeble shadows onto the deserted promenade. The early evening air was crisp and cool - a refreshing precursor to the heat of the coming summer. Most of the boats in the harbour still wore their protective winter shrouds as they waited to be cleaned and prepared for the coming season. Boats were an indispensable accessory for preening owners to flaunt their wealth before their peers and hordes of gawping day-trippers.

Susie was attending a charity reception with a small group of friends in an exclusive boutique hotel on the Cannes seafront. She'd forgotten the name of the charity but knew it had something to do with refugee camps in the Middle East. No matter, the main thing was seeing her friends again after a week of stultifying tedium in her Mother's boyfriend's Villa in Cap Ferrat. It had become a recent custom amongst her friends to meet just before the Summer Season started. It had been a few weeks since their Winter Season had ended in Gstaad. In between, Susie had tried to stave off boredom with shopping sprees in New York, Paris and Rome, but three weeks of consumer indulgence had eventually become dreary, even for a committed consumer like her. Her friends, too, were like deprived addicts, too long without a hit on their credit cards. Back together in their bubble, they could catch up on the latest gossip and decide which parties they were going to attend.

This evening she was glad to be out of the house. Her Mother's boyfriend, Bilic, was becoming more antagonistic with every passing day. He was a brute. Lean and wiry, a psycho with a short fuse. Rumour had it his gains were ill-gotten. He'd become very rich very quickly; he was cunning and aggressive, not someone to be crossed. The plain fact was Susie was frightened of him; she didn't like the company he kept or the way he treated her Mother.

"More champagne, Madam?" An immaculately dressed waiter bowed and proffered a tray of bubbling flutes. Susie dismissed him with a flick of her glass. The waiter deferred and moved on, "These people are so well mannered!" he grumbled, making his way through the crowd. Periodically someone snatched a glass or discarded an empty flute onto his tray. To members of this exclusive circle, Europe's social elite, he was invisible and unworthy of acknowledgement. As the evening wore on, the reveller's inhibitions loosened, and the chatter and dancing became wilder as they consumed more and more champagne. The waiter was making yet another circuit when an outflung arm knocked his tray flying. Crystal glasses shattered on the marble floor. Red wine drenched a woman's immaculate white silk suit. Furiously she spun around and slapped his face hard, leaving a bright red mark on his cheek. The room fell silent as everyone turned to look at the commotion. The inebriated occupant of the suit screamed incoherently at the crestfallen waiter. "You fucking idiot! Look what you've done! Do you know how much this outfit cost? More than you'd earn in a lifetime, you cretin! Get the Manager!" she shrieked. A Maître d' hurried over. "Out!" He hissed at the waiter. "You're fired." He turned to the leathery perma-tanned socialite, "Madame, I apologize. He will be dealt with. May I offer to clean and repair your suit?"

Petulantly the woman turned her back. "Don't bother! A charity can have it now; it's soiled."

Susie left her friends gossiping over the drama and returned to the view over the bay. She felt disgust at the foul-mouthed woman's behaviour; she was typical of the conceited super-rich. . Browbeating a waiter was undignified. 'In God's name, why am I socializing with these idiots? What sort of culture do we live in, when even respectable-looking middle-aged women launch into drunken, foul-mouthed tirades.'

She wondered if the woman would even remember the incident when she sobered up. Susie was beginning to find the arrogance of the élite nauseating. Bitterly, Susie ruminated, "I'm sick of this; everything and everyone is so shallow".

She had followed the European Season for five years: Wimbledon, Monaco, Deauville, Paris, London. Same old places, same old faces. It had been fun, to begin with – the newfound freedoms after her finishing school days and a few years studying a Fine Arts Degree in Paris. The sophisticated parties, the allure of stylish, rich young men after the awkward village boys of her youth.

Susie had been too naive to realise that the glittering, hedonistic lifestyle masked a superficial, demeaning existence. The constant pressure to be a headline-grabbing consumer and socialise with celebrities became an addiction, which then infected you with a shallowness that turned you into a disdainful husk of a human being.

After Paris, she'd had a part-time job with Justin Urquhart, an art dealer just off Regent Street. It was just something to get her out of bed in the morning. Urquhart used her social connections shamelessly in return for little or no work. Other than a few hours at the Gallery, her days were filled with social engagements with her circle of 'friends'; the nights with previews, premiers, and dinner parties. She should feel contented. Her lifestyle was something plenty of people aspired to above all else, but she felt empty, lonely, and directionless. She had every possible advantage: money, position - and yet it was not enough. Susie had no idea what she wanted, yet she knew this existence would eventually destroy her. She had seen what years of partying had done to previous generations of the social elite. They either died young or existed in a living coma, their brains addled by years of drink and drugs. Hedonism extracted a high price for its transient pleasures. She felt trapped in her gilded cage, and like all of her acquaintances, was stalked by paparazzi and fortune seekers.

Bilic was a case in point. Fifty years old but still acting like a twenty-five-year-old Lothario. His taut shining skin, perma-tan and dazzling teeth were fine from a distance. But if one looked closely, his eyes were black and pitiless - reptilian. He embodied everything she had come to despise about her life. She looked across the salon at him - a young groupie on each arm, a lecherous smirk on his face, swaying after too much champagne. He was addicted to sex and money and regularly left her poor mother languishing at her estate in Budapest while he gallivanted about all over Europe – the gossip magazines routinely carried pictures of him cavorting with third-rate celebrities.

The opening bars of 'Riders of the Storm' brought her out of her musing and brought her down to earth. She turned from the balcony and walked towards the stairs, and headed for the ground floor. Perhaps it was time she finally decided what mattered most. At the Hotel entrance, she summoned the bell boy who called her car. Wearily she climbed in and instructed the chauffeur to drive home. On the way, she gazed at familiar landmarks and the gaudy ostentation juxtaposed with the silent, barely visible blanketed beggars tucked into dark alleys between grand gated villas.

Chapter 8: Minor Reprisal

Forbidding saturnine thunder clouds glowered over a large anonymous business unit in East London, the headquarters of Vanquish Security. The firm specialised in contract military personnel supply to Multi-National Corporations and Governments. Their activities in various parts of the world protecting their patron's assets were veiled in secrecy - hidden from public scrutiny by zealous bureaucrats.

It was past midnight, and the offices lay in darkness. A woman walked briskly down a dimly lit corridor. Every now and then, she glanced behind, certain she could hear a faint echo of following footsteps.

In the basement lobby, she collected her cleaning trolley and called the service lift. Her movements were brisk, economical and confident. A loud ping broke the silence as the lift doors hissed open. She listened again. The footsteps were faint but definitely getting nearer. The woman frowned, then closed the doors. She pressed the button for the twenty-first floor. They always gave her the top floor. She leaned against her trolley, pondering as the lift ascended, "I hope that damn creepy Supervisor keeps away tonight!" All week she had struggled to avoid him after he propositioned her. His persistence was exhausting.

The lift hissed softly as it slid to a stop. Lobby and corridor lights sprang into life as she walked purposefully towards her destination, the CEOs office at the far end of the corridor. The suite of offices was designated restricted access, and the offices were locked when staff left for the day. The woman took a slim wallet from her overalls and, selecting the precise tool, unlocked the door and closed it quietly behind her. She had memorised the layout of the office suite. Without hesitation, she turned left and walked past a Secretary's desk into the main office. Once inside, she moved to the right and opened a mahogany cabinet to reveal a safe with a digital lock.

Taking a small black box from the trolley, she attached two suckers near the safe's keypad, then pressed a button. A six-figure display rapidly began counting down combinations. Each time a pin was unlocked, a LED lit. The door opened in less than two minutes - not bad. She tugged open the heavy door - two shelves: the top was filled with neat bundles of new fifty Pound and one hundred Euro notes. The woman ignored them; donning a pair of black cotton gloves, she carefully removed a stack of files tied with brightly coloured ribbon together with a grey metal cash box from the bottom shelf.

Whilst she bent over a desk examining the files, she felt a faint draught on her neck. There was no time to react before a grey garbed arm seized her in a chokehold; she was lifted off her feet and dragged backwards. The woman was experienced enough to know not to expend energy unnecessarily at this point, so she didn't struggle. Her assailant pinned her against the wall with his forearm jammed against her windpipe. His movements were quick but erratic. Plainly he hadn't done this often, but he hadn't positioned his body to defend against a counterattack. An opportunistic pervert.

Hot, fetid breath scoured her face; it was the damn supervisor. He had a weasel face and greasy strands of lank hair dragged over a bald dome. His claw-like hands held her in a vice-like grip.

"Gotcha! What ya doin' in 'ere? This office is locked after hours. How'd ya get in? Never mind. That's by the by. Now then, darlin', I've been meaning to have a chat with you all week. Trying to avoid me? It won't do. We need to get a few things straight. Being caught in here means you're in deep shit. If I was to report it, that is."

Filthy claws began to wander. The woman gasped for air.

He wanted the bitch conscious, so he loosened his grip. It was his second and last mistake. The sneer on his face transformed into bewilderment at the woman's unexpected strength as she grabbed his overalls and slammed her knee into his testicles with a practised ferocity. He spasmed in crushing agony as she discarded his flaccid body and left him mewing quietly on the floor.

Once again, her movements were swift and measured as she resumed her task. She hid the files and metal box under a pile of rags on her trolley. Then returned to the lift. Her work was done for the night; she had what she came for. As the lift came to a stop in the basement, the hollow sound of an alarm shrieked out from above. "Damn!" There wasn't an alarm in the office; the bastard must have called security. Abandoning the trolley, she bundled the files and box into a sturdy cotton bag and sprinted, hell for leather, toward the exit.

Twenty yards from the door, shouts sounded behind; two guards were in pursuit, one of them shouting instructions into a two-way radio. Just as she reached the exit, it burst open and two more guards, brandishing tasers, charged in. Without breaking stride, she jumped high and kicked the lead guard in the chest as she sailed over him, sending him tumbling into the second guard. They crashed to the floor as she burst through the fire door and sprinted the fifty yards to her car. "Amateurs", she grinned.

Later that morning, the atmosphere in DCI Gittins' interview room at Paddington Green Police Station was tense, putting it mildly. The four guards who had chased the suspect sat around a table nursing bruises and cuts and bad cases of wounded pride. Gittins wasn't one to spare their feelings.

"Bloody useless, the lot of you. A woman, for Christ sake! How could you let her get away? Four grown men can't catch a woman! Call yourselves security guards! You're bloody useless! I don't know why Vanquish pay you good money for that piss poor performance!"

A Sergeant knocked timidly, then sidled along the wall to the back of the office. Gittins turned his attention to his detective constables. "Five thefts this month; last night's makes six. Christ! What's going on? The Commissioner's going ballistic; he's complaining like hell. The Home Secretary is giving him grief on a daily basis. The biggest corporate crime wave in living memory. And what have you lot found? Sod all! That's what!"

One of the detectives piped up, "They've got an excellent description of her, Boss! It should be easy to pick her up."

"Bollocks! There's been a decent description after every theft! Problem is, they're all different. Never had an old woman before though, that's a first. If she can outrun four Security Guards, she's got to be a pretty fit old girl!"

In a rundown warehouse at the edge of London's Docklands, the 'old girl' stood before a brightly lit mirror. A slight smile played across her careworn features. She had enjoyed her night's work. Humming softly to herself, she dabbed her face with smooth, practised movements, removing makeup from around her eyes and hairline. Reaching back, she unpinned a lustrous black wig and placed it carefully in a box beside her dressing table. She regarded her reflection in the mirror. Lifting her chin, she smoothed the sagging skin around her neck. Then digging her fingers into the skin on the hairline, she began to pull back latex. Carefully, so the mask didn't tear, she slowly peeled away the prosthetic.

Masquerade

Shorn of the disguise, George Dark scratched his face, relieved to be free of the chafing facade one of his alter egos demanded. He smiled. Six thefts, six different disguises: it would keep the Met busy for weeks. He held the mask up so that it sat over his hand, next to his reflection. "This is what I do; this is what I am - the Masquerade."

Chapter 9: Trojan Horse

A restless herd of commuters milled around the entrance to the tube station, unwilling to tolerate the soaking drizzle of a grey London morning. Chester pushed his way through, then, turning right, walked briskly until he came to a double fronted shop: 'Dave's Café'. He paused before the steamed-up windows. The muted sounds of the bustling café drifted out to him as he surveyed the street. No one looked away, no one suddenly found something interesting in a shop window, but if he'd had the presence of mind to look upwards, he would have seen clusters of black plastic domes suspended from the rooftops - the dispassionate omnipresent CCTV surveillance, installed for everyone's safety. But Chester was an amateur and didn't look.

He opened the café door and was immediately enveloped in a blast of hot air and the cacophony of boisterous workmen fortifying themselves for another day on the treadmill.

"Seat at the back, Luv," the waitress greeted him.

Chester craned his neck and spied the empty table in a back corner, "Perfect".

Weaving his way through the maze of chairs, bags and coats, he put his raincoat on a spare peg and sat facing the door.

Eventually, the waitress huffed and puffed her way over to him.

"What will it be, Luv?"

"Full English, please, and a mug of tea."

"Right you are. Won't be long," having barely paused on her perpetual circuit of tables, she nodded a tired half-smile at him, scribbled the order on her pad, then fixed her attention on the clutter at the next table. She shouted Chester's order across the hubbub to a chubby, red-faced man sweating behind a counter crammed full of steaming mugs.

Chester smiled. He felt safe in here - just another anonymous face amongst the multitude. He unfolded his paper and settled to wait for his companion - a source. Meeting like this was routine for him, a way of collecting information quietly, without attracting attention. His breakfast arrived with a mug of tea. He read the paper as he ate, enveloped by the clamour of the café. He finished his meal, ordered more tea and sat back to wait. Abruptly the chatter died down, and the café emptied en-masse, one sitting of workers fuelled with breakfast and gossip, immediately replaced by another set; this time office workers, the clamour started again. It was a comforting daily ritual.

Finally, his source, Sants, arrived tagged onto a group of suits. He looked around and gestured towards Chester as the waitress' greeted him, then went over and slumped down, red-faced and blowing hard.

"Sorry, mate. Tube was full. Had to wait for the next one."

"I thought you'd bottled it," Chester complained.

"No way! Those bastards need bringing down a peg or two!"

"What have you got for me?"

"Oh, you'll enjoy this one. Money Laundering rules apparently don't apply to Civil Servants."

Chester inclined his head.

Sants glanced around, lowered his voice and continued. "Any bank transfers for more than five thousand pounds are recorded in line with the Money Laundering regs. At the end of the month, a report is emailed to the Fraud Squad to check for suspicious transfers. After your suspicions about the Home Secretary's European friends paying him 'fees' for his 'Consultancy' work, I wondered where he kept it; none of his UK accounts had anything like the amounts you were describing. And anyway, he would need to hide them from the Parliamentary Standards Committee's inspectors."

Chester was cynical, "Do they really check up on the politicians with their snouts in the trough?"

Sants shrugged, "Who knows. Anyway, I thought about the Bank Transaction System. It tracks money transfers between banks everywhere. Ostensibly it was set up to catch drug dealers and gangsters, but everyone knows it's so the Inland Revenue can check up on everyone. The System plugs into a worldwide Bank Transaction Network controlled by the major American banks. America used its muscle as the Global Reserve Currency provider to force non-US banks to join. The IRS were determined to stop Americans from hiding money offshore."

"Yes, I remember; the Swiss weren't too pleased about that."

Sants continued, "I was convinced that once the money entered the system, it would show up somewhere. Well, guess what? It doesn't! Every transaction has a code, an IBAN and a SWIFT number. I should be able to trace the money from one bank to another until it reaches its final destination. As I didn't know which Banks the Corporatists use, I started with the Home Secretary's. There were no lump sums deposited in his accounts, just regular salary credits and some dividends. I should have been able to find a match between the Fraud Office Report and the Home Secretary's account. It's as if there were a black hole that money disappears into.

But this takes the biscuit; I discovered there are two reports. The original unaltered report is sent by encrypted email to the Home Secretary; a second filtered report is sent to the Head of the Fraud squad. It seems certain names are deemed too sensitive for the Police to see. No doubt for security reasons. Where have we heard that excuse before, eh? MPs expenses?"

Sants settled back in his chair and gulped his tea, letting Chester digest the information.

Chester swore, "Bloody outrageous. One rule for us and no rules for them. But we're expected to pay the bill every time they screw it up! How much money is involved?"

"Difficult to say at the moment. I'm still working on it. I've only just worked out this stuff. If we start with names of people we suspect of getting bungs, it's relatively easy to hack into their bank accounts and see the amounts. But the best solution would be to get the encrypted report sent to the Home Secretary that would give us everyone's name in one go."

"Can you do that?" Chester looked doubtful, "The security must be phenomenal."

Sants was aggrieved, "How do you think I've got all this stuff? I'm not some spotty hacker spreading viruses!"

"All right! All right! Sorry. Keep your voice down! Just be careful, I'm no expert, but they must be monitoring those systems for cyber-attacks, especially after the breach last year. Then you'll be disappeared. Suicided!" Chester sat back. This was getting to sound dangerous. He had heard rumours from colleagues about people, activists, who just dropped off the radar, never to be seen again. Sants was venturing into dangerous waters here, and like the idiot he was, Chester had asked him to do it.

"I've saved the preliminary stuff on this." Sants pushed a memory stick across the table. "I was in a hurry, so I had to copy the entire contents of the laptop in one go. There is a pile of other crap on there. Maybe worth a look; you never know, there might be something juicy for you."

Chester casually cupped the stick in his hand and slipped it into his pocket. "Encrypted?" he asked.

"Yes - usual password."

"Good, in that case, the usual fee applies." Chester glanced at the newspaper.

Sants picked up the paper with the money tucked inside.

As Chester left the café and headed towards his office, a driver in a car parked thirty yards down the road puffed on a cigarette then reported Chester's movements on a two-way radio. He turned and nodded to his companion, who got out and followed Chester. A few moments later, Sants left; this time, a woman got out of the car and followed Sants, who walked in the opposite direction to Chester.

Chapter 10: Chameleon

Dark pushed open a large metal door at the service entrance of the Debden Oil and Gas Offices. It clattered shut behind him. Another night shift, another job: tonight, he was looking for evidence of bribes paid to junior ministers in the Home Office by Debden Oil and Gas. He was going to 'clean' Debden's offices. Dark was going to find the 'little black book' every blackmailer used when they recorded their 'favours'. His footsteps echoed across the bare concrete floor, bouncing a hollow discord off the breeze-block walls. He grasped the handrail and clattered noisily down a metal staircase to the basement where the cleaning equipment and locker rooms were located. He gradually slipped into character as he walked. His posture stooped, his gait changed to a shuffle. He mumbled to himself when someone approached. He transformed into an ageing itinerant odd job man.

George Dark was a twenty-four-year-old fugitive. He was on the 'Most Wanted' list of every major Western security service. They did not know his real identity, but they knew all about his activities. The theft of sensitive information from some of the most closely guarded and secure Government and Corporate offices in Europe was one of his specialities. 'The Establishment' and their Corporatists cohorts were desperately trying to catch Dark and stop his activities. The underground media published the material he stole, which caused uproar within 'The Establishment'. They were desperate to hide details of their corruption from the public and label it fake news. Dark knew full well if he was caught, 'The Establishment' would kill him. To frustrate the security service's persistent efforts to identify him, he adopted a series of personas. Tonight's disguise was an office cleaner. He adopted the dishevelled grimy appearance of someone who didn't take personal hygiene too seriously. He was anonymous amongst the tide of humanity that inhabited the overcrowded cities. Scruffy jeans and oversized t-shirts camouflaged him to the point of invisibility, making him appear much younger to a casual observer. He used wigs and facial prosthetics to drastically change his appearance from one character to another. When he walked the streets, his habit was to keep his face down and avoid CCTV.

Dark was the antithesis of the popular view of a secret agent: his skin was pale from too little exposure to sunlight, and his head lolled forward as if holding it upright was too much effort. His shoulders were rounded from too many hours in front of a computer. He didn't look as if he would pose the slightest threat in a fight. Yet appearances were deceptive; he was skilled in Krav Maga and could climb like a cat.

Once at the bottom of the basement stairway, he ambled down a long dim corridor. Widely spaced fluorescent lights cast pools of cold light that were interspersed by patches of darkness. Dark rounded a corner into the locker room, a small space twenty feet square. Harsh lighting gave the room a cold, austere atmosphere. Battered grey metal lockers lined one wall; there were wooden benches set out before them. A doorway to the left of the lockers led to a washroom. The only sounds were the muted rustling of people changing into their grubby uniforms; cleaners, mostly illegals, removed watches and rings for safekeeping, leaving them on the top shelves of their lockers. No one spoke. It was an unwritten rule: ask no questions, tell no lies. Most of them had cherished photographs of loved ones taped to the inside of the locker doors - long-distance memories that kept them going through the grubby drudgery of the job. Dark followed the example of his co-workers and quietly donned his overalls. The odd nod of recognition was the most interaction anyone gave.

Dark had picked up the habit of a fugitive unconsciously from his father's friend Heinz Gombricht - the nondescript appearances and disguises, the ability to blend into almost any type of crowd or background. Never letting his guard down, never trusting anyone. The unrelenting stress of hiding her family from the authorities had led to his mother's death. Dark knew that in the end, she had just given up hope of ever getting justice or leading a normal life.

But Dark vowed he would never give up. The only life he knew was a fugitive's, hunted and self-contained. He had become an expert in living outside the boundaries of normal society: parallel to it, but separate from it. Heinz had trained and guided him in the tactics of identity creation; he had developed his own methods of hacking and cyber-attacking and was part of an elite group of people who could break into any computer system in the world.

In the far corner of the locker room, opposite the washroom, was a small office with a large glass window where the supervisor and his lackadaisical assistant resided throughout the entire duration of the night shift.

The supervisor was an old, stick-thin Rastafarian whom everyone deferentially called Mr Michael. Dreadlocks dangled around his shoulders, and a roll-up cigarette, a permanent fixture on dangled from his bottom lip.

Masquerade

His custom was to perch upon an ancient wooden swivel chair. He sat ramrod straight, head held proudly high. He gazed slowly and deliberately around his domain. He was an even-handed supervisor, respected and trusted by the cleaners. He never enquired into their affairs and, once he had distributed the job sheets, left them alone to complete their work. During the night, he might send out his assistant, Arthur, to check everything was running smoothly and that no one was sleeping on the job, which was about the only thing you could be dismissed for.

"Ah, the last one Mr Michael," said Arthur, "the quiet one's here." Which was quite a compliment considering none of the crew spoke to each other.

Mr Michael selected a card from a pile on his left and noted the time in a slow, deliberate script on Dark's card, which bore the name Lewis Goodman, before replacing it in alphabetical order in the stack on his right. Thirty cards, one for each cleaner booked in.

"Distribute tonight's job sheets Arthur, give the crew their rounds or else they will be talking all night long. I'll get no work done."

Arthur habitually printed the job sheets as soon as he clocked on and spent the next thirty minutes filling them out. He enjoyed the small amount of power he wielded. He decided who would get the easy jobs. He was not above taking a consideration for this favour, and as long as Mr Michael got a cut of the action, he was allowed to enjoy his influence. One thing he always made sure of was giving Dark the most difficult job, the one on the top floors where the bosses had their offices. Everyone else grumbled about dragging their trolleys all the way up there and then having to be so particular about the cleanliness of the place. The slightest speck of dust and the managers were on the phone complaining. With Dark, he never had to worry about all of that crap. Dark kept the place spotless.

"Always on time, that fella. Same time to the minute. Takes some doing that does. Attention to detail. Same as his work - never changes his routine. Same job, same time, every time he's on. That's the sort of cleaner you need!"

The funny thing was, he had never actually seen Dark work. His areas were always spotlessly clean, and he was usually one of the first to finish. Arthur wondered how he did it. On reflection probably best not to ask. It was done properly, and that was all there was to it.

Masquerade

If Mr Michael had been aware of Dark's activities, he wouldn't have been so sanguine. When Mr Michael thought Dark was busy dusting furniture or vacuuming corridors and offices, he was, in fact, meticulously rifling through the desks, emails and computer files of senior managers, methodically stealing secrets that could be used to expose the company's clandestine criminal activities.

Dark closed his locker door and walked to the office to collect his job sheet. He gave a deferential tap on the door and waited. Arthur took his time to open up then scowled at Dark, "What do you want?"

Dark took off his spectacles, wiped them on a grubby rag, then mumbled, "Just after my job sheet, Boss."

Arthur harrumphed, "You're early! You know we start at nine o'clock sharp."

Dark stared at his feet, "Well, if you are going to send me up to the top floor again, I could do with starting early. There's a lot of work up there, you know. Takes all night." He hoped Arthur would allocate him the top floor; it was where he needed to break into the finance director's safe.

Abruptly Arthur turned back and marched over to his desk. He shuffled through the pile of job cards and, with a grunt, paused at the one he was looking for. "Here, you can make a start. I'll be up to check on you later, so no mucking about."

Dark mumbled, "Yes, Boss," and turned to collect his trolley. He knew Arthur and Mr Michael would both be asleep in the office before the hour was out. Arthur wouldn't be sent out for another couple of hours. The security guards would cause him the most concern. There were ex-military, and they took their duties seriously. Their rounds were unpredictable and covered every inch of the building. Twice Dark had nearly been caught in the last week. He had abandoned one attempt to break into the safe when they had stopped outside an office he had broken into. It was supposed to be locked permanently and only cleaned by a supervised technician. He would have no way of explaining how an ordinary cleaner gained entry to an office secured by a Triple-A Security Grade Vault door. They were almost impossible to break. Unless you used a copy of the Director's biometric key.

Chapter 11: Kalyptra Genesis

A shrill ring from an ancient telephone roused the old man from sleep. It was the Albanian. "The girls will be ready tomorrow - the usual address in Paris. There are seven, all white as specified. Your clients will be satisfied; these are high-class girls."

Marat grunted into the phone; the arrangement was satisfactory. He replaced the receiver in its cradle and thumbed a remote control. Seconds later, a highly polished door behind him opened. One of his aides walked softly to his side, "Yes, Patron?"

The old man selected a cigar, "After the girls have been collected from the squat, I want them taken straight to the warehouse in Marseille. Pick them up at the usual time tomorrow. Make sure everything runs smoothly. Have you made the arrangements with the Swiss for Bilic's step-daughter to be delivered to the squat?"

Later that morning, a heavily built security guard methodically scanned the manicured parkland looking for any untoward movement. He was part of a small army protecting one of the most powerful men in Europe. Bright early morning sunshine dazzled him as it reflected off the dew-laden grass. He rested his machine gun in the crook of his arm whilst he reached into an inside pocket for his sunglasses. As he put them on, he heard the distant thrum of a helicopter engine, the first of many scheduled to arrive that morning at Kalyptra's European headquarters. In the woods surrounding the estate, more than two hundred men secured the perimeter. They were part of a guard billeted permanently on-site to protect the building and its occupants. There were four other estates owned by the Kalyptra Group in other European locations. Each of them had identical security arrangements.

The guard watched as the helicopter landed and an electric buggy drew up to the helipad, ready to carry its passengers the half-mile to the house. The Polish representative Jan Sobieski struggled out of the helicopter then gestured impatiently to his assistant to keep up as he climbed into the buggy. Just as the helicopter's turbines increased their thrust, ready for take-off, the heavy whump of a second helicopter could be heard approaching from the East. The guard looked over his shoulder and saw a dark green Augusta Eurocopter slow its approach to a hover as it waited for the first craft to leave the helipad.

Masquerade

This estate was the original headquarters of Kalyptra. The building itself was a beautiful 15th century fortified Chateau set in extensive grounds on the banks of the Loire River in northwestern France. The founder of Kalyptra, Louis Marat, had acquired the war-ravaged estate and its farms from a penniless aristocrat at the end of the Second World War. He had made a fortune during the war by supplying cigarettes and meat to the German army. He made similar deals with the Allies when they came along. After the war, he made another fortune on the black market, finding petrol, importing meat, fresh fruit and vegetables, then selling them at highly inflated prices to industrialists, the aristocracy, and the French establishment.

The guard knew the scene would be repeated throughout the morning as the fifteen delegates arrived for the regular management meeting. These delegates were creatures of habit; they even arrived in the same order. Sobieski was invariably the first to arrive. The guard checked his watch; it was time to make his rounds. He turned to his right and walked along a path, frosty gravel crunched under his heavy boots in the unseasonal chill of the early morning.

As Kalyptra's delegates arrived for their meeting, over in Geneva Heinz Gombricht had returned from London to his base. He sat at a battered wooden desk in the basement of the St. Jean Hostel for Lost Souls. In his late fifties, Heinz was tall, distinguished; he was descended from Austrian nobility. He had followed his forebears into the Austrian Diplomatic Service but had retired early after losing his two closest friends in separate incidents which he knew to be suspicious. The three of them had been covertly investigating corruption in the highest ranks of their respective Governments. Somehow their activities had been discovered, and his comrades, Julian Dark and Ferdinand Esterhazy, had been murdered. Heinz had narrowly escaped being pushed in front of a train at a Moscow station. He'd got the message and immediately went into hiding. He had no wife or children to worry about, and using his familial connections, had established a cover and new life in Switzerland. But he still fought corruption in the European Establishment. Heinz understood in the twentieth century, conflicts would be fought with technology, so using intermediaries, he had established a global network of insurgents with expertise in IT, cryptography and surveillance, the 'Hacker Network'. His best operative was George Dark, Julian's son, codename 'Marlowe'. Dark's skillset of disguise, hacking and burglary unearthed many of the Corporatists' most

Masquerade

closely guarded secrets. They were infuriated by the exposure of their deceitful practices and had ordered their henchmen in Kalyptra to kill Dark on sight.

On the other side of the world, in a cramped apartment in Kowloon, Hong Kong, was home to Jimmy Chan, his brother and his parents. Jimmy was a prodigy; at nineteen, he was studying for a PhD and was one of the world's foremost experts in cyber-security. He was also an insurgent hacker and a lynchpin of Heinz's network. After his parents lost all their savings in a stock market crash, Jimmy joined Heinz, determined to make the bankers pay for their recklessness. He sprawled on a sofa dividing his attention between a mobile, a laptop and a console game. His mobile buzzed; it was Heinz.

"Hey, man!"

"Hi, Jimmy. What have you got for me?"

Jimmy flopped back on the couch, scrolling through notes on his laptop. "Jose was right about the fighting in South America. There are three groups of guerrillas waging a sustained campaign against left-wing governments. They are all funded by Blackwood, an arms dealer owned by the American Corporatists. They claim to be protecting their assets in the area, but they're really engaged in regime change; they're trying to instal an American-backed President."

Heinz grunted, "Same old story. What's the prize? Oil leases?"

Jimmy, "Yeah, plus they get to influence neighbouring countries; Cuba was always an itch they couldn't scratch."

Heinz closed the call with Jimmy and looked over at his old grandfather clock. It was after midnight, but he still needed to read through a well-thumbed file. Aromatic cigar smoke swirled in the light from the desk lamp. He opened a section headed 'Kalyptra'; a faded black and white photograph of a street urchin dressed in rags fell out. The boy, holding a Mauser pistol, was guarding a pile of Red Cross ration boxes, cigarette cartons and crates of whiskey. Gombricht picked up the photo; this had been his adversary for decades. Replacing the photo, he picked up a copy of an old Sûreté arrest warrant, dated 1960, made out in the name of Marat, accusing him of black marketing and keeping a brothel.

Back at the Chateau, Marat, dressed in silk pyjamas and dressing gown, gazed thoughtfully out of his bedroom window at the bright, crisp winter morning; the estate's preened parkland was made even more beautiful by an unseasonal frost. The view lifted his spirits. Marat took great pride in his chateau and its estate. It had taken many years of meticulous cultivation to create the verdant sanctuary into which he escaped from the pressure of his position. A homeless orphan of war-torn Paris, the chateau was the prize he dreamed of all those years ago. After creating one of the most powerful secret organisations in Europe, all he wanted was the peace and quiet of his beloved estate in France and his winery in Mendoza, Argentina. His passion in life now was growing prime beef and quality wine.

Soon though, his mood darkened as his thoughts turned to the difficulty he faced naming his successor. This would be his final act as Patron of the Corporatists' enforcers, Kalyptra. It sounded a grand title; he enjoyed the pageantry he had introduced over the years, mimicking ancient secret societies. His position carried so much influence that he manipulated most of the senior politicians and bureaucrats in Europe for the benefit of his Corporate Masters.

In his search for a suitable successor, he had considered the members of his own Council and arrived at a shortlist: Bilic and Stryckland. Marat alone would make the choice. Someone to continue his traditions. Today at their quarterly meeting, he would announce his retirement then watch as the jockeying for position began.

The position would need a ruthless leader. Tough enough to control some of the most ruthless and brutal businessmen on the continent. He knew the Council would follow any instruction if they could see a viable plan that gave them a profit.

Marat's masters were a secretive group, defined by their vast individual wealth. They owned global corporations but did not necessarily have the political influence of the Oligarchs. For the most part, these two groups joined in a symbiotic relationship for their mutual benefit. Trivial arguments often broke out amongst minor members, but these disputes were quickly resolved, usually with a killing. The pact between the two power structures was sacrosanct. Marat considered the United States to be a Plutocracy, whilst Russia and several Asian countries were Oligarchies. Europe was a hybrid of the two systems, but which, if his master plan succeeded, would mutate into something he called a Corporatocracy. This would make government and state functions commercial and profitable, involving all departments in capitalist mercantile activity to extract as much profit as possible from the population. Marat was well on his way to making this a reality.

These two groups, which consisted of a number of ancient families, put simply, ruled the world. They owned and controlled the wealthiest businesses the world had ever seen. For decades, their organisations accumulated vast wealth and power by manipulating markets and politicians globally. Smaller companies and men of principle who tried to compete with them were ruthlessly eliminated.

The Oligarchs and Plutocrats tolerated no argument. They demanded and received absolute obedience from their underlings. Marat reported directly to the Corporatists' senior committee. He was viewed as a senior subordinate who ruled his department as a despot. The Head of the Families had accepted his resignation with apparent equanimity two weeks previously. Now he was looking forward to a peaceful retirement dividing his time between his estates.

The Kalyptra Group had grown over the years from a loose collaboration of black market racketeers operating in Europe amidst the chaotic aftermath of the Second World War. Today it was a highly organised and secretive enterprise. If one were able to look, superficially, its activities were entirely above board and legal. However, the means by which they came to control those activities were most certainly illegal. In the late 1940s, as shortages of basic foodstuffs and luxury goods gave way to plentiful supply, the racketeers' profits began to dwindle. The more astute racketeers quickly realised they could improve their profits by seizing control of perfectly legal established businesses. This would have the major advantage of avoiding the attention of the police and inevitable jail time if they were caught. So by a combination of coercion and money, they camouflaged their illicit operations behind the veil of legitimate business. To begin with, they seized control of family companies, often where the owners had been killed or were missing, presumed dead after the war. They either paid off or forced the remaining family members to hand over the businesses. Then they set their sights on larger, more profitable businesses. Again their methods were to try an amicable first approach to buy shares. If that was refused, they either blackmailed or killed shareholders until they gained majority ownership of the company. Once they had constructed a satisfactory portfolio of companies, they set about managing them legally then expanding the enterprise until it became a prominent national business. They were fortunate that this growth coincided with the blossoming of the media industry. Companies anxious to make consumers aware of their products underpinned the increased use of advertising agencies throughout Europe. They copied the brash American method of unsophisticated, provocative marketing. The agencies, in turn, sustained and nurtured a nascent television business as well as creating the glossy magazine trade in which celebrities glamorised and endorsed their products. The success their companies derived from this promotion helped them to grow into pan European corporations reaping the benefits of the newly created trading zone. By the early sixties, youth pop culture provided a huge pool of disposable income for these companies to chase. The newly successful corporations now felt powerful enough to pressurise governments to relax legislation allowing them more leeway to advertise and control consumers in exchange for huge sums of money paid to the government in tax revenues. Not to mention large donations to party funds, or indeed individual donations to selected influential politicians. European governments and the European Union eagerly complied. New businesses sprang up to satisfy the masses' addiction to consumerism. These new corporations built exciting new shopping Malls or 'Temples of Consumerism' on the outskirts of towns, bypassing traditional high streets. By the mid-eighties, these retailing corporations became the major driving force in national economies. Their tax revenues and contribution to GDP gave them unparalleled power, able to influence politicians and civil servants alike. Their shareholders became used to a steady income from dividends and demanded year on year increases. Over the course of forty years since the war, the racketeers became extremely wealthy and accepted as respectable members of the establishment. The more astute members of that group understood that to continue growing their profits, they would need to stop wasting time and energy competing with one another and work together to share the by now gigantic spending consumers were willing to fund with credit.

So, after a series of secret meetings, the current Kalyptra CEO established his seniority by virtue of his vision of how their new organisation could increase profits and a viable plan to implement that vision. Dissenters or lone wolves were ruthlessly disposed of, and their corporations subsumed into the collective. If approached, you were either in or out; there was no middle ground.

Marat wasted little time in using the newfound strength of the organisation to generate larger and larger profits from a seemingly insatiable appetite for the Corporatist's goods. Of course, this appetite could not be created or sustained without the connivance of the media industry. Realising Kalyptra members needed to sustain demand, they duly acquired majority shareholdings in leading advertising agencies, television companies, newspaper and magazine groups. The job of these companies was to create and sustain demand for Kalyptra members' products. In order to achieve this goal, the companies encouraged the pop culture of the sixties, where freedom of choice of lifestyle and relaxation of social rules created a demand for goods aimed at young people. Month after month, glossy magazine photographers were invited into the homes of celebrities who gushed about their trophy homes, cars, holidays and lifestyle to an audience eager to emulate them. Advertising agencies and television reinforced the message that a happy and fulfilling life could only be achieved by buying the latest fad. Banks provided the means for consumers to acquire the object of their desire by providing easy credit to everyone.

The Corporatists soon realised how easy it was to manipulate people's behaviour with their advertising campaigns and the tenor of their television programmes. If a program showed a particular beauty spot in a foreign country, demand for holidays to that location mushroomed overnight. So-called independent experts appearing on TV warning of the possible health risks associated with a rival's product could bring a company to its knees in a matter of weeks. These were the tools in Kalyptra's armoury when vying for its member's supremacy. Not only were they more effective than the old methods of physical violence, but they were also legal and actively encouraged by Governments.

With this understanding came power, and with this power came the realisation they could make or break politicians and governments. Very soon, governments and politicians also recognised this supremacy. And in recognising this, they accepted they had lost control of their voters and so accepted the inducements offered by Kalyptra in a bid to retain a modicum of self-esteem. If they did not, their political opponents would, and they would be out of the game altogether.

By mid-morning, helicopters had deposited all fifteen members plus associated lackeys to the Chateau. They had assembled in a large, sparsely decorated salon. Its walls were plain white, and there was no adornment apart from a huge relief of Kalyptra's icon, a blood-red Tanburg Eagle mounted high on the wall. Before it was a large oval table around which were seated members representing each European country where Kalyptra operated. The Rt. Honourable Giles Stryckland and Milan Bilic were both allocated prominent seats near Marat, emphasising their seniority. At intervals around the room, assistants and guards waited silently.

Background chatter in the room grew louder as more delegates arrived and began to take their places. Bennetti, the Italian delegate, a lawyer by profession, walked leisurely towards his seat. He was an elegant patrician with a deep Mediterranean tan. Politically skilled and ruthless.

Fabian de Braganza, the Portuguese delegate, caught up with Bennetti, and, like old friends, they embraced and walked arm in arm towards a table serving coffee, chatting amiably. Braganza was tall with a rower's physique. He preferred a traditionally tailored Saville Row suit to Bennetti's modern Milanese designer clothes.

Butzi Schneider, the Swiss delegate, strode across the reception area; his cropped blonde hair framed a broad face which cracked into a smile as he spied Sobieski, Marat's minder. They were joking about a recent inebriated night on the town in Paris when Butzi nudged Sobieski. Stryckland had walked in and made his way to his seat. He looked drawn, with shadows underlined his eyes. "There goes a man under pressure," Butzi remarked.

"Talking of pressure, where's Bilic?" asked Braganza.

"The Alchemist, the man who turns crap into gold. He won't be far from Marat," Bennetti mused. "I spoke to him last week. He was in an unusually good mood. Maybe he knows something. I wondered if Marat has given him the nod."

Sobieski, ever the loyal supporter, growled, "Maybe he has maybe, he hasn't. But Patron will keep his cards close to his chest. He'll play those two off against each other, you'll see. Test their metal, see which is stronger. Anyway, whoever wins will still have to be endorsed by the American bosses."

They watched Stryckland studying the meeting documents. Sat at the far end of the table, ignoring those around him, he looked isolated.

"It's going to be an interesting meeting, gentlemen," Bennetti murmured as the group drifted apart.

Sobieski watched the rest of the delegates take their seats. He felt dismayed by what he saw. The men who created Kalyptra had been little older than young boys who fought tooth and nail to survive the lawless aftermath of the Second World War. Ordinary men of fighting age were either dead or incapacitated. The rest had starved or had been killed fighting for food or shelter in the bloody chaos. Circumstances had turned those boys into ruthless survivors with killer instincts. Now the delegates were corporate types, either lawyers or accountants. He didn't trust them, "devious bastards, the lot of them - always get someone else to do their dirty work... too squeamish, cowards to a man."

Marat waited quietly for the hum of conversation to die down. When the room fell silent, he spoke softly. "Number One! Your report, please."

Sobieski wasn't interested in the organisation's bureaucracy - he was a man of action. At six feet eight and nineteen stone, he was built for trouble. He took a seat and daydreamed wistfully of the time when he could ruck and maul with the best the Toulouse Rugby Club had to offer. Of course, he was much slimmer in those days - before injuries had taken their toll. That was when he began to work for Marat as a 'facilitator'. He snoozed, engrossed with his memories: the money, the girls. But it had been the deals and the fights that he loved. He remembered helping Marat resist a double-cross by the Unione Corse over a tobacco shipment. Habitually suspecting treachery, Marat had taken him along as an enforcer on a seemingly straightforward deal. Whilst the Boss and his accountant were making the exchange, he had crept up behind the opposition with a silenced automatic and kneecapped three men waiting to ambush them. The deal had proceeded without further incident, much to the irritation of the Capo, who expected to walk away with both the money and the cigarettes.

Chapter 12: Recount

In the East End of London, Dark's alter ego wearily pushed the cleaning trolley along the dimly lit corridor. Tucked safely in his pocket was the evidence he had come for. Debden Oil had been bribing senior Civil Servants to guarantee their gas fracking licenses in southeast England. His work was done for the night. He just needed to throw out the rubbish, and he could go home. A cold beer and a film were in order.

He banged his trolley through the fire doors into the service area. A chill night breeze hit him like cold water hitting a drunk. Shaking off the lethargy, he crossed the yard, then stopped. He listened intently. The night was unnaturally quiet. He looked up; the city and the river were bathed in silvery moonlight, city lights glazed the scudding clouds a deep orange. A rumble of thunder softly shook the air. Eastward over the estuary, lightning flickered fitfully above the clouds. Dark watched spellbound as the storm moved towards him.

Since childhood Dark's senses had been heightened by electric storms. Static - he felt it pulsating - waves of energy vibrated through his body as the gathering storm moved swiftly westward and abruptly unleashed its fury above him. Explosive thunderclaps detonated with growing power. Jagged bolts of lightning stabbed through the clouds, matching thunderclaps blast for blast.

In the millisecond of a lightning bolt flash, Dark glimpsed a black van in the murk beyond the yard. As the lightning flash died, the van melted back into the gloom. Dark was drawn towards the fence. Another jagged flash illuminated five men, clad in black, emerging from the van. Dark had a sense of uniforms, boots, helmets, masks - then blackness again as the lightning faded. Another incandescent flash, and he saw a body thrown to the ground. Suddenly the storm paused as if catching its breath. In the ominous vacuum, Dark heard the rhythmic pounding of heavy boots thudding against soft flesh. Abruptly the pounding stopped, leaving a brooding stillness broken only by a chorus of rasping breath.

Subdued, the storm began to move away, its fury spent. Dark became aware his hands were slick with blood; the wire fence had cut deep. Anxiously he scoured the darkness beyond. "What the hell was happening?" Lightning stubbornly refused to illuminate. Somewhere in the blackness, he heard the soft crunch of gravel as the van moved quietly away. Appalled by the sickening spectacle, Dark raged at the night, tormented by his helplessness in the presence of casual brutality. He spat sour, steaming bile. Then collecting his wits, he ran through a service gate leading to the road. Perhaps there was a flicker of life in the poor wretch yet.

Stooping low, he used his torch to search for the body. Had they even left it? Something glinted before him; without thinking, he reached and picked it up. Then with a snort of disgust, he dropped it. It was slick and warm; he examined the object in the dull light. "Dear God!" A severed finger with a ring. He fished a handkerchief out of a pocket and gingerly picked it up. Dark turned the ring over and found an engraving. It brought him up short. "My God!" He was shaken. The ring was engraved with a Tanburg Eagle. His stomach crawled; this was the insignia of his deadliest enemy – Kalyptra.

Dark finally found the body thirty yards away, half-hidden in a pile of rubble - all but invisible. Then the rain came back in sheets. There was nothing to be done for the victim; he was dead. Apart from the ring, there was no means of identification. This was no ordinary beating; this was an execution - a carbon copy of Dark's own father's murder - the most recent in a string of murders of high profile businessmen. "But why?"

Carefully Dark wrapped the severed digit in a handkerchief and pocketed it. The ring might lead him to the victim's identity.

Hurriedly he returned his trolley to the cleaning station, collected his coat and left. He needed to speak to Heinz. With luck, his network could be able to track down the black van's owner.

Dark returned to his base on the top floor of the ancient crumbling warehouse– located on a wharf tacked on to the bank of a tributary feeding the Thames. By land, the only access was a narrow, overgrown lane which was all but invisible to a casual glance. Property developers hadn't considered the area development material, so it was left alone, hidden on its little spit of land, surrounded by ostentatious concrete and glass developments.

His father had bought the tumbledown ruin years before the property boom as a quiet bolt hole. Ramshackle on the outside, its dilapidated appearance belied a state-of-the-art apartment and workshop. Its obscurity suited Dark perfectly.

Masquerade

A garage in the basement housed a rusty old Mini and a battered Hilux pickup. On the riverside, an integrated boathouse contained a tired river launch. A refurbished tugboat was moored midstream alongside a line of barges. Add in a tunnel that ran eastward, and there were several options, should Dark choose to leave quickly unobserved.

Dark came out of the shower and dressed quickly, made a mug of tea and walked over to a large bench - his nerve centre. The upper floor of the warehouse had been converted into a workshop and living space. Workbenches full of electronic equipment lined two walls; on another side of the room was a stainless-steel bench crammed full with costumes and makeup paraphernalia. Several head mannequins held an array of latex masks. A bank of screens ran the main news and business channels broadcasting the latest propaganda the establishment characterised as factual news. Nearby, an aluminium and glass cabinet housed racks of customised black box computers and routers, Dark's anonymous backdoor into the Corporatists' cyber-world. A Faraday Cage enclosed every room in the building, this blocked electronic signals and prevented the NSA and GCHQ from eavesdropping.

From here, Dark was able to communicate instantly with Heinz's network of fellow insurgents. They were a small band fighting the might of the Corporatists across the cybernetic jungle. They picked off established corporations as well as the new wave of technology companies that made enormous profits selling personal data from their vast data farms. Technology did that to people - depersonalised them and turned them into automatons.

A laptop was the first to boot. Dark checked the private forums for updates. It was too early for there to be much activity. He was impatient to speak to Chester. "But what would he tell him? That he had witnessed a murder in the midst of an electric storm?" A couple of milli-second flashes of lightning and teeming rain in which he saw and heard the briefest glimpses of a murder. Not the best conditions to absorb something happening fifty yards away in a storm.

He needed more detail. Dark settled down to visualise those fateful few moments. His subconscious would give him the detail. He relaxed to meditate.

Masquerade

The van was large, matt black - almost invisible in the storm. Its sidelights glowed dimly in the murk. It had rolled noiselessly down the road; wisps of white exhaust vapour trailed behind. Quietly it had stopped. A side door had slid open. Five men clambered out, brisk but silent. Dark had the impression the men were Police, though there were no obvious badges. Besides, the Police wouldn't keep a suspect in the van with them. He would be locked in a cage in the back.

The men had dragged the victim onto the rubbish-strewn waste ground and begun the beating. Something about the van bothered him. Why? He replayed the scene again. Wait ...there was something. It wasn't completely black. A thin fluorescent stripe ran down the side of the van and on the door... or was it a symbol? What was it? Relax. Don't force it. A logo of some description? A shield, perhaps? Two lines crossed behind it. Spears? No, too short. Swords? Yes, swords! So a shield and two swords. There was a script below. Small, just too small to make out clearly. 'V' something. Possibly 'A'? What else? Damn can't see. The door was closed again. Quietly the men had returned to the vehicle. It had disappeared silently behind a curtain of torrential rain like a ghost.

Dark roused himself and pulled a laptop towards him. He ran a search for a shield and two swords. Nothing. The parameters were too broad, thousands of logos filled the screen, all useless – this was a job for Heinz.

Dark stifled a yawn. He had been up for more than twenty-four hours, but this was no time for sleep. He needed to get Chester digging out details of the murder. He used cheap pay-as-you-go mobiles to communicate with his contacts. He destroyed the phones every couple of weeks; paranoia was his friend. He dialled a number from memory.

"Fancy a coffee?"

"Yeah."

"Usual place - an hour?"

"Sure."

He cut the call. The contact would understand the conversation. They would meet at a prearranged place. The time was the code. An hour meant the Serpentine Bridge at two pm. Half an hour was a small café in Soho at eleven am. There were a dozen variations. Dark preferred practical fieldcraft to bypass the ubiquitous technology trap of mobile phone cells and the internet.

Chapter 13: Circularity

At Marat's Chateau, the meeting was in progress. Nicolescou stood and nervously read his report. "The Romanian Government have awarded the new Budapest rail link contract to Constanta Construction AV. We have negotiated with the Transport Minister for over six months. So I am pleased the Minister has listened to our advice. The 'Banker' has checked the estimated accounts for the contract, and he confirmed that Kalyptra will receive a commission of one hundred million Euros. Also, there will be an annual fee of two million Euros for security services."

Marat jotted down notes, then waved for Mannheim, the German delegate to begin. "The Schiller supermarket chain has been given permission to build ten new supermarkets in greenbelt on the edge of large towns. The environmentalists who stalled the project have been dealt with."

Next came Poland - Czerwiński reported Kalyptra would receive a Three Hundred and Fifty Million Euro fee for arranging a deal between the Polish Army and an American Arms supplier. Every delegate gave a positive report. Substantial fees were due to Kalyptra. Their Corporatist overseers would be satisfied that their insatiable quest for profit was proceeding to plan. There were two regions left.

"Explain to me, Petrakis, why are our cigarette deliveries being disrupted?"

Petrakis shuffled around in his seat; this would be uncomfortable, "Patron, we have four of the eight Customs superintendents on our payroll. But the Ministry in Tirana is replacing staff so quickly we can't keep pace swiftly enough to prevent the deliveries from being disrupted. We're at our wit's end. There is so much demand, we can't keep up with it. We could easily supply twice our current capacity if there was safe passage for the goods."

"Why haven't you persuaded a senior official that they should turn their attention to other matters? Do you know of such a person?"

"Of course, Patron, we have investigated two potential candidates, but they have impeccable characters and no family. We have found no weaknesses to exploit."

There was silence in the room; no one dared speak. The only sound was the slow rhythmic tick of a clock high on the wall behind the delegates. Marat considered his options. Petrakis was a loyal delegate; he was normally successful. Marat would help him, but he let the silence hang for a while. Eventually, he turned to his secretary. "Take a note for Signor Leppardi to contact the two officials in the Albanian Interior Ministry. Instruct them to make arrangements for our shipments to be given free passage with immediate effect. I have dealt with these people before, they will be aware of the correct course of action.

He turned back to the delegate, "Petrakis, in return for this favour, we will require an additional commission."

Mightily relieved, Petrakis replied, "Naturally, Patron. Your assistance in this matter is most gratefully received." He nodded acknowledgement of the favour.

Marat, "Now we have been updated on regional business, let us proceed to one of the main items on the agenda. You will be aware we have been tasked to reorganise the supply of cheap labour by the Corporatists. Bilic has nearly finished negotiations with Hellenic Travel Group to acquire their European chain of budget hotels. The hotels will provide a plausible cover for us to move a workforce freely around Europe free from political interference. You are all conversant with the substantial profits earned from people migrating to Europe looking for work. We take a minimum of €10,000 per person. We arrange the necessary paperwork and take care of the relevant officials. That still leaves us with a respectable profit. Even at this price, which amounts to ten years wages in many countries, our gang masters are inundated. They turn away dozens for every one they take.

With the acquisition of the hotel chain, not one migrant will be turned away. We also control the whole supply chain from recruitment to finding work and controlling their wages. We are instructing the recruiters in Afghanistan, Iraq, Nigeria, Uganda, and Eastern Europe to find as many people as they can. There is a high demand for unskilled manual labour in the construction and services industries.

On a different note, we have replaced the traditional suppliers of these men with our own recruiters. We can now be sure we are not being cheated as often as we used to be. This is not only a *bona fide* business venture; it is the cover story for infiltrating the squads of our militia into the UK disguised as hotel workers in the weeks leading up to the coup.

Bilic will outline the plan placing these people with our members. Make sure the members know their responsibilities as far as ensuring the correct paperwork and documentation needed to enter their countries legally, and also there is to be no interference when the workforce is crossing the border. All necessary contacts to smooth these fundamentals must be in place as soon as possible. Our first shipments are just beginning. We have work lined up for them; we do not want to lose face by failing to fulfil quotas. Bilic, continue."

As Bilic began to outline his plan, Marat sat and weighed the pros and cons of his two preferred candidates. Marat weighed Stryckland's personal characteristics. He had known him for fifteen years or so ever since he approached the organisation when he was made a junior minister. Stryckland came from a privileged background, educated at Harrow, Oxford, then Sandhurst. He had enjoyed the advantages of an upper-middle-class childhood. His character was patrician, ruthless, and Machiavellian – he was much like Marat himself. He was completely at ease in the society of the heads of corporations and senior politicians that made up the European establishment. These were significant advantages for Stryckland. His organisational and planning skills were well known. Strategically he was a visionary, an excellent Counsellor for the Corporatists, much better than Marat. Well versed in the dark arts of political intrigue, he circumvented or removed political opponents or obstacles before they became problems. His weakness was that he had little or no idea when it came to the enforcement side of the business. If he were given the job, he would need a team of aides around him to act as enforcers to put his plans into action and advisors to rein in his more outlandish schemes.

Bilic, however, was a master of man management, a man of action, willing and able to engage with his men to achieve their goals on time, whatever it cost. Time and time again, Bilic had got his hands dirty and worked with his troops to ensure a successful outcome. His major strengths were his ruthlessness and cunning: a nimble mind able to draw conclusions without the need to rely on anyone else. He worked well under pressure. He had, after all, dragged himself out of the slums and chaos of war-torn Serbia and made himself a multimillionaire.

Yet that was his major weakness; his peasant roots made him feel insecure and therefore overly antagonistic and given to impetuosity. He was out of his depth socialising with executives and owners. His background and lack of education limited him in those circles. His habitual air of menace also frightened the life out of these people; usually, they quickly made an excuse and left.

Marat massaged his temples; this decision was not becoming any easier, how ever much he thought about it. In many ways, the obvious choice would be for both of them to be joint chairman. But that way was fraught with danger. Each despised the other. They could barely bring themselves to speak to each other civilly. He was well aware that Bilic was trying desperately to undermine Stryckland's pursuit of the job. And equally aware that Stryckland would only tolerate this attack for so long before retaliating.

These two were the only viable long-term prospects. If he ignored these, then the only real candidate he trusted with the custody of the society was Sobieski. But he would want to retire in five or six years, and this choice would present itself once more.

Bilic's voice brought Marat back to the meeting.

"And so I want you to make sure the government ministry responsible for immigration in your countries has prepared the necessary documentation and visas for these workers to enter the country at the appointed time. I want you to review the document pack in front of you. You need to understand the importance of this project; the Corporatists are expecting significant revenue streams. We all know failure is not an option."

Now Marat stood. "Thank you, Bilic."

He turned to the delegates, "As you are all aware, at Kalyptra, we must safeguard the interests of our Corporatist masters. Up to now, we have used blackmail and persuasion to encourage politicians to pass legislation that enhances our profits. However, recent events have exposed flaws in this strategy. Our methods are being exposed to public scrutiny; this must not be allowed to continue. Stryckland will explain."

Giles Stryckland stood, "In order to ensure Kalyptra's continued success, we must make changes. There are obdurate politicians and even low-level members who no longer wish to co-operate with us. They are being dealt with as I speak. One solution is acceptable to us, one which we have quietly been building towards for decades. Kalyptra will seize total control of every Government in Europe - our heartland. Britain will be the first coup d'état. Their political system is broken, and the electorate is easily manipulated. Kalyptra will assume command when I replace the Prime Minister after…"

Impatiently, Bilic stood interrupting Stryckland, "My friend Stryckland needs to get to the point. The coup will happen like this; the British media will report outbreaks of public disorder spreading across the country. In the midst of this chaos, the Prime Minister will have an unfortunate accident and die."

Stryckland retorted, "A rudderless Government will need a visionary leader to restore order; that will be me. A suitable scapegoat will be found to blame, and we will have seized control of the country with no one being any the wiser."

Annoyed at the interruption, Bilic glared at Stryckland, "The hotel workers we discussed earlier are, in fact, mercenaries posing as migrant workers. I am infiltrating thousands of them into Britain; their mission is to capture and commandeer strategic media installations like television transmitters, radio stations, power stations. The country will be on lockdown and under our direct command. Allowing us to control the flow of information to the British public."

Now Marat stood, "In these circumstances, the British public will believe what we tell them are the facts. And they will believe completely. After all, everyone understands an attractive news presenter wouldn't tell lies."

A ripple of laughter spread round the table.

"I will update you on progress during the week. Thank you. And now all points of order and action points having been addressed, I bring this meeting to order and offer any other business before we close the meeting."

Marat briefly looked around the table; he knew no one would offer a comment at this point, but he had kept the most important point of order until last.

"However, before we close the meeting, I want to bring your attention to a significant issue. Having reviewed the financial data which you all provide before each meeting, it is apparent one delegation has been underperforming for some time now. I have been monitoring the situation closely and have made my own enquiries into the shortfall in revenue."

He discreetly signalled an enforcer, Dubois, who moved noiselessly into position behind the victim. Quietly Dubois slipped on a pair of fine black leather gloves then pulled a wire cheese cutter from his jacket pocket.

Marat continued, "It seems one of us is being greedy. Money has been stolen from us. This person is falsifying the data he sends in a futile attempt to cover up his crime. But I have been in this game for far too long to be so easily duped. So now let us hear what the culprit has to say for himself before I decide his fate."

Marat let the silence linger. He held each delegates' gaze, except one, who tried to avoid Marat's stare. His evasion only served to confirm his guilt.

Marat had no intention of making the next part quick or easy. It was essential that he instilled fear in the minds of his subordinates. He stared at the Spanish delegate, who slumped forward on the table, arms held out in supplication.

"It seems Signor Daugaard admits his guilt."

Daugaard gathered himself and clenched his fists, summoning a show of defiance. He lifted his head and began to speak just as Dubois slipped the garrotte around his neck and heaved, slicing easily through the flesh and muscle. A fine mist of blood sprayed the table red as Daugaard writhed and kicked out. His hands clawed at the wire. His death throes beat a loud, irregular tattoo against the underside of the table. The horrendous cacophony stopped abruptly the moment the wire severed tendons, then the carotid artery. Dubois maintained his grip for a long, silent minute, his face, hands and clothes sodden with blood. At that point, with all muscle and cartilage severed, the head fell forward and rolled along the glass table, leaving a bloody trail of glutinous gore.

A pungent tang of fear hung heavily in the air. One delegate leaned and retched.

Marat allowed the shocked silence to linger. He was completely unaffected by the brutality.

"If that is all, I declare the meeting closed. Good day, gentleman."

The remaining delegates hastily exited the room, eager to put some distance between the gory spectacle and themselves. As Stryckland boarded his flight back to London, his mobile rang.

"I want the money you promised me for the sting job. You told me the money would be in my account a month ago," Gittins shouted.

Stryckland was astonished by the intensity of Gittins' anger. "I don't know who you think you are talking to, but you had better calm down!"

Masquerade

"Sod that! I'm sick and tired of being fobbed off. I want my money! You owe me for the last two jobs, and for the two before those you didn't pay the full price. Enough is enough. "

Stryckland bellowed, "Don't threaten me, you bastard! If it wasn't for me, you'd still be sat at a desk processing parking tickets."

Gittins' temper was getting the better of him, "And if it wasn't for me, you'd be stuck in some backwater committee in Westminster. Don't forget I've cleaned up your dirty little secrets for years. I know where the skeletons are buried, and if you don't pay me what you owe me, I'll let your enemies know how you ruined them."

Stryckland's voice became little more than a whisper, "If I were you, Ronald, I would think very carefully about my next move. It might prove terminal. You're not the only enforcer I use."

Gittins took this to be a bluff; he had never seen Stryckland talk about using anybody else to do his dirty work. It was bluster.

Chapter 14: Wages of Sin

Sam Chester was editor in chief at the 'Enquirer'. A radical magazine with a distinctly belligerent editorial policy, especially towards the Government's insatiable appetite for power. Every issue contained an editorial exposé that denounced the latest transgression. It railed against the Establishment in an attempt to arouse righteous anger in the population. To counter this, Bullmore and the Corporatists diverted the public's attention toward the banality of celebrity. It was their version of Rome's 'Bread and Circuses'. The unpalatable truths of the public's mechanistic dehumanisation had to be kept quiet. Chester's confrontational editorial policy dovetailed neatly with Dark's agenda. They both fought to break the Corporatists' stranglehold on Western Civilisation.

The consequences of this passion had created an uncomfortable existence for the magazine - police harassment and constant media attacks to discredit the magazine and its journalists. In one particularly vicious attack, the Corporatists targeted one of the 'Enquirer's' more vocal journalists, Ralf Gillingham. They concocted a story about soliciting and subjected him to a very public show trial. Carefully coiffured TV presenters dispensed the party line discrediting the journalist and saying, effectively, "You don't really believe this conspiracy theory, do you? Why on earth would Government Ministers lie to you? These public servants are a model of probity." Their siren calls mesmerized an already indoctrinated public. Everyone believed attractive journalists were impartial. The lie was so great, no one could possibly believe it wasn't true, and so the massive scale of Corporatist deceit remained hidden in plain sight. Chester knew only too well if a lie was repeated often enough, people accepted it as the truth.

Chester killed some time before his meeting, drinking coffee and browsing the newsfeeds. At half-past one, he checked his watch, grabbed his jacket and walked out to meet Dark, whom he knew as 'Marlowe'. A brisk thirty-minute walk later, he was leaning on the Serpentine Bridge watching two drakes squabbling loudly over a dowdy female. "Bloody typical." He muttered caustically.

He was always tense when he met an important contact; there was a reasonable chance he was being watched by MI5. Furtively he checked. The park was almost deserted after lunch. The office workers had retreated to the tedium of the office. A few joggers panted past. A wizened old man shuffled along the gravel path. All seemed normal. Chester turned back to the ducks. The old man, leaning heavily on his stick, puffed his way up to the handrail.

His rasping breath gradually subsided, "Smoke?"

The question startled Chester. Not just the impertinence, but the voice didn't quite fit the owner. He turned around and looked more closely, letting the question hang for a moment. He was mistaken, just an old man.

"Excuse me?"

"A cigarette. Would you like a cigarette?" The old man glared at Chester through bushy eyebrows. "It's a simple enough question." He lit a cigarette and blew a stream of smoke at Chester.

Chester regarded him with mounting annoyance, "No. And neither should you." He turned from the proffered packet.

The old man turned to look at the ducks, sniggering quietly to himself.

A moment passed, then the penny dropped. Chester turned to the old man, hissing, "It's you, isn't it? Come on, own up! Marlowe?"

"Keep your voice down! Of course, it's me, you idiot."

"Damn. I wasn't sure. You need to work on the voice... wasn't quite right - disguise is OK, though."

Dark grunted. "It was deliberate. Let's find a seat. Over there, it's quiet."

They walked to a solitary bench in the middle of a wide-open space.

Chester glanced around. "So what's new? It's only been a couple of weeks since our last meet."

"Something's happened."

Chester noted the anger, "What?"

"Last night, I saw a group of riot police beat a man to death. That's the sixth death in the last couple of months. Last night wasn't a beating gone wrong; it was an execution."

Chester was taken back by the rawness of Dark's fury. "Where was this?"

"Outside Debden's offices, East London. The end of the night shift. There was a humungous thunderstorm. A van pulled up on some waste ground over the road from the building. Next thing, five men, all in black, balaclavas, uniforms, the lot, dragged this guy out of the van and started kicking him. After a couple of minutes, the guy on the floor isn't moving. They get into the van and drive off."

Chester, "What? Just like that? Any idea who it was?"

Dark, "Unbelievable, it was so… so mechanical. There was no urgency; it was as if they were swatting a fly. They didn't shout at him; in fact, they didn't speak at all. They were like robots, just mechanical, calculating. I want you to find out who the victim was."

Chester pondered, "Sounds premeditated, right? You're the only one to have seen one of these executions. Don't you think that's strange? You'd think with six deaths, someone else would have seen something before. Who's behind it?"

Dark blurted out, "Christ! Come on, Chester! Who do you think? It's the bloody Corporatists."

Chester's training wouldn't let him jump to conclusions. "We can't be certain yet."

Dark exploded, "Bollocks! You damn well know who it is. When people speak out against the Corporatists they disappear. What the hell happened to one of your contacts after the G20 in Rome last year. Arrested, never seen again. Probably met the same fate as that poor bastard last night. Anyway, I happen to have some evidence."

Dark passed the crumpled handkerchief to Chester. "Look at the ring. Remind you of anything?"

Chester gasped when he saw the severed finger. Repulsed, he carefully turned it over until he could see the engraving.

"Christ Almighty! Is this for real?"

Dark replied, "The Tanburg Eagle."

Chester was disbelieving, "Was he Kalyptra? Is this some sort of signifier? And then be careless enough to leave this behind?"

Dark shook his head.

Chester, "Was there anything else?"

Masquerade

"Actually, there was... on the van. It was absolutely hammering down, I couldn't see clearly, but I think there was a logo. I'll get one of Heinz's hackers to track it down."

Chester, "OK, I'll contact a couple of my guys who have contacts with the cops. They know when something big has happened. Someone always talks; when they do, we'll find out."

Dark fumed. "Why? It's like they're having a purge. We need to find out why before it's covered up. "

Later that afternoon, Chester was at home. A canted lamp cast a small puddle of light on his desk. The rest of the room was in darkness. He scribbled on a scrap of paper, drawing columns with dates and names; he listed the person's name, together with the media outlet that reported their death. He surveyed the list for a while, then wrote 'Terminated' against the relevant name. Finally, he wrote the name of his source against each entry, 'Sants' or 'Marlowe', being the most frequent. The last victim's name was unknown so far, but 'Marlowe' aka George Dark, was the source. Beneath his list, he drew and re-drew a large question mark. He concluded it was obvious that looking at the increased incidence of deaths portended a dénouement; these events must foreshadow a climactic event. As ever, he was concerned about the most effective way of rousing the public. For the thousandth time, he wondered: how could they light a fire under public opinion? What in God's name would it take to make them angry enough to take action and cast off the Establishment shackles?

The phone rang, rousing Chester; it was Sants. Chester reached for a notepad, "Yes? I know who Malcutt is…. Home Office."

He scribbled on his pad.

"OK, thanks. You'd better lie low for a while. I'll be in touch."

Chester replaced the handset; it rang again immediately. This time it was the Magazine co-owner Polly Enderby-Smythe.

Chapter 15: Business and Fratricide

Milan Bilic leaned back in his seat, hooked his thumbs into his waistcoat pockets and gazed out of the French windows to the azure sea of the Mediterranean. Thoughts of his new yacht moored in the harbour at Marseille kept intruding. He wasn't in the slightest bit interested in the detail of the negotiations going on behind him. Normally he wouldn't bother to attend a meeting like this, but he wanted to finalise the deal quickly. The hotel business was needed urgently for the Kalyptra's latest Project – the coup. The business owner - an idiot, Baggio, a longstanding business acquaintance - had agreed to sell but was haggling over the price. Bilic was not accustomed to being kept waiting; he intended to make sure Baggio paid for his lapse of judgement. First, there was the satisfying spectacle of watching his lawyers dismantling the opposition's demands to a level where he was prepared to deal.

The incessant drone of negotiation lulled his senses. The haggling was proceeding according to plan. According to Bilic's mole in the opposition team, Baggio's company was virtually insolvent and days away from bankruptcy. They had desperately borrowed money to service loans, hoping they would win a profitable contract for which they were shortlisted. Alas, the contract had gone elsewhere, and they were now forced to sell the Hotel chain before it ruined the whole group. Bilic held another ace card; he knew the precise amount of money Baggio required from the sale to remain solvent.

He straightened his cuffs and flicked some imaginary fluff from his designer jacket. Absentmindedly, his hand smoothed an imaginary strand of jet black hair into place. Bilic's *modus operandi* was to know exactly which cards his opponent held before he began negotiations. Anything else would be like walking into a room naked. By fair means or foul, he knew his opponent's moves before negotiations began. He was driven to win at all costs. It was the only game that mattered. Only fools gambled or took chances.

This strategy had paid off handsomely many years ago. He had amassed a huge fortune and had acquired the usual wealth trappings of an arriviste billionaire: ostentatious homes in Europe, private jets, yachts, socialising with the latest celebrities. There were only two things that motivated him now: acceptance by the upper echelon of European society, and power. Socialising with Old Money would grant him the prestige he craved. But more important still was the need for power – a need etched into his psyche since he was a feral urchin prowling the streets of Belgrade. He craved to be the undisputed alpha male.

After working his way through Slovakia, Poland and Germany, he had found a job as a security guard in the European Parliament in Brussels.

Within six months, he had secured a permanent position as a clerk in the Public Works Procurement Dept. His job was to process bids for various civil engineering contracts in Europe. After another year, he was head of his own section. Two years later and he was running the entire department. This rapid rise was due to Bilic's ruthless self-promotion and even more ruthless disruption of rival candidates' applications. He was usually the only choice for the next promotion. He sabotaged his competitor's personnel files, making them appear unsuitable for the post. Several times he had resorted to administering a mild poison, which caused them to feel so ill they were unable to attend the selection panels.

That he was allowed the scope for such rapid promotion was a testament to the extraordinarily lax security and checks made on new employees. Not even the most rudimentary checks were conducted; these would have revealed that Bilic's educational certificates were forgeries. The university where he was supposed to have gained his degree did not even exist.

Bilic cemented his position as Chief Secretariat for European Infrastructure and Development Procurement Projects. He also discretely cultivated closer contact with the CEOs and Chairmen of the large Civil Engineering Companies that undertook the majority of large scale infrastructure projects in the EU. As these relationships developed, he selected those CEOs whose discretion could be trusted. He was now in a position to make substantial sums of money by offering contracts to people who would accommodate his demands. In his eyes, there were no losers, only winners, as the EU would have its project completed on time and on budget - something he insisted upon. The companies that played the game had the most profitable contracts, and he was able to make millions of Euros for every contract he put their way. He was even able to help the companies find cheap labour from his contacts in the Balkans. This often gave the company a pricing advantage to place a lower-priced bid. Conversely, if a company did not play the game, he always made sure there was some sort of delay on the project. They weren't given another chance.

In one case, he took a secretive majority share in a company owned by a reclusive old Irish industrialist. The target was carefully chosen because he was single and had no living relatives or dependents. Once Bilic had seized control of the company, he murdered the recluse, disposing of the mutilated body in the Atlantic. Using his EU position, he then awarded the company bigger and bigger contracts. Eventually, his greed got the better of his hitherto impeccable judgment, and whispers began to circulate that there was something crooked about the bidding process. Bilic retired immediately, citing ill-health.

He could have enjoyed his freedom; a substantial fortune sat in a Hong Kong Bank. Whilst the money was initially reassuring, it soon lost its novelty. He found he still needed his particular drug - power. From an early age, his forceful personality allowed him to coerce many of his contemporaries, getting them to go along with his ideas or perform tasks for him. But he had not realised how potent this ability could be. Being able to outwit or bully almost anyone with whom he did business was the real source of satisfaction he derived from his business dealings. He became dependent on the exhilaration of manipulating a business opponent. The more it happened, the more he needed to savour the sensation. Eventually, he became dependent on it. He was an addict, obsessed with winning, sadistically crushing his opponents. There would never be enough power to satisfy his desire.

Abruptly he refocused on the bickering lawyers; his yachting daydream vanished. His relaxed mood evaporated. "Enough!" he shouted. The assembly fell silent.

Bilic took a deep breath, "Signor Baggio, let's conclude the deal. Our proposal would relieve your company of the burden of servicing the debt on your Hotels. Our research tells us this is costing you a considerable sum of money. I want you to think of the benefits of my proposal. Disposing of an unprofitable business will allow your other companies to survive. In these circumstances, I think our offer is very fair."

Bilic paused for a moment, gauging his opponent's reaction, then continued, "The hotels have never achieved the occupancy figures you estimated. You bought at a bad time for International Travel. They have been a drain on your Group's resources for too many years now, and in the current global slowdown, things are unlikely to improve in the short term. We are offering you a generous way out of your predicament. You will still

Masquerade

have a solvent company. Come now! It makes sense to accept my offer. You must have paid for the loan ten times over by the time you include fees and interest. Just think of that money staying in your bank accounts instead of paying it to the bloody bankers. If you accept my offer, you can be free and clear of any debt. A fresh start."

Baggio's bloodshot eyes narrowed involuntarily as he considered Bilic's honeyed inducement. He was close to accepting in any case. Bilic was right; he had very little choice - the damned banks were near to foreclosing on the loans. At least he could save the rest of the Company this way. Bilic's offer was good, he thought; he couldn't really see any negatives, but the businessman in him still did not want to give up the hotels too easily. Despite any way out at this stage looking like a godsend, one thing still nagged at the back of his mind: how had Bilic found out about the company's financial situation in the first place?

An hour later, the late afternoon sun dipped low in the western sky. The hotel staff quietly closed the salon curtains. Bilic closed the deal with a firm handshake. As both sets of lawyers filed out of the room, Bilic turned to his adversary, "Finally, Baggio! Why the hell didn't you do this earlier? You could have saved us both a lot of time and effort. Good luck with your new lease of life." Baggio shrugged and walked away, looking pleased with himself. For his part, Bilic regarded his back with malicious anticipation; soon, he would have his retribution.

Thirty minutes later, Bilic walked down the steps of the hotel towards his limousine. His chauffeur-cum-bodyguard held the door open for him. His gang of lawyers clambered into a people carrier behind.

Inside the car, he flipped up the lid of the centre console and took out a mobile phone. It was a secure line. He hit a speed dial button and waited for a response.

A curt voice commanded, "Give me your report."

"The deal has been completed satisfactorily," Bilic replied.

"Good, I will expect a detailed report at next week's meeting."

The line went dead.

A humourless smile spread across Bilic's face as he replaced the phone in its cradle. The committee had expressed doubts about his ability to acquire the hotel chain, his most vocal critic being the Englishman, Stryckland. He would take a great deal of pleasure from his discomfort when he presented his report. The deal would also cement his position within the organisation; he would be second only to the Patron, dealing a hammer blow to Stryckland's aspirations of being the Patron's successor.

No one in the Organisation had been able to generate as much profit as he had. He completed more deals as well as organising new revenue streams.

Now the first stage of his plan to succeed the Patron was successful. The hotels would be used as cover to infiltrate thousands of mercenaries into Europe, posing as cleaners and porters. Their first mission was the coup in the UK, due in July when the Government was in recess for the summer. He would discuss plans to bring in the first batch of soldiers with his recruiters in Northern Africa. With luck, the deal would be complete in a few weeks, and then he could bring them in time for the summer season. They wouldn't be too obvious amongst the thousands of seasonal recruits starting at the same time.

"Is the Italian still behind us?"

"Yes, Monsieur. Jadic is monitoring their car. They are three kilometres back."

"Good, it's time to teach him a lesson. Give the signal to the others."

Just as they passed the brow of a hill, Bilic's driver pulled over to the verge and parked the Mercedes limousine. Behind them were two large black four-wheel-drive vehicles with eight bodyguards. "Go and tell Giorgio to run back to the other side of the hill and let us know Baggio's convoy is closer. Tell the drivers they are to run the bodyguard's cars off the road and shoot them. You will stop Baggio's car. No one is to touch him; I want to deal with him."

They didn't have to wait long. Baggio didn't take security seriously. He only had one extra car with bodyguards. Bilic's drivers watched in their mirrors for the convoy to come speeding over the brow of the hill. As soon as they saw them, three sets of accelerator pedals were floored, and three car's tyres threw rooster tails of dirt and gravel high into the air as they accelerated hard to match Baggio's convoy, who were not minded to slow down. They were soon racing side-by-side up the mountain road then along straights. Tyres smoking and screeching around blind corners, racing through tunnels, neither side holding back, somehow realising to lose the race would mean death. Each time Bilic's driver was able to draw slightly in

Masquerade

front of Baggio's driver, the road favoured Baggio, and Bilic's car lost ground again. Eventually, they came to a very long straight and with both car's engines screaming at maximum revs, slowly Bilic's driver was able to draw out a car's length lead. Bilic screamed from the back, "Now! Now! Stop." Faced with the prospect of crashing into the rock face or Bilic's car cutting across him, Baggio's driver stamped on the brakes, leaving two thick black lines of rubber; it screeched to a halt behind Bilic's limousine. Behind them, Bilic's bodyguards forced the bodyguard's car into the rock face where it crashed in a crumpled heap, rolled several times onto its roof, then exploded and caught fire. As the flames took hold, Bilic's bodyguards emptied the magazines of their automatic rifles into the wreck. The occupants lay still, engulfed by the inferno.

Bilic smoothed back his hair and waited for his driver to open the door. Cool and unruffled, he stepped out of the car and walked past his bodyguards to the rear window of Baggio's limousine. He tapped with exaggerated politeness on the darkened glass. Hesitantly the window lowered, revealing a sweating and dishevelled Baggio trying unsuccessfully to calm his companion, a tall, lithe blonde who was screaming hysterically.

Bilic gave Baggio a look of pure malice, then with a theatrical sigh, "Alfredo! Please! Shut her up!"

Still, the blonde screamed, arms and legs flailing, resisting Baggio's efforts to calm her. Bilic's hand slid behind his back; slowly, he pulled out a Beretta. He kept his arm close to his side - the gun hidden.

"Alfredo! I implore you. Stop this racket! "

Still no response. Bilic's eyebrows arched in exasperation, "Alfredo, your hand."

Baggio paused his attempts to silence the girl and half turned towards Bilic, surprised. His hand fell away from the girl's mouth. Abruptly Bilic raised the gun and shot the screaming girl in the head. There was stunned silence.

Calmly Bilic continued. "At last! Peace and quiet; now I can hear myself think. Please, get out of the car."

Shakily Baggio eased himself out of the car onto unsteady legs. He swallowed nervously; his Adam's apple bobbed up and down. He felt a warm stickiness on his face and tried to wipe it away. He looked at his hand; it was bright red. A large thick globule of redness slid down his fingers and dripped onto his white shirt. Bilic gently took his arm and led him to the side of the road. Baggio was bewildered; what the hell was going on? He'd just done a deal with this guy, and here he was ambushing his convoy and killing his bodyguards!

He knew Bilic was a psychopath, but everything had been normal thirty minutes ago; what had changed? Bilic put an arm around his shoulders.

"Milan, what is the matter?" Baggio implored. "What is going on? Why have you done this? Those were four of my best men in that car."

"Alfredo, we made a good deal this afternoon. But you need to learn some respect! You know I don't accept bad manners. We should have concluded our business more than a week ago. But no, you had to push your luck! This put me in a very dangerous position; I was forced to lie to an extremely powerful man, someone who doesn't tolerate lies. You must suffer the consequences for this."

"But Milan! I spent years building up that business from nothing. I didn't want to sell; I was forced into a corner. I had to make sure there was no way to save the business before I let it go."

Bilic stopped abruptly and slapped Baggio's face, shouting, "That is the point, you fool. It was me! Me! I removed your options. You had no choice but to deal with me. Don't you understand? I put you in that corner. Me! Accepting my offer was your only choice. By making me wait, you made me look weak. You cost me a significant loss of face with my associates. Now you must pay the price. Stay where you are!"

Baggio stood trembling, rooted to the spot, wondering what was about to happen. Bilic took two paces, turned to face Baggio. Their eyes met and held momentarily, then Bilic raised the Beretta and put two bullets into Baggio's knees. Baggio screamed and hit the ground hard, clutching his shattered legs.

Bilic's face was expressionless. He ignored the whimpering bloody heap on the road and walked calmly to his car, got in the back seat and instructed the driver, "Take me to the villa."

Chapter 16: Spectre of a Thief

A knock on the door.

Palmer reluctantly looked up from his computer. He was reviewing an internal video of an interrogation at the Frimley Rendition Unit in Hertfordshire.

"What is it, Smalling?"

"Sergeant Brittle told me to show you this, Sir."

"Is it important?"

"Yes, Sir, I think it is."

"Right! Bring it here."

Smalling plugged a memory stick into Palmer's computer.

"I was just checking last night's operation when I noticed something unusual, Sir."

"Well, what is it?"

Smalling pressed a button. A black-and-white picture appeared on the screen.

"It's a night vision camera, Sir, so there's no colour. As you know, it was a filthy night with the storm, so the pictures from our standard cameras weren't much good. Look at the yard on the left of the screen; keep your eye on it when the van comes into shot."

They waited a few seconds; a figure pushing what looked like a trolley walked across the yard. It stopped, looked upwards. Then the van came slowly into shot on the right-hand side of the screen. As the men got out of the van, the figure in the yard turned and moved towards them. The figure stood next to the fence as the police carried out the beating. As the van drove away, the figure ran back through the yard then reappeared near the spot where the van had stood moments before. It crouched down, searching the ground, stopped and picked something up. Then it began searching once more, gradually moving out of shot.

Palmer swore, "Damn! He saw everything! Did he find the body?"

Smalling grunted, "We must assume so, Sir. He was looking in the right area."

Masquerade

Palmer spun his chair around and strutted over to a window. "Those bastards at 'Vanquish' are getting sloppy. What did he pick up?"

"Not sure, Sir. We'd have to ask the team if they've lost anything."

Palmer grimaced, "Do that."

Smalling hit a button on the keyboard, "There's more, Sir. I can identify the figure in the yard. At least, I think I can ID him as he leaves the office."

Palmer leaned forward. "Show me."

"This is from a camera at the front of the building. It's the end of the shift, and the weather has cleared up, so the picture is much clearer. You can see everyone is leaving."

Smalling's finger hovered over the screen as they watched a trickle of men hurrying out of the main entrance.

"There!" Smalling traced a solitary figure walking out of the gates, who then turned right.

Palmer stared intently at the screen, following the figure's progress down the service road and across some waste ground. He recognised the scale of the threat the anonymous figure posed.

Palmer grimaced, "Clever bastard. See how he walks, cap pulled down over his face. Head down, hands in pockets. His walk is not too fast or too slow. Look, he glances behind every now and again. How many cameras did he pass? Must be three. Not one shot of his face. This guy's a pro. How much more footage is there?"

Smalling was confident, "This is all I have at the moment, Sir, but I'm positive I can track him down. We have plenty of CCTV coverage in the area."

Palmer was well aware of the pressure the Home Secretary was capable of exerting when he wanted something done quickly. He sat back at his desk, looking intently at the screen, "Smalling, I don't need to remind you its bloody imperative we catch this bastard." Palmer gestured at the recording. "Vanquish is supposed to be a covert operation. If this gets out, we're all screwed. We need to find this guy and silence him and bloody quick before he tells anyone else. Find where he lives; we need to take him out. I'll be down in an hour to see what you've got."

Masquerade

"Christ." He thought, "Stryckland will go berserk when he finds out. Better get it over with."

He took his mobile from his pocket and dialled a contact, "Put me through to the Home Office - Permanent Secretary." He drummed his fingers on the desk as he waited.

"Sir Miles? ... it's Palmer ...is the Minister free? ...yes, it is urgent – very! ...I'd rather speak to him in person if you don't mind ...right, two o'clock it is."

At one forty-five precisely, Palmer walked through an imposing gatehouse into the Home Office quad. He always had to grit his teeth when he visited Stryckland. This was an alien environment, a bastion for elite Whitehall Mandarins. He was from the wrong side of the tracks. Twenty years working for the Establishment was enough for him to understand they were amoral; they kept it hidden behind their mask of false smiles and courtesy. He loathed them with every fibre of his being, but he was trapped by past misdeeds – inextricably tied to the devil.

Sir Miles Lansdowne, the Minister's Permanent Secretary, was waiting for him at the top of the staircase, hands clasped behind his back like a spiteful schoolmaster. "Ah, Palmer. You're on time! Good. The Minister has a busy afternoon. All I can give you is fifteen minutes. I'll get you when your time is up." He led Palmer through an outer office filled with secretaries busily typing. He knocked quietly at a padded leather door before gesturing Palmer inside.

Palmer found Stryckland reclining on a sofa, reading a thick sheaf of papers. Without looking up, he beckoned Palmer forward to a seat opposite. After a few moments, he put the papers on a coffee table and looked over his spectacles at Palmer.

"Well? What's so urgent you can't tell me on the phone?"

Palmer was Stryckland's man in MI5. Senior enough to lead investigations, but like Gittins, not powerful enough to cause problems. He operated outside the normal command structure and reported directly to Stryckland.

Palmer paused a moment before replying, "We have a security breach."

Stryckland put his spectacles on the table and waited.

"Vanquish were supposed to eliminate a defector last night. They made a hash of it; there was a witness."

"Jesus Christ!" Stryckland's composure vanished. "What the hell happened?"

"They were seen by a night shift worker when they were terminating Neuberg."

"Have you arrested him?"

"No, we're trying to trace him."

"Then what the hell are you doing here? You should be using every bloody copper in the Met hunting this terrorist. How do you know he saw the termination?"

"We were making a routine check of the recording – to make sure Vanquish did the job, and he... the night shift worker, showed up on CCTV."

"What are you doing to catch him?"

"I've got a technician tracking his movements on CCTV. Fortunately, the area is saturated with cameras. We are confident we can trace him; it's just a matter of time."

Stryckland banged his fist on the coffee table, "Time is something we don't have. There are important plans due to start in a few days. They would have to be shelved if the activist press hears of this. You need to find this bastard and quickly, or I'll have your head! Use whatever you need but find him. Do you have a description?"

Palmer bristled, "I wouldn't be trying to find him if we didn't!" Stryckland's arrogance always needled him at some point. "I'll use extra men to check the CCTV recordings."

Stryckland hooked his thumbs into his waistcoat pockets as he stood. He gazed at the traffic on the Mall. "And put the snatch squads on standby. I want to take this irritant out without delay. Keep me posted."

Sir Miles knocked and held the door open for Palmer, "Don't let us detain you."

Stryckland waited for the door to close before he walked over to his desk and made a call to his other fixer. Stryckland turned to Sir Miles, "We need a news blackout for this witness situation; speak to the editors of the main papers and TV stations. Make sure they toe the line. Also, have a word with the Met Commissioner, remind him that he owes us a number of favours, and we expect his full co-operation for this investigation. I'll need to speak to Gittins urgently. Finally, tell Anthony Granger I need to use MI6's expertise. I want to see him this afternoon."

The news was a bombshell for Stryckland; it jeopardised Kalyptra's coup project. Marat would go berserk if he found out. Stryckland decided to handle this on his own – using Gittins, of course.

Chapter 17: Shadow Stalker

Gittins nodded understandingly. "Same old crap," he thought, "he needs me to dig him out of the shit."

Stryckland carried on oblivious, "The one solid lead we have is a location. We're sure he was caught briefly on CCTV. Talk to Palmer at MI5. He has the recording. In my opinion, this person could well be the thief behind the recent spate of thefts. We don't know if we are dealing with some sort of genius cat burglar or if there is a gang. Whichever, we have been given the runaround, and it's got to stop! It's one thing to steal from a company, but stealing from the government is treachery. It is imperative you find whatever it is he has stolen and where he is taking it. Starting with the time of the murder, GCHQ will run scans on all communication systems, voice, text and emails. There are no limits on your resources here, Gittins. Whatever you need from GCGQ or MI5, just ask for it. I'll get them to co-operate. But you must catch him. Both our careers depend on that. Understand?"

Gittins was staggered by the scope of Stryckland's investigation. With the blanket surveillance used to monitor the public, it could take weeks or even months to trawl through the recordings.

Stryckland interrupted his thoughts, "Report directly to me. I will be managing the situation personally."

"Wouldn't this normally be handled by Cobra?"

"Normally, yes. But this is a special case. We don't know how far our systems have been compromised. So the information I have just given you stays confidential for the time being. This is 'need to know only'. Tell your team we are searching for an industrial espionage thief. Here is some background: a body was discovered on waste ground in the Docklands area... it was a Government courier. We don't know why he was in the area, and it's pretty rough – a war zone where local gangs settle their disputes.

The important thing is that he was carrying highly classified information on an SD Card. The card is now missing; MI5 searched the area and found nothing. It is vital the card is found and returned to me. MI5 have discovered someone witnessed the murder. This is the person you must find; he probably now has the card. I don't need to highlight the consequences if the press gets hold of this. We need to control the information given to the public. They will be fed our official version of events. Before then, I need the witness safely under lock and key and the card in my possession. We'll close down these magazines using anti-terrorist legislation, so we can hold these people for as long as we want.

In the meantime, MI5 have increased security at all airports, railway stations, ferry ports – all departure points from the UK, in fact. Although this is more in hope than anything else. It's all we can do at this point in time, as we have no definitive description.

Get your team together tonight. Don't worry about the niceties; find the information any way you have to. Remember, time is of the essence. I want a progress report tomorrow morning. Come to see me in my office at 9:30am."

Gittins rose to go when Stryckland called him back.

"Gittins! I hardly need to remind you about extracting information. Use whatever you need to get the information... and also, ask Palmer about the GCHQ recognition software; it may help with CCTV searches."

Chapter 18: Network Exposé

Dark tapped a few keys and logged into a secure chat room he used to communicate with the Hacker Network and its Controller, Heinz.

He scrolled down a list of members until he came to Heinz's alias, then clicked to open a chatbox.

"Need to re-arrange the party. Are you available?"

The cursor blinked at him for a few moments before kicking into life.

"When were you thinking?"

"As soon as possible."

"Why?"

"Another termination. I was there."

A long pause.

"Who?"

"Not sure yet."

"What do you need?"

"To identify a logo... a shield with two crossed swords with the letters V and A beneath, I think – I need to know whose logo it is."

"No problem. What's the plan then?"

"We go public with the corruption scandal and carry out 'Judgement Day'. It will bring down the British government, the Corporatists and the Establishment."

"How are we going to do that?"

"God knows. Enough people have tried to wake the public from their torpor. Who knows if we'll succeed? All I know is I have to try, or we'll end up with as much freedom as lab rats. Best guess, for now, is to use their own propaganda weapons against them."

Heinz was puzzled, "How can we do that? The government controls security."

Masquerade

"We do it the usual way. I walk in, place a few remote control devices in the right areas, then we can override the TV control room in London and transmit our own programme with our version of events."

"God! Who's going to be the person in front of the camera for that?"

"We'll have to work something out. We'll find somebody. The main thing is that we expose these bastards while we still can. If we don't act now, it will be too late. I'm guessing these murders are a precursor to something big."

Heinz, "OK, leave it with me; call you later."

In a tenement building in the Kowloon district of Hong Kong, Jimmy Chan was relaxing after a strenuous week at University. He had handed in his dissertation the previous day. Professor Li had smiled surreptitiously as he took it from Jimmy. He was intimately familiar with Jimmy's research. Jimmy was confident his PhD was in the bag. He was an expert at making and breaking advanced encryption algorithms.

As he settled down to play a game with some online friends, his laptop bleeped. He recognised the tone; it was his handler, 'Khan'. He sighed deeply, "Sorry guys, something's come up. Got to go."

A persistent buzzing dragged Dark out of a deep sleep. He fumbled for his laptop. Four-thirty am. He had fallen asleep at the kitchen table.

"George. It's Heinz. We've tracked them down. The letters you saw on the van belong to Vanquish Securities. Jimmy just called in; he searched the CCTV system for the London Metropolitan Area and traced the van's route backwards from the execution to the time it left the Vanquish compound at nine the previous evening.

The execution was planned. Vanquish had driven directly to Drapers Hall in the City. CCTV showed crowds of people milling around on the pavement outside: a gang of men approached the victim and his female companion. They began to jostle the man, seemed like a mugging at first, then it got rough. The woman called for help, none came. Seconds later, uniformed paramilitaries turned up. They used riot sticks to hack a path through the crowds directly towards the victim. This was no random extraction; they knew exactly who they wanted. They very nearly killed the female companion. She's in critical condition in St. Thomas' with a fractured skull. The gang restrained the guy until the paras grabbed him and bundled him into the van.

Masquerade

Vanquish's compound is in the East End of London. We ran a background check on them. They're a privately owned company with contracts with most European Governments, mostly high-risk situation support for the Police. They are a longstanding government partner. They don't seem to have a website, but we broke into their IT system and found what we needed. They have five hundred field operatives, mainly ex-British army and mercenaries. They are extremely well-armed and experienced in combat. They are often embedded with the British Army. The Americans used them in El Salvador in the Eighties to replace an uncooperative President. Democracy American style! It turned into the usual blood bath."

Dark interrupted, "What the hell? Since when are private armies allowed to carry out operations in the UK?"

Heinz grimaced, "Oh, it gets better. Vanquish's Board of Directors includes an ex-Cabinet Minister, as well as a Chief Constable and the head of some Quango you've never heard of. Over the last financial year, they've invoiced a hundred million for covert support on police, terrorist surveillance and organised crime operations. There is no doubt they are private paramilitary working for the Corporatists."

Dark thought about the possibilities, "Any background on the victim's movements that night?"

"Just the meeting at Draper's Hall – some sort of political rally, it seems. We haven't got any further than that at the moment. Though it's a bit strange for a possible Kalyptra member to get involved with political activists. For some reason, he was picked up by the Police and held at Paddington nick for a couple of hours. Then he was taken for his final ride. We are trying to find out background intel on him; I'll keep you posted."

Dark grunted, "Christ. These people are mad! Abducting people off the street and murdering them. I've asked Chester to do some digging too. I'll call you later."

Chapter 19: The Trappist

Four-thirty in the morning, an exhausted Gittins walked into a darkened incident room. The Met's Facilities Department had set up a temporary office in the basement of Paddington Station. "Out of sight out of mind, eh?" Gittins muttered. Decrepit desks and chairs lined the sides of the room; blank whiteboards faced the empty desks. Trolleys laden with equally shabby computer equipment queued in the central aisle. Gittins scratched his head. Where to start? He had absolutely no information with which to find the witness. Yet again, Stryckland was asking for the impossible. All Gittins had was a CCTV tape that MI5 had put together. A hooded man had been tracked from the office block next to the murder site to an area miles away, close to the river Thames, whereupon he had disappeared. Gittins massaged his aching neck and walked upstairs to his office. Resigned to another frustrating investigation, he pulled a severely depleted bottle of Johnnie Walker from a filing cabinet. He dropped his raincoat onto a chair and surveyed the untidy pile of files on his desk with distaste; he slumped in a chair and took a large brooding swig. He had lost count of the number of disasters he had covered up for the Home Secretary. Stryckland always covered his own back but treated Gittins with disdain. But Gittins was indispensable for two reasons: he could root out information like no other detective in the Met, plus, he could be relied on to keep his mouth shut. This case bothered him, though; Stryckland was uncharacteristically edgy. In fifteen years, he hadn't seen Stryckland look concerned before. Normally he carried off the proverbial stiff upper lip. Why was he so anxious? The consequences of not finding the witness must be catastrophic indeed. Stryckland was obviously lying about the murder of the Government Official. The Met was rife with rumours of hit squads sent out to 'discourage' anyone who was becoming a nuisance. Government Officials didn't walk alone through London ghettos late at night. The murder had 'assassination' written all over it. The problem was, a phantom had witnessed it, and Gittins had a matter of days to catch him somehow.

By six o'clock on that damp London morning, a glowering sky kept the office lights burning. A weary Gittins walked disconsolately back down to the basement. His investigation team had arrived and lounged around, chatting quietly.

"Boys and girls. Your attention, please. I won't take up much of your time. The team leaders will brief you in more detail, such as it is, in a moment.

Masquerade

You all know each other; we've worked together many times before. Yet again, we have to dig the top brass out of the shit!"

A ripple of resigned laughter spread through the room.

"But this time, there is a difference. We have to track down and catch a terrorist who, by all accounts, knows how to stay off the radar. I'm told his actions have triggered a National Emergency, and we have just a few days in which to catch him. A political activist has been murdered, and secret Government documents have been stolen. This has posed a major security threat to the country. Thousands of lives are in imminent danger. I hardly need to tell you the pressure from the top brass will be unrelenting until we find this bugger."

The room fell silent as they digested the information.

Gittins suddenly felt exhausted; he hadn't had a chance to sleep since Stryckland had summoned him to his office. He needed to give the team the few details he was allowed to divulge. It was barely enough to get them started on the enormous task.

"It is understood that he has stolen documents which contain details of the security arrangements for the Prime Minister's upcoming attendance at a rally. In addition, it's thought he is behind the recent spate of thefts from Government contractors. We have as yet no motive for these robberies, but one must assume this person intends to sell the information to the highest bidder. We should also assume such info may be bought by persons or agencies who are enemies of the UK Government.

So, this is being treated as a terrorist incident, and as such, we have been authorised to use any means at our disposal to apprehend this person. At this point in time, we have no clues about the person's identity. I need hardly point out this is an extremely difficult investigation because there are no concrete leads. Therefore we need to gather the facts about the crimes committed as quickly as possible. Let's see if we can find a pattern."

"Yes, Guv," a burly detective at the back of the room called out. "Do we have any information at all about this person's identity? Where do we start?"

"We have one lead. MI5 have obtained a CCTV recording of the cleaning staff leaving the building opposite the murder site. They have traced a suspect to an area close to the old East India Docks. I need a house to house search of the area as soon as possible. Sergeant Malinger will

Masquerade

coordinate that. Apart from that, no Haskins, we have bugger all. It seems we are dealing with a 'phantom'. We have no idea whatsoever about this person - what sex they are, age or appearance... no name... nothing! It is possible they were one of the cleaners, so a team needs to get over there and interview the management; let's see if we turn up something. A list of everyone on their night shift for a start. The team leaders have a file for each of the break-ins. Check them again, see if anything was missed, go back to every crime scene and recheck them. Interview the witnesses again. Find me something to kick-start the investigation."

There was nothing to do for the moment but wait and let the officers in the field get on with the job; Wearily, Gittins took the stairs back to his office and threw the pile of files from his desktop to the floor. Stryckland's attitude kept niggling him: the assumption Gittins would simply carry out his latest dictate like some faithful pet dog. Well, this particular pet dog was getting fed up with no bone; he was still owed for the last two jobs. Things had to change, or there would be no more extracting the Right Honourable Gentleman from the mire. He decided to get some fresh air; a smoke would calm him down.

Meanwhile, at GCHQ in Cheltenham, a dozen young technicians sat before a wall of computer screens monitoring thousands of phone conversations and messages, waiting for keyword algorithms to flash alerts. They were searching for the proverbial needle in a haystack. The GCHQ system was connected to the NSA supercomputer in Langley, Virginia. Together they screened every electronic message sent anywhere in the world. The young men and women had the same skills as those who worked for Heinz's Hacker network. Many of the GCHQ techies were there because they had been given reprieves from substantial prison sentences for hacking; a small minority were there out of a sense of patriotism. Every one of them was patiently waiting for the alert to pop up, showing the keywords indicating another suspected terrorist was active.

Back in London, Sergeant Malinger had set up several desks in a corner of the incident room. He had manned it with three junior constables who were given the job of scanning every reported incident from border control over the last twenty-four hours. Heathrow was a scene of chaos; its Police station held fifty young men who fitted the suspect's loose description complaining loudly about their interrupted travel plans. A similar scene played out at Dover, with twenty young men being held. The border guards were going mad; they wanted to know what they had to do with the detainees and how the hell they were going to interview this lot and do their day job and where the hell were the police when they needed them. Malinger had also contacted regional airports in Holland, Belgium and northern France, asking for any unusual arrivals from the UK as a matter of some urgency.

On Gittins' desk, there were two notes to phone Palmer at MI5 to arrange a viewing of the CCTV recordings.

"Hey, you! Constable. Come here." Gittins shouted at a young policeman staggering into the office under a pile of box files. "Have you been seconded onto this investigation?"

Nervous Constable, "Yes Sir, Sergeant Malinger told me to bring those files from the archives."

"OK. I've got a job for you. Do you know where MI5 is?"

"Yes, Sir, I had to go there the other day."

"Good, I need you to go there now and collect some more files. Go to the Duty Officer at the front desk and tell him you are to collect the files for DCI Gittins. Under no circumstances are you to let those files out of your sight. You are to come straight back here. No calling in at a shop or any nonsense like that. If you lose those files, I'll have your head. Do you understand? Good! Now go quickly."

He watched the young constable skitter out of the office, then picked up the notes to call Palmer.

Masquerade

Chapter 20: Chasing Shadows

"All right, All right. I'm coming! Give me a bloody chance to get to the door!"

Rachael Taverner pulled her grubby dressing gown tighter as she opened her front door. "What's all this racket? Do you know what time it is?" she yelled at the figures beyond the door.

A young policeman and woman stepped back as they came face to face with a belligerent young woman. The policeman took a step forward, trying to regain control.

"Hold on a minute, sunshine! I told you lot last week my Alec ain't showed up 'ere! I dunno where he is! But he ain't here. So stop harassing me and piss off!"

"Excuse me, madam. We're not here about Alec; we're conducting door to door enquiries about a local missing child."

Rachel Taverner was wise to the wiles of coppers, put her hands on her hips and stood her ground. "What child? From where? I ain't heard of no missing kid. People round here wouldn't be tucked up in bed with a kid missing. The whole street would be out looking! What's this child's name?"

The policeman consulted his clipboard. "It was only reported late last night. A girl, five or six years old. He looked at his notes again and asked the question written in large bold letters. "Have you seen anyone suspicious around recently? Male, six feet tall, mid-twenties, wearing a hoodie."

He waited, nervously anticipating another salvo.

Ms Taverner glared at him contemptuously, "Do you think we're fools? What's this cock and bull story really about? Who is this hoodie person? Don't you realise that applies to half the blokes on the estate? Now piss off, the lot of you. All you bastards do around here is cause trouble. Just leave us alone! Go!

Shaken, the young constables turned on their heels and quickly made their way back to the incident van to report.

"Right, you pair. What have you got?"

"Not much, Sarge. All we got was a load of abuse. Nobody believed we was looking for a missing kid. They all thought we was after this bloke for something. Gave us a right load of verbal they did!"

Masquerade

The sergeant sighed, "Show me your clipboard then. How many houses have you been to? Bloody hell, what have you been up to? There's only six addresses here! Is that all you've done?"

The WPC volunteered, "But they wouldn't tell us anything, Sarge."

"What do you mean they wouldn't tell you nothing? Who's the bloody copper? You make 'em tell you. You put the frighteners on them. Didn't you learn nothing during your training? You're in charge. You scare them shitless until they do what you want! Else you'll never make a proper copper. Understand?"

Just then, Gittins walked into the incident van. The sergeant jumped to his feet. "Off you go, you two." He turned back to Gittins, "Morning, Sir. It's been hard work; these buggers don't trust us."

Gittins looked askance.

"But I think we may have something for you. There have been two sightings of a man similar to the description given, close to the river next to those posh new flats."

Gittins flicked a drooping tail of ash from his cigarette. "Well?"

"A bloke walks back there quite often, not every morning. But pretty regular, usually early, sixish. No description beyond general height and build."

Gittins' intuition rang out… no description? "Righto Sergeant, let me have the reports. I'll take it from here."

Once he was far enough away from the van, he called Palmer. "Right, we have a sighting, close to the river, there's a new development of apartments in the area. I want you to be careful; I don't want you lot scaring him off!"

"Bollocks! We've done this often enough to know what we're about. I'll send in some plainclothes boys to check the area, then we'll use the snatch squads. You'd better tell Stryckland we're bringing his witness."

Gittins smiled sardonically; he knew this wasn't the time to make rash promises. "Just make sure you do. It's your head on the block if you come back empty-handed." He closed the call then paused, still holding the handset. Better report to Stryckland… but bare facts only.

Chapter 21: Prima Facie

"George Darling! Not like that! Remember, less is best!"

Dark froze at the sudden memory of his mother's voice. The emptiness was still felt years after she'd died. He turned and gazed at his reflection in the illuminated mirror for a moment longer, then continued applying foundation with small dabbing movements, just as she had taught him.

She had always chided him about his sloppy application. She was such a perfectionist. When she taught him the art of theatrical disguise, she was at the height of her powers. The most celebrated female character actor of her generation. She took Dark with her as she played the grand theatres of Europe for a decade until she had died. Her grief for her husband had inexorably worn her down. Now Dark used the skills his mother taught him and refined them into a formidable weapon which he used to great effect against those responsible for his father's murder.

He selected a mocha foundation powder, dark brown shadow and a lighter brown highlight powder. He picked an aquiline nose from one compartment, eyelashes from another and a silver-grey wig from a third.

His mother had been too gentle to consider revenge. Dark was not. At an impressionable age, the horror he had felt had seared itself into his memory. Unable to forget the horror of the witness report, his grief had turned little by little turned to implacable anger, which in time morphed into an unyielding determination for retribution upon those responsible.

With some effort, Dark cast away his melancholia and continued his preparation for the night's disguise. He secured his mop of curly brown hair in an elasticated hair net. Then he continued with the foundation, which aged his appearance with every layer. Pulling a frown, he applied shadowing with a fine brush along the furrows on his brow and put two prominent lines down the sides of his mouth, then wavy lines along his forehead. With a finer brush, he drew lines along the top and bottom of his mouth and at the corners of his eyes. Using a medium brush, he drew hollow cheeks and prominent bags under his eyes, then conspicuous lines along his neck. When he was satisfied with the shadow, he used a highlighter on either side of the shadow lines to blend the effect into the background colour of his face. Then he carefully glued and adjusted the aquiline nose until he was satisfied with its positioning. Finally, he glued a pair of large hirsute ears in place and affixed the wig.

Masquerade

He noticed his hands trembled slightly. A flicker of a smile creased his face; he savoured the effects of adrenaline build-up. The anticipation of approaching danger always invigorated him. He regarded his disguise in the mirror. It was good: a cap and uniform would distract a casual gaze from his face anyway. He knew people only noticed general features; his face wouldn't attract too much attention.

Dark lived and worked outside the normal conventions of society. You would not find any record of his identity number or passport, nor any medical, financial, or criminal records. He was invisible to the web of Corporate databases that monitored and controlled the world's population. That was the way he liked it, freedom writ large, a nobody – invisible to 'The System'.

To complete his disguise, Dark strapped an aluminium brace to his left leg - designed to give him a pronounced limp - then stood to check his appearance in a full-length mirror. He hobbled across the bare concrete floor of the warehouse, the brace chafing his thigh. At a huge wooden bench, a bank of computer screens displayed a constant flow of information: stock prices, streamed business news, chat room conversations. Piles of paperwork littered the bench; large A-zero sheets of building plans masked a mess of pens, screwdrivers, soldering irons and various artefacts Dark used every day. Dark rummaged around the cluttered desktop looking for the new ID badge. He caught sight of it partly hidden beneath a heavy leather-bound business directory.

He made a final check that he had everything he needed, and nothing he didn't, before slamming the door behind him for another foray into the dissolute underworld of corporate crime.

Chapter 22: Divided Loyalty

After witnessing Bilic's latest indiscretion, Susie had decided she needed to confront her mother about their wedding. Susie harboured an intense dislike for the man, and after his drunken display at the premiere, she had determined to make her mother see what a monster Bilic really was. She knew that her mother would be attending a fine art auction in Paris and had decided to catch up with her there.

The salon was crowded, but Susie spied her mother sitting in the VIP seats in the front row. An avid collector, Klara – Countess Esterhazy, often attended auctions when staying in her Paris townhouse, which housed part of her collection; the rest were housed at the family seat in Hungary. Klara was every bit the Countess: tall, elegant, and dazzlingly beautiful. She had remained a widow and alone after the death of her husband, Susie's father, until the commencement of her bizarre attachment to Milan Bilic.

An attendant escorted Susie through the chattering audience to the enclosure; her mother looked up.

"Susie! Darling, whatever are you doing here? I thought you were staying in Cannes?"

Susie kissed her mother, "Oh Mama, it was so boring! I just had to get away. Everything irritated me, especially Bilic."

Klara's good humour evaporated, "You can use his first name, you know."

Susie sat, "I can't! He's frightful! He made such a fool of himself at the premiere. He was so drunk he couldn't stand upright. And he was carrying on with some tarts! He didn't even try to hide it from me!"

Klara glared at her daughter, "Susie! We've been through this before! Once we're married, it will be different."

"Oh Mama, you're so naïve; men like that never change. He's a coarse and vulgar brute! The only thing he wants is your titles and land. Once he gets those, you'll never see him; he hardly spends any time with you now."

"Susie! Stop being so melodramatic. I refuse to discuss this any further. Please just enjoy the auction... look, it's about to start."

Chapter 23: Gittins Responds

Stryckland's call to brief the Prime Minister about the murder of a Government Official had not been pleasant, but the PM didn't worry him; he was feeble and easily outwitted. It was the head of Kalyptra he feared. If he didn't catch whoever was responsible for the missing plans, Marat would have him killed in a most unpleasant way.

Stryckland reproached himself. He was powerful, the most powerful man in the country. The Prime Minister was too weak and indecisive, so Giles naturally took the reins; he was the power behind the throne. Nature abhors a vacuum and all that. In normal circumstances, it meant he could do as he pleased. With the powers he held under the Prevention of Terrorism Act, he basically had carte blanche. He could order the police and MI5 to search out and detain indefinitely any person suspected of involvement with terrorists. Who defined who was a suspected terrorist? Why he did, of course, and he wasn't obliged to explain his reasons to anyone. It meant he could do whatever he wanted without being held accountable. So, now he needed to use these powers to their full extent if he wanted to stay alive and enjoy the benefits of twenty years of political manoeuvring.

To prevent the collapse of Kalyptra's most ambitious project, Stryckland had to catch the witness to the murder and retrieve the missing memory card. The witness would be branded a terrorist, discredited, his whole life history reconstructed to portray him as an enemy of the state. His 'perverted' values were exposed as he plotted to induce a revolution. The government security services would find tangible evidence with an array of weapons of mass murder, links with known terrorist organisations, a recorded final message and a well-publicised confession. To convince the Great British Public that their ever-vigilant government had once again saved them from the nightmare of bloodied and mangled bodies, a show trial would be televised, so everyone could see the plain truth.

The character assassination was easy; MI5 had done this innumerable times. It would only take a matter of hours to modify the man's life history to suit their purposes and then start to drip feed the story on TV news channels. The public would accept the story at face value; they never questioned anything. Stryckland could – and often did – dress an adverse news item in a half-believable story; the general public would swallow it whole. Helped by a few friendly newspaper editors, who all just happened to be in receipt of OBEs, and TV commentators, who belonged to the lower echelons of the Establishment. He even had an ex-newspaper editor write the crap for them. The whole system worked like a well-oiled machine; their enemies never really stood a chance. The public had read so much negative propaganda about the perverted opposition that they were deemed to be guilty even before they had opened their mouths to protest. Television was the Corporatists most effective weapon; they had used it to manipulate public opinion since its invention – promoting their agenda while discrediting opposing views. The general public had been well and truly brainwashed. Television had, in fact, destroyed people's capacity for critical thought. If those nice-looking newsreaders gave them the information, well, it was bound to be right. What possible reason did they have to lie?

The difficulty lay in catching the witness. It seems that it was no ordinary passer-by who saw the deed that would have been easy to deal with. No, this person was a much more formidable obstacle. According to Detective Chief Inspector Gittins, he had disappeared off the face of the planet.

A jangling ring from Stryckland's direct line interrupted his musing; he answered promptly, "Well? What have you got?"

"Here we go!" Gittins thought to himself; he knew how this conversation was going. "Nothing yet, but I've ordered a house to house search in the area surrounding the last CCTV sighting. A team are checking the companies we suspect were burgled to see if anything is missing. There are no concrete reports for the ports or airports as yet. We just have to keep digging."

"Christ Almighty. What are you people doing?"

"Sir, you know as well as I do these things take time. When we get some info to work with, we'll start to make progress."

"I'm not so sure about that. If this witness is part of the group responsible for all these burglaries, you'll be lucky to find anything. They have managed to remain completely anonymous for the last twelve months; there hasn't been the slightest clue as to their identity. For the life of me, I can't understand why we haven't intercepted any of their phone calls or messages. Damn it, if we can follow the conversations of a group of jihadists in the middle of Afghanistan, you'd think we could track people in our own country. I'm going to convene a COBRA meeting in the morning. We'll extend the operation and see if we can't flush them out."

Gittins cleared his throat, "Why don't we try shaking up the radical press? You keep complaining they are getting too close to your associates. How do you know this group isn't feeding them the information they keep reporting? Look. This group is good; we haven't been able to get anywhere near them after years of trying. Most of the companies and Government offices are not aware they have been hacked. It's the same with the physical burglaries. There is no trace anyone has been in the office, never mind accessing every secure hiding place in the room. One office even had an underground secure room which took up half the floor area – most people wouldn't even consider there was a hiding place, but it was broken into, and it was three weeks before they even realised something was wrong."

Stryckland replied, "I know, they couldn't understand how it was reported; they were working on a banned substance. They thought it must be conjecture... guesswork. Until one of the directors was working in the safe and found a fragment of cloth, just a thread snagged in the edge of a box file. The safe is sanitised, the floor and walls and shelves are packed with pressure sensors, infra-red beams trigger movement alarms, it is positively pressurised, so anything that might contaminate the files is blown out of the safe. Anything heavier than a pin will set the alarm off. Staff wear a sealed forensic suit and gloves into the safe, and yet here was a thread of cotton, snagged where no cotton had been before. How the hell did someone get in? It was impossible, but in they had been."

Gittins, "One person surely can't be responsible for all these robberies; he would have to be superhuman. It must be a group. There are too many break-ins for one person. Look, relying on the CCTV surveillance stuff is getting us nowhere; let's grab some of those journalists, put the frighteners on them. They'll bloody crap themselves at the thought of being held indefinitely."

Stryckland worried, "You're right; we need to change tactics, seize the initiative."

Gittins nodded, "It always comes down to some old fashioned tough police work."

Masquerade

Stryckland pursed his lips, thinking aloud, "We need to take the fight to them; you're right, close the 'Enquirer' down and seize the staff, especially that editor. That will put a stop to the bad press, at least. Go on, get on with it!"

Stryckland slammed the phone down. "Bloody journalists!"

Masquerade

Chapter 24: Resilience

Searing morning sunlight streaming into the room, roused Susie. Slowly regaining consciousness from a drunken stupor, she tried to work out where she was but failed miserably. Her body ached; her eyes felt gritty and glued together. Her mouth was as dry as the Kalahari. The slightest movement of her head made her wince. Unaccountably, her legs and arms were too heavy to move. A chill breeze caressed her naked body. Shivering, she felt for her clothes. She lay on a rough sodden blanket. Tentatively she reached further; she felt splintered, jagged wood. Then, unexpectedly her hand touched skin, calloused, cold and inert. Unnerved, she jerked upright.

The faint roar of traffic filtered through a broken window. Out of a powder blue sky, a low hanging morning sun cascaded brilliant light into the room. Painfully, Susie prised her eyes open and looked around, trying to make sense of her surroundings. She found herself in a large salon, with a high ceiling pitted with broken plasterwork. Torn and faded wallpaper peeled off the walls. In places, the plaster had been ripped off, exposing wooden lathes like a decomposing body's skeleton. Thick curtains of cobwebs hung over a window in a far corner of the room; the bare floorboards were covered with shattered plaster and hundreds of empty wine and beer bottles. Piles of dirty clothing and rags had been shoved into a corner. Comatose bodies were strewn about the floor like cast-off dolls – most of them half-dressed. Susie gagged; she had never seen such a squalid mess in her life.

"Where am I? How the hell did I get here?" She thought long and hard. Slowly, she began to piece together the previous evening's events. She had gone to 'The Beat Club' with Annabel, a friend from Cannes. They had met some old friends from Zürich. She seemed to remember some guys had crashed their group. They were from where? Yes, that was it, Hamburg. They were flashing the cash... bankers, maybe? She remembered a lot of champagne, dancing to loud music. Smoking something disgusting. Then on to shots and lustily throwing up in an alley. They had gone on to another club. Anything else was a blank. She certainly couldn't remember getting to this hell hole. The strange thing was, as a seasoned party goer, she was usually more resilient to the effects of boozy nights. She earnestly prayed the pain would stop pulverising her head.

Increasingly she became aware of a sickly bitter-sweet odour. Body odour, vomit, stale urine. She gagged again. Half remembering her hand had

Masquerade

touched something gross, she slowly turned to see what it might have been. She recoiled from the sight. Lying a foot away from her was a man, completely naked, grimy grey skin, broken nails and filthy nicotine-stained fingers, a mass of shoulder-length hair – matted Medusa-like into an unruly thatch. He had one arm flung over another equally dirty naked body, the sex of which was indeterminable.

Susie drew her knees up to her chin, repulsed. Just beyond the inert body, a sudden movement caught her eye. 'Oh my God!' A rat languidly climbed through a man's hair then sat in its midst, gnawing at something. That was too much; Susie moaned and jumped up, looking for an escape. As she did, her foot scattered a pile of empty beer cans with a loud crash. The rodent immediately took flight, skipping over and around bodies towards a large hole in the skirting. Susie felt scratching on her feet and let out a full-blooded scream as she saw more rats following the first. In a blind panic, she grabbed some clothes scattered on the floor next to her and ran towards the door.

She was nearly at the portal when something grabbed her hair, bringing her to a skidding halt.

"Thinking of leaving us without saying 'Goodbye', petite Cherie? So rude! And you such a lady. You should know better. After all, we have been waiting such a long time for you."

Susie was spun round to face a filthy half-naked giant. Seventeen stone of barrel-chested muscle, at least six and a half feet tall. She dangled helplessly in an iron grip, toes just scraping the bare floorboards. She aimed a punch at his face in a futile attempt to make him release her. Then screamed with all the power her lungs could muster.

"Shhh, quiet! You'll wake the others. We don't want them disturbing our little tête-à-tête, do we? After all, it will be your last taste of freedom before the sheikh comes for you. You wouldn't want to spoil that special moment for me, would you? The giant grinned lasciviously. "Here, put these on". He threw some clothes at her. "You will need to look presentable for your new master. Stop snivelling, pull yourself together."

Unable to wriggle free, Susie gasped, "All right, put me down. Put me down! What do you want?"

"You know what I want, Cherie. You must get dressed. But first, I want a little taste, eh? They never let me try the merchandise. All those beautiful women... what a waste! But you are too good to pass up. There is time to spare, and you will be my reward for staying in this stinking hole all night with these damn rats!"

Desperately Susie squirmed.

"Are you going to behave, or do I need to get rough?" He raised a gigantic hand and slapped her face.

Scared as she was, Susie had enough sense to look as if she would co-operate. She nodded. The giant let go, and she fell to the floor. Smiling broadly and drinking in every detail of her lithe naked body, he began to make appreciative grunts as he anticipated the delights to come. He watched closely as Susie picked herself up and searched for the clothes he had thrown at her. "Ahh, Chérie, we have been waiting all night; Bilic said you would come. He was right. Those two German guys didn't look your type, but they won't bother you anymore. He nodded towards two bodies lying in the corner. The two bankers from the club. Susie rummaged around on the floor for the flimsy skirt and stockings he had thrown at her, when her hand found one of her shoes. Instinctively she grabbed it, and in a blur of movement, slammed the stiletto heel into her captor's face. The appreciative grunting stopped abruptly – a look of astonishment frozen on the giant's face, as his body dropped to its knees, then crashed to the floor, a black stiletto pinned to its face like an incongruous eye patch. A bloody red tear rolled slowly down its cheek to mourn its demise. Susie sat quaking for a few moments, stunned. The implications of the giant's remark about the sheikh dawned on her. She had been kidnapped to be sold as a sex slave. And the giant had named Bilic.

Now she made the connection. The men that had gate-crashed their group the previous night must have brought her here, and Bilic must have paid them? Were her friends from Zürich involved in this set-up?

Abruptly she threw up over the dead body of the giant. For a second time, she searched frantically for some clothes. She grabbed some rags, not caring what they were.

Pulling herself upright, she stumbled out of the room, walking out onto a derelict landing – bare boards and more crumbling plaster. She called out for her friends; her voice echoed around the abandoned building. No one answered. Once more she called, still silence. Where could they be? No matter. She had to leave.

Masquerade

She dressed hurriedly. A man's trousers and a grubby tweed jacket with no lining and torn pockets. The captors might be back at any moment galvanised her will and drove her towards the nearest exit. An open door led out to a garden at the rear of the house. Once outside, she picked her way through the overgrown grass of a large rambling garden. At the back of the garden, partly covered by an overgrown privet hedge, she saw a small gap. On the other side was a quiet residential street. She stepped through and began walking quickly down the tree-lined road. She reasoned she was probably still in Paris when she saw a street sign with an arrondissement motif. She could find refuge in her mother's house. She ignored the curious stares her bare feet and unkempt appearance attracted.

Susie felt wretched. How could she end up in such a terrible situation? Her life had very nearly ended this morning. That was surely a sign that things had to change. This was not the first time she had woken up in a strange place, not knowing how she had got there. But this was much worse – to end up unconscious and naked in a filthy squat deserted by her companions. Who knows what had happened while she was asleep. The sickening realisation was enough to bring her to her senses and make her realise she should stop thinking about change and do something positive to make it happen. Where the hell was her mobile? Was it in her handbag? That must still be in the squat somewhere.

At the same time that Susie had scrambled through the gap in the back garden, a large black Mercedes limousine had crunched quietly up the gravel drive leading to the squat. A driver opened a backdoor for a tall patrician Arab, who paused briefly, waiting for his assistant to take up station. After scanning the facade of the house, he walked toward the front door. The sheikh had sent him to collect the new girl. He stood at the front door waiting while the assistant ran inside. Moments later, he reappeared, "She isn't there, Master."

The man's face hardened into a cruel mask, "Foolish! Bilic will pay for this." He strode back to his car, the assistant scurrying after him.

A quarter of a mile away, Susie could see the unmistakable outline of the Sacré-Cœur in the distance. Her mother's house was in the seventeenth arrondissement adjacent to Montmartre. She would be there in under an hour, even walking without shoes. Her heart lifted at the thought of a safe haven and a hot bath.

Masquerade

As she walked, Susie took stock of her life. She had lurched from one party to another. Always following the crowd to the most fashionable night spots.

Preoccupied with her transgressions, Susie arrived at her mother's house. She was greeted at the door by Matilde, her mother's housekeeper. The enticing aroma of a casserole drifting towards her. "Ahh! Mademoiselle, what an unexpected surprise. Mathilde diplomatically ignored Susie's bizarre attire.

"Ça va, Matilde. Where is Mama?"

"She's meeting friends, Mademoiselle. She will be back for dinner. Will you be staying?"

"Yes, Mathilde, I shall. I'll wash and change before we eat."

"That will be nice. I'll set an extra place for you."

Now that she was safe, Susie felt exhausted. Slowly she walked upstairs to her room, threw her rags onto the floor and ran a steaming hot bath. Leaning on the washbasin, she looked at her reflection in the mirror. Unexpectedly, a vague recollection of her father's work came to mind; he had been a diplomat. But she knew little more than that, and one thing she did remember was he used to keep a diary. Now, where were her father's papers; they would be a way to reconnect with him? She would ask her mother over dinner. With that thought, she turned and sank into a steaming hot bath.

Susie's mother's joy at seeing her daughter home was palpable. "It's such an unexpected surprise to see you, Darling. I'm sure Milan told me you were attending a party?"

"Oh, Mama! I'm so happy to see you too!"

Klara's face clouded over at Susie's tone of voice, asking, "Why, Susie darling, whatever is the matter?" For a moment, Susie's composure slipped, and she looked close to tears.

"Mama, I've had such a terrible fright, and I've been such a fool!"

"Come now, tell me what this is all about?"

"It's difficult to know where to begin. For such a long time, I've been leading such a shallow lifestyle: one party after another, empty-headed friends. My life is empty of any real meaning. You are the only tangible relationship I have. I don't like Milan one little bit. I never have, and I'm sorry to say, I don't think you should marry him. I know you can't see that, but it's true."

Susie took a deep breath and related the story, "Last night, I got into a terrible mess. After a film premiere, a group of us went to the Beat Club. As usual, we got rather drunk... so my memory is a bit hazy. I remember we met the Strauss girls from Zürich. We were partying with them, and they introduced some boys that they knew. I can't remember very much after that, but I'm sure the boys put something in my drink. When I woke this morning, all my so-called friends had disappeared, and I was a squalid squat somewhere in the suburbs. There were rats and tramps, and God knows what else in that horrible place. As I tried to leave, a man attacked me; I hit him with one of my shoes... I think I killed him." Susie broke down again. "I don't want to go to prison Mama... he said I had been taken there to be sold to an Arab sheikh. They had kidnapped me! I had to hit him to get away." Susie collapsed into her mother's embrace, her body shuddered with racking sobs.

"Darling, I'll talk to Milan. He will get to the bottom of this. If those people tried to kidnap you, they need to be arrested. Milan has connections within the Sûreté. I'm sure he can find out what happened."

Susie blurted out, "But that's just it, Mama. The man said Bilic had arranged for me to be taken there."

"But Darling, that's preposterous. Why would he do such a thing?

"Because he wants me out of the way. He wants to stop me from telling you the truth about him. Believe me, Mama, he's dangerous. I've heard some really bad stories about what he's done to people. "

Klara looked at Susie sceptically, "Darling, you've just been through a terrible trauma. I think you are letting your imagination run away with you. Why don't we talk about this later?"

"Okay, Mama. Just for a little while, let's talk about something else. But afterwards, I need to talk to you seriously. I've made up my mind I want to change my life."

"Darling, that's wonderful."

Eventually, Susie calmed down, "Mama. Are father's papers still in his study in Ticino?"

"Yes, they are; why do you ask?"

"I just feel I'd like to find out more about what he was doing before he died. I think I'd like to go to Ticino for a few days and rest. Would that be okay with you?"

Klara was thoughtful; it could at least bring peace of mind to Susie. "Yes, Darling, I think it would be good for you. In fact, a change of scenery might be the best thing in the world for you right now. I'll phone Hans in the morning and let him know you will be coming. You'll be safe there, and Louella can keep you company. You will have space and time to relax and go through your father's things if that's what you want. Yes, it's a very good idea."

Susie, "Will you promise me one thing? Don't tell Milan about this. Just tell him I've gone home to Budapest for some peace and quiet. And don't tell him why I want to read father's papers; I'd like to keep that secret between you and me."

After dinner, the phone rang. Susie answered it in the drawing-room. It was Bilic wanting to speak to her mother. When he realised it was Susie who had answered, he raged, "Where the hell have you been? My bodyguards have been searching for you all day. Your handbag was found in some filthy squat in the suburbs. What the hell are you playing at? You spoilt bitch, you don't realise how much trouble you've caused me."

Susie blurted out, "Why? Did you have to do some explaining to your sheikh? You don't own me."

Bilic sneered, "Think so? Once I marry your mother, I'll control the entire estate. Then you either do as I say, or I'll cut you off without a penny."

"My mother won't stand for that," retorted Susie.

"She won't have much choice! Once the marriage certificate is signed, she'll do as I say. Trust me, I'm not someone you want as an enemy."

Susie, "We'll see about that. "

"Your mother will agree to anything I suggest."

Susie yelled, "Just like those tarts in Cannes."

Bilic laughed, "That was just harmless fun – a bachelor having a final fling before he marries the woman he adores."

"Looked more like habitual debauchery to me. I can see right through you. I know you want our titles and money. Well, you won't get them!"

"Tell her if you like, she won't believe you. Anyway, it's too late, the arrangements have been made. The priest is booked, the guests are invited. To cancel it now would be a complete humiliation in front of all her friends; your mother wouldn't countenance that."

At that moment, Susie realised she could kill again, and next time it would be Bilic. If she had to do it to stop him from marrying her mother, she would.

Chapter 25: The Brief

Back at the 'Enquirer', Sam Chester was nursing a half mug of Black Label. 'Marlowe' wanted Chester to find out the identity of the victim he had found on the waste ground. Many favours had been offered, arms twisted, and much cash dangled. So for the last six hours, a small army of the homeless, petty thieves, street cleaners had been sniffing out any information about the events leading up to the murder. These people were the oil lubricating the city's vital services. Invisible to the general public, this network of unseen dogsbodies absorbed careless gossip and tittle-tattle and passed it on to Chester. In turn, he used these nuggets to lambast the establishment. Chester was impatient; he stared moodily at his list of names.

At six the next morning, Chester was jerked awake as the phone jangled; his spies began calling in. Most had heard nothing useful. But two separate informants had heard rumours that something had been planned for the Draper's Hall meeting, and the Police were told to stay away.

"Pat! What have you got?"

Patrick was a bouncer working the West End pubs, "Some cops from Paddington were joking about some action at Drapers Hall... some sort of political meeting."

"Thanks, mate." Chester put the phone down. It rang again immediately, "Speaking... Bernie mate. Any news?"

Bernie was an under-chef at a Chinese restaurant, "I overheard some customers talking while they were having a fag, round the back of the restaurant. It seems that murder victim's post mortem is happening tomorrow at Holborn. Some bloke called Malcutt has been called in to do it."

"Thanks, Bernie; I'll leave your fee in the usual place."

Chester slumped back in his chair; he smelled a rat. Malcutt was an infamously corrupt pathologist, appearing whenever a dirty deed needed covering up. Chester just so happened to have a contact working at the mortuary for such an eventuality.

Chester made the call, "Spencer? ...what? ...I know it's six o'clock. This is important. I hear on the grapevine that Malcutt is being called in tomorrow. What's the story?"

Masquerade

Spencer's voice trembled, "Christ! How the hell did you find out?"

Chester concealed his eagerness, "A little bird told me."

Spencer became agitated, "I'm saying nothing. And if you know what's good for you, you'll stay clear."

"Come on, mate. I've got nothing for this week's edition: give me a break. You must know something?"

Spencer clammed up, "It's quiet; there's nowt on."

"A body found in the Docklands? Is that for Malcutt? Come on, spill the beans... You know I never reveal my sources."

The mention of the docklands body terrified Spencer, "No way! More than my life's worth; I'm saying nothin'."

Chester, "What?"

The line went dead.

Why was Spencer terrified? Deep down, Chester knew.

Chapter 26: Choppy Waters

Palmer sat with Gittins in the incident van. Some monitors had been rigged up, and they watched MI5 agents work their way methodically through the apartment block. Finally, someone came out and signalled the snatch squads to stand down. He wasn't in there. Quietly they made their way back towards their vans. Suddenly a dog handler, searching close to a heavily overgrown hedge, called in; his dog had picked up a scent. The lead MI5 agent ran over to confer. The other agents and snatch squads ran to the perimeter of the copse and crouched down, watching the dog work the scent. A few minutes later, the lead agent returned and motioned a squad to follow him. They disappeared behind some overgrown bushes.

Palmer grunted, "Looks like they found something."

Gittins nonchalantly puffed on a cigarette, "Don't get your hopes up!"

Abruptly, Palmer stabbed a finger at another monitor, "Look!"

Gittins snarled triumphantly, "Gotcha! You little bastard!"

Palmer banged his fists on the desk, "It's him, I know it! He fits the body profile; we've got him."

Gittins remained calm in the face of Palmer's exuberance. "Steady old son, we're not there just yet. Can your cameras follow him?"

"Sure"

"OK, get the snatch squad to move up behind him, but make sure they keep their distance. I don't want to spook the little swine now."

Palmer made the call then, "You're an East End boy, do you know this neck of the woods?"

Gittins snorted, "Long time ago, son… long time ago. This was all warehouses and docker's homes. All gone now – full of thieving bankers. I'd like to nick those bastards, but they do their thieving legally."

"Doesn't look as if he could afford to live here?"

"Probably not, but there might be places he could squat; it's like a rabbit warren down there."

Palmer was exasperated, "It'll be tough for our guys to corner him then."

Gittins smirked, "They only need one shot."

Masquerade

At the warehouse, Dark towelled sweat away from his face. He'd had a good run this morning until he noticed police activity on the nearby estate. Ordinarily, it wouldn't have disturbed him, but he was edgy since the murder. He had seen dog handler vans tucked away in a back street, plus two large, unmarked minibuses with blacked-out windows. He smelled trouble. This wasn't coincidence; it was time to move. He sat at his computer and typed a message to Heinz, 'Suspicious activity nearby, possibly Police or Anti-Terrorist Squad. Taking no chances. I'll take the boat and meet you at the hostel.'

Dark grabbed a large waterproof canvas bag pre-packed with several sets of clothing. From another shelf, he pulled a smaller waterproof case containing his disguise props. He opened a wall safe and selected several sets of ID documents: Russian, Portuguese, French, German, Malayan and Chinese. Each set contained passports, driving licences, credit cards and hard currency of various denominations. He shoved them into the bag along with his disguises.

There were several escape routes from the warehouse; all of them allowed him to exit the building at a safe distance away. Airports, train stations and passenger ports would be monitored closely. Commercial ports were often overlooked: they would provide his best opportunity to escape. That's why he'd decided to use the tug and sail to Rotterdam, then sail up the Rhine to Basel. The Rhine had plenty of small commercial harbours to hide the tug if a change of plan was needed. Dark had taken the precaution of registering the boat at Tilbury and Duisburg in Germany. It would mingle with other working boats on either side of the Channel. The route to Heinz had been memorised long ago.

Heinz Gombricht's headquarters in Geneva were located at the St. Jean Hostel for Lost Souls; it provided a suitably deceptive cover for the Hacker network. Its neglected façade belied the state of the art facilities installed in the basement; from here, the Hackers constantly monitored Corporatist activity. The hostel also provided the perfect cover for hackers wishing to come and go unnoticed. Disguised as an itinerant, Dark would be able to visit without arousing suspicion.

The hostel was the control centre for a group of rebellious hackers spread around Europe and Asia. They were Heinz's eyes and ears. Once in the heart of Europe, Dark could move freely from country to country if needed. He would be much safer there.

Dark ran down the tunnel leading to the boathouse; it stank of rotting river waste. The river current had trapped all manner of rubbish against its doors. He hadn't been down there in weeks, and the lack of fresh air concentrated the stink. Dark threw his gear into a small tender and five minutes later was on board the tugboat, moored midstream. He dropped his kit into the wheelhouse cabin and made his way down to the engine room. He checked oil and fuel levels before starting the generator, which stuttered fitfully into life before settling into a regular rhythm. After turning on the engine room lights, he made a cursory check for signs of fluid leaks. Satisfied, he turned the lights off and made his way back to the wheelhouse. Normally Dark was meticulous and ran through a checklist to make sure the boat was seaworthy before getting underway. This time, however, he was keen to put some distance between himself and the warehouse. For all he knew, the police were close; they may even have reached the apartment. He needed to make himself scarce.

A gusting easterly wind blew a heavy drizzle against the wheelhouse window in a thick pitter-patter; the weather was closing in. Dark quickly punched Rotterdam's port coordinates into the boat's auto-pilot navigation system. Then he ran outside to cast off the bow and stern lines. The current pulled the tug slowly from its mooring before Dark nudged the throttle levers to slow ahead, edging the tug into midstream.

As the boat made its way into the downstream channel of the Thames, Dark checked behind. Four hundred yards away, he could just make out three figures dressed in black. They appeared from the side of the boathouse. A split second later, the apartment's upper floor dissolved in a flash of orange as the incendiary devices took out the windows at the front of the apartment. The blast knocked all three figures to the ground before they staggered back to the shelter of the boathouse. Thankfully they looked unhurt.

With any luck, Dark thought grimly, the explosion would have diverted their attention away from the river.

He took out the charts and studied the crossing to Rotterdam in more detail. He should reach the mouth of the Thames estuary just before lunchtime. Crossing the North Sea to Rotterdam's Neue Port should take another six or seven hours, depending on the weather and traffic. He estimated an hour to get through the port and into the Rhine. With luck, he should be looking for a berth on the Dutch Rhine at about seven or eight o'clock in the evening. He would spend the night there.

The radio blared out the weather forecast. Gusting winds would lighten by midday with a medium swell in the Thames. Dark noted the forecast with satisfaction; the weather shouldn't cause any problems on the first leg of the journey.

The rhythmic hum of the boat's engines calmed Dark somewhat. He analysed his movements after the murder. How had the Police found him so quickly? What clues had he left? He was preoccupied and barely noticed familiar riverside landmarks. First was Galleons Hill to starboard, then he sailed past Tilbury and Gravesend as the mouth of the estuary widened into the North Sea. Dark kept the tug close to shore, losing sight of the bank on the starboard side.

Dark set the autopilot and went to the galley and brewed a strong cup of tea. As he got back to the wheelhouse, he checked the navigation system and noticed they had swung north-east following the Essex coastline a mile or so to sea. As they passed Clacton-on-Sea, a squall drove a curtain of heavy drizzle in from the open sea. Visibility would remain poor for the next few hours at least. That suited Dark admirably. The autopilot would follow this heading until they reached Felixstowe. Then they would turn to starboard and join the main shipping lane over to the Dutch coast. Dark settled himself into the captain's chair for the crossing.

As he neared Felixstowe, a heavy swell began to pitch the boat about and the horizon filled with whitecaps, whipped up by a strengthening wind. Visibility was reduced to a few hundred yards as a thick band of rain merged dark grey seas with the sky. He checked the anemometer, which showed a gusting north easterly was hitting his port side. Typical North Sea weather, rough seas and blustery winds; there would be no relaxation on this trip. He turned on the shortwave radio and listened to the chatter of surrounding shipping. After a couple of hours of being buffeted, he picked up the navigation lights of a fleet of fishing boats dead ahead. Powerful waves pitched the boats up and down in a manic jig. Every few minutes, Dark checked his heading against the waypoints on the navigation system. The fishing boats were struggling to maintain their heading and were forcing him off course. He cursed them roundly as he took evasive action to avoid their random changes of direction. Gradually he had worked his way through most of the fleet and was checking his position on a chart. Looking up to check the navigation system, he froze. A hundred yards in front of him, a line of heavy orange buoys wrapped around a heavy trawl net rose and fell on the swell. It must have fallen from one of the fishing boats. It was a miracle he had seen it at all. Dark gave the engines full throttle and spun the rudder hard to port. Whatever happened, he couldn't afford to snag the semi-submerged netting on his propellers. The diesel engine bellowed as it fought for traction against the surging waves. The tug shuddered as it healed over as the rudder finally began to bite. The buoys were only fifty yards away. Slowly at first, the boat began to change course, then the rudder bit into the rough swell and the tug swiftly came to port. Dark cursed at the nets; this was going to be too close to call. The buoys scraped down the side of the boat, and Dark's curses turned to prayers. If the propellers snagged, he would be a sitting duck. He would need to call the Coast Guard, and that would mean a report. A report would mean the Authorities would have his location. The boat juddered; Dark checked behind. The buoys wallowed in the tug's foaming wake. He prayed harder. Again the tug juddered then surged on. The props must have cut the net – he was free. Dark pulled the throttle levers back, the high-pitched whine of the engines quietened to a steady thrum. Dark resumed course; that was too close for comfort.

Only then did he notice a huge commotion on the shortwave radio, and although he didn't understand Dutch, he guessed he was the cause of the fuss. There was nothing to do but stick to the plan. By six-thirty, the rain was easing, and Dark could just about make out Rotterdam's Europort. The autopilot made a small adjustment to the boat's heading to enter the harbour in the correct shipping lane. Once completed, Dark switched it off, taking control himself. As he sailed through the port, he hoped he looked just like any other tug making its way through Rotterdam's massive docks. Running at the harbour's speed limit, it seemed to take forever to pass mile upon mile of containers from all parts of the Globe, stacked in regimented ranks on the dockside. The harbour walls had damped down the pitching waves of the channel into a flat gentle swell. A slight sea mist and the gathering evening gloom concealed Dark's passage through the port. At seven o'clock, the tug entered the Dutch Rhine. Dark needed to bed down for the night, so he quickly set the coordinates for Nijmegen. There was bound to be a berth there. By next morning he would be miles down river. The Rhine was the gateway to Europe; from its mouth to Basel would take about three days sailing. But he was in no hurry, now that he was out of the UK and immediate danger. He would be safe mingling with the other traffic

Masquerade

plying the River and the Neue Port. His best disguise would be to behave exactly like the other boats. But right now, he could do with a meal and rest. It had been a long day.

Back in London, Nelson Abe was one of Malinger's junior constables. He had completed his training at Hendon only two weeks before and was determined to make his mark, so he diligently studied every message that popped up on his computer screen. However, after six hours of staring at the computer, he had a splitting headache and was losing the will to live. Every message had been a report from a ferry company, airport security, or Transport Police. Then he noticed a message from the Coastguard. They'd picked up radio chatter between fishing boats off the Dutch coast complaining about a UK-registered tug disrupting fishing. The Rotterdam Harbourmaster had joined the altercation when it became apparent the tug was entering the port at Rotterdam. The harbourmaster put out a call for seafarers to identify the tug. The Harbour Master sent a boat to search for the tug.

Nelson decided to pass this on to the Sergeant just in case

Chapter 27: Road to Redemption

Five hundred kilometres away from Dark and Rotterdam, Susie eased her Porsche Carrera slowly into the chill grey light of a Parisian dawn. She drove quietly along damp deserted boulevards heading southwards towards the autoroute for Nemours. She was calmer now she had made a decision. She settled back into the sports seats, gripped the tactile steering wheel a little tighter and began to enjoy the drive. The horror of the previous day, if not forgotten, was put in perspective. For the first time in years, she felt a sense of purpose. She should be in Ticino by afternoon, then she could spend a few days reading her father's diaries.

An hour later, she reached the autoroute. Gradually the slower traffic thinned out, and she settled the Carrera into a fast cruise. Half a kilometre behind her, a powerful black Mercedes saloon discretely held station with the Porsche. Susie was an accomplished driver and relished the sensation of driving a thoroughbred sports car, finding it therapeutic. Her father had collected sports cars from the sixties and seventies, and together they had frequently spent time driving the mountain roads and passes of the Alps and Dolomites. He would regale her with stories of his rallying exploits; they had developed a strong bond on these drives. Susie cherished those memories, and she suddenly realised how deeply she missed her father.

Susie noticed a sign for Nemours and decided to stop for coffee. Turning off the autoroute, she remembered a small cafe close to the river, deep in the National Park forest. Behind, the black Mercedes slowed and followed her. Thirty minutes later, she was driving through the forest. Tall trees marshalled a narrow road through the dense dark woodland towards the river. Susie let the Porsche amble at a walking pace down the narrow lane. The car travelled so quietly that the burble of its engine failed to alert a herd of deer; they only reacted as the car rounded a sharp bend. Susie delighted in their lithe beauty, highlighted by shafts of dazzling sunlight glinting off their sleek red-brown coats as they bounded for cover into the murky wood. A few kilometres later, Susie pulled into the café car park. She had expected the place to be deserted so early in the season, so she was surprised to see crowds of chattering couples milling around. Inside, the cafe buzzed with conversation, clinking china and the hiss of espresso machines. So much for a quiet coffee! Susie collected a tray and joined a queue at the counter.

Outside, the Mercedes parked discretely behind a tour bus, out of sight of the café but where the driver could keep an eye on the Porsche. Two men clambered out of the back seats and strode toward the café. They looked out of place in their black suits – standing head and shoulders above diminutive elderly couples in their brightly coloured anoraks. The men joined the queue for coffee, failing spectacularly not to look conspicuous as they searched for their mark. They found her sitting at a window table on the far side of the cafeteria, looking out at the river.

The chattering crowds, unsettled Susie so she decided to powder her nose and carry on to Ticino. As she left the restroom, the two thugs were waiting. One twisted her arm viciously behind her back and jammed her against the wall. He placed a large fleshy hand over her mouth. "Stop struggling bitch! You're coming with us."

Susie squirmed and kicked but to no avail. The brute was stronger. Her breath came in gasping sobs as she began to heave; bitter bile flooded her nose and mouth, she began to lose consciousness.

Recognising the girl was passing out, the thug slowly loosened his grip. Desperate to bring her round, he slapped her face a few times. Slowly her eyes fluttered open, and she gulped fresh air.

"You and I are going to walk out of here arm in arm. We're just an ordinary couple on a day out. Listen to me! Snap out of it! We'll go to your car and drive somewhere quiet. Don't even think about shouting out, I've got a knife, and I'll cut you bad if you so much as make a squeak. Are you going to keep quiet?"

Susie nodded. She started to think that maybe these two were not as formidable as the giant who had confronted her in the squat – these guys were smaller at least. Part of her was calculating how she could disable this brute, then he grabbed her arm.

Susie snarled at him, "Take your hands off me, you bastard, or I'll scream!"

He relaxed his grip slightly, "Smile bitch, or you'll regret it."

Desperately, Susie tried to think of a way to escape as she was frogmarched towards the door.

She tried to make eye contact with someone. Anyone who might see the desperation in her eyes. But everyone was too engrossed to pay any attention to her. The cashier glanced at her momentarily then looked away

Masquerade

as a customer called. None of the diners paid any attention. Susie's determination wavered, then lifted again. He said they were going to her car, his accomplice would have to leave them. One to one, she would have a chance of escape.

They crossed the car park towards her car, threading their way through the crowds. A light drizzle began to fall. Susie tried to wrench her arm clear, but the thug yanked it back.

"Don't be stupid." The thug hissed, "See that car?" He pointed at the Mercedes. "My associates will follow us to a more private setting; we'll conclude our business there. Now get in the car and no tricks. Don't forget the knife... and his gun." He nodded towards his smirking accomplice.

Susie weighed her options. Paris had given her a measure of confidence. Years of falling out of nightclubs had taught her the most effective ways to deter unwanted advances.

So she acted – terrified and helpless. "Okay, just don't hurt me."

The thug smirked, "Don't worry, you won't feel a thing. Get in, and don't start the car until I tell you."

As she walked around the Porsche away from his line of sight, Susie quickly hitched her skirt up well over her thighs. She opened the car then played for time by taking off her jacket; the thug was struggling to manoeuvre his bulky frame into the sports seat; then he noticed her lithe stockinged legs and stopped, half in half out of the car. He was completely distracted.

By now, his colleague was a hundred yards away, making for the Mercedes. The thug's knife was in the hand furthest away from her. He was transfixed by Susie's legs and reached over to touch them. Susie responded to his advance; her hand briefly caressed his cheek before jabbing her thumb deep into his eye socket. Her attack was so unexpected that the thug barely whimpered before Susie had punched him in the neck with all the force she could muster. The thug crumpled, dazed. Quickly Susie started the engine then ran round to drag her unwanted passenger away from the car.

The thug's accomplices in the Mercedes hadn't yet noticed anything amiss. Susie heaved on the thug's coat. His bulky body resisted her attempts to move it, but her desperation gave her strength, and after what seemed like an eternity, the thug lay inert on the ground. But one leg was jammed between the seat and the dashboard. Try as she might, it wouldn't budge. Frantically she ran back around to the driver's side and somehow managed to pull his leg up and out of the car. Suddenly a horn blared out. The occupants of the Mercedes had seen their colleague lying on the ground. Their car started, and engine howling, headed rapidly toward her. Susie flicked the Porsche's gear lever into reverse and floored the accelerator. The Carrera catapulted backwards in a hail of gravel; Susie flicked the steering wheel, spinning the car round and accelerating away. A flawless demonstration of car control her father would have been proud of.

Everyone in the crowded car park craned forward, looking for the cause of the commotion. As they surged forward, they blocked the accelerating Mercedes, which swerved and bounced off the side of the bus before taking off again, after Susie.

The Porsche roared up the lane. Checking her mirror, she saw the Mercedes disappearing into the distance. But she knew they would not give up the chase. Sure enough, she soon heard a horn blasting and saw flashing lights as they tried to catch her. A quick check saw the Mercedes was a couple of hundred yards back. "Okay big guy, let's see what you're made of." Susie dropped a gear and floored the accelerator, trying to remember the layout of the road. The car leapt forward, racing along a lengthy undulating straight through the forest. The Porsche bucked and weaved over the gravel surface so that Susie had to make constant corrections at the wheel. The Mercedes was still just visible in the mirror but wasn't gaining. Susie remembered a sequence of bends were coming up. She knew the race-bred Porsche would be far more agile than the heavier Mercedes. As she approached the first turn, she downshifted two gears, trail braked into the apex, then, with a swift dab of opposite lock, accelerated hard out of the corner. The engine howled as the car executed a perfect drift and accelerated hard down the lane. When she reached the end of the next straight, she checked her mirrors again. The Mercedes was nowhere to be seen. Breathing a sigh of relief, Susie kept her foot down. "By the time I get out of the forest, he'll be miles behind." These must be Bilic's men, God; they must have been waiting for me at Mother's house. After the failed attempt at the squat and their row on the phone, he seemed even more determined to get rid of her. She wondered if there were more thugs waiting somewhere. Now she was undecided about going directly to Ticino or taking a detour to lose them. She decided on the direct route, the route nationale.

Back in the Mercedes, one of the thugs made a call on his mobile. "Patron, the girl nearly killed Franco, and she's escaped ...No, we've lost sight of her

...Yes, the tracking device is still working. I'll call you when we find out where she is going."

Chapter 28: New Ally

Dark bent over a sheaf of charts; he needed a place to moor the boat and change its nameplate. Suddenly he heard a klaxon wailing behind. Glancing over his shoulder, he saw a harbour master launch closing at speed. Dark steered closer to the bank to let it pass. However, as it came alongside, it slowed to match his speed.

"Ahoy, Rosetta. Heave to."

"Damn, damn!" Dark cursed loudly and at length. He had no choice: he couldn't outrun the powerful launch. He would have to stop.

Dark came about, idling the engines to hold the boat against the current. The Harbour Master launch drew alongside in a smoothly executed manoeuvre, allowing a boarding party to step onto Rosetta. Two men in dark waterproofs, both armed with automatic pistols and assault rifles, took covering positions for a young lieutenant. He marched purposefully along the deck towards the wheelhouse. He sized up Dark while casually resting his hand on his automatic. Dark would need to be careful.

"Good evening. Are you the captain?"

"Ja." Dark responded.

"Your papers?"

Dark thought quickly, "Damn, I haven't sorted out the passports." The last thing he needed was for them to search the boat. Abruptly Dark turned away. "Eine moment bitte."

The lieutenant, astonished at Dark's peremptory manner, called out, "Stop where you are!"

Dark stopped in his tracks as he heard a gun being cocked.

"Show me where you keep the papers. I'll get them myself."

Dark had no option but to comply. "This way," he gestured.

The lieutenant was too experienced to fall for that trick. He gestured for Dark to walk back to the wheelhouse.

"Did you cross the Channel today?"

Dark kept his back to the lieutenant, "I followed the Dutch coast into Rotterdam."

The lieutenant persisted, "A boat like this was reported disrupting fishing operations off the coast earlier. Was that you?"

So that was it, bloody fishing boats. Dark lied smoothly, "Sorry, don't know what you're talking about."

They had reached the wheelhouse. Dark pointed to a box file on the chart table. "The papers are in there." He glanced towards the deck; the other two guards were momentarily out of sight.

The lieutenant squeezed past Dark to reach the file. "If you weren't near the fishing boats, why do you have netting snagged on the back of the boat?"

Dark thought quickly; he wasn't going to be able to talk his way out of this. The lieutenant knew Dark was lying. However, Dark still had a small chance to escape. The box file contained nothing but old receipts.

The lieutenant, thinking he had the situation under control, looked away from Dark as he opened the file. Seeing only scraps of paper, he rummaged through them, looking for official documents. Then he looked up, confused, "There's nothing here but …." That was as far as he got. Dark punched him in the temple. Instantly the lieutenant collapsed, sliding silently to the deck, unconscious. Dark sneaked a look on deck. The two guards were looking back towards their launch. He only had a few seconds. "Bloody hell, this was the last thing I needed." He turned back to the wheelhouse, grabbed his bags and ran through the door opposite the guards. As he reached the rail, there was a shout – "Halt". Then two loud cracks. Dark felt something sharp slice his cheek.

Without breaking stride, Dark dived over the railing into the freezing black waters of the Rhine. A hail of bullets scorched past him as he swam back under the tug. The two guards sprayed automatic fire into the water where he had dived in. But Dark surfaced on the other side of the police launch, close to the middle of the river. The current was slow but strong; he dived again. His lungs were bursting by the time he was able to surface next to a train of barges slowly making their way upriver. Grabbing the end of a wayward tarpaulin, he carefully looked around the stern at the commotion on the Rosetta and the police launch. They were using spotlights to search the water around the boats as well as the bank. The two guards were shouting at the launch pilot as the lieutenant stumbled along Rosetta's deck.

Masquerade

It took all of Dark's strength to haul himself and his bags into the barge and scramble under the tarpaulin. It was going to be a long cold night. He burrowed down into the filthy mound of rubbish, shivering uncontrollably. The stench was overpowering, but at least the stinking rubbish would provide some protection. If he hadn't found shelter from the chill night wind, he would have died from exposure. Exhausted, he managed to wriggle around to create a small nest. He rubbed his arms and body to keep his circulation going. The next couple of hours would be critical if he was going to make good his escape. It was completely black in his small burrow. He estimated it was about nine in the evening. The sun had been setting as the Rotterdam Harbour Police boat had boarded his tug.

He hadn't slept for thirty-six hours now and was dog tired, but he needed to stay awake and fight off the onset of exposure. Sleeping might prove fatal. Considering the overpowering stench of rotting food, Dark thought it highly unlikely staying awake was going to be a problem.

On the river, Police patrol boats had arrived and raced up and down, searching for the fugitive. On the first pass, the Police had hailed the tug pulling Dark's barge. They questioned the captain briefly before peeling back downriver. Dark wasn't too worried by their search; they were just going through the motions. He was certain they would concentrate their efforts in the area where he had been stopped. Swimming out to mid-stream away from the river bank had been instinctive for him. But the Police's instinct would be to focus on the bank; they assumed that would be the obvious escape route. Their blunder gave him the necessary time to make his escape.

After a long uncomfortable night, slivers of grey light filtered into Dark's burrow. It was time to go. The half-light of dawn would cover him as he swam ashore.

A couple of hours later, Dark was seated at the Emmerich quayside, soaking up the warm mid-morning sunshine. The harbour buzzed with activity: cargo was being loaded and unloaded from barges lining the quayside, stevedores shouted orders, the clang and thump of cranes drifted on the balmy air. At the far end of the harbour, a river bus pulled in and exchanged one set of passengers for another. Dark considered it... "no, too many people, too busy." He wandered down to the other end of the harbour; it was quieter there – older, smaller boats. Sure enough, after a few minutes, he found what he was looking for. A battered old barge, smoke rising lazily from a blackened chimney stack. A grizzled old man pottered about on deck. A large pile of wooden crates were stacked on the quay; no one seemed to be loading. Dark waited for thirty minutes or more and, seeing no one else aboard, decided to try his luck.

He wandered past the barge then back again. The old man appeared on deck. Dark called out. "Hello! Are you sailing today?"

The old man looked up and gave Dark a sour look. Watchful eyes shaded by bushy eyebrows sized up Dark. "Maybe. What do you want?"

"I'm trying to get to Basel. You look shorthanded. I wondered if I could work my passage."

The old man looked dubious. "What can you do on a boat? Have you crewed before?"

Dark lied, "I have a mate's certificate and plenty of experience on coastal merchant boats."

"Why are you going to Basel?"

"I'm travelling. I'm meeting some friends in Basel on Saturday."

The old man was wary. He didn't like sudden change, but his cargo was due in two days, and he was late because his usual crewman had broken his arm in a drunken brawl. He was desperate: his loan repayments were two months in arrears, and business was hard to come by in the recession. His customers were feeling the pinch as well; they were weeks late paying him. Perhaps this guy could help him out of a hole.

"Maybe I can take you as far as Strasburg, but there won't be any pay."

Dark grinned: "That's all right, I just want a lift. I'll work my passage, as I said. How long will it take to get to Strasburg?"

"All right, come aboard. What's your name? Bags?"

"Just these. Call me Marlowe." Dark shook the old man's hand.

"It should take two days, maybe three depending on the river." the old man shrugged. "Take the port cabin. Drop your gear off. Then I'll show you where I want those crates. As soon as you load up, we'll be on our way." He was suddenly business-like.

Dark manhandled his canvas bag down the narrow gangway to a small but comfortable cabin. She was an old boat but solid, built by craftsmen. He

Masquerade

quickly checked the layout, then went back on deck; the cargo was waiting for him.

The old man gave him his instructions, then added. "I'm going to my cabin to sort out some paperwork. Don't be long."

Two hours later, sweating and grimy, Dark wandered into the wheelhouse, wiping his hands with an oily rag. The old man was peering at some charts.

"What do you make of this?" he enquired of Dark, stabbing a finger at a point on a chart of the river.

Dark flipped the chart around. It showed some narrows with a depth restriction. Dark told the captain what he saw.

"So you can navigate?" the old man demanded.

"Yes, I told you!" The old man scrutinised him, still unsure. Dark feigned indifference and studied the chart, waiting for the next test.

A short wave radio crackled into life. It was the German River Police warning shipping to be on the lookout for an escaped prisoner wanted by the Dutch authorities. He was dangerous and should not be approached. A description was given, male, mid-twenties, dark hair, 1.8 metres tall. Last seen in the vicinity of Nijmegen.

The old man hunched over a chart and puffed on his pipe, one finger tamping down the tobacco as his calloused hand traced their route upriver, seemingly oblivious to the radio. He regarded Dark surreptitiously from under bushy eyebrows.

"He's good," the old man thought, "a slight twitch, but otherwise, not bad." The old man had some experience in these matters; both he and his father had been the subject of many interrogations. His father during the war by the Nazis and himself during the Cold War by the Russians and the Germans. Their transport business was a front for a family smuggling operation moving contraband along European waterways, between East and West. They moved anything that was in demand, no questions asked. Europe was a difficult place in which to survive the immediate aftermath of the war. Especially in Germany. They survived as best they could, living like the rats they ate.

Abruptly the old man said, "Well, let's be on our way. We should reach Koblenz by nightfall, then we can top up with fuel and get some supplies. Do you have any money?

Masquerade

Dark smiled, "I have some, enough for supper perhaps."

"Cast off then. Mate!"

Dark shook his head, relieved and resigned in equal measure. The old man hadn't said anything. But Dark guessed he suspected something was amiss with his new crew.

The barge chugged steadily upstream in the afternoon sun. Its diesel engines sent a rhythmic vibration through the deck beneath Dark's feet. He gazed idly at the low lying banks, making the most of the respite. Cattle grazed in lush bulrush fringed meadows. The homely smell of aromatic wood smoke drifted out to Dark from picturesque villages on the river bank. There was something about the old man that Dark liked. Outwardly he seemed a crusty character and didn't give much away, but Dark had felt no antipathy in the earlier scrutiny. On the contrary, there had been a glimmer of a suppressed smile in response to Dark's replies. Years as an outlaw had made Dark finely attuned to nuances of voice and body language. The old man might try to take advantage of Dark as a deckhand, but he had shown no appetite to confront Dark when he had heard the news on the radio.

A slight bump and slowing of the engines woke Dark. He had dropped off. Quickly he ran up on deck as the old man manoeuvred the barge into a fuel bay. The jetty was deserted, apart from the owner of the fuel depot, waiting, hands on hips for the barge to dock. "Gunther, you old reprobate! He called out. "Where have you been? I was beginning to worry you'd run off without paying me."

The Old Man grumbled, "Mate! Get that for'ard line, will you? Ernst, you heartless old bastard. How can you say that? When have I ever let you down?"

The two men clasped hands then rocked in unison in a vice-like bear hug. Ernst slapped Gunther heartily on the back, "Come and have a beer, old friend." They walked into a wooden hut.

An attendant walked out to take Dark's order, "Fill both tanks, will you... filler caps at the stern, I'm just going to the general store."

"No rush, it'll take a while", the attendant yawned.

Dark wandered slowly down the dock. Glad as he was for fresh air, he shivered in the chill evening. There weren't many other businesses at the depot, just a dilapidated river cruise business, and that was closed. Dark made his way to the general store. A single naked fluorescent tube dropped a cold pool of light beneath its door, and a weather-beaten sign attested to a laid back approach to life.

Dark walked into the dimly lit shop; it looked like a throwback to the fifties – bare floorboards, metal shelves stacked with anything you could imagine and many things you couldn't. He looked around; the counter by the door was empty. He spied a bell on the counter and gave it a tap. The ring hardly penetrated the heavy atmosphere – silence. Eventually, a distant door grated somewhere at the back of the shop, and a slit of light announced the shopkeeper. Slowly, a hunched old man shuffled along a gloomy aisle toward Dark. He blinked curiously at the visitor as he reached the counter.

"Bitte?" he squeaked.

"Guten abend," Dark began, "do you sell food?"

"Ja, ja. Behind you, three aisles along... halfway down. There is fresh and frozen food." The old man busied himself with paperwork at the counter and switched the radio to a classical music station. Dark tugged a trolley out of a stack and started to inspect the shelves.

Fifteen minutes later, Dark had chosen the groceries he thought would be needed for the next couple of days. The hunched old man was sitting quietly, listening to his radio, absentmindedly tapping his fingers in time with the music. Dark's presence startled him. But, without a word, he began to check Dark's trolley. The headline on a stack of newspapers caught Dark's attention. It was asking the public to report sightings of Dark. Had the old man noticed the headline, he wondered?

Dark diverted the shopkeeper's attention, "Can I borrow the trolley? This is heavy, and the boat is down at the fuel depot."

"Ja, ja. Leave it there; Ernst will bring it back," the old man squeaked. He peered at Dark through grimy spectacles and stroked his chin thoughtfully as the door slammed shut. He closed the evening newspaper and studied the headline about the manhunt.

"I wonder, I wonder. It could be him, but then what would he be doing here? He was miles away... it's probably nothing... just my imagination."

Masquerade

Absentmindedly, he turned to his ledgers and entered the details of Dark's purchase.

Dark was putting away the groceries and supplies in the galley when he heard the captain grumbling and stumbling at the gangplank. He had obviously enjoyed more than a few beers with his old sparring partner.

As Dark closed the last cupboard door, the captain stumbled into the galley. "Ah, there you are. I wondered where you'd got to. I don't suppose there's any coffee in the pot, is there?"

"How was your long-lost pal?"

"Ahh, Ernst talks too much about the old days. It's okay every now and again, but every time I see him? Bah! It's getting tedious."

Dark ventured, "Only, I wondered when we would be leaving."

The old man regarded him speculatively. "In a hurry?"

"I suppose so; I would like to get to Basel as soon as we can. I promised my friends I would be there by Thursday. And as it's Tuesday, it doesn't leave too much time."

The old man walked past Dark and opened a cupboard, took out the coffee jar, and spooned some instant coffee into a mug. "Want some? Oh, and by the way, call me Gunther." He put a kettle of water to boil on the stove and turned to face Dark, leaning back against the counter and crossing his arms. He thought for a moment. He distinctly remembered Dark telling him he was going to meet his friend on Saturday. What had changed his mind, and why lie about it?

Gunther looked at Dark carefully. The boy was anxious, and he was sure he knew why.

"We stay here tonight. I'm tired, and I want to rest. If you're in a big hurry to meet your friends, then we can start early in the morning. We'll have the whole day to get as far upriver as we can. Unless, of course, you want to find an alternative way of getting to Basel?"

Dark began to mouth a protest but thought better of it and quietly accepted the old man's decision. "OK, I suppose it will have to do. I'll be awake early. Good night!" Dark turned on his heel and went to his cabin.

Masquerade

Gunther gave a tight smile and took a sip of scalding hot coffee. "So we'll see. He is not prepared to give anything away yet. Let's see what tomorrow brings."

Dark lay on his bunk. He could hear Gunther manoeuvring the boat away from the refuelling jetty. Dark fell into a deep sleep, his first for over forty-eight hours.

Next morning Dark woke with a start. He'd overslept. Damn! From the rocking motion of the barge, he guessed they were underway. He dressed quickly and went to find out where they were. He was halfway up the steps to the top deck when Gunther, standing with his back to him, hissed, "Stay where you are. Don't come on deck."

The old man's tone stopped him dead. Dark froze, not moving a limb. He tried to look beyond Gunther but could only make out a blue sky.

"What's the matter?"

Gunther stood quite still, looking straight ahead. Doing his best to appear as if he were doing nothing more than enjoying the morning air as he steered the boat. "Customs and river police have been very active this morning. They have been patrolling the river with their high-speed RIBs. They're checking every boat on the river. We're being followed right now. We'll be stopped and searched very soon - I think they're looking for you?"

Dark said nothing. Unsure if he trusted the old man enough to confide in him.

Gunther took his hesitation as confirmation. "Go below and stay in your cabin. Do you want them to find you if they search us?"

Dark hesitated. "No, I don't. Can you hide me?"

"Wait in your cabin; I'll be there as soon as I can."

Dark's nerves were on edge as he made his way back to his cabin. In London, Seargent Malinger was experiencing similar emotions as he called Detective Inspector Gittins with news he knew would irritate Gittins. He wasn't sure how but he knew there had been a screwup.

An hour later, after consuming several cigarettes and developing the least incriminating version of the bad news, Gittins drew a deep breath and made the call. Five long minutes later, Gittins sat and lit another cigarette. All things considered, he thought the call had gone reasonably well.

However, the receiver of the call was not so sanguine. Stryckland had slammed the receiver down in a furious rage.

"Incompetent bloody fools!" They had him in their grasp, yet he still managed to get away. This was the second time, damn it! What sort of man were they dealing with? This was no gifted amateur looking to make headlines or a quick buck. It was obvious he was a professional. This man posed a serious threat to Kalyptra's plans, more than that, he was getting under Stryckland's skin. Would Gittins be able to deal with him? Maybe it was time to call in one of his enforcers."

Chapter 29: Rural Retreat

"Chester? Chester? Is that you?" A taut whisper. It was Polly Enderby-Smythe, the magazine's proprietor.

"Polly? What's the matter?"

"Oh my God! We've been raided. Some MI5 bastards are shutting us down. They're using some bullshit about Prevention of Terrorism. They've even slapped a Black Notice on this week's edition." Her voice was hysterical

In the background, a cacophony of loud noise, screams and shouting drowned out Polly.

"Somehow, they have found out we knew about the Draper's Hall murder. How? How did they know that? Christ! Do we have a mole? Who the hell would do that?"

More screaming.

"My God, these people are animals! A copper just punched Janice in the face; Christ, she's a bloody mess. They don't even use handcuffs anymore, just tie wraps. The bastards! They're tearing the place apart! Chester, you need to get out! Hide. They've been asking about you. Remember Leo's place? I'll meet you there in a couple of days. There's a key in the garage behind the paint pots. Hurry up, for Christ' sake; these bastards must be on to you. If they catch you, we've got no chance of exposing their lies. I'll get ……"

The line went dead. Chester felt sick. He could barely take in what he had just heard. So, it was the 'Enquirer's' turn. The Corporatists were out to stifle the last bastion of free speech. Chester wondered how a nation that had remained fiercely independent for a thousand years could allow itself to sleepwalk into fascism. Using terrorist legislation as an excuse to curtail free speech just because people had the temerity to disagree with them. It was a dark day.

Abruptly he came to his senses. He yanked a couple of disks out of his computer and stuffed them in his pocket. That would take care of the last couple of articles he was composing. He grabbed two notepads and shoved them into a briefcase. Emails? The bastards will be able to read them if they get the PC. Chester swept away the monitor and keyboard, grabbed the computer and ran outside. He threw everything into the back seat of his car and sped away in a shower of gravel.

Chester took the main route south out of London; throwing caution to the wind, he drove as fast as he dared. He tried to think clearly, but his mind was a whirl of indecision. The shriek of a siren behind him jerked him round. Checking his mirror, he saw a barrage of strobing blue lights. He froze, his heart thumped hard against his ribs, followed by a surge of relief as an ambulance sped past. Fingers fluttering, he turned on the radio to calm his jangling nerves.

As Chester was escaping London, Gittins was sat in his office in the middle of a conference call with Palmer at MI5, "Did you pick up everyone at the magazine?"

Palmer chuckled, "Most of them; we even got the owner… a loopy aristocrat."

Gittins took a drag on his cigarette, "What about the journalist?"

"He's on the run, but our agents are monitoring him. God, he crapped himself when the owner told him they were being raided."

Gittins snorted, "Typical! Don't lose him, for God's sake. Stryckland is giving me enough grief for letting the thief escape. The last thing I need is for this bugger to go AWOL."

"You worry too much; we'll take him when he goes to ground."

Thirty minutes later, Chester picked up the M3 motorway heading for Hampshire. There wasn't much traffic on the road at that late hour – it was past midnight by then – and he could at least see what was following him.

He pulled in at a twenty-four hour service station on the outskirts of Basingstoke. He tried to remember where the hell Leo lived. He could barely think straight. A road atlas might jog his memory. He bought a Driver's Atlas of the British Isles and a mobile. He tried to remember the last time he had visited Leo and Polly. He scanned the map, desperately looking for recognisable names. He knew the village was somewhere on the South Downs. He remembered they used to walk to the pub for long lunches. What was it called? The Royal Oak! That was it! He scanned the page, his finger moving slowly over the map. He knew that once he found the pub, he would be able to retrace the walk back to the cottage. Now, what was the village called? His finger hovered, uncertain. He trawled his memory… and then, there it was; he had it!

Masquerade

Chester drove down a country lane into Moreton Bolas just as dawn was breaking on the eastern skyline. But he didn't recognise the road, was he mistaken? He drove slowly down the narrow high street, searching for a pub. "Why in God's name don't they have street lights in the sticks?" In the half-light, there was no sign of a pub. He decided to try again before moving on to another village. He turned around and retraced his steps. There! A narrow gravel lane on the left, a faded hand-painted sign 'Old Smithy Brewery'. The car crunched its way along the track, hemmed in by banks of dark red rhododendrons. After fifty yards, Chester turned a corner to find a row of ancient black-and-white timber-framed houses. The ground floor was made up of shops. And there, opposite the shops, was a sturdy wooden post with a sign for the Royal Oak. Further around the bend, he could see the pub – a timber-framed redbrick building with a thatched roof that looked reassuringly familiar. Chester parked the car at the back of the pub and relaxed for the first time in six hours.

He decided to leave the car and walk to Leo's; he was on familiar ground. Once he had settled in, he would collect the car. Chester collected his bags and walked to an overgrown hedge of yew trees at the back of the car park. Hidden in its midst was a rickety lichen covered gate. Chester pushed through and walked along a short avenue of yews into the graveyard. Following the boundary path, he passed through another decrepit wooden gate which led to Leo's cottage a quarter of a mile away. To a casual observer, the overgrown path was all but invisible. It took a good ten minutes for Chester to reach the cottage.

Just as Chester stumbled, exhausted, into Leo's garden, two MI5 agents drove quietly into the village. The passenger studied a map of the area on his laptop. They parked in a lane, guessing their mark was close. Being in the middle of nowhere, the laptop was suffering from intermittent signal loss, meaning they couldn't pinpoint their exact location. They weren't worried; they knew the journalist was here and running scared.

Chester found the key behind the paint pots as promised. In the hush of the morning half-light, he let himself in. Once inside, his first thought was to hide his disks and notebooks. He checked a couple of rooms downstairs, nothing suitable. There were dirty cups on the kitchen table; "strange," he thought. He wandered back out to the tool shed. Looking around, he found an ideal spot high up in the thatch hidden by a beam. He stretched and pushed the items far back into a knothole. Satisfied, he walked back to the cottage. Gradually the dawn chorus began. The garden was large, full of trees, rhododendron bushes, and secret pathways lined with clipped yew hedgerows. Leo obviously spent a lot of time maintaining it. As he walked past the garage, Chester noticed Leo's old pickup was missing. He wondered where it had gone, "Leo loved that old bus; he would never have got rid of it. Chester's wits were dulled by exhaustion, but something nagged at him. Going into the kitchen, he decided to contact his main sources and tell them he had gone to ground. He brewed a mug of strong black coffee and sat at the kitchen table with the new mobile and his address book. "It's unlike Leo to leave these dishes lying around; he's normally obsessively tidy." First, he needed to alert Marlowe... a text on the hackers' message board, "Police closed down the magazine. Am in hiding. Story censored and seized. Be in touch asap, Chester."

As the message was dispatched, the clatter of a diesel engine announced a visitor. "Who on earth could that be? It can't be Penny?" Chester hurried into the kitchen, only to find a man, dressed in rags, and covered in blood. The tramp spun round when he heard Chester, grabbed a large carving knife and lunged forward as Chester appeared.

"Wait!!" Chester yelled.

The tramp stammered, "Back, I kill you!"

Chester backtracked rapidly, "OK. Just take what you need and go; I won't interfere."

The tramp slowly lowered the knife, "Food and water."

Chester motioned toward the cupboards, "Help yourself. What's wrong with your arm?"

The tramp backed up to the fridge, trying to stem blood seeping from his forearm, "A fight. My friends and me were escaping from gangmasters. We were betrayed and got into big fight. My friends die. But I got away."

"Look, put the knife down; I'm no danger to you. Take as much food as you want... it's OK."

The tramp warily sized up Chester, then, deciding he was harmless, put the knife on the countertop and opened the fridge.

Chester asked, "What's your name? What happened?"

"Rafa. I come from Bulgaria. A man in Germany tells me and my friends he can get us work in UK. Easy money, he said... use your skills."

Chester shook his head – another example of corporatists getting cheap labour. "This happens a lot; organised criminals take advantage of people desperate to find work and keep them in servitude... working on farms and stuff... you're lucky to escape."

Rafa retorted, "Lucky, really? Four of my friends are dead, killed by gangmaster bastards. They say they can't let us live because if we escape, we are a big danger to them. So they shoot us. Bastards." Rafa banged the counter. "But not farms... was hotels. We are soldiers; they pay us to fight for them. Not now, I will avenge my friends: I kill these guys."

Chester leaned forward, his journalist nose for a story screamed there was something big here, "Whose army?"

"Big boss-man. I hear his name when I steal cigarettes. Polish guy... I think. They talk about operation... another Boss... *Bil*... maybe. Then some other guy, *Strick* something. I don't remember."

Chester sucked in air, "Christ Almighty! It's them, must be; Marlowe's targets. Did they say what the hell they were up to?"

"Not so much. But we all soldiers. So we must fight, yes? In UK, we must fight someone."

Meanwhile, the two MI5 Agents had now checked the roads leading into and out of the village. The sleepy community had shown little inclination to rouse itself. A solitary tractor trundled down the main street, but otherwise, the place was silent. After they called in their report to Control, Gittins came on the radio, "What the hell's going on?"

"We've found the journalist's car in a pub car park near the edge of the village... so he can't be far away; he must be in one of the houses near the pub."

Positive news – that would get Stryckland off his back. "Right, you two stay where you are. I'll get extra men down to you. I want the bugger back in Paddington sharpish! You two take charge, and no mistakes: it's vital this guy is in custody tonight."

Thirty minutes later, two black helicopters disgorged a snatch squad into a field close to the waiting MI5 agents. Twenty men squatted down under cover of the hedgerow, waiting for orders. Then a dark blue armoured minibus pulled up. A uniformed Sergeant leaned out, "I've been told to report to you to do a house to house. What's the crack?" Thirty minutes

Masquerade

later, twenty constables were rousing the village. They used their usual tactic; they were looking for a runaway teenager. Had anyone seen anything unusual? Any strange men wandering around? It took them two hours to work their way around the village. At ten-thirty, a sergeant and five footsore constables wearily made their way up a gravel track to a black and white timber-framed cottage.

"Have you checked the map? This has to be the last section. Let's hope the blighter's in here. I'm getting pissed off wandering around this dump without the prospect of smacking someone. Let's hope we get lucky in here. You two, you know the drill, let's go."

Two Constables peeled off and walked around to the back of the cottage whilst the other three went to the front. A knock at the front door produced no response. Ignoring the careful cultivation, they trampled over manicured borders peering through windows. After five minutes of searching, they were just about to leave when a PC, checking the back garden, noticed the door to the garage had been left open – the lock dangling from its clasp, "Hey, Sarge!"

Cautiously they pushed open the door. A rusty red pickup ticked and clicked as its engine cooled. The sergeant needlessly felt the bonnet, "Still warm. There must be someone around. Look in the back." The youngest constable, eager to please, walked to the back of the pickup and lifted a canvas cover, then recoiled in horror. "Christ Almighty! Sarge, look!" The bed of the truck was covered in blood-soaked straw. There was a sodden pile of clothes and four very dead bodies.

Meanwhile, in the kitchen, Rafa warily looked out of the window, "I must go. The Police can't find me" He peered through the half-open door and hissed, "Bastard! You call police?"

Chester looked stunned, "Oh God! No! No! They're after me, not you. Listen, I know you won't understand this, but it's important! Call this number. Ask for Marlowe; speak to no one else. Tell him everything you told me. Tell him to check the murder victim's autopsy in London. Don't get caught, for Christ's sake, they'll kill you."

Chester stuffed a wad of cash into Rafa's hand. "Find somewhere safe in London. Now run!"

Rafa hesitated for a moment, then hearing the sound of approaching voices, dashed out of the back door into the cover of a nearby hedge.

Masquerade

Chester waited a moment, then calmly walked outside, hands held high.

Half a dozen anti-terrorist agents confronted him. One screamed, "Show me your hands! Down! Now! Get Down!"

The two MI5 agents stood triumphantly in the cottage kitchen.

One called to control, "Put me through to Gittins; it's urgent." A short pause. "We've got him, Sir. He was in a cottage just outside the village. He seems to have been busy, four bodies... ...Yes, Sir, the snatch squad have secured him... ...so, they need to take him to Paddington Nick, for processing. I understand... ...Yes, Sir, we'll get Home Office Forensics to search the premises."

From the cover of a large clump of bushes at the back of Leo's garden, Rafa watched the Anti-Terrorist Police bundle Chester into a black van, where he was locked in a cage. The rest of the squad stood around waiting for instructions. Rafa checked the coast was clear, then slipped away through the undergrowth – destination London.

Chapter 30: Nascent Rebel

It was late evening when Susie drove up the steep gravel road cut into the heavily wooded hillside skirting Lago Lugano. Lights over the heavy wooden gates guarding the entrance greeted her. She stopped the Porsche and got out to ring the intercom. Maria, the housekeeper, answered. "Susie! At last! We were getting worried. Come in, come in."

The heavy gates swung open slowly. Maria's husband, Hans, stood on the porch, waiting to carry her bags.

"Hi, Hans. Sorry I'm late, but I had to take a detour. It added so much time. If it's all the same, I'm so tired I'll go straight to bed."

Susie woke late the next morning after a fitful night's sleep, troubled by visions of Bilic and Sheikhs. Maria served her breakfast on the terrace overlooking the lake with a view of the Italian shore. Susie wore shirtsleeves in the warm Ticinese morning. A sharp contrast to frigid Paris. She had forgotten how beautiful the view was – the snow-capped Alps in the distance, the deep blue waters of Largo Lugano below, the verdant green hillside of the lakeshore. It was so beautiful; why had she stayed away for so long? Deep down, she knew: the place was full of memories of her father.

After she had eaten, Hans took Susie to her father's study. "Maria cleans every week, but we don't move anything. It is as it was the day he left us. I'll leave you to look around."

Susie was grateful for Hans' tact; she wanted to study her father's papers in private. As Susie walked around the room, half-forgotten memories of her father slowly came back. She was gripped by a sudden melancholy. What would her life have been like if he were still here? She would have been happy, fulfilled. She sat in his favourite chair and looked around. She gazed at his collection of watercolours, the shelves stacked with his beloved detective novels. This room was the essence of her father. A cultured, principled man who had been murdered by ruthless businessmen.

On one wall, a series of posters for 1960's Grand Prix surrounded an original Le Mans '60s racing scene by Michael Turner. She suddenly remembered his car collection. They must still be in the garage neglected, gathering dust. Why was it only now, five years after his death, that she realised how big a void he had left? Were the constant parties and spending sprees an excuse to block out reality and numb the void he left behind? Now she was forced to confront her grief at her father's murder.

Eventually, her attention was drawn to a large Louis XV Style walnut cabinet. Her mother had described it the previous evening. It held her father's confidential papers and diaries. She had to read them; she knew intuitively that her new direction in life would be revealed in these journals. She turned a small brass key and opened the door. Below five shelves, there were drawers to the left and right, separated by a plain wooden panel. Susie examined it carefully. It seemed solid; there wasn't a sign it could be moved at all. Her mother had told her to push firmly on both edges. There would be a click, then the panel would slide down to reveal a large cavity; it would contain her father's journals and keepsakes. The journals would reveal her father's real work, his opinions and principles.

She settled down with half a dozen volumes in an easy chair and began to read. What she found was astonishing. She knew her father was a senior civil servant in the French Diplomatic Service, based mostly in London, with intermittent postings to Lisbon, Rome, Istanbul and Stockholm. But his journals read like a spy film. He had played a part in the country's more clandestine foreign and domestic activities.

The entries in the 1986 journal were the most interesting. In the course of his work in London, her father had become suspicious of payments made by the French Government to several prominent businessmen who owned large companies operating in Europe. His attention had been drawn to a group of senior civil servants and long-serving ministers. With the assistance of a trusted source, he was able to prove that they were receiving substantial sums of money from a secretive company based in Switzerland. To what end, he was unable to discover. He was able to find many cases of low-level corruption by government officials all over Europe, but he was convinced there was a mastermind behind all of the corruption he had discovered. The question was: who?

On the last page of the journal, he had written two names. They made her hair stand on end. One of them was the French Prime Minister, the other the Duc de Toulouse – the most powerful landowner in France

Susie wondered if the suspects knew they were being watched.

His later entries were less organised, more hurried somehow – as if he hadn't had time to organise his thoughts coherently.

Masquerade

Susie now knew she had found her new vocation. Her father's journals inspired and intrigued her. She knew that corruption within the Establishment was still happening: Bilic was proof of that. She must uncover it.

Her father must have had help. Surely the journals would tell her someone her father trusted. Impatiently she picked up another journal and started skimming through pages.

In the third journal, she found what she was looking for. Her father described a reception for the President of Chile held at the British Embassy in Vienna. He seemed to dwell rather more on the description of a Senior Attaché to the Austrian Ambassador than he did on other guests. His name was Heinz Gombricht. In later journals, he was referred to as HG or H.

Susie needed to find 'H' and talk to him.

But how? Her mother would know; she knew all of her father's friends. A forty-minute phone call later, she had the background for Heinz Gombricht. He had been her father's opposite number in the Austrian Embassy. They often met at conventions and conferences around Europe. They had collaborated on several projects concerning European Energy Infrastructure. Her mother remembered they had become concerned that funds were being siphoned off. Suspicion lay with the European Procurement Office.

Heinz's wife died in a car accident five years ago. Her mother seemed to think it was just before he was due to retire. Her father was away from home a lot at that time. Her mother was sure he and Heinz were working together. But her father had never divulged what the secret might be. Six months after Heinz's wife died, her father was murdered. Heinz retired soon afterwards. He immersed himself in charity work based in Geneva.

Susie's mother began to reminisce during the call. She told Susie her father was a leading figure in the student riots in 60's and 70's Paris. From an aristocratic family, he turned his back on the family business to campaign against large petroleum companies; he was one of the first eco-warriors.

His group of activists formed an underground network to fight for several causes prevalent in the day: environmental protection, endangered species, and multinational corporate corruption linked to government corruption, amongst others. Her father seemed to have formed a close friendship with an Englishman who held a senior position in the UK's civil service. (His codename was 'Merlin' – Dark's father). Together they gathered evidence of corruption in the British government and civil service and a shadowy European organisation. Merlin had been caught stealing confidential data by the British secret service and had been murdered, the victim of a street gang beating. Her father had given up trying to expose the government corruption at that point and changed his attention to environmental issues.

Susie called her mother again. She hesitated at first, then blurted out, "Mama, was Dad murdered too?"

Klara wept, "I'm sure he was. I'm sure the Corporatists knew he was working with Julian and Heinz. They knew if the truth got out, people wouldn't stand for it; the public would rise up against them. The only way the Corporatists could prevent that was to silence the whistle-blowers."

Susie closed the call. Why hadn't she asked these questions before? So much wasted time. Well, she was damn well going to do something about it now.

Drawn towards her father's desk, she picked up a small battered leather address book. It was filled with his neat handwriting from cover to cover. On the first page was an entry for Heinz with the address and phone number in her mother's handwriting. She picked up the phone and dialled the number. After many rings and just as she was about to hang up, a male voice at the other end answered. "Oui, St. Jean Hostel for Lost Souls."

Susie, "Hello. I am looking for Heinz Gombricht. Do I have the right number?" A long silence followed, then, the voice replied.

"Who is this?"

"My name is Susie Esterhazy. I think you may have known my father?"

She was about to tell him about the address book when he cut in sharply,

"Your number, please? I'll call you."

Nonplussed, Susie gave him her mobile number and replaced the handset. She waited.

The next morning, Susie woke early and left for Geneva. After driving for an hour, Susie's Porsche pulled into a layby. Grey clouds filled a leaden sky; a storm was brewing. A signpost indicated two ways to Geneva, the old circuitous route for cars and general traffic, plus the more direct autoroute.

Susie plumped for the right-hand turn. The autoroute would take her around the top of Lac Leman. She glanced at Heinz's address scribbled on a pocketbook on the passenger seat.

A few miles back, a Mercedes slowly coasted to a stop; it was approaching a junction. Which way did the Porsche go? The guy doing the navigating was panicking. He knew the consequences of failing Bilic. The driver tried to reassure him, "We've got the tracker, you idiot. We can't lose her. We can pick her up anywhere within a hundred kilometres. The worst case is that it takes some time to get to her. There's no point in panicking."

But the hoodlum wasn't convinced, "Christ no! I knew we should have stayed closer. Bilic will kill us if we lose her. What the hell are we going to do? Which way did she go? It's too mountainous to get a signal; it could be hours before the tracker can pick her up again... and she's in a Porsche, for Christ's sake, she could be halfway to Spain by then. God! If we find her, we take her! No more mucking about."

Bastien, the co-driver, turned to his companions, "Just grow a pair! Think! Where can she go from here? She's probably driving through a valley, and the mountains are blocking the signal... let's take the old road and wait for the tracker to work again!"

Lucien, the driver, impatiently floored the accelerator and drifted the Mercedes around the left-hand turn and the old road.

Anxiously, Susie checked the rear-view mirror; had she really lost Bilic's henchmen? She knew he would not let things lie. Huge raindrops splattered against the windscreen; the warm droplets reinvigorated her. Her life was taking a new direction with all the uncertainty that brought, but what most appealed was the chance to carry on her father's work. She was desperate to consign her consumer lifestyle to history. She wanted to be judged as a force for good and not as a parasitic butterfly. With her mind made up, Susie closed the car's hood and pulled onto the autoroute towards Simplon.

The Porsche cruised down the autoroute winding its way between towering Swiss peaks. She was eager to meet Heinz. The windscreen wipers thumped hypnotically as Susie pictured her father and Heinz: two young guns fighting against amoral corporations. Still, she kept a wary eye on her mirrors. Still no Mercedes. "That gorilla will be needing a long stay in hospital," she mused. It was barely conceivable she had taken on two thugs in as many days and won.

Masquerade

Meanwhile, the occupants in the Mercedes were feeling slightly more relaxed. A flashing red dot on their tracker showed their target was making progress along the north side of Lac Leman, albeit they were on the opposite side of the lake. At least they now knew where she was. There was no rush. Everything was under control; their only instruction was not to damage the goods or draw attention to themselves. Otherwise, they were free to take her at a convenient time then transport her to the remote farmhouse in the hills above Menton that Bilic used as a safe house. Bilic's client, the Sheikh, wasn't expecting his consignment for a few days yet.

On long the straights, Susie accelerated effortlessly past slower traffic; she was making good time. The Mercedes, on narrower roads, fell even further behind.

Susie stopped for petrol at Villeneuve. A cool wind coming off the lake chilled her and made sure she wasted no time getting back into her car, heading for Lausanne. She should reach Geneva in time for dinner.

As she got closer to Geneva, Susie began to feel nervous. But she was determined to start life afresh, and her instinct told her this was the right thing to do. At least she would be safe from Bilic once she was with Heinz.

Heinz would be able to tell her more about her father's work. She was intrigued by Heinz's decision to run a hostel. It seemed a strange choice after his activism. Perhaps he just needed some normality. She could always stay at the hostel even though Heinz wasn't involved in the struggle anymore. It would give her time to plan and consider her next move. The change would be good for her. But she hoped there would be some way she could be useful to Heinz.

Chapter 31: Dark Dilemma

Back on the Rhine, Gunther burst into Dark's cabin, "Quickly! Come with me! We have very little time."

Gunther shoved him down a narrow passageway towards the stern, "Hurry." At the far end, a door led to the engine room. He pushed Dark inside. The noise from the diesel engine was deafening. Gunther beckoned Dark to one side of the cramped chamber, then he squeezed between some machinery and dirty grey panel and reached down to lift a heavy wooden board about two feet square. Cupping his hand over Dark's ear, he shouted, "Let yourself into the hole feet first. There is plenty of space in there. It's used to access the underside of the generator. No one knows about it. You'll be safe there for a few hours. The air supply is good, but there is very little light. It's dry, so you'll be fine. Go! Go! Quickly we've got visitors."

Dark hesitated momentarily, then lowered his legs into the gap and squeezed through the narrow opening and lay shivering in the gloom as Gunther replaced the floor panel. He was trapped, not something he allowed to happen very often.

Dark lay quietly, letting his eyes adjust. He noticed small slits of light at the far end of the hold, which was by no means empty. He crawled around blindly; as he moved toward the light, he came upon cigarette cartons, a crate of brandy, and finally, a box filled with plastic packages. He picked one up and sniffed: marijuana.

Dark, "Hmm... a bit of extracurricular cargo."

He continued to rummage, and his hand brushed against a small, heavy, wooden box. Dark took it over to the only source of light and opened it. It was full of coins, mostly gold. He poked around; one coin felt markedly different. He picked it up, held it to the light, then he froze as he recognised the crest: the Tanburg Eagle – just like the ring on the murder victim in London.

"God! Was Gunther working for them?"

Dark examined the cracks of light more closely; they appeared to form the outline of an opening. As he looked for a handle, a loud blast from a ship's horn announced the arrival of their visitors. There was a dull thump as the boats were tied together, then footsteps above, again Dark froze.

Carefully he slid the panel back, revealing Gunther's cabin. Gingerly, he climbed out and tiptoed to the door, then cracked it open to listen - nothing. Quietly, he slipped through and inched along the passageway. Hearing faint voices, he followed the sound toward the galley. Two men sat at a table, a pair of Uzi machine guns were propped casually against a cupboard. Dark shuffled closer for a better look. One of the men was heavily built, about fifty. The other was younger, wiry, hard, with a thin scar running along his jawline. Gunther climbed down the steps from the wheelhouse, wiping his hands with a rag.

The giant lit a cigarette, "Is Rainer steering?"

Gunther nodded. As he looked up at the giant, he caught a glimpse of Dark lurking in the shadows; quickly, he turned to pour himself a coffee to hide his shock.

The giant snarled at his back, "Come here, we need to talk."

Gunther, "Yes, Mr. Sobieski."

Sobieski, "We have a situation. We need you to carry a shipment next week. Fifty men… you pick them up in Constantia and deliver them to the usual drops."

"I told you I was finished with that cargo… it's not right what you're doing."

Scarface grabbed Gunther by the throat, "You'll finish when we say so, old man."

Sobieski stubbed out his cigarette, "This is an emergency. We've just lost a boat with all hands off the English coast; they must be replaced. You know the routine, so it has to be you, no arguments. Last time for sure. Understand?"

Scarface glowered at Gunther, "Don't mess with us! We know where your family lives."

Sobieski lit another cigarette, "Like, I said, the shipment is fifty men. You will load up at Constantia, on the Danube, and deliver to the usual drop off points in Holland. You know the drill."

The two men got up to leave.

Sobieski turned and peered down the corridor where Dark was hiding, "Carrying anything interesting? That last crate of whisky wasn't bad."

He took a step forward, but Gunther blocked his way, "Just machine parts."

Sobieski, "Mmm... maybe next time."

Gunther, "I told you: there won't be a next time."

Scarface grabbed Gunther's arm, "You'll finish when we say so."

Dark tensed as he watched the thug manhandling Gunther. Scarface heard a faint noise, turned and peered down the corridor. Swiftly, Dark shuffled back into Gunther's room. Scarface drew a 9mm from his waistband and rushed along the corridor. Reaching Gunther's cabin door, he flung it wide open and took aim. The room was in darkness. He flicked the light switch... nothing. Just a neat, orderly cabin.

Scarface turned and marched back into the galley and shook his head in Sobieski's direction.

Sobieski shoved Gunther against a wall, "Don't forget! Constantia." Then he turned on his heel and left with Scarface.

"Marlowe? Marlowe? Where are you?" Dark stepped out of Gunther's cabin.

Gunther bunched his fists and snarled at Dark, "What the hell do you think you were doing?"

Furious, Dark stepped into Gunther's face, "Me? What the hell are you up to? You're working for these people, you bastard!"

Gunther stepped back, "Not out of choice. They find you, they suck you in and force you to do their dirty work."

Dark leaned on a bench, "Are they Mafia?"

Glumly Gunther shook his head, "No, much worse. They're Kalyptra. They are dark ops criminals. They control politicians, officials, police... anyone with power. You're caught in a trap; they'll kill you and your family if you don't cooperate. I've seen it done. I love my wife and kids, so I have no choice."

"How long have you been mixed up in this crap?"

"Me? Ten years... others I know have been doing it for thirty."

Gunther sat opposite Dark and lit a cigarette, "I followed my father. We smuggled stuff behind the Iron Curtain. You'd be surprised how much contraband passed down the Danube in the old days. The Soviets needed dollars and their little luxuries. There was always someone ready to oblige them for a price. We still move the odd cargo for their successors, but they weren't as ruthless as Kalyptra."

Dark asked the obvious question, "Did they ask about me?"

Gunther regarded Dark speculatively, "Perhaps... Scarface asked if I had seen anyone unusual on the river. There is a European wide search for a British national. Why? What have you done?"

Dark grimaced, "Wrong place, wrong time... especially for Kalyptra. I saw something I wasn't supposed to." Dark took the Tanburg coin from his pocket, "Like you, I operate outside the system. The authorities don't like that. This was in the hold; what do you know about it?"

Gunther threw the butt of his cigarette out of the porthole, "It's a Tanburg Eagle. Kalyptra's icon... so they know who belongs."

"I heard the big guy talking about picking up people in Constantia... so, what's it all about?"

"That was Sobieski, one of the top guys. Looks like they lost the last load of illegals in the English Channel. He wants more men in the UK."

Dark was appalled, "So they're people trafficking?"

"Yeah, but this isn't the usual cheap labour. The last dozen trips have all been moving hard fighters. They're planning something big, and whatever it is, it will start in Britain. Mark my words."

Chapter 32: Alta Heist

As Dark was confronting Gunther, Marat was being briefed by each of his directors on their latest financial returns.

As the meeting came to a close, a pair of footmen resplendent in royal blue frock coats, powdered wigs and white breeches stood to attention on either side of the salon's huge mahogany double doors. Stryckland brought up the rear as members made their way out to their helicopters. He gazed at the floor deep in thought and at first did not notice a footman approach.

Expressionless black eyes fixed on Stryckland. The footman leaned close and whispered, "Le Patron wants to see you; follow me."

Obediently, Stryckland fell in as the footman led the way through a concealed doorway. Marat's sense of theatre was mildly comical. He was obsessed with cultivating a despotic image. Part of which was designed to promote an air of omnipotence. However, Stryckland considered it was an absurd affectation, the footmen being a case in point. Their outdated costumes were so cumbersome it was impossible to carry out their bodyguard duties. Marat's threats when dealing with members of the council, whilst graphically real, were dramatically contrived to instil terror.

Stryckland grimaced, "Vanity makes fools of us. Without doubt, when I succeed Marat, I'll do away with this pretentious nonsense". The footman led him along a winding subterranean passage; their footsteps echoed off the rough limestone walls. Hearing footsteps behind, he half-turned and saw another footman with Bilic in tow. The reason for the appointment was now clear, the succession. Stryckland wondered how Marat was going to handle it; he hoped this was just a preliminary discussion.

A little way down the passage, Bilic decided to unsettle his rival and walked shoulder to shoulder with Stryckland. He gave him a predatory smirk, which Stryckland acknowledged with a curt nod, then fixed his gaze on the footman's back. They walked on in silence. At an alcove, the footman turned and led them up a steep stone stairway. A draught of cool air blew down an ascending passageway. After an interminable climb, they reached the top and faced a stout iron-banded teak door. The footman tugged a massive iron handle and heaved, the hinges grated as the door swung slowly open. Hot sunlight flooded into the tunnel, dazzling them as it reflected off the white walls. Taking the opportunity, Bilic moved swiftly toward the unmistakable bird-like figure pecking at his lunch in the shade of a huge umbrella. The late afternoon sun burned Stryckland's neck. He felt the heat seeping into his dark business suit. He began to perspire and not only from the heat.

As they neared the table, Bilic placed himself directly in front of Marat, staking his claim. Stryckland remained at a little distance and waited, hands clasped behind his back. Bilic began gabbling, desperate to be heard first. Stryckland happily let Bilic blunder on. Pointedly Marat concentrated on peeling a clementine. Eventually, he pointed his dessert knife in the direction of some chairs arranged around the table. Bilic stopped midsentence, looked flummoxed, then sat quietly. Stryckland took a seat apart from Bilic, crossed his legs and relaxed, calmly waiting for Marat to begin.

Eventually, Marat sat back and studied them. He folded his hands on his lap, "There is an important matter to discuss. For some time, I have been considering retirement, and I want to start discussions with you today with a view to finalising this matter within the next few months."

Bilic and Stryckland both looked surprised at the candour but knew better than to say anything.

Marat suppressed a smile; he was well aware that they knew that he planned to retire but decided to keep them in suspense for a while. Better start with the matter of seizing control of the British government.

Marat kneaded a hand, "Give me an update on our plans to remove that idiot Prime Minister. How much progress have you made?"

Stryckland, "The project is on schedule. We are making excellent progress. During the last six months, we have co-opted the command structure of each branch of the British Armed Forces, and we have a firm commitment to support us in return for complete autonomy to manage their organisations as they see fit. Furthermore, they know the rank and file are so angry with the political class that they will follow strong leadership and carry out orders to enforce martial law when we implement it. They swear allegiance to the Queen anyway, not political pygmies."

Marat picked at his lunch, "Who are these people? Do we have guarantees we can control them?"

"They are impatient to regain control of their troops and exasperated by spineless politicians constantly reducing the size of the armed forces. For the army, we have the Chief of the General Staff, the Assistant Chief of the

Masquerade

General Staff, the Quartermaster-General, the Master-General of the Ordinance and the Commander Land Forces. That gives us complete control of land forces.

The Navy recruits are: First Sea Lord & Chief of the Naval Staff - Admiral Sir Horatio Urquhart, Fleet Commander - Admiral Sir Jasper Harvey, Second Sea Lord - Vice-Admiral Toby Ponsonby, and the Controller of the Navy - Rear Admiral Louis Botham.

We also have the head of the RAF, Air Chief Marshall Sir Frederick Jakes, and Air Commodores David Parry and Luther Scanlon.

The pretext for the coup will be an unprecedented level of terrorist attacks. The Prime Minister will be killed, and strategic installations around the country targeted. The Deputy Prime Minister will appear to be a dithering idiot, overwhelmed by events and lacking the necessary competence to regain control. I will step in as a safe pair of hands to restore order from the chaos engulfing the country. The combined heads of the Armed Forces will pledge their support for the interim government in the fight against the insurgents. Due to the widespread nature of the threat and the inability of the Intelligence Agencies to apprehend the perpetrators, I will declare martial law.

My only concern is the senior Civil Service... the bureaucrats. These people have built their own empires, which they guard jealously from any political interference. As you are aware, these are the people who really govern the country. Politicians are useful idiots who milk the system then disappear. The bureaucrats will be extremely reluctant to relinquish control when martial law begins. Their pernicious tentacles spread into every facet of government. They have the most to lose in terms of power and influence."

Marat drummed his fingers on the table, "They may be persuaded by an argument which gave them more power and influence. Why don't you promise them a share of the rewards certain to come their way if they assist our members? Of course, we needn't make good on that promise."

Stryckland frowned, "We have tried many times in the past to break their hegemony, but they are stubborn. Perhaps the inducement of more power will finally persuade them."

Marat, "Well, if they won't co-operate, what about the regional civil servants – the ones that manage public services? Are they open to bribery or coercion?"

Masquerade

Stryckland mused, "Strangely, we don't think these people will cause too much trouble. They just follow orders from their masters in Whitehall. After all, they obey every edict issued without question, however ridiculous. Why would their mindset change?"

Marat, "Controlling the population's mood and temperament using the media will be fundamental to the success of the coup. This is undoubtedly the most important element along with the armed forces. If we cannot convince people of the necessity for martial law, then our plan will fail before it starts."

Stryckland, "Of course, Patron, you are quite correct. With that objective in mind, we have infiltrated the state broadcaster, for some time, in fact. We have hundreds of sleeper agents planted throughout the organisation, waiting for our signal. They are spread through all levels of the organisation: from senior managers to journalists and studio floor managers to technicians, all ready and waiting to broadcast our agenda and message. After all, they have been promoting the wider message for other members for twenty years. This is a tried and operationally proven group of people. We will have nothing to worry about with them."

Marat "Well, the support mechanisms seem to be in order just as long as we can control the Whitehall civil servants and the judiciary, they are our main threat. What event are you going to use as the trigger for the introduction of martial law?"

Stryckland looked smug. "That's relatively straightforward. The agents and mercenaries Bilic has imported will initiate simultaneous attacks in London, Birmingham, Manchester and Newcastle. Substantial bombs strategically placed will cause mass hysteria. Such concerted, widespread and violent attacks on British cities will make martial law a logical response. The public will welcome mass troop deployment to patrol the streets while MI5 and MI6 track down the perpetrators. We can manipulate this situation for as long as we need until we control all elements of government needed to run the country. As I mentioned, after the assassination of the Prime Minister, I will seize control from the Deputy PM. A few timely reports from the BBC and broadsheets reassuring the population they are safe under martial law will calm the situation. I will be credited with the authority and vision to bring the country through a difficult time into a more stable and prosperous future. After all, we're all in it together."

Marat, "How do you plan to terminate the Prime Minister?"

Masquerade

Stryckland smiled, "An unfortunate accident – the one terrorist attack that got through. Most unfortunate!"

Marat sipped his coffee thoughtfully, "And the police? We have most of them on board anyway, but are you sure they will follow it through to the end?"

"We have the whole Metropolitan police command structure, as you are aware. Additionally, we have more than fifty per cent of the chief constables in the regional command structure. These people operate a closed shop; the only reason we have not approached the other chief constables is that we just haven't had time. These people wholeheartedly believe in rigorous surveillance and authoritarian control of the public. Their mindset is completely aligned with ours. They are determined to retain their current powers and, if at all possible, extend them. Not only will they welcome martial law, I think they will do their utmost to persuade us to retain it permanently."

Marat nodded; he knew the British police were well known for their authoritarian conduct. Kalyptra would have a fervent collaborator in the police.

"Have you a date in mind to initiate the coup?"

Stryckland, "We are considering two possibilities. The first is the early August Bank Holiday. Bank Holidays are three day weekends; the Sunday and Monday would see large crowds gathered in our target areas. During these holidays, the emergency services are habitually busy – close to breaking point. Widespread panic would compound the situation, stretching the emergency services enough so they lose control. Thus creating the necessary circumstances for a national emergency. In fact, the public will demand it. This date has the added benefit that the PM will have been out of the country on a State Visit to Brussels and so will be flying back into a storm. Also, we know his whereabouts for the assassination plan. The second possibility is another Bank Holiday and long weekend at the end of August when the conditions would be replicated, weather permitting. We are targeting the first weekend with the possibility we could fall back to the second holiday if we encounter problems with the initial target date."

Masquerade

Marat sat back and pushed away his empty plate. He looked at Stryckland with respect. "Very good, Giles: an exceptional plan. You seem to have covered all possibilities. I see no difficulties with your plan, do you?"

For the first time during their conversation, Stryckland felt apprehensive. "With the plan Patron, no. However, there is a possibility we have a security breach. We think a copy of the plan is missing. One of our junior aides was about to betray us, so we were forced to terminate him. He may have had a copy of the plan on him, but we cannot find it. It may have been taken from his body by someone who witnessed the termination. We are urgently searching for this person; we believe it to be a thief who has been stealing our corporation's data.

Marat's expression froze. His voice, when he managed to control himself, was ice cold, "Are you serious? Which incompetent fool has been so inept as to allow details of our activities and plans to be stolen? Why in God's name are you not tearing the UK apart looking for the plans? Are you able to sit there and tell me you are exerting every muscle and sinew to catch this person?"

Stryckland struggled to retain his composure; he waited for a pause in the tirade, "Patron, the situation is under control. I have Scotland Yard's most able thief-taker hunting the suspect. We have complete use of the intelligence services hunting this person down. Our anti-terrorist squad are managing the British police, and our own agents around the world are also hunting this person. We only just missed him at his hideout in London, and we are sure he is in Europe at the moment. It is only a matter of time before we catch him."

Marat jumped to his feet, knocking his chair over and threw his napkin at Stryckland, "You'd better be right Giles, your life depends upon it." Then looking at Bilic, "So does yours." Marat paced up and down along the terrace. Stryckland and Bilic remained seated and kept very, very still – both understood a wrong word at this point would be fatal. Eventually, Stryckland noticed Marat's shoulders drop, a sure sign the red mist was dissipating. Slowly Marat walked back to them, looking at the ground, hands behind his back. "Giles, I'm placing a great deal of trust in you to resolve this matter. Your future is in your hands."

And then, as if nothing more serious than a conversation about the weather had taken place, Marat continued, "And now, let us discuss the question of my successor. As you know, I have decided to retire in the next three to six months. It is my prerogative to appoint someone to take my place –a new CEO. Following the rules of the organisation, there can be no discussion or argument about the outcome.

"I consider you two to be the ablest people on the council, although your latest newscasts some doubt on that!" He glared at Stryckland before continuing. "The choice is extremely difficult. Who should succeed without causing our organisation to become fractured by internal rivalry, especially from the individual who fails?"

Marat noticed how Stryckland was able to maintain an air of unflappability when Bilic looked decidedly anxious. Frankly, he was surprised. He had thought Bilic's strength of character would have made him immune to nerves. Perhaps Stryckland would be the better choice after all.

"Therefore, I must be sure that having made my choice, the person who was unsuccessful swears an oath to the council to accept my decision and support the new leader. Would you both be willing to make that commitment? Before you answer, let me say that I'm still undecided."

Silence. A warm breeze fluttered the chequered tablecloth and flapped at the umbrella's canopy while the two protagonists digested Marat's comments. Stryckland was aware that Marat was studying their reaction. He was determined to remain calm and collected. He was well aware of the importance Marat placed upon the smooth running of the Society and the slightest indication that someone might upset that would ensure instant dismissal, if not elimination.

Masquerade

Chapter 33: Rendition

Interrogation Room 14 was identical to the other nineteen in Marsden Green Correctional Facility: a simple box room fifteen feet square, bare walls, ceiling and floor painted an antiseptic white. Two chairs sat in the middle of the room. One was high backed, substantial, constructed of wood and fixed to the floor with steel bolts. The chair's occupants were restrained by stout leather straps, which were stained almost black with blood and sweat. An acrid tang of disinfectant could not conceal the ingrained reek of urine or the fear which permeated the atmosphere. Gittins, however, found it reassuring; he knew it would terrify the chair's unfortunate occupant. He stood watching as Chester lay semi-conscious on the floor. Gittins prodded him sharply with his foot. Chester's eyes fluttered, then clamped shut against the dazzling glare of spotlights.

Gittins gestured to two guards to lift Chester's limp body off the floor and strap it into the interrogation seat. The men were stripped down to t-shirts and wore combat trousers and boots, ready to begin the inquisition. Sweat droplets dribbled down their muscular arms; the room was stiflingly hot. Later, when the first phase of the interrogation was complete, Chester would be left in the chair while the room temperature was set to freezing. Every aspect of the room's design was intended to disorientate a prisoner, to break their resistance.

Gittins walked quietly around Chester as he began to regain consciousness. Suddenly, he grabbed Chester's hair jerking his head back, then slapped Chester's face. Chester blinked rapidly but kept quiet. A small act of defiance.

"Why have you been printing terrorist propaganda? Who are your sources?"

Chester stayed silent. Another slap.

"You will talk. Everyone does… eventually. How much pain are you willing to tolerate? Take my advice: save yourself the agony. Tell me everything; no one will be any the wiser."

Chester grimaced and stared at the floor, trying his utmost to stop the room from spinning.

Gittins' predatory smile, "OK, it's your funeral. Let's get down to business." He nodded at the guards. Nonchalantly he checked his mobile as the guards began the beating. The room was silent apart from the guard's

Masquerade

grunts. After a few moments, Gittins put his mobile back in his pocket and sent the sweating guards back to their bench.

Gittins lifted Chester's sagging head, "Now do you feel like talking?"

Chester squinted at his interrogator through puffy eyelids but said nothing.

Gittins called the guards, "Again."

Four times they beat Chester with gloved fists and sand-filled leather coshes. They were well practised; there were at least a dozen prisoners on remand at the facility at any one time, and each one received several sessions a week to prepare them for the final interrogation. Chester was a special case, so Gittins was managing the process. He needed to find Chester's sources, and he only had a few hours in which to do it.

After a few moments, one of the guards, breathing heavily, nodded at Gittins. Angry, bloody welts covered Chester's face, blood streamed from his smashed face, uneven gasps hissed out of swollen lips, and bloodied, black eyes were slits in a grotesquely puffed-up face. Gittins regarded him dispassionately; the guards had done well. Chester was suffering but still conscious and aware of Gittins. "Are you with me?" Gittins grasped Chester's broken nose and twisted it. Chester screamed long and hard. "Listen. This is just a warm-up. Next, they will use the hammer and pliers on your hands and feet. You don't want that. You have lasted longer than normal. Give me the name of your main source. Then it will be over, I promise."

Chester mumbled, then shook his head weakly.

Gittins shrugged and nodded to the guards. They pushed a stainless steel trolley over to Chester. He recoiled when he saw the implements laid out neatly on a crisp white cloth. Stainless steel hammers, wedges, sharp-nosed pliers, scalpels and incongruously an old Bakelite box with two wires and a winding handle.

Gittins tapped Chester's face lightly, his voice gentle, even persuasive, "Are you sure you want to go through with this? If you are undecided, now is the time to talk. You will never be the same after this – the memory of the pain, the violation of your mind and body… it will never leave you. And for what? You will talk; everyone does in the end. No one can tolerate agony indefinitely. Think man!"

Chester stared at the floor and said nothing.

Masquerade

Tersely Gittins replied, "If that's the way you want it. You had your chance."

Picking up one of the pliers, he jabbed it under a fingernail. "A name, the source giving you the classified data?"

Chester's body jerked back and forth as he frantically tried to pull away from the pliers. He shrieked as he felt the pliers dig deep into his finger, then let out a guttural scream as Gittins yanked out the nail. Unbearable red hot pain shot up his arm.

"Give me a name!"

Chester sucked in air as he moaned incoherently, "Don't know!"

"Why not? You have spoken to him... met him."

"Code...."

Gittins grasped a hammer. "What does he look like?"

"I don't know." Chester hardly finished speaking before the hammer smashed down on the mutilated finger. Again he screamed long and hard. Spittle dribbled down his chin. The guards looked on disinterested.

Gittins toyed with the hammer, "You don't know his name? You can't tell me what he looks like? Yet you publish the lies he tells you about the government. What sort of journalist are you?"

He leaned forward and jabbed the pliers under another nail. There was no question this time; the nail was just ripped out. A long scream reverberated around the room.

"Again! A name. What does he look like?"

Now Chester's willpower was all but broken. Between waves of nausea, he sobbed, "Don't know... I don't know his name... every time different. Can't tell... looks like."

"How do you contact him?"

"Phone... Oh, God! Stop!"

"What does he sound like? Is he English?"

"Uhh. Different ... accents... but English."

"OK, so give me his name."

Masquerade

"Told you... don't know."

Gittins stood and wiped the sweat from his brow; the room was getting suffocatingly hot. He gestured to one of the guards. "Get the box. He's about ready to spill his guts."

One of the guards attached small crocodile clips to Chester's nipples, two thin wires led back to the Bakelite box.

Gittins checked Chester. A dozen years' experience interrogating for Stryckland allowed him to gauge a prisoner's capacity for punishment. Chester could tolerate a session with the box. He would have to; Gittins needed the name.

"A name, Chester. Quickly, this is about to get extremely uncomfortable."

Spittle and sweat and blood oozed down Chester's battered face onto his heaving chest. Hoarsely he gasped, "Don't know ... Don't know..."

"Foolish, very foolish." Gittins shook his head at this misplaced loyalty then briskly wound the handle. A flick of a switch and Chester was propelled violently against the leather straps by a massive unseen force. His eyes gaped out of his swollen eyelids, misshapen lips convulsed into a manic grin. He shrieked long and loud as a fiery electrical current surged through his body.

Gittins leaned in close and whispered, "A name Chester, just one name, and then it will stop, I promise. I want the special name. The one that feeds you with the good stuff."

The scream was cut off as Chester vomited. Another twist of the handle – his hand hovered over the switch, waiting. Chester moaned and sobbed incoherently. The switch moved, and once more, the electric current convulsed Chester's body which spasmed like a deranged marionette. The switch flicked off.

Ignoring the stench of vomit and piss. Gittins leaned closer. His voice was soft, "Chester, you have endured enough. Tell me what I need, and I can make the pain stop. Then you can rest, maybe even sleep. Tell me. Stop this madness!"

Then he waited. He knew Chester was broken.

Slowly Chester's eyes flickered, bloody slits. "Phone... my phone."

Gittins' voice was soothing, "Very good, now I can stop the pain."

Masquerade

He turned to the guards, "You. Get me his phone and get a shot of morphine ready: I want him out for a while."

Gittins scrolled through the contacts on Chester's phone. All were names, no indication of who the source might be. "Chester, which contact is the source?"

Chester was in shock. His body convulsed violently. He gasped for breath. "Marlowe," he gasped.

Gittins scrolled down the list to Marlowe, a '41' prefix for the number. Where the hell was that? He turned to Chester, "Rest for an hour, then you are going to phone your contact and arrange to meet, understand?"

"Take him to a cell and give him the shot. Wake him after an hour and bring him back here."

After a leisurely meal, Gittins walked back to the interrogation centre; he brushed droplets of rain from his jacket as he walked to the Control Room. One of the Guards stepped out, "He's ready. Bastard's spilling his guts, can't stop gabbling."

Gittins nodded curtly. "I'll be with you in a moment. Make sure he stays conscious." He poked his head around the Control Room door, " Anything important?"

"Not yet, but he is at stage three. Very efficient those two. He won't be typing any time soon."

Chapter 34: Key Node

Throngs of homeward-bound commuters hurried along rain-soaked pavements as Susie guided the dark blue Porsche Carrera along the narrow cobbled streets of Vielle Ville to her hotel for the night. Welcoming street lights reflected brightly off the wet tarmac. She knew the city well. She was a regular at many of the city's social events. Once she had left the main arterial road and entered the city from the west, she found familiar streets leading to her favourite stopover, Les Armures. The hotel was located close to the lake and, importantly, just a ten-minute walk from Heinz's Hostel. At the end of a short private road, she pressed the buzzer on the security gate and announced herself. Heavy steel doors slowly rolled back to reveal a steep ramp down to a subterranean garage. Susie parked the Porsche close to a lift then gave a sigh of relief as the garage doors shut behind her with a loud clang. She turned off the engine and sat quietly for a few moments; she was nearly safe. Once she was with Heinz in the Hostel, she would be out of Bilic's reach for the first time. She looked around. The garage was empty. The only noise was a faint hum from the fluorescent lights. Hers was the only car in the garage; the Hotel wouldn't have many guests. That suited her nicely.

The next morning, after a leisurely breakfast, Susie walked to the hostel. It was a large sandstone and redbrick Gothic structure, built in the early years of the Twentieth century. The front doors were set within an ornate limestone arch; they were massive oak affairs, reinforced with stout weathered brass hinges and straps. As she looked up, Susie could see arranged across three floors, arched windows mimicking the shape of the main entrance. All in all, a building of substance, albeit one that had seen better days. The street was busy with tourists and shoppers. She noticed a bakery, ironmongers, newsagents and a greengrocer. But there were shops with boarded-up windows too, their doorways sheltering the dispossessed and homeless, wrapped in grubby blankets waiting for the hostel's doors to open. Their unseeing stares were oblivious to the crowds of shoppers, who in turn ignored the grubby hunched bodies. Apprehensively Susie walked towards the hostel doorway. The doors were as heavy as they looked, and she struggled to push them open. Once inside, she stopped in her tracks, overwhelmed by the ominous murkiness of the cavernous, dimly lit hallway. As her eyes adjusted to the gloom, she saw several doorways on either side, while at the far end, a light glowed faintly. The building still wore its original decor and was in dire need of cleaning. Dense cobwebs draped themselves over light fittings and faded pictures. A thick blanket of dust covered every surface. Further along the hallway, she could just make out the lower steps of a staircase. Opposite this, a faint light illuminated a counter. Susie wondered why any homeless person would enter such a forbidding place. Hesitantly, she walked towards the reception counter, conscious of her footsteps ringing off the cold tiled floor.

On top of the counter, a jumble of papers and leather-bound ledgers sat in an untidy pile. Behind the counter was an office, its walls lined with box files; a table completely covered with stacks of documents occupied the centre and in the midst of all the clutter sat an ancient Adler typewriter with a shredded ribbon strewn over its keys. A tweed jacket occupied the back of an old dining chair, and a plume of smoke rose lazily from somewhere within the chaotic jumble. On the wall directly opposite the counter, an old-fashioned wall clock lethargically counted the seconds. Susie reached over to a large brass bell and tapped it. She waited patiently. The place smelled like an old, much-loved grandfather: worn leather, aromatic tobacco, sherry; she liked it. Eventually, the faint tread of footsteps approached, then an unseen door opened, and a man appeared. Susie regarded him with open curiosity. He was late middle-aged, tall, with greying curly hair atop an open, friendly face framed by laughter lines. Twinkling grey-green eyes returned her frank stare. Susie trusted him immediately.

"Hello. I'm looking for Heinz?"

The man inclined his head, "That's me. What can I do for you?"

"I'm Susie Esterhazy. We spoke on the phone; you asked me to meet you."

Heinz replied, "Susie, yes, indeed. Come, let's go to the refectory. We can talk over coffee." He stepped out of the office and led Susie up the wide oak staircase.

Its threadbare carpet had seen better days, but at least it was clean. At the top of the stairs, they walked down a wide corridor into a large common room. Sunlight streamed in through the three tall windows, which Susie had seen from the front of the hostel. A dozen tables and chairs were randomly arranged before the windows. Susie chose a seat where she could see the street below.

Masquerade

Heinz set the coffee on the table and began without preamble, "I'm pleased to meet you. Actually, we have met before, but you were very small. You wouldn't remember. Your father was a dear friend and colleague."

Susie smiled, "I'm afraid I don't know very much about my father's professional life. He moved a lot. Mother said it was easier for her to live in Paris and look after me. One of the reasons I wanted to meet you was to find out more about his work. I read his diaries yesterday. They are rather cryptic in places."

Heinz nodded, "I know. The reason you and your mother stayed in Paris whilst your father moved around Europe was because it was safer for both of you that way. Due to his preoccupation, your father ended up in some dangerous situations."

Susie sipped her coffee before framing her next question carefully. "So I understand; I read his diaries. Why would a Commercial Attaché with the French Diplomatic Service get involved with such dangerous people? What was happening?"

Heinz scratched his chin and pulled a wry face. "Your father and I were both Diplomats; Ferdinand for France, myself for Austria. We bumped into each other by chance while we were each trying to persuade a large Pharmaceutical company to set up a manufacturing plant in our respective countries. Ferdinand was quite aggressive in his sales pitch and tried to sabotage my efforts. We had many arguments. Eventually, we realised the Pharma was playing us off against each other, so we walked away from the negotiations.

For a couple of years, we kept bumping into each other. Sometime during the '80s, we attended a conference in Istanbul. We were both the worse for wear after a session at the hotel bar. We were complaining about how the multinationals were making life difficult for us. This was a time when international trade was expanding very quickly. Credit was flooding International markets, and new American technology companies were expanding at a phenomenal rate. They circumvented traditional routes to market. If they couldn't persuade companies to buy their products, they used government ministers to force the companies to buy their goods, effectively cutting out local competition. Slowly, Ferdinand and I began to see a pattern. The same companies began dominating markets in one country after another. We often heard of an American company failing to secure a contract, then weeks later, miracle of miracles, its original bid was reinstated, and the company was given the contract. We began asking around to see if colleagues had also noticed this trend.

Then out of the blue, a friend warned me. He said, 'You know Heinz, you are being too inquisitive for your own good. You're getting a reputation for being meddlesome. Spend some time with your family while you can. You never know what's around the corner.'

I was completely taken aback. Such an obvious threat to a Government official was unprecedented. But it also meant that there was substance to our suspicions. We decided to do something about it."

"What could you do?" Susie was shaken to find her father had been in such danger.

"I'll tell you. But first, you should know that earlier I took the precaution of phoning your mother to confirm she knew of your intentions. The work we were involved in brought your father and me into contact with extremely dangerous people. These people are still around, and they haven't forgotten how we damaged their cause. They will go to any lengths to maintain their anonymity. So we need to be extremely careful about what we say and who we speak to. But before we go any further, tell me, why the sudden interest? You have been the definitive hedonist, an original wild child since you were sixteen. What made you suddenly take an interest in your father's work?"

Hesitantly Susie began her story. "Three nights ago, I was plied with drink and drugs and taken to a squat in a suburb of Paris. I found out that I had been kidnapped to be sold as a sex slave to some rich Arab. I'm certain this was arranged by my soon-to-be step-father, who wants me out of the way so he can steal my family's fortune.

Can you imagine how close I was to disaster? I don't know how I managed it or where I found the strength, but someone tried to rape me. I had to kill him to escape. It took a long time to reach Mother's apartment. But during the walk, the scales fell from my eyes. I saw how empty and meaningless my life had become. I've wasted so much time spent with shallow people. Then I began to think about my father. I was sixteen when he died, and I still don't really know what happened to him – he just disappeared from our lives.

I drove to our house in Ticino – you know, getting my head straight after Paris. I read his diaries, trying to understand his life, what sort of person he was. I knew he was a diplomat. But I had a nagging feeling there was more to him than that. From what you say, it seems you were both mixed up in some sort of spy ring.

My father wrote a lot about a man he used to work with. This man saved my father's life once. My father trusted this man, someone he considered to be a close friend. That was you; you were my father's friend. Now I want you to be my friend. Please!"

Heinz found her appeal hard to resist. He had kept his friendship with her father, Ferdinand Esterhazy, a closely guarded secret for many years. No one knew about it apart from Susie's mother.

"Heinz, please! I'm being hunted. On the drive from Paris to Ticino, I was followed. The bastards tried to kidnap me again. I have nowhere else to go. Please! You must help me. I don't know if you are still involved in that work or not, but you have some experience in these matters. I want to carry on my father's work. If you have retired, please put me in touch with someone. I'll work with them."

Heinz was horrified by Susie's story. "Who was this step-father?" he wondered. Heinz explained to Susie, with the creation of this new world order came nascent seeds of opposition. There were still some public-spirited politicians and civil servants who were disgusted by their government's capitulation to corporate greed. The more rebellious fought to counteract the corrosive effects of global trade and consumerism on their cultures, the French being the most successful. They despised the superficiality and general vulgarity of the consumer society philosophy promoted by corporations, as Heinz eloquently paraphrased the adage, "The Corporatists know the price of everything and the value of nothing".

Heinz sipped his coffee quietly for a long time. Abruptly he stood. "One problem at a time. We need to put these thugs off the scent. Where is your car? We'll hide it. Then you can tell me all about Klara's villainous suitor..."

Heinz's mobile buzzed. He checked it, "Excuse me; this is important. I should take the call." He stood and moved to an empty table.

"George? Are you alright?"

Dark, "I'm in Basel."

Heinz cut the call; he gestured to an aide and turned back to Susie, "Your car keys?" The aide took them and left. "Now, the suitor…"

Masquerade

Susie grimaced, "Milan Bilic, a monster, a loathsome beast. Bilic is a millionaire and a dangerous bully. I think he made his money by skimming money from European construction projects."

Heinz, "Interesting, where does he live?"

"Cannes."

"How did Klara and Bilic get together?"

"Bilic is desperate to be part of the European social A-list. He goes to all the social events and manages to wheedle his way into the upper echelons somehow. That's how he came to be at Longchamp when Mama attended last year's Prix de l'Arc de Triomphe. He gate-crashed our enclosure and set about ingratiating himself with all the guests. Mama was so naïve that she believed everything he told her; he can be very charming in a common way."

"How did they get to you in Paris?"

"I was tired of Cannes, so I visited some friends in Paris. We were having a quiet drink in the Ritz when these German guys crashed our party. We'd never met them before, but they seemed OK, so we had a few drinks then went to a nightclub. Next thing I know, I woke up in a filthy squat. They must have spiked my drink; I was the only one of my friends who was there."

"Then what?"

"I tried to leave, but this giant stopped me. He said they'd been waiting for me, and Bilic wouldn't like it if I left before the Arab came to collect me. The bastard actually sold me to an Arab sheikh!"

"What happened then?"

"I killed him!"

"You?"

"He tried to rape me. That wasn't going to happen."

Masquerade

Chapter 35: Suspicion

Dark jumped off the omnibus into the warm afternoon sunshine. He mingled with the tourists as they ambled along the Old Town's narrow cobbled streets and alleyways. At the Place de Bourg de Four, he found an empty table at one of the pavement cafes dotted around the square. He sipped a leisurely cappuccino as he watched the crowds drift by. Eventually, satisfied the coast was clear, he dropped a few francs on the table and made for the hostel.

Five minutes later, he stopped outside the imposing façade of St. Jean Hostel for Lost Souls – finally, sanctuary. He needed somewhere safe to lie low, and this was his safest refuge. Many others in the hacking community used the hostel as a temporary stopover. It was a 'mother ship' for itinerant insurgents. Heinz coordinated the activists' assignments all over the world. The Hacker network was slowly succeeding in persuading ordinary people to look beyond the smokescreen of media disinformation and see an alternative interpretation of events.

Dark took a last precautionary look at the street then heaved open the heavy doors. The murky, cool corridor was familiar, as was the ubiquitous musty odour. The place was deserted; it was too early for the evening influx of visitors, and all the staff would be meeting in the refectory. Before he looked for Heinz, Dark wanted to leave the Tanberg ring he had found on the severed finger after the murder with one of the analysts. He walked straight through the mountains of paperwork in the admissions reception into what appeared to be a storage cupboard. Closing the door behind him, he pressed and held a light switch; to one side, a wall panel slid back, revealing a stairway leading down to a modern suite of spacious offices in the basement. The offices were filled with communications equipment and computers. Every room was in darkness, except the last and largest – the control room. One of the senior analysts, Manfred, was hunched before a screen, concentrating intently. He looked up as the door opened.

"Ah! Hello George! We've been expecting you. Good trip?"

"Eventful, I would say... Where's Heinz?"

"In the refectory, I think... interviewing a new recruit. Though why someone like her would want to join us is beyond me, but there you go." Unexpected arrivals always made Dark suspicious. The Hacker network faced a relentless onslaught from Kalyptra's media cronies. A favourite

Masquerade

tactic was to try to infiltrate their agents into groups they labelled as conspiracy theorists so they could undermine them. "When did she turn up?"

"Last night. Staying at Les Armures ... obviously loaded."

"If she's loaded, what does she want with us?"

Manfred shrugged, "God knows."

Upstairs, the refectory was busy. Noisy chatter filled the room. Heinz was near the window talking animatedly to a stunningly beautiful girl. Dark caught Heinz's eye and impatiently gestured to him.

As Heinz and Susie walked toward Dark, Heinz was emphatically pointing out, "You know Susie, if you do work with us, your life will change dramatically. Kalyptra are doing everything in their power to destroy us. They are experts at killing any opposition. They frequently resort to murder. But often they are more astute and use more subtle methods to quash opposition. You're making a big decision; you should think seriously before you commit."

Susie shrugged and asked, "Who or what is Kalyptra?"

"It's what we call the Corporatists' enforcers. The Corporatists are so secretive that no one really knows who they are. It's rather like peeling an onion; there is layer upon layer of camouflage. As well as conducting much of the Corporatists' business affairs, Kalyptra make sure no outsider can get close to the Corporatists'. Kalyptra is the ancient Greek term for a 'Veil' or a 'Mascque'. This is their function, conceal the identity of the Corporatists and their Establishment cronies at any cost. It's extremely difficult to fight an enemy you can't see. Our problem is that the only way we can expose these people is to tear down the veil, which means we have to destroy Kalyptra. Only then will the culprits be exposed, and we can see who is really ruining our lives."

Susie wasn't about to be dissuaded, "If my father was part of this fight, then I want to be part of it too. I can take care of myself. Don't forget, I've escaped two kidnap attempts in the last twenty-four hours. Besides, once I make my mind up, I stick to it."

Heinz shook his head. "Just like your father. Stubborn as a mule."

He gestured to Dark, "This is our lead field operative. George Dark."

Masquerade

"Hello. I'm Susie Esterhazy." She appraised Dark. Handsome in a bookish way, shame about his dress sense, he looked as if he'd slept in his clothes for a week.

"Would you excuse us for a moment? There's something urgent I need to discuss with Heinz." Dark was brusque.

Susie was nonplussed. She turned and strode off. Then, it suddenly dawned on her, this was part of Heinz's warning – no more privilege. Well, that was fine with her. She was happy to be judged on her merits. She called over her shoulder, "See you later, Heinz."

"That was rude."

Dark shrugged, "I'm not good socially, you know that."

Heinz sighed, "Come, let's go to the Control Room. We've just received some news."

They walked quickly to the basement, Heinz punched in a code, and they entered an air-conditioned room full of computer servers at one end and rows of benches at the other. Manfred was sitting at a bench and gestured as Heinz and Dark walked in.

Manfred, "It's confirmed, and he's for real; the story checks out."

Dark looked at them both, "What's confirmed and who checks out?"

Heinz looked worried, "Chester is in police custody. We received a message from someone called Rafa. He maintains Chester asked him to contact us and tell you the murder victim's post mortem is scheduled for tomorrow. You need to examine the body and his belongings; Chester thinks he was murdered because he had stolen something important."

Dark swore, "Christ! It's taken me two bloody days to get out; now I'm supposed to go back when the whole bloody country is on high alert? And who the hell is this Rafa?"

Heinz grimaced, "Rafa is a refugee, a soldier, smuggled into the UK to use his military skills, now who do you think would do that?"

Dark paced back and forth, "That's what Gunther was talking about. Another thing. What about this girl Susie? She could be an informant. Have you checked her out?"

Masquerade

Heinz sat on the bench and took out a pack of Gauloise, "Sure she could. But she isn't; she's Old Money. They don't like the bourgeoisie Corporatists' any more than we do. Anyway, I knew her mother many moons ago; she's kosher. Plus, she gave us a name ... Bilic."

Dark looked up sharply, "That's the second time I've heard that name; the first time was on Gunther's barge yesterday."

"So, he's Kalyptra? Why haven't we heard of him before?"

"Don't know, but according to Gunther, he runs their people-smuggling operation."

Manfred butted in, "So he must have smuggled this Rafa?"

Chapter 36: Special Delivery

The weather front covering Southern England changed direction and moved north. The storm's intensity began to wane. The thick grey cloud that had enveloped the small plane since it crossed into France was at last beginning to break. Every now and then, Molby the pilot glimpsed the dull orange glow of street lights four thousand feet below. He double-checked his heading then rubbed his aching shoulders. Four hours of intense concentration had left him with a vice-like headache. The journey from Switzerland had been tense. Normally he would have refused to fly in such severe weather. The plane's operating ceiling of 20,000 feet meant it had to fly through the teeth of the storm. A severe weather front had suddenly changed direction and moved swiftly across northern Europe. It had caught the small Piper, pummelling it like a toy. Molby had needed every bit of his vast experience to stay in the air and stick to the flight plan. His destination was a small airport in southern England. He hadn't flown to this particular airfield before, though he was a frequent visitor to small private aerodromes all over the continent. These places were pretty relaxed about visitors turning up at unusual times. They made easy pickings for professional smugglers like him. A couple of whiskies in the clubhouse should revive him. He was twelve miles out and preparing his final approach to Elstree, a small airfield on the outskirts of London. He had radioed his Prior Permission Required half an hour ago and had made a point of being overly effusive towards an overbearing club official. Using the glow of the instrument panel, he checked a scribbled note for instructions to deliver his package. The package was fast asleep in the baggage hold at the back of the plane, hidden under a pile of blankets. The package wasn't about to report his arrival in the UK to the authorities.

Molby had been given strict instructions by his friend Gunther: after landing, he was to make his way to Taxiway B and park as close to the boundary fence as possible. That was fine with him; he was being well paid for a routine journey delivering medical supplies to a clinic just outside Watford. But he was cutting it fine; his ETA was 2100 hours, so he had ten minutes to land.

"Elstree Control. This is Cessna Papa Alpha four one six. Six miles South East Commencing joining pattern."

Private airfields weren't always manned, but it was common practice to inform them and other aircraft in the vicinity of your intentions. Molby had

Masquerade

studied the 'Standard Overhead Join' before he took off. Now he settled into the routine. He would make a complete sighting circuit of the airfield before landing. He eased back the throttle and descended to two thousand feet, ready to commence a circuit of the aerodrome. He was just below the cloud base - visibility was good in the clear night air. Runway lights glinted into the distance. He banked to port and began a gradual descent to a thousand feet. "You awake in the back?"

A muffled grunt replied in the affirmative.

"We'll be down in five minutes. Better get yourself ready. I'll let you know when the coast is clear."

Another grunt.

Molby focussed on the approach. The runway was clear, and no other aircraft were in the immediate airspace. Gunther had told him to leave the plane unlocked when he went to the clubhouse to sign in. He banked into the Base Leg and dropped to six hundred feet to begin the final approach. He could see maybe twenty aircraft parked near the Maintenance Hangar. There were less than a dozen cars in the car park. He was in luck, a quiet night: perfect. The fewer people around, the better. A gentle bump and the Cessna was down, Molby braked and throttled back the engines. The Cessna shed speed quickly and chuntered its way to Taxiway B at the far side of the airfield.

"We're down. I'm going to park the plane on B. I'll be five minutes getting my stuff, then I'll be gone. I'll leave the door unlocked; I'll be in the clubhouse having a drink for an hour. Then I'll come back to lock up. There aren't many people around, so you should be able to get out without being seen. Good Luck."

Another muffled grunt.

Molby turned the plane on the apron, applied the brakes and switched off the engines. He hung his headset on a hook and, rubbing his temples, looked over to the faded white paint of the clubhouse. A large whiskey beckoned. Quietly, without a word, he got out.

Later a shadowy figure slipped quietly out of the plane and crept through the darkness to the woods at the edge of the aerodrome. The package had been delivered safely. In the clubhouse, Molby raised his third glass to the club captain, "Salut!"

Masquerade

At thirty-six minutes past twelve, the package walked out of Embankment Station into the cool night air. George Dark was back in London to find the evidence that would destroy Kalyptra.

Chapter 37: Cold Calling

As the door closed behind him, Dark dropped his bags on the floor and inspected the cramped hotel room. It held a single bed and a rickety pine wardrobe. He checked the minuscule grimy shower and stained toilet. It was a grubby dump, perfect for Dark's purpose. Heinz's team's speciality – crappy hotels where Dark could hide unnoticed. This particular dump was frequented by migrant workers, who followed cash in hand jobs around Europe. They were an ethereal workforce unaccountable to anyone. Over the years, they established their own support network, places to eat and stay, basic medical care and private cash only banking. This hotel was one such establishment. The migrants used it when cheap labour was needed in London. Their last big job had been tunnelling the new cross rail links in the capital. The owner of the hotel, Benny, was Lithuanian and distrustful of any authority. He asked no questions, dealt in cash of any recognisable denomination and habitually failed to keep any record of his guest's identity or their stay. To the outside world, the hotel looked like an ordinary terraced house. In fact, it occupied six houses out of the ten in the terrace. If you stayed at Benny's place, you merged into the cultural melting pot of East London, anonymous and unseen by the authorities. The migrants were tight-lipped about their support network; they knew information was power. Without information, the authorities were clueless about their existence and whereabouts. Benny acted as a trusted counsellor, lawyer, banker and protector. The hotel was ninety minutes from the coast. Migrants drifted in and out of the country like spectres.

Dark closed the sliding door to the bathroom and looked out of the cobweb encrusted window. It was a corroded aluminium double glazed unit that did little to reduce the noise of a busy rail line yards from the room. A rusting fire escape clung perilously to the outside wall within a few feet of the window. He had noted the sign in the corridor: it would give him an additional escape route if needed. Turning to unpack, he smiled. He would be inconspicuous here. The owner had barely looked up from his reality TV show as Dark scribbled a name in a tatty exercise book.

Luckily the bathroom mirror was just about good enough to apply his disguise. Dark propped his prop bag on the wire tray sitting across the bath. A flickering light above the mirror was completely useless but allowed him to place his own more powerful light on top. His most important asset, a disguise, was now available. When he had arranged everything to his liking, he peeled back the duvet cover and lay on the grubby bed to rest.

Dark woke with a start; he'd overslept. He took a London A-Z map out of his rucksack and spread it out on the bed; he wanted to study the route to the mortuary. He marked CCTV locations provided by the team in Geneva. He estimated if he took the underground to Mile End and changed to the District Line, it would take him to Westminster, and he could walk the rest of the way. Ten minutes is all it would take. If he joined the morning rush hour, he would be unremarkable in the crowds.

The next morning Dark awoke early; a watery sun barely penetrated the thin grey curtains. His shower was a tepid trickle. All the better to emphasize the characteristics of a scruffy student. He began applying his disguise. He pulled his hair back into a thin net cap and pencilled in a new hairline on his forehead. He selected a long unkempt wig as part of his disguise. Carefully he manoeuvred the wig into place. Next, he glued a scruffy beard in place. With a pair of thick-rimmed spectacles, much of his face would be obscured. He would look like any other overworked junior doctor. He stuffed a lab coat, stethoscope and notepad into a rucksack that would complete the character. He surveyed his handiwork in the mirror, confident he would fit in. He knew most people were deferential when faced with uniformed figures, and a doctor was as potent as any. Satisfied, he grabbed his parka and rucksack then left.

He boarded the Tube at Leytonstone and wedged himself into a corner close to the doors. The carriage was stiflingly hot, packed full of sweating bodies. At Mile End, he joined the crush leaving the train and changed to the District Line. Another boiling airless tube took him to Westminster. The irony of passing so close to the seat of power he was trying to emasculate wasn't lost on him.

Outside the station, he joined the procession of workers. He pulled the hood of his sweatshirt over his face and kept his head down. He headed for St Thomas' Hospital; within ten minutes, he walked past the main entrance then around the corner to a service entry used by staff. There were only rudimentary checks made as dozens of people made their way into the building. He took a service lift to the third floor. Alone in the lift, he wondered what else Chester's sources had found out. He slipped on the lab coat, hung the stethoscope round his neck and stuffed his coat into the rucksack.

Masquerade

Exiting the lift, he glanced to his right down a long corridor full of people hurrying back and forth. Dark walked briskly to a stairwell and took the steps two at a time to the Pathology Department. Casually he peered around the door. At a reception desk twenty yards away, he could see the head and shoulders of a nurse and receptionist poring over a computer screen. Assorted personnel in light blue scrubs walked back and forth along the corridor. Dark slung his rucksack over his shoulder. He took an ID card from his pocket and slipped the lanyard around his neck. The building plans had shown the Morgue was located at the end of this corridor as it branched off to the left.

No one took the slightest notice of him, and to avoid conversation, he fished a Walkman out of a pocket and adjusted the headphones. He stuffed his hands in his pockets and rounded the corner to the Morgue. "Shit!" – two WPCs almost collided with him. One held his gaze briefly, but she was so engrossed in her colleague's gossip that she might as well have been looking at the wall. A radio crackled into life, then they ran towards the lifts and passed out of sight.

"So far, so good," he mused. He had expected there might be a few Police around considering the nature of the victim. Another thirty feet and he reached the corner of the corridor leading to the Pathology Department. As he rounded the corner, two more policemen barged into him. He looked up and found the whole corridor packed with Police. "Damn!" They appeared to be waiting, chattering noisily. Dark put his head down and carried on. He shouldered his way firmly through the crowd towards the double doors leading to the Morgue. As he reached for the door, it burst open. A distinguished-looking elderly gentleman in pink scrubs confronted him, peering over half-moon spectacles. Dark checked the man's lapel badge, then muttered "Professor" and moved to one side. The Professor frowned as if trying to place Dark, then remembering his audience, he cleared his throat and turned to a pretentiously decorated Policeman. The chatter in the corridor subsided.

Dark muttered, "Excuse me," and then continued on his way. He exhaled deeply as the double doors swung shut behind him - that had been close. This corridor was deserted. He could see doors leading off to offices. Signs suspended from the ceiling guided visitors to various departments. Dark strode down the corridor looking for the 'Morgue'. He passed a lecture theatre with a sign written in black marker taped to the door, "Forensic

Pathology: recent techniques for the acquisition of evidence. An introduction for Year Two recruits. Presentation by Prof. Malcutt."

That was why there was a gaggle of coppers. Then Dark noticed a sign pointing to his destination, straight ahead. Fifty feet away, the sign guided him to a set of wooden doors. Another directed "Visitors report to receptionist - Room 628a." Dark gently tried the Morgue doors; they weren't locked. He put an eye to the crack; it was dark. He turned off the Walkman and listened for a moment. As soon as he stepped inside, fluorescent lights flickered on, revealing a room approximately forty feet square.

Dark surveyed his surroundings. Immediately in front of him was Reception: two desks and chairs, a computer on each desk. One desk held a thick visitors log, its corners worn and battered. It was closed, but a red biro marked the most recently used page. Dark opened it out of curiosity, nothing remarkable. Next, he turned his attention to the rest of the room. Behind the desks were shoulder height temporary partitions. Beyond these lay the working area of the morgue. A row of six stainless steel tables. Opposite these were fridges for storing cadavers; Dark counted eighteen. Over each table, suspended from the ceiling, were spotlights, video cameras and microphones. A viewing area was set out opposite the freezers behind a floor-to-ceiling glass partition. The far end of the morgue housed the scrubbing area and sterilising equipment. Immediately beyond the partitions, there were three trolleys, each with a black zipped body bag. When Dark noticed these, he became anxious. The technician wouldn't leave a body like this unless it was due to be collected. So there was little time to find the evidence.

He began to walk to the freezer cabinets but, after a few paces, returned to the reception desk. He hit the spacebar on a computer's keyboard, a screen flickered into life. It prompted for a password; Dark typed "password" but got an error message. Then "123456". The desktop screen appeared. Dark quickly found a register icon. He clicked on it and was presented with a database listing cadavers and the stage they had reached in the pathology process. He looked for an entry dated three nights previous. It was the fourth newest entry. He clicked on the name to display more details. Malcutt had performed the post mortem late yesterday. The cause of death was noted as bruising to the brain and internal bleeding caused by a ruptured spleen. The body was in fridge number six. Personal effects and relevant evidential items had been bagged, labelled and stored in bin six.

Dark quickly cleared the screen and hurried over to the locker. The storage bin door was locked. Dark surmised the bin would be chilled to keep organic evidence stable for delivery to the forensic laboratory. He tried the handle again before reaching for his lock picks. A minute of skilful probing sprung the lock. The draw slid smoothly outward, releasing clouds of vapour. Inside were sealed plastic containers with tissue samples. Three heavy-duty plastic bags contained clothing. Dark pulled out the larger bag and broke the seal. He took out a pair of trousers and felt the pockets, nothing. Then he searched the shirt, nothing. He paused as he heard the outer doors open then voices at the computers. For the moment, he was hidden by the partitions. Hurriedly he pulled out a heavy tweed jacket. Nothing in the outer pockets. Then he searched the inner pockets, nothing. Then, as he folded the jacket, he felt something hard in the lapel. Quickly he examined the area; the stitching was recent. He felt a surge of anticipation. He tugged the seam open to reveal an SD Memory Card. A cursory search would have easily missed it. Hurriedly, he put the card in his pocket and hastily shoved the clothing back into the locker. His jubilation was cut short as the crowd of rowdy police cadets surged into the room hard on the heels of the white-haired Professor. At first, they were too preoccupied to notice Dark, who quickly zipped his rucksack and slung it over his shoulder. Quietly he closed the drawer; it shut with a quiet click. Then he made for the door.

Just as he reached the portal, a voice called out, "Excuse me?" The room fell silent. Dark turned, the Professor beckoned to him. "Do I know you, young man?"

"You may, Professor; I'm a junior house doctor."

"What are you doing here on your own?"

"Ah, one of your assistants thought he had left his notes here; he asked me to check as I was passing."

The professor frowned. He was about to ask Dark something else when the doors burst open and an assistant wheeled in a trolley bearing the subject of his lecture to the cadets. Immediately he forgot Dark and encouraged the cadets to take their places around the examination table.

Masquerade

Dark seized the opportunity and hurried to the door. His heart was pumping, but he forced himself to stay calm. Most of the cadets had surrounded the Professor, but two stragglers loitered by the door, totally indifferent to the lecture. They smirked as they watched Dark approach; he ignored them. But instinctively knew they were trouble. He would have to deal with them quickly. He glanced over his shoulder at the rest of the group; everyone was focused on the professor.

As Dark walked near, one of the weasels stuck his leg out, blocking Dark. Dark paused, feigning surprise. The other weasel sneered, "What's in there?" He jabbed a finger at the rucksack. Without warning, Dark landed a heavy blow on the cadet's neck. The cadet made a quiet choking sound before collapsing. The other cadet began to shout when Dark landed a punch in his solar plexus. Dark risked a glance over his shoulder, the professor was droning on, and no one had noticed. He closed the doors and tied the handles together with his belt. That would give him a few extra minutes once they discovered the two cadets.

Chapter 38: Riot

Heavy grey clouds pelted fat droplets of rain on Dark as he hurried along Fleet Street, mingling with tourists and office workers. As he walked, he considered Chester's predicament; he wouldn't last long once the interrogation people went to work. A few hours in isolation, freezing cell, no light. He would give them anything they wanted in a few short, painful minutes. Although Chester hadn't seen Dark without a disguise, he could still give them broad details such as estimates of height and build. Dark was so preoccupied he didn't notice a low rumble from a crowd of demonstrators until they were on top of him. A large mob carrying placards and banners were in disarray, racing down the road, every one of them looking over their shoulders at something in the distance. Pedestrians quickly became embroiled in the confusion as fear turned the demonstration into a melee. As he was jostled, Dark searched for the cause of the crowd's unease

At the back of the throng, Dark heard a soft rumble gradually build until it reached an ear-splitting crescendo. Then as abruptly as it started, a heavy silence fell. Dark looked for a side road down which he could escape.

During the lull, everyone stopped, mesmerised. Anxiously, everyone looked back. Intermittent drops of rain became more frequent, quickly building in intensity. A whisper rippled through the crowd, then faded to silence. Then far back in the crowd, a solitary shout: "RUN!" Instantly the crowd roared and surged away from the threat. Blind panic gripped the throng; demonstrators stampeded from the now visible massed ranks of police horses galloping at them. Behind the mounted squads, Riot Police banged their shields in a deafening cacophony. Their black helmets and dark visors dripped with condensation as they yelled incoherently back at the demonstrators.

Dark felt the deafening wall of sound vibrating through his body. Caught in the mob's hysteria, he was flung around like flotsam in a raging torrent. Abruptly he was catapulted headlong, caught in a human rip-tide. He clung to those around him desperately, trying to keep his footing. However, the people in front of him stumbled over fallen bodies. Dark's ankle gave way, and he was thrown headlong over a writhing scrum of people. Such was the force that propelled Dark that he sailed over them and hit the pavement hard. He tasted warm salty blood. Concussed, he looked up at a young girl, perhaps only seventeen or eighteen, who had dragged herself up into a sitting position. Her ripped banner lay discarded on the road. Dazed, she looked at her bloodied hands, then tried to stem the blood streaming from her nose. Dark reached out to help her when a horse's hoof smashed into her temple; she was flung to the ground like a rag doll. Her lifeless eyes stared accusingly at Dark.

The phalanx of police horses trampled heedlessly through the stricken protesters. Dark curled into a ball in the midst of bloodied and broken bodies. He lay quietly until the last of the Mounted Police had passed over them. Then, as the remaining battered protesters tried to get to their feet, they were kettled by riot police, then herded into awaiting black marias.

A loud, insistent beeping dragged Dark grudgingly out of a deep and luxurious sleep. "What the hell was making that din?" His arms and legs refused to move. Gradually he became aware of voices close by. He gave up trying to sit and lay, trying to remember what had happened. He remembered escaping from the mortuary. He had been walking down Fleet Street, and there was a demonstration. He remembered the Police charging them. But that was it; his mind was a blank from then on. The smell of disinfectant told him he was in hospital as if the bed had left him in any doubt. Suddenly the curtain was thrown back, and a severe-looking nurse escorted two doctors to his bed. The younger doctor looked thoughtful as he measured Dark' pulse. The other consulted a thin file. No one looked at or spoke to Dark. The Doctor put the file down and shone a bright light into Dark's eyes, then he pulled back the sheets and tapped the soles of Dark's feet. He glanced at the nurse. "Has he been conscious before?"

"No, Doctor. He's been unconscious since the ambulance brought him in."

Seemingly satisfied, the doctor pulled the sheets back and moved onto Dark's neck. Then, swiftly working his way down to Dark's arms: "Any pins and needles?"

Dark grimaced but shook his head, "No, but it hurts like hell when you move it."

"It's badly bruised. I think the horses got you. I don't think there's anything broken, but we'll take X-rays to make sure. Hopefully, a few days rest should see you back to normal. Any aches and pains, just take paracetamol." Then, as suddenly as they'd arrived, they left.

Masquerade

A younger nurse came and peeled back the curtains. She was more sympathetic. "Can I get you some tea?"

Dark smiled, "Thanks, where are my clothes?"

"I've folded them up and put them in the bedside cabinet. Do you want something?"

"Would you be a darling and pass my coat. I want my glasses."

Dark had secreted the SD card in his spectacles case, the nurse unfolded the coat and passed it to him. He felt the inside pocket. Thank God the case was still there. He took it out and gave the coat back to the Nurse. As he took his spectacles out, he felt for the card. He breathed a sigh of relief; it was still there safe. Now his head had cleared, he could remember pretty much everything. He thanked his lucky stars he hadn't worn any prosthetic disguises this time as that would have been rather difficult to explain.

A little while later, the curtain parted, and a different nurse came in. She smiled and said, "Awake at last. We wondered when you would put in an appearance." She looked over Dark's shoulder as she checked his readings. She studied his face briefly as she pulled a small machine towards her. "Let's see what your blood pressure is doing, shall we?" She strapped a sleeve to Dark's arm. The machine began to whir. She looked at him speculatively.

"You were at the demonstration, weren't you?"

"No, I just got caught up in it."

"Ah right. What were you doing before that?"

"Why do you ask?"

"Well, I don't mean to be rude, but you've got foundation running down your neck. Are you one of those street performers or something?"

Instinctively Dark reached up to feel his neck. Damn, he'd forgotten about the rain. He must look like a prat. Pale face and an orange neck.

The machine stopped whining, the nurse kept chatting, "The ambulance brought you in about six hours ago. Can you remember what happened?"

"Not sure. I remember walking down Fleet Street. I think there was some sort of demonstration. There was a lot of shouting. But I can't remember much after that."

Masquerade

The nurse leaned forward and said in a conspiratorial whisper, "There are a few of your friends on the ward with you. You all came in at the same time. It seems there was a bit of crush when the police tried to break up the demonstration. There were quite a few broken bones, I'm afraid. A policeman wants to talk to you. It's nothing to worry about. I think he is just taking names and addresses." She turned, "You can come in now Constable, he's ready."

Dark felt his heart sink. How much had the copper heard?

"Just a few questions, Sir."

"Sorry mate, you'll have to wait." A burly porter barged past the Policeman. "He's needed for a check-up. Won't be long."

Dark felt the trolley moving. He called to the porter leading the trolley, "Where are you taking me?"

"Down to X-ray, mate. They are going to give you the once over. So lie down and take it easy; we won't be long."

Dark was feeling nauseous, so he didn't argue, "Good timing. I didn't want to talk to that copper."

The porter grunted, "Who does? Bloody arrogant bastards. They've been giving all the demonstrators a hard time. You'd think those students were a bunch of terrorists, the way they are treated. All they were doing was marching down the road."

As they got to the ward door, another policeman jumped out of his chair and barked at Dark, "What's your name? Have we got your details?"

The porter snapped, "Give it a rest, mate; he's not well. He can't exactly run away now, can he? He'll be back in in a bit; you may be able to talk to him then if he's awake."

The policeman pulled a face but didn't argue, "I'll be waiting when you come back."

As the porter wheeled Dark's bed down the corridor, he saw three other bloodied and bruised protesters being hustled away in handcuffs. Each one flanked by burly policemen. Two of the prisoners were young girls, desperately trying not to cry. They all carried war wounds of some description - livid red and blue bruises on their faces and arms. The policeman leading them pushed his way down the crowded corridor.

Masquerade

Dark stifled a snort of disgust; it was as if they thought a girl of nine stone would be so dangerous she needed two sixteen stone policemen to escort her. If it weren't so ludicrous, it would be laughable.

It was past midnight when Dark was woken up by someone shaking his arm. He looked up to see the policeman who had tried to stop him from going for his X-ray. Across the room, more policemen were shaking other patients awake. "Right! We've wasted enough time in 'ere; we need to process you lot and go. What's your name?"

Dark complained, "What the hell? It's the middle of the night, can't this wait?"

The policeman glared at him, "Watch your lip, or I'll 'ave you down the nick! You've been given the all-clear. I need to check your ID." He moved around top dark's locker, "Your stuff in 'ere is it?"

Dark sat up. "What do you think you're doing? Don't you need a warrant to search someone's belongings?"

"Don't get smart with me, mate! I know the law better than you, so shut up and do as you're told." He began pulling clothes out of the locker onto the floor. He found Dark's jacket. "What have we got here?" He emptied the contents onto the bed: wallet, keys, coins, mobile, glasses case. "Wilson! Bring that terminal over here and check this ID. Make sure it's legit; see if he's got any priors. Fill in the MP2374 form and get him to sign it. When you've finished, come and find me."

A young constable hurried over. He opened Dark's wallet, then sat on the edge of the bed and carefully made a note of credit cards, library card – all in the name of Justin Lawrence. Then he picked up the bulky terminal and entered the driving licence number.

"Here goes," thought Dark, "let's see how Heinz' handiwork stands up to scrutiny."

As the constable waited for the confirmation to come through, he absent-mindedly picked up Dark's glasses case, opened it, and began fiddling with the SD card.

Dark held his breath, "God."

The constable grimaced and mumbled, "Bloody machine, we'll be here all night." He began tapping the SD card on the terminal.

Dark willed him to put the card down. What the hell was taking the damn terminal so long?

At last, the terminal came to life and started to beep; a green light indicated it had connected to the System. Dark looked as his image flickered on the terminal screen. A brief physical description followed.

"Damn. Where has he put the card?" thought Dark.

The machine whirred for a few more seconds., then flashed a message: "DVLA match. Subject Verified as Justin Lawrence." The database thought Dark's ID was valid. Heinz's guys had done their usual thorough job. It was all Dark could do not to laugh.

The Constable looked disappointed. "Very well, Mr Lawrence, the system seems to recognise you. So, why you were taking part in the demonstration? I need to take a statement."

Dark's natural inclination was to argue about freedom of speech, but he decided it was better to play the game and get the hell out of the hospital. First, he needed to get the card back from the copper.

"Can I put my stuff away?"

"Fine."

Dark quickly collected his belongings and put them back in the Cupboard. Then as if he just remembered, "Can I have the SD card?"

"What?"

"The SD card. You were playing with it as you waited for the terminal."

"Ah, yes, the card." The constable patted his pockets. "Now, where did I put it?"

"In your trouser pocket."

"Did I?" he fished around, "Ah, yes, here." He held it out, but as Dark reached for it, he snatched it back.

"Anything interesting? You seem a bit keen to get it back."

"Yes, there is some personal stuff that's important to me."

"Should I take a look? Nothing compromising, I trust!"

"No, there's nothing compromising. And if you do want to look, you'll need to get a warrant."

The constable looked uncertain, then handed the card back to Dark. "Stop wasting time; let's get this statement out of the way."

"Fine with me." Dark put the card back in his glasses case.

The policeman cleared his throat and studied the form, "Name?"

Dark asked, "Why are you interviewing me here and not at the police station?"

"There are too many of you to take down to the station. Sarge says I have to process you here. So what's your name?"

"You know already - Justin Lawrence."

"Address?"

"32, Roundtree Gardens, Greenwich."

"How long have you lived there?"

"Three years."

"Occupation?"

"Office cleaner."

"Mobile number?"

"07854 321452."

Finally, the constable turned the page and smoothed the form down the middle with the heel of his hand. He sat back in his chair and asked, "Why were you demonstrating?"

Dark, "I wasn't. I was just walking down Fleet Street when the demonstrators came running towards me and knocked me over. The next thing I knew is I'm in the hospital with a suspected broken arm. Can I go now?"

Policeman, "Not just yet; we need to corroborate your story before we let you go."

Dark, "Am I under arrest then?"

Masquerade

"Not yet, but you are suspected of taking part in a very serious public disorder event. In the event of us finding enough evidence, you could be charged, and when you are found guilty, you will face a custodial sentence."

"But I just told you I wasn't part of the demonstration."

"Well, you'll have to supply me with evidence that you had no connection to the demonstration before I let you go."

Dark, "That's funny; I thought it worked the other way around. I could swear you were innocent until proven guilty. I thought the police had to find concrete evidence to prove beyond reasonable doubt that I was guilty of a public disorder offence before you could arrest and charge me."

The young Constable smirked, "Oh, we'll find the evidence don't you worry. You're bang to rights."

"I repeat: I wasn't part of the demonstration. I was going about my lawful business."

Policeman, "Where were you going?"

"None of your business."

"Where had you been prior to walking down Fleet Street?"

"None of your business."

The constable was getting angry; his training had indicated that members of the public would be cooperative. Instead, he found he was dealing with an obstructive and difficult individual who seemed to know his rights. He wasn't quite sure whether he should knock him about a bit or ignore the provocation and carry on asking questions. He decided he would come back to this one later. He had another half-dozen people to process, and his sergeant had told him he needed the paperwork at the station by 8 o'clock before his shift finished. After all, the nurse had said this guy was going to have to stay in hospital for another two days at least. There would be plenty of time to deal with him later.

"I'm going to cut you a break. We'll leave it here for now, and I'll come back tomorrow, and we can finish off the forms in the morning." The policeman gathered his equipment and, with a parting glare, marched out of the ward.

Dark couldn't believe his luck. He stood up and made a show of swaying and moaning and groaning.

Masquerade

All the other beds in the ward were empty. The nurses were scurrying around cleaning and making up new beds.

Dark slumped back on the bed, "I need to make myself scarce."

He waited half an hour until the nurses went on their break. There were only two left covering the ward. When he was satisfied the coast was clear, he quickly retrieved his clothes from the locker and got dressed.

He made sure his strapped up arm was covered and peered around the door at the nursing station. One nurse sat at a computer with her back towards him. He could hear another nurse talking to a patient in a darkened ward off to his right. This was his chance; the exit off to his left was clear. Quietly he walked down the dimly lit corridor and shouldered his way through some heavy wooden double doors into another corridor. He froze. Walking towards him were two policemen: the belligerent Sergeant and the Constable. Dark ducked into a sideward and waited for them to pass. The Sergeant was lecturing the Constable in a loud, hectoring tone. "It's not good enough, Jones. This is the second time I've had to pull you up. One more time, and you're back for a refresher. Now go and find that Lawrence bloke and finish the forms straightaway. I want them back at the station in an hour."

Dark sucked in his breath and walked as naturally as his bruised legs would allow. As he walked out of the front door of the hospital, the cool night air tasted sweet. Freedom is the freshest air of all.

Chapter 39: Express Delivery

The trip from Folkestone in the French HGV had exhausted Dark. He had been surprised at the relative ease with which they had passed through British checks at the dock. Although he had taken precautions, the HGV was driven by a Belgian well trusted by Heinz. Dark had posed as a hitchhiker. A Border Agency officer sullenly carried out his checks, ticking items off on his list as he inspected the lorry. However, the inspection had been drastically curtailed when the official hoisted himself onto the top step of the lorry to check the cabin. When he noticed Dark lounging on the bunk behind the driver, the checklist suddenly lost all significance. The official's chin dropped as he took in Dark's day old stubble, ill-fitting shoulder-length blonde wig, exaggerated eyelashes and rouge. He froze as Dark reached out to caress his hand while stretching his fishnet-clad legs invitingly, minute leather hot pants barely covering his modesty. The flustered official gulped and beat a hasty retreat slamming the lorry door shut behind him. "Bloody foreigners!" he muttered.

Dark was always amazed at how easily strict protocols and routines could be disrupted by overt displays of excruciating behaviour. People's discomfiture caused them a great deal of anxiety; Dark relied on this discomfort and used it frequently.

Having just arrived at the hostel, Dark was seated with Manfred, who was booting a laptop into life. After a few keystrokes, a large wall-mounted screen flickered into life. Heinz rushed in to join them.

Heinz turned to Dark, "How did it go?"

Dark grinned, "Not too badly, though I nearly got caught when Malcutt brought a group of police cadets into the morgue."

"What happened?"

Dark slipped the SD card into the laptop's memory slot, "Nothing really. I was disguised: I just bluffed my way out.."

Heinz shook his head, "I don't know how you do it."

"All in a day's work. Now, where are we with the motive for the murder?"

Heinz pulled a notepad from his briefcase, "Chester thought the increase in murders in London was not coincidental; there were eleven. The MO for the murders was similar to normal gang-related killings. To a casual eye, the six murders Chester and you identified were just gang-related. But there is a difference. The six victims were professional people, every one of whom was either in some way connected to the government or companies bidding for government contracts."

Dark looked for the holes in Heinz and Chester's argument, "What about robbery; isn't that a simple explanation?"

"No, not with your victims... there was nothing stolen."

Dark looked perplexed, "Ok, what then?"

Heinz tapped his pen on the notepad, "The only explanation we can think of is that they're tidying up loose ends. The question is ... Why?... So, what else did you discover on your trip?"

Dark exhaled, "Something is brewing... the bastards are up to something for sure. I met that guy, Rafa; he told me there have been thousands of soldiers trafficked. Bilic is running it – the sheer scale means something extraordinary is going to happen."

Heinz folded his arms and challenged, "Does that mean you're going to let Susie help us?"

Dark grimaced, "Let's see what's so important about this memory card first."

Manfred, head down over the laptop, interrupted, "Why don't you two leave me in peace. I'll call you when I find something."

Upstairs in the refectory, Heinz, Susie and Dark got some coffees and made their way over to a table looking over the Old Town.

Heinz turned to Susie, "Let's try the introduction again. This is George Dark. His father, Julian, was a close friend and colleague of your father. As you know, much of our work uses computers to monitor the Corporatists. When we need physical evidence, George is the person who goes and gets it. He does the dangerous stuff and finds plenty of evidence the Corporatists would rather we didn't know about."

Susie sat arms crossed; after their last meeting, she was in no mood for pleasantries. Besides, he looked even more of a mess, three days' worth of stubble, hair tousled and wild, his clothes were dirty and torn. "Hopefully, your manners have improved. What happened to your arm?"

Dark scowled; he was about to respond when Susie carried on, "You don't look like a spy."

Dark retorted, "Looks can be deceiving; you look like you should be 'doing lunch'. The fact I don't look like a spy is why I'm sitting here. Heinz says, you know Bilic?"

"Yes... he wants to marry my mother."

"What do you know about his business activities?"

"Not much. He's very secretive. He travels a lot... mostly Europe and the Middle East."

"Any close friends?"

"None that I know of. It's why he's so desperate to marry mother – he wants to make connections in European society."

"You said he tried to kidnap you?"

"Yes, once in Paris and then again when I travelled to Switzerland. He wants me out of the way so he can control my mother."

"Will he try again?"

"He's very determined. If he can find me, he's bound to."

Dark looked over to Heinz, "She'd better stay in the Hostel. He appears hell-bent on getting her out of the way, and he seems to be able to find her at will."

Heinz nodded, "We've moved Susie in already, but I'll get one of the porters to keep an eye on her; they're used to dealing with wayward clients."

Dark turned to Susie, "It's important you stay inside; you've ridden your luck twice, the third time you may not be so lucky. We are sure Bilic belongs to Kalyptra, a front organisation for the Corporatists; these are ruthless people. They will kill you if you get in their way. So stay inside, understand?"

"As you wish." Susie turned to Heinz, "If you need me, I'll be in my room."

Alone in her room, Susie went over the turn of events since she had met Heinz. "So this is what a new beginning feels like?" It felt strange; she needed to speak to a familiar voice. Picking up her mobile, she made the call she'd promised her mother.

"Hi, it's me; I'm staying at the Hostel. Heinz thinks Bilic will keep trying to kidnap me, so I'm staying here for a while. I'd better keep a low profile for the moment."

Klara was astounded, "So Heinz is sure Milan wasn't bluffing?"

"No, Mother, Heinz is pretty sure Bilic is part of a criminal group he is investigating called Kalyptra."

There was a sharp intake of breath at the other end of the line. "God! Not them."

Susie didn't take much notice, "I'd better go now; I'll let you know what happens. Bye"

Disconsolately, Susie gazed out of the steamed-up window. Crowds of umbrellas meandered across the wet Square. Why had her family suffered so much? Since her father's death, they had endured one misfortune after another. Initially, Bilic appeared to be a knight in shining armour. The estate had needed a man to run it properly. Quickly she had discovered he was a monster. His only interest was cashing in on her mother's social status.

Chapter 40: Setup

Bilic's Mercedes limousine sped through the early morning sunshine along La Grande Corniche. He was on his way to meet an old acquaintance, a capo in the Unione Corse, the notorious criminal cabal that ran organised crime in Southern France. The two had known each other for twenty years, ever since Bilic had used Fabien on a contract killing to remove an obstinate mayor blocking one of his property deals.

At the moment, though, his thoughts were far from this meeting. The men who were tailing his would-be stepdaughter had reported they had lost track of her Porsche. It was their second mistake. It was a simple task, for God's sake: follow her, wait for a remote spot and kidnap her. How difficult could it be? He would have to make an example of these idiots. When they returned to base in Marseille, they would be taking a trip to the bottom of the Mediterranean. One of the quiet inlets in a bay near Marseille. They would be in good company with the fools who had left the giant Busard alone with the girls in the Parisian squat. They had made the trip yesterday. Bilic felt a grudging admiration for his stepdaughter after that episode. How a feeble girl had managed to kill a seasoned combat veteran was beyond him. "Christ! Why can't these people ever do as they're told?" His mood swung back and forth from calm to blind fury.

He glowered at the scenery speeding by. Anger gnawed away at him. In this mood, he was powerless to resist the saturnine madness. It could only be purged by physical violence. Whoever was nearest when it gripped became a target. His men, who frequently witnessed these episodes, dreaded the mood swings.

"Jean-Paul!" he barked. "I need coffee. Find somewhere!"

The driver glanced in the rear-view mirror and recognised the signs. Immediately he floored the accelerator, sending the Mercedes surging down the road. Its powerful engine howled as its driver raced to avert a melt-down. Anxiously he scanned the road for a service station or cafe.

"Thank God," Jean-Paul breathed a sigh of relief as they sped into a small village; there would be a small bar here. "Two minutes, Boss, we'll be there."

"Don't tell me! Just get me there and get an espresso. Triple shot," Bilic snarled.

Masquerade

The 'TipTop' bar was squeezed between a rundown drapery and a pharmacy. The car screeched to a halt outside. It was barely stationary as Jean-Paul leapt out. Drowsy customers jerked awake as Jean-Paul ran through the open door. Bilic, too, jumped out of the car, unable to contain himself. Agitated, he paced back and forth beside the car. His fists clenched and unclenched as he tried to contain the building rage. A cigarette would help; Bilic leaned against the car and lit one with shaking hands. He took a deep drag, threw back his head and slowly exhaled smoke. He let the nicotine work its magic, and slowly, the rage began to abate. Several drags later, Jean-Paul scampered back carrying two espressos.

"Just in case you need extra, Boss." Bilic glared at him, then dismissed him with a jerk of the head; he downed both cups.

His first priority was to find the girl and honour the deal with the Sheikh. The incompetent idiots would have to wait until he returned to Marseille.

He considered his next move. He pulled a phone from his sports jacket. He needed his most trusted fixer, Vargas.

One of Vargas' technicians would be able to track Susie's mobile even if his idiots couldn't. All she had to do was make a call. She would be his prisoner again within hours and then the small matter of closing the deal with the sheikh.

Two hours later, Bilic was sipping a large glass of chilled Chablis as he reclined on a lounger taking in the view of the setting sun from the veranda of his clifftop villa. It had been a tough meeting thrashing out the details of a construction deal with his old Unione Corse friend Fabien Turlot. Now he was determined to have an equally enjoyable and relaxing evening. He'd booked an escort provided by a discrete and expensive local madame. The naked blond, an expert masseuse, was in the process of removing his shoes when the call came in.

"Yes! Bilic."

He smiled encouragement at the girl to continue.

"Monsieur Bilic, its Vargas. We've found her... Geneva... She just called her mother... Yes, I'll keep tracking her."

Vargas let out a deep sigh. He had monitored the girl's mobile for three hours straight; luckily, she'd made a call. Bilic had insisted he find the girl urgently. Failure wasn't an option. He prayed his laptop alerted him to any further calls the girl made.

Bilic sounded satisfied, "Keep monitoring the phone. We'll meet at your base in Zirl once you have picked up the girl. We'll go on to Budapest from there. I'll deal with her and her mother at the estate. I have to persuade the woman to do something she would rather not. Once we have finished, you will terminate her. Do you have enough men to attack the estate?"

Vargas, "My men are professionals; they can deal with farmers."

Bilic closed the call and took another sip of wine. Wearily, he rested his head against the lounger and closed his eyes as the girl rhythmically massaged the soles of his feet. He felt the tension draining away and began to feel relaxed for the first time in days. He knew where his targets were and what he was going to do with them. He would deal with the Sheikh after he'd seized the estate. Then it would be his English rival's turn. He couldn't terminate Stryckland; he was too well connected, but he was going to destroy his reputation, especially in the eyes of the Corporatists. Then he would be the only logical choice to succeed Marat.

Bilic's sources in the Metropolitan police had informed him no one knew how the secret plans had been stolen from Stryckland's office or why the plans had been copied to an SD card. But Bilic knew it was Stryckland's responsibility. If the card wasn't retrieved within days, Kalyptra would have to call off the coup. If that happened, the Corporatists would execute Stryckland then he, Bilic, would lead Kalyptra

The blond masseuse was well versed in Bilic's requirements. After the prescribed time, she rose softly from her knees, moved to his head and began massaging his temples. One hand always maintained contact with his body, how ever light the touch. She watched Bilic's body progressively relax. His breathing became shallow and regular as he drifted deeper into delta sleep. One of the girl's hands slid softly to the base of Bilic's skull and began softly kneading his neck. With her other hand, she deftly scooped up his mobile and, with a few dexterous clicks, located and memorised the last two entries in the call list. Then, just as smoothly, she replaced the phone exactly as it was before – it took less than five seconds. The massage was uninterrupted as she moved both hands down to work his shoulders.

A few hours later, in London, a light shower had caught Giles Stryckland and his companion Camilla Lethwaite as they walked to a discreetly fashionable

Italian restaurant in Knightsbridge. His mobile vibrated in his jacket. "Just a second, darling. Must take this... it's important." Stryckland cupped his hand over his ear and sheltered against a wall, "Yes!"

"He is driving to Budapest."

"Can you follow him without being detected?"

"Of course."

"Then eliminate him at the earliest opportunity."

"Understood. Usual fee?"

"The usual fee."

Stryckland grinned as he closed the call. Smiling, he turned to his companion, "Come, darling. Let's eat; suddenly, I seem to have developed a great appetite."

At the other end of the call, the blond escort made a last check on the contents of her gun case. Satisfied she had left nothing out, she slotted the Mercedes SUV into 'drive' and accelerated hard down the AutoRoute slip road. She would arrive in Budapest with plenty of time to prepare a welcome for Bilic.

Chapter 41: Kidnap

As Stryckland was dining on beef carpaccio in London, in the darkened Control Room at the hostel, Heinz rubbed aching red eyes; it had been a long day. The three hackers in the control room, along with Hayato in Osaka and Jorge in Seville, had been monitoring the Metropolitan police manhunt for Dark. The Metropolitan Police Commissioner had made a brief announcement on the BBC. The version fed to the public was: they were looking for persons unknown who were suspected of stealing highly classified documents. If the information were to fall into the wrong hands, it would compromise National Security. Taken at face value, it seemed they were making slow progress. In reality, the hackers knew precisely how clueless the Met really were in their hunt for Dark. What they learned from hacking the Mets computers was that having drawn a blank in the UK, the Met had called upon their colleagues in Europe.

By pure coincidence, forty-eight hours after the murder, a young constable had passed a file of seemingly innocuous events to a senior detective on Gittins' team. Interpol had compiled a list of suspicious activities in a daily report. There were three. Two involved known drug traffickers. The third concerned the reported escape of a possible illegal immigrant from a cargo barge on the Rhine. Although the description was extremely vague, Gittins had decided there was nothing to lose by following it up, and he had ordered two of his teams to liaise with police forces in Holland and Germany, as well as customs officials monitoring shipping on the Rhine.

Next, Heinz's hackers moved their attention to see what the Dutch and German police files were saying; they noted a report filed by the Koblenz police of an unusual customer, a young man who had bought provisions at a twenty-four hour supermarket in the port. He had caught the shop assistant's attention as he didn't see many British crew in the shop. A visit to the harbourmaster's office and CCTV recordings had shown them travelling upriver on a barge, later accosted by the River Police. Somehow the young man had escaped. Heinz knew if the German police had picked up Dark's trail, it would eventually lead them towards Geneva.

By pure chance, the net was beginning to close. The network's only advantage was that the police wouldn't know it was their fugitive on the barge. Heinz smiled to himself. They would be furious if they knew Dark had travelled back to the UK to retrieve the SD card from underneath their noses. He wondered how long it would take them to connect the dots and if they would find him. Wearily, he walked to his desk and flipped open his contacts list; he called three more hackers. He needed to rest his current team, they had been hard at work for over ten hours, and tempers were beginning to fray. On the plus side, the network was swinging into action, working as a team, the way he'd always planned it. He knew they were fighting a formidable enemy. But Heinz had gathered the most brilliant young minds of the computer generation. People who were able to out-think and out-manoeuvre the technical geniuses, the cream of MIT, Cambridge, Socal, CIA, NSA, NASA and GCHQ. His people were able to sniff out information whose creators had determined should remain hidden. Heinz considered it his moral duty to expose the industrial scale of personal data held by the Corporatists for their dishonest schemes.

Heinz called, "George, come and look at this: a recording from earlier this evening. We seem to have visitors. Do you see two men sitting outside the cafe? They've been there since lunchtime, too long for tourists, don't you think? Despite their apparent casual behaviour, they are studying the building. Could you have been followed?"

Dark, "No, they're not homeless – too well dressed. They could be police, they tracked me up the Rhine, but I covered my tracks after that. Maybe they're Bilic's goons?"

Dark, Manfred and Heinz studied the SD card's file listing as it scrolled down the giant flat screen in the control room. Manfred's fingers flashed across the keyboard, "It's taken a while to break the encryption, but Jimmy in Hong Kong managed it."

Heinz leaned forward, studying the screen intently, "So what have you got?"

Manfred frowned, "Well, I can't see a 'smoking gun'; everything seems routine, ordinary emails and files."

Late next morning, a befuddled Susie wandered into the refectory; she'd had a fitful night's sleep, disturbed by malevolent fantasies of fleeing from Bilic's brutal thugs as she frantically searched for sanctuary with Heinz. Now kitchen staff were busy clearing the vestiges of breakfast from deserted rows of tables.

"What time is it?" she mumbled to a waiter.

"It's 11:30; we're getting ready for the lunch sitting. They're queuing outside already."

Masquerade

"Oh my God! I'm so late. Is there any coffee left?"

"Yeah, there's still some left." The waiter pointed to a table near a window containing a stainless steel urn and crockery.

Susie sat brooding. "Bloody hell!" She was vexed she had overslept; she'd wanted to start working with Heinz that morning. Now the chance was gone. She determined she was not going to miss the next opportunity.

Later Susie was in her room searching high and low for a pair of practical shoes. She was determined to be with Heinz when he came out of that damned Control Room. Frustrated, she threw her bags on the bed. Nothing she had packed was remotely suitable; she would just have to buy a pair. She was used to getting her own way, so Dark's warning about leaving the hostel didn't carry much weight. After all, she had evaded her pursuers, and no one knew where she was. She wandered down from the refectory looking for Heinz, but his office was empty. Likewise, the basement door was closed. Oh well, she would only be thirty minutes at the most.

She flew out of the front door, oblivious to the whisps of cigarette smoke emanating from the reception desk. Satisfied she had everything, she walked quickly along the Place de la Madeleine's crowded pavement struggling into her coat whilst checking her handbag for keys, cigarettes and a purse. She was completely engrossed and so was unaware of a middle-aged couple of tourists who folded a tourist map then followed thirty yards behind.

Behind her, the couple were perspiring freely in the warm sun. As experienced as they were, they couldn't keep up with their mark without making it glaringly obvious they were tailing her. "Ok, we're going to lose her; I'll call the extra teams in." The woman made a call on her mobile and spoke breathlessly, "The mark is leaving us behind. We'll break cover if we try to keep up. Damn it, she's almost jogging. We need the backup teams."

A dark blue Citroen van, seemingly belonging to the City's Street Maintenance Department, had parked in a side street just off the Rue Verdaine. Complete with orange flashing lights, it barely merited a second glance from the busy shoppers as they squeezed by. Inside six men were studying video feeds on a bank of monitors through a dense fog of cigarette smoke. The atmosphere was stifling. The team leader, Vargas, was hot and irritable. Bilic had ordered the team to snatch the girl once she was away from the hostel. At such short notice, they could only make generalised plans – much depended on the girl's movements. Vargas hated these situations. A professional soldier, he considered meticulous planning essential. Ad hoc operations were liable to go wrong very quickly. However, Bilic was in no mood to compromise. They would just have to cope with the situation. Vargas didn't like the topography; it was impossible to cover every alleyway. He didn't want to mess this up, not when Bilic wanted a result so badly. Now the operation had only just started, and already they had a problem. He could see on one of the monitors the mark disappearing into a crowd of people. "What's the girl's location?"

"Rue de Toutes-Ames, heading down this street... there are several options she could take Rue de la Fontaine or Rue de Barrieres. But she must end up on the Rue Verdaine for sure."

He grabbed a two-way radio. "Zimmerman take the mark on Rue Verdaine. She's moving quickly, so you'll have to have your wits about you. The van is waiting; we'll count you down." The snatch itself was a well-rehearsed routine the team had used dozens of times. A van waited at a secluded spot; as the mark passed the van, they would be bundled inside gagged and tied. Often a mark could be snatched off the street in seconds with nothing to alert passers-by. "She may take either Rue de la Fontaine or Rue de Barrieres, so make sure you don't lose her. Turn on your head-cam and keep me updated."

A tall dyed-blond tourist ambled down Rue de Toutes-Ames, stopping to inspect window displays like most of his fellow day-trippers. He nodded his head in time to the music playing in his headphones. A light blue sun hat, the inevitable sneakers, and a garish short-sleeved shirt worn outside his shorts completed the American tourist caricature. However, his attention was focused on the approaching crowd. Why the hell do these people walk everywhere, he wondered? Back in California, sensible people used a car. "Europeans are freakin' mad!" Suddenly he spotted the mark walking towards him, casually he stopped and fished his mobile out of a pocket and pretended to answer a call. Just as casually, he finished the call as she walked past. She was certainly stepping out. He spoke into a concealed microphone, "Zimmerman, I've got the mark; she's heading towards Rue de la Fontaine. Headcam is on. Confirm you're receiving me."

Back in the van, Vargas quickly checked a large-scale street map. He traced the route Susie was likely to take, then he found what he wanted: an area of narrow streets just off Rue Verdaine. He tapped the spot, "That's where we'll take her." He turned to the technicians, "If she follows this route, we'll take her here. Get the van on standby. There are a couple of alleys there we could use. Give the snatch squads a heads up; she'll be five minutes. I need some air." Vargas pushed open the back door of the van and inhaled deeply. He worried about the snatch. His team were good, but this was bad ground; too many things could go wrong. Not that Bilic would care, he was only interested in results. If they got the girl, they'd be in Budapest in the morning. If not… well, he preferred not to dwell on that possibility.

Dark hurried along the Rue Verdaine. He scanned the crowds as he hurried down the street, but there was no sign of the girl. Mrs Berger, the formidable receptionist at the Hostel, had noticed Susie leaving in a hurry and had called up to Heinz. That was ten minutes ago. "Damn, she could be anywhere... What the hell was so important that she had to rush out without telling anyone?" mused Dark. She'd been warned it wasn't safe outside. Finding her was going to be a lottery; if they lost her, they would never get Bilic.

He reached the end of the street when he saw Susie coming towards him. Without a care in the world, she meandered along, engrossed with the window displays, oblivious to the crowds around her. Dark checked the street for signs of a tail but saw nothing unusual. He was still cautious, though; the street was too crowded to be certain she wasn't being followed. He decided to hang back and see.

Zimmerman had tailed Susie for the length of Rue de la Fontaine; his practised eye spotted Dark almost immediately. Then when Dark changed direction and followed the girl, he knew they had trouble. He studied the rest of the street, looking for the guy's backup, but there was none. Dark wasn't one of theirs. He clicked the transmit button on the two-way radio. "We have a guest. He spotted the mark and turned and followed. We are nearly at Place du Bourg-Four."

Back in the van, Vargas swivelled round in his seat to check the video feed from Zimmerman's headcam. "Look in his direction and describe him."

Zimmerman did as he was told, "Six feet; dark jacket." Vargas couldn't see anything sufficiently distinguishing to ID the man: he wasn't wearing anything that would stand out in a crowd. Vargas swore; this was going to be as awkward as he thought. Who the hell was this guy? If he was a friend

Masquerade

of the girl, why didn't he speak to her? Was he police? Unlikely, they always worked in pairs. So why was he following her? Vargas decided it would be safer to take them both. He would let Bilic decide the man's fate.

He picked up the two-way radio, "Okay, standby, everyone. In three minutes, the mark will be in the snatch sector. I want everyone ready. Zimmerman... Kramer, you're going to be on point. You need to call it when we take her. Take the tail as well. Repeat, this is a two-man snatch. You know what to do: same routine as always."

Immediately four teams of four operatives raced towards the snatch zone. The technicians in the van had briefed them on their positions while they waited for their cue. The dispatch team had moved another dark blue Citroen van into position. It was soundproofed and was prepared for a hostage to be restrained. The snatch team waited in the alleyway concealed behind a rubbish skip. A backup team was located in the next alleyway, and two more teams were placed on the side of the snatch site to prevent any interference.

Dark walked thirty yards behind Susie. The alley's late night's revellers were long gone from the subterranean bars and clubs. Tourists were still out and about shopping and sightseeing, but the alleys were deserted. Susie turned into Pass. Mathurin-Cordier. Around a corner, Dark and Susie were the only people in the alley. Dark felt naked without a crowd. Susie carried on walking, oblivious.

She was passing a narrow opening when she seemed to disappear into thin air. It happened so quickly Dark doubted his own eyes. Muffled sounds of a struggle dispelled any doubt she was in trouble. Instinctively he sprinted to the alleyway, just as three men bundled Susie, kicking and screaming into the back of a van. She had a black cloth bag over her head, with two men holding her arms and a third struggling to hold her thrashing legs.

"Susie! Hang on!"

Dark launched himself at the man pulling Susie's legs. The guy was so preoccupied that he didn't hear Dark. He only felt a sharp stab of pain as Dark kicked his legs away before landing a heavy blow to his neck. He fell to the ground unconscious.

Behind Dark, three thugs rushed him; the point man hit Dark hard with a cosh sending him flying to the floor.

"Leave him! Someone's coming. Get the girl out of here. Quickly!"

Masquerade

Vaguely Dark heard shouting, then tyres screeching. Moments later, willing hands pulled him to his feet.

"Monsieur. Are you alright? Did they steal anything? Don't worry, we have called the Police."

"It's OK. I'm fine." Dark was dazed but still cognisant. "Did you get the registration?"

Fifteen minutes later, Dark related the events to Heinz in the Control Room.

Heinz was furious, "Christ Almighty! How many times was she told not to go out on her own? Where the hell was the damned porter?"

"Never mind that. We need to get her back before Bilic sells her or worse. Who have you got checking the CCTV footage?"

"Jules in Sydney. He thinks he'll have something for us in a few minutes."

"I can't do anything here, is her car in the garage?"

"Yes, Mathieu has the key."

"Give me a mobile. Keep the line open; I'll need directions."

"No problem, it won't take long to scan the database."

Heinz turned back to the technicians in the room.

"Manfred, we need to access the Traffic Monitoring System. I want to track those vans. Use the licence plate recognition system."

Dark floored the accelerator as he blasted along the slip road onto the AutoRoute. The Porsche's flat-six emitted a guttural howl as he accelerated hard through the gears. Mathieu had found the van carrying Susie. It was part of a convoy of three identical vehicles heading east. They hadn't wasted any time getting out of Geneva; they were well clear of the city. The question was: where were they going? Heinz knew Susie's family estates were located somewhere beyond Budapest. Dark didn't think they would drive that far – surely they would have taken a plane. Assuming the convoy was going to meet Bilic at some point, why drive all the way there?

"George, they've just passed Nyon. I haven't the faintest idea where they're going."

"OK, no problem. Just keep me updated. I think I'm about twenty kilometres behind; I'll close to four or five clicks and hold station. I should be close enough to get her out when they stop."

Dark rainclouds soaked busy evening commuter traffic as Dark skirted Zurich on the autoroute. As he reached Winterthur, Heinz called, "It looks as if they're stopping probably a service station."

"I need fuel too. Are all the vans the same colour, the same type they used in Geneva?"

"Yes, they're identical to the one you saw."

Cautiously, Dark pulled into a service station. As he parked by the fuel pumps, he could see in a far corner – well away from the café and shop – three black Mercedes vans; they looked deserted. Dark ignored them and fuelled up. In the back of the control van, the men ate a late lunch washed down with a few glasses of wine. They were in good spirits. The package was secure in the other van. A tricky job well done. They bragged about the best way to spend their bonus. They all assumed they just needed to collect the money. If Vargas had bothered to look at the monitors, he might have wondered why their tracker showed the mark's car was located next to them.

Four hours after leaving the service station, Dark picked up Heinz's call, "George! They're turning off the AutoRoute; you should see a sign for Starnberg, the E353. Take that road. Wait…. they've turned off onto another road. They seem to be heading towards the outskirts of Zirl... in a forest, it seems."

For the next hour, Heinz's team guided Dark along a maze of small back roads and tracks. He was deep in a forest. There were no houses or lights to be seen in the evening gloom.

The lane turned into a rutted track. But there were no tyre marks to indicate vehicles had passed that way. Dark turned back and drove slowly, looking for signs of a turn-off. After five minutes, he found something: a narrow trail, barely wide enough for a car. If it hadn't been for the disturbed bracken, he would have missed it completely. He parked the car and crept down a rough pathway that twisted and turned through the dense wood. The night was completely still and very dark. Eventually, he caught a glimmer of light through the trees. Keeping to the side of the track, he gingerly crept to within a hundred yards. A substantial wooden chalet lay in a clearing. In front were three dark vans and two Mercedes limousines. "Bilic?" Dark wondered. He was about to creep closer when the acrid tang of cigarette smoke stopped him dead. Behind and to his left, a dark red spot glowed and faded in the darkness. Soon it was joined by another. Soft voices conversed. "No fireworks this evening then?"

"No, Bilic wants them to see each other suffer... the sick bastard. He thinks the mother will give in more easily if she has to watch the daughter being worked on. He'll wait until we get to the estate tomorrow."

Dark was so preoccupied with the two guards that he didn't hear soft footsteps creeping behind him; he only felt the cold barrel of an AK47 against his neck.

Masquerade

Chapter 42: Bad Blood

On the Castle Esterhazy estate, a concerned farm manager paced around the farmyard glowering at the threatening grey clouds tumbling across a lowering morning sky. Strong winds whipped the avenue of cypress trees lining the winding drive that led to the castle. He grunted his disgust at the wind. There would be no work today; the wind had beaten down vast swathes of corn, making it impossible for the combine harvester to work. He ordered the farmhands into the barn to rest with an early lunch while they waited for the weather to turn. Then he marched towards his Land Rover. He would need to tell the Countess about this latest problem. In all likelihood, the harvest would be late again this year. "Yet more bad news," he thought grimly. The estate had been dogged by misfortune for a long time, ever since the Count had died. His beloved wife Klara had existed in a state of limbo ever since. She persevered for years, determined to keep the estate in the family. Yet all the estate workers knew she was slowly but surely running out of money. But she was as stubborn as her late father, Count Lazlo Esterhazy. She had kept on everyone who worked on the estate and absorbed losses without complaint. Bearing this in mind, the manager was not looking forward to seeing her disappointment when he gave her the bad news.

Preoccupied with his thoughts as he steered the bucking old Land Rover down a rutted track leading to the castle, he didn't notice the convoy of black Mercedes vans preceded by a black Mercedes limousine speeding up the main drive.

However, he had been spotted by one of Vargas' henchmen, sitting next to the driver of the Mercedes limousine. He half-turned to speak to Bilic in the backseat. "Seems to be a busy place, boss. That pickup is heading to the castle. We've seen a few tractors on the way in. There are going to be a lot of witnesses – difficult to keep things quiet with so many people around."

Bilic looked out of the car window at the immaculate lawns and gardens being tended by a group of gardeners. "So this is how the bitch lives," he mused. Although Bilic and Klara had been intimate for some time, Bilic had never actually visited the family estate before today. He flicked imaginary fluff from his jacket. A mixture of envy and resentment that someone should own this magnificent property whist he didn't was brewing nicely.

Masquerade

However, he was certain that soon, it would all belong to him. "Who the hell needs all this? I do," he thought; "soon it will be mine, everything."

They were still travelling at high speed as they entered the turning circle in front of the castle. All three vehicles braked hard, coming to a stop in a hail of gravel. Even before they were stationary, the back doors of both vans were flung open, and a dozen men jumped out and sprinted toward the front door. They were dressed from head to toe in black, their faces hidden behind ski masks. Each man was armed with an Uzi submachine gun, a Glock automatic holstered at their side, and a large hunting knife – strapped to the thigh. A webbing waistcoat carried flash grenades, smoke grenades and spare magazines. The lead gunman raced up six broad limestone steps and put all of his six foot six, seventeen stone bulk behind a vicious kick against the sturdy oak front doors. They didn't budge, and he cannoned backwards, landing heavily on his back. Another gunman sprang forward with a heavy sledgehammer ready to smash the door.

Bilic called out, "Leave it!" He was in no mood for niceties; he paused to prime a grenade launcher. "Stand back!" He lifted the weapon then watched with satisfaction as the heavy oak doors disintegrated in a huge explosion that rocked the castle walls. He half-turned away from the lethal shower of splinters as they embedded themselves in the gravel at his feet. "Go! " he shouted at his men, "Bring the bitch to me."

Twelve men raced into the great hall, spreading out and taking different doors on the ground floor; another group ran up a wide mahogany staircase. They vandalised rooms as they searched, determined to spread confusion and fear, screaming whilst firing short bursts with their machine guns. The terrifying cacophony of sound quickly spread through the castle as the black-garbed killers swept through each room. Bilic sauntered through the shattered remains of the front door, picking his way through the rubble. He avoided the slick pools of blood that smeared the polished floor: the grenade blast had mangled two corpses that now lay in the hall. An old man lay bleeding at the foot of the stairs, whilst twenty feet away, a smaller figure slouched against a wall, bleeding from a head wound. Bilic stood in the middle of the great hall, hands clasped behind his back, taking stock of his prize. Five hundred years of family history lined the walls. Huge oil paintings of long-dead ancestors outfitted in their finery, displaying their military or hunting prowess. He despised it and yet was jealous. From his impoverished upbringing, this ostentatious display of wealth was difficult to comprehend. He understood the accumulation of

Masquerade

money and the gaudy exhibitionism of the nouveau riche. Even Bilic realised money did not confer sophistication; that character trait was instilled by growing up in a place like this. The self-assurance and awareness of generations of a familial bond infuriated him because he could never have it. It wasn't something you could buy. He had decided long ago that if his birthright denied him these trappings, then he would buy or take them forcibly. Klara Esterhazy was the means to achieve his ambition. One side of the Hall contained a large collection of antlers which attested to the family's hunting traditions. Bilic smirked, "The hunters have become the hunted – survival of the fittest; C'est la Vie!" On another wall, a dozen huge broadswords were arranged around a massive shield. Next to this display, pikes and halberds were placed in an arc. A massive fireplace took up half of one side of the hall. Mounted high on the chimney breast was the Esterhazy Coat of Arms – a griffin and a lion supporting the family shield of sky blue with six fleurs-de-lys. The motto, "Honor Virtutis Praemium", was written in large gilt letters on a furled banner below. If Bilic could understand it, he would have derided it, believing there is no such concept, only the right of the strongest.

He clasped his hands behind his back and listened to sporadic gunfire, followed by screams and the explosive crack of stun grenades. Bilic turned to his driver, "Bring me a chair; this may take some time." The driver disappeared through an arched doorway then returned, dragging a colossal high backed dining chair.

Eventually, the shouting drew nearer, stumbling footsteps echoed down a flagstone corridor then a group of cowering women were herded into the Hall. They cowered before Bilic. He assumed his most charming expression, "Where is the Countess? Tell me quickly, and I won't hurt you."

Everyone in the group looked at the floor. Bilic smiled, motioned to his driver, who handed him an automatic pistol. Bilic slowly and deliberately cocked the gun and rested it nonchalantly against his leg. He repeated the question more forcefully. "I will ask once more only." He smiled encouragingly, but the look was wasted; the women were frozen in abject terror. Bilic shook his head, "Shame." He took aim and shot a young chambermaid at the front of the group. The sound of the gunshot was shockingly loud. The women clutched each other and screamed hysterically as they stumbled away from the dead body; one woman slipped on the dark red pool of blood and fell to the floor. Bilic rested the gun on his knee once more, "Do I need to ask again, ladies?"

Masquerade

Once again, he lifted the gun but was interrupted as a group of roughly dressed men was marched into the room; behind them, Susie and Dark, both bound and gagged.

"Good of you to join us. Remove the gags. You may be able to instil some sense into these stupid bitches. I'm not having much luck. They seem to be ignorant of their mistress's whereabouts. Even a little gentle persuasion hasn't jolted their memories. How about yours? Where is the Countess? We will find her eventually, and the sooner we do, the more of you will live." It was, of course, a complete lie; he had no intention of leaving witnesses capable of identifying him, but it always gave a victim's hope in such circumstances.

Bilic called, "Jules, let's persuade one of these. That one, hold him."

The soldier in question grabbed one of the gardeners, a gnarled and weather-beaten old man. Sadistically he twisted one of the old man's thin arms high behind his back and then immobilised him in a headlock. The gardener tried to wriggle free, but he was no match for his younger, stronger captor and could only kick out with his legs.

"Relax, my friend, you will only hurt yourself if you struggle. Just give me the information I need, and then Jules here will let you go back to your duties." Bilic smiled encouragingly at the old man, "The Countess, where is she?"

The old gardener gave Bilic a look of utter contempt and uttered a stream of unintelligible Hungarian. He paused, hawked and then spat a copious stream of phlegm in Bilic's face. For a second, there was stunned silence; the spittle dripped slowly down Bilic's face. Bilic uttered a primaeval scream, raised his hand and smashed the gun into the old man's face once, twice, three times. At the third blow, the old man's eyes fluttered shut and the soldier, feeling resistance fade, dropped the lifeless body. Now Bilic's rage consumed him; any semblance of self-control vanished. He strode over to the body of the old man and fired four shots into the head, a pause, then another fusillade. He ejected the magazine and, loading another, fired three shots into the dead girl's body. His breath came in quick heavy pants overlaying the faint whimpers from the huddle of women. Bilic's shirt was stained dark with sweat; his pungent odour filled the room.

Bilic, grunting like an animal, grabbed a hunting knife from a guard and strode over to the estate manager; he seized a handful of hair then, jerking the man's head back, pressed the knife against his throat. The man gagged but had the sense not to move.

Bilic, wild-eyed and all self-control lost, screamed in his face, "Where is the bitch?"

Above them, from the top of the staircase, a light voice rippling with nerves, yet somehow crystal clear floated down. "I take it you mean me? Well, here I am, Milan. What murderous intent brings you to my home? What causes you to slaughter my staff in cold blood?"

Bilic spun round. When he saw her, he looked crestfallen like a small boy caught out. Her calmness in the face of the carnage made Bilic even more irate. She was dwarfed by the two muscular guards who had found her in an upstairs office, yet her strength of character dominated the room. It was obvious she was afraid, but she resolutely held her head high.

Klara demanded, "Why are you doing this? "

Bilic shoved the estate manager to one side and walked slowly back to the chair. He paused, holding one of the carved eagles on the back of the chair. In the distance, they could hear faint gunshots and shouted protestations as Bilic's soldiers rounded up the rest of the household. Bilic cupped his ears in the palms of his hands.

"Jules. Put these people somewhere secure... one of the garages will do."

He gestured to Klara's guards to bring her down. He sat on the chair, oblivious to the pools of dark red blood.

Bilic, peevishly, "It seems I'm too vulgar to fit in your circle of friends. Let me demonstrate evolution's basic lesson: survival of the fittest. Coarse I might be, but I'm stronger than you. I'm a predator. I am the one who makes money with the courage to risk everything! You and your kind are too comfortable and set in your ways to stop people like me from taking your power. And I'm going to take everything you have. When I have your signature on these documents, it won't matter whether you live or die. I would prefer it if you and your damned daughter both died, but my associate Mr Al-Haroun has taken a fancy to your daughter's nubile body, and so he shall have it. I'll be rid of her for good." Then another thought struck him, "What took you so long to come down … after you heard gunfire?"

"I was on an important call," Klara said dismissively.

Masquerade

Bilic looked at her dumbfounded; then, taking a folder from one of his aides, placed a file on an ornate gilt table and drew two chairs close. "If you please?" He gestured for Klara to sit. With a flourish, he produced a Mont Blanc fountain pen from his jacket. With a smug look, he pulled a wad of documents from the file. A guard brought a stick of red wax, a tea light and two wooden-handled stamps. The guard lit the candle and then stood waiting for Bilic to begin. A notary had affixed adhesive tabs to pages needing signatures, Bilic quickly signed half a dozen pages. "Your turn, my dear." He offered her the pen.

For a long time, Klara looked at him defiantly, "You don't frighten me, Milan, so stop trying." Bilic thrust the pen right in her face. Klara ignored it and glared at him. Bilic slapped her hard, knocking her to the floor. Blood oozed from her mouth and nose.

Susie screamed, "Stop, leave her alone, you bastard!"

Bilic, "Sign the deeds, and it will stop!"

A guard grabbed Klara and threw her back in the chair. Once more, Bilic shoved the pen in Klara's face. She pushed it away and glowered at him. Again he slapped her – harder. This time Klara did not cry out or fall over but held Bilic's gaze before looking pointedly at her watch.

Bilic was astonished. The bitch was actually defying him. Incredulously he exclaimed, "Are you late for an appointment?"

Klara snorted, "No, but you are!"

Bilic snorted, "You're mad! You're about to die, and you look at your watch?"

Susie started to weep as the hopelessness of their situation sank in. She had known Bilic was ruthless, but she couldn't comprehend this.

She began to plead. "Please for the love of God. Don't do this. You don't need this." She gestured. "You could buy this place a thousand times over. You don't need it for the money, you don't understand our way of life. You only understand money, power. Well, I can tell you how you can make a lot of money and if it's power you want, I can tell you how to take that too, but first you have to let all of us go."

Bilic regarded her speculatively. What was she talking about? How much money? How much power? He drummed his fingers on the documents. Klara was bound to sign, wasn't she? She glared at him defiantly, and that look sowed a seed of doubt. Susie's offer might be interesting; he could always kill them later.

Bilic threw open his hands, "Okay, what have you got?"

Susie exhaled heavily, "Untie me first." She demanded. Bilic gestured to the nearest guard. Susie rubbed her chaffed wrists. She glared at the guard, "Towels, one damp, one dry. Move!"

Bilic sat back and folded his arms, "Come on, I haven't got all day."

Susie studied him; he was hooked. "I can tell you how to make a great deal of money within the next couple of weeks. When I say a great deal, I mean hundreds of millions. In return for this, you must let us go and give up any ambition to take over my family's estates and titles. I will give you part of the information now, enough to get you into negotiations with the purchaser and twenty-four hours after you and your men leave, I will give you the information to guarantee you win the contract. Do we have a deal?"

Bilic watched the guard bring the towels, "It sounds tempting, I grant you. But you'll need to give me a little more than that to consider giving up all of this." He waved his hand in the general direction of the castle.

Susie smiled, "It will be worth it, I guarantee. And you will be dealing with people who have the power to more than adequately reward your endeavours with titles and estates far more prestigious than our modest and remote properties." Susie left the bait hanging. Knowing Bilic's weakness for prestige, the thought of a title would seduce him into agreeing.

Bilic, "You have my attention."

Susie stemmed the flow of bold from her mother's nose and frowned as she considered her words. "I know you have contacts and dealings with a number of... shall we say – newly installed governments in Africa and South America. You have experience in supplying the means by which your business associates assume power. What if I were to tell you there are plans afoot to assume control of a major European power. Your contacts in the arms business would allow you to enter negotiations to supply the resources needed." Susie looked at Bilic speculatively. Would he swallow the story?

For his part, Bilic was doing his best to conceal his shock at Susie's proposition. Did she know about the coup? It was inconceivable that she could have stumbled upon the information. Hell, if she had mentioned this to anyone else, then the cat was out of the bag, Kalyptra would have to abort the plan. He had to find out if she had told anyone else about the plan.

"That's ridiculous. How do you know about this stuff? It sounds preposterous. Without stating the obvious, for such a plan to work, only a very small number of people would be privy to it. You don't fit that description. How do you know?"

Susie grinned, certain he was hooked. They would be out of here very shortly, she was sure. "Why? What does it matter? Do you want to make a small fortune and gain a bucket full of titles or not?"

Bilic couldn't stand the smug look on Susie's face; he wanted to knock it off. However, glancing at Klara, he could see she looked apprehensive. What was she thinking? Bilic stood and paced around. His intuition told him the girl knew something, something important.

But what was he missing? She had been picked up in Geneva. Susie had been working in that grubby hostel for a couple of days. His agents had mentioned a couple of men who seemed to be supervisors or managers of some sort. But nothing unusual. Why had she gone there to do such menial work? She wouldn't work there for charity; she was too self-centred for that. What was she up to?

Susie watched Bilic paced up and down, feeling rather pleased with herself.

Abruptly Bilic stopped and stared intently at Dark. Why had this guy got involved? He had followed her ... Why was he so keen to catch her? What if this was the witness for whom Stryckland was turning half of Europe inside out; then he must know about the coup. Was he the thief who had been terrorising Kalyptra? And Susie knew him; therefore, the people at the hostel knew about the coup. Now Bilic realised that the planned coup was perilously close to being exposed and would have to be aborted, but he had the thief. Better still, he had Stryckland in the palm of his hand. Bilic almost shouted with joy. This was too good to be true. Not only was he going to assume his place in society, but he was also going to destroy his opponent in the leadership battle for Kalyptra.

Masquerade

He turned on his heel and barked at the guard, "Guard them with your life. I have to make a call." As he turned towards the hall, Karla called him back, "Just a moment Milan." Bilic turned on his heel, Klara stood, then moved very deliberately to one side. Puzzled, Bilic opened his mouth to speak. He couldn't see the small red dot that had appeared on his forehead. A quiet ping of breaking glass and Bilic flew backwards as a high-velocity bullet emulsified his head, plastering the white wall behind him with bloody gore.

Half a mile away, in the shadow of an ancient yew, Bilic's lithe blond masseuse slid her rifle back into its protective canvas bag. Calmly she rolled onto her back and made a call on her mobile. "Darling, the package has been delivered."

In the back of a chauffeur-driven Jaguar, the Rt. Hon Giles Stryckland smiled a grim smile, "And then there was one."

Chapter 43: Revelation

Back at the Hostel, Heinz and Manfred were in the Control Room. Manfred was still trying to make sense of the files on the SD card while Heinz paced the floor puffing away on a large cigar, "Where the hell has George got to?"

Manfred was only half-listening, "Don't worry, he always comes back, you'll see. He'll waltz in as if nothing has happened."

Heinz muttered, "I'm sick of looking at these files. I need some shuteye."

Manfred called out, "Heinz! George has just messaged; he's coming back... says he'll update us in the morning when he gets here."

"Bloody Hell!" Heinz muttered. "OK, I'm going to get some sleep; see you in the morning."

Hours later, as the cloud-filled sky was tinged pink by the first rays of sunlight, Dark parked Susie's Porsche outside the hostel. He switched off the engine and sat quietly for a moment, collecting his thoughts. The streets were deserted apart from the odd early morning jogger. Birdsong filled the fresh morning air. Wearily Dark clambered out of the car and walked into Heinz's hostel. No sooner had he reached reception, he bumped into Heinz. "Christ! Where have you been? We've been worried sick."

They walked down to the Control Room together. Manfred had pulled an all-nighter was still scanning the SD card.

"Well?" Heinz demanded.

Dark pulled out a chair, "Do you mind... I'm knackered. I've just driven back from Budapest."

Heinz exclaimed, "Klara's Estate?"

"Yeah, right."

Heinz butted in, "Klara called. She told me Bilic was dead."

Dark grimaced, "It was obvious Bilic was going to kill Klara – the rest of us too probably. Apparently, Klara had other ideas."

"How did you escape?"

Dark yawned and rubbed sticky eyes, "Some of the farmworkers heard the shooting and called the Police. The snatch squad panicked when they heard the sirens. They forgot about me in the confusion, but they grabbed Susie."

Heinz, "Klara overheard the gang leader on the phone; he was asking for instructions from a 'Patron'. Also mentioned Marat, Klara seemed to think he was 'Le Patron'. The leader mentioned somewhere near Paris. Maybe that's where we'll find Marat, and I'm pretty sure I know who Marat is."

"Dear Mother of God! This is the first real breakthrough we've had about one of their bases in ten years of trying. If they are taking Susie back to Paris, this person must have some sort of connection to Kalyptra. If he is le Patron, then he might even be the head of Kalyptra. Can we trace them?"

Heinz glanced over to Manfred. "What do you think?"

"Shouldn't be too difficult. They're using the same vans as they drove to Budapest. In theory, all we have to do is follow the vans on CCTV. If they deviate from the AutoRoute, we will struggle. But if they stay on it, we'll find them."

Heinz, "OK, let's get moving on this – can you get hold of the CCTV tape for yesterday afternoon when they left Hungary? "

"Sure, no problem."

Heinz mused, "I'll get Xiyang and his mates on it. What time is it in Shanghai?"

Dark looked pensive, "I've waited a long time for this. I want to look these people in the eye and see them for what they really are. At last, we have a chance of exposing the Corporatists."

"You realise the irony of that, don't you?"

"What, the fact we've had to hide our real intentions to catch them?"

"That's only part of it. All of us have had to assume a false identity to stop them finding us, you more than anyone."

"Listen, to try to oppose these people openly is to invite annihilation. They force you to live a lie just to exist on your own terms. If they had any idea you weren't conforming to their diktats, they would destroy you to stop the idea of individuality from spreading. It's an unfortunate fact that you cannot be who you really are if you want to fight them. Let's get back to this memory card."

Masquerade

Manfred looked doubtfully at Dark, "The tech guys and I have been all over this... can't find a damn thing."

Chapter 44: De Facto Foe

Susie dreamt of water. Lots of it, large chilled bottles with condensation dripping down the neck. It had been so long since she had drunk anything. She had been gagged for the whole journey. Her tongue was dry and swollen.

She was shaken roughly. "Wake up! Le Patron wants to see you." Rough hands dragged her to her feet. Bright sunshine streamed through a large open window. She was vaguely aware of a lawnmower somewhere. Susie swayed, trying to regain her balance. Waking up in sunlit, strange places was getting to be a habit. At least this place had more class than the Paris squat.

"Drink?"

He was a mind reader. The guard watched in amazement as Susie gulped a whole bottle down. "More," she demanded. A second bottle went the same way.

Susie wiped her mouth with the back of her hand. Now her raging thirst was sated, she looked about her. It was a substantial salon; the ceiling must have been over twenty feet high. She sat on a sofa before a large soot-stained fireplace. Easy chairs were set next to French windows at the far end of the room. Richly decorated oriental rugs covered the floor. Enormous portraits of long-dead aristocrats covered the walls. She could see well-tended lawns through the French windows. A large writing desk sat to one side of the window where she had heard the mower.

The guard snatched the bottle off her, "Enough, the Patron is waiting." Forcefully, he propelled her towards the door.

A small bird-like man sat behind a large writing desk. He was the most extraordinary person Susie had ever seen in her life. Though small in stature, he exuded power and menace. Pitiless reptilian eyes regarded her dispassionately. He was dressed formally in a suit and tie. He stood as she entered.

"Please, sit." He gestured to a sofa then sat in an easy chair opposite her. Now he seemed an attentive host, charming even.

"May I offer you some refreshment? Coffee, tea?"

"Coffee, please"

A guard went to get the order. "You are Susie Esterhazy?"

"I am," Susie replied nervously.

"Milan Bilic was your step-father?"

"Almost… he and my mother had planned to marry soon…. you know he was killed last night?"

"Yes, his men told me. Why had Bilic kidnapped you and taken you to Budapest?"

"Bilic was trying to coerce my mother into signing her estates over to him."

"He was always hot-headed. Did you see who killed him?"

"No. I didn't even hear the shot. It was horrible. He was thrown against a wall ten feet from where he stood. He was … unrecognisable. Who are you?"

The birdman held her gaze for a moment, "My name is Marat."

"Did Bilic work for you?"

"I would like to catch whoever murdered him."

"Did you know he was going to sell me to a sheikh? He abducted me a few days ago."

"You escaped?"

"That's why he kidnapped me. He wanted to get rid of my mother and me at the same time. Bastard."

Marat studied Susie for a long time, "I'm not sure what to do with you. Bilic was an extremely useful asset to my organisation. His death causes me a great deal of inconvenience. If I find you were responsible, you will die. In the meantime, I will delay the sheikh. He is insistent the deal with Bilic is honoured. Apparently, you are worth a great deal of money to him. I admit I'm tempted to accept his offer."

Marat stood as a manservant brought coffee.

"You didn't know me when you were brought in?"

"No, I haven't met you before."

"And have you heard of me?"

Masquerade

"No."

"Did Bilic ever speak of his work?"

"No. It infuriated my Mother. He was very secretive. He would brush aside any questions about his business dealings."

"So he didn't speak of my organisation or me?"

"No, I told you, he was very secretive; he never spoke about his work."

"So you are unaware of his immediate plans for the future?"

"I know he wanted a title and was prepared to murder my Mother and abduct me. Other than that, no, I don't."

Marat wanted to be sure the girl knew nothing about the coup. If Bilic had disclosed anything, their plans would be in ruins. Bilic's operation to smuggle thousands of mercenaries disguised as immigrant workers into the UK was pivotal to the success of the coup.

"I would like to believe you, but I have to be sure Bilic told you nothing of our work. We are determined to keep our business dealings private."

"Honestly, I don't know anything about that. Bilic's only interest in my Mother was to socialise with people he wanted to impress."

Intuitively Susie realised she had to appear clueless in the face of the incessant questioning. Marat was nervous Bilic had let something important slip. She realised the conversation she had overheard between Dark and Heinz was true. The UK Government was going to be brought down.

Marat returned to his seat. He crossed his legs and sat back, studying Susie quietly. The girl was a well-known socialite. Beautiful certainly, but he detected no guile in her face. He thought she was the bedraggled personification of a vacuous jet-setter. On balance, he decided she should be confined to her room in the Château until the coup was finished. He had no love for the Sheikh, a rival oligarch. One of the groups the Europeans had been fighting ever since the Arabs had reneged on a building contract in the Gulf.

"Guard." He turned back to Susie, "You will stay with us for the time being, my dear. Confined to your room, of course. You will be quite comfortable there. Let Guillaume know if you need anything. He will stay by your door."

Chapter 45: Blood Ties

Stryckland walked through the gates to Downing Street with a spring in his step. His plan was coming to fruition. His rival had been dealt with, so he was the only viable candidate to succeed Marat as head of Kalyptra. Now he was about to set in motion the next phase of the coup, which would see him installed as the British Prime Minister.

An hour and a half later, the British Prime Minister was bringing his weekly cabinet meeting to a close. "A late item... I'm attending a meeting of European Leaders in Rome tomorrow. The day after, I shall be in Manchester for the Artificial Intelligence Conference. The UK has invested a great deal in this new technology, and it's important to raise the profile of the event with my attendance."

Murmurs of assent rippled around the table.

"As usual, the Home Secretary will hold the fort in my absence. If that is all, the meeting is closed."

The meeting broke up, and people filed out of the room chattering. As Giles Stryckland walked past him, the Prime Minister reached out, "Giles. If anything does crop up, make sure you call me. Don't do anything rash."

Stryckland smiled a slick smile, "Of course, Prime Minister, but as you say, you have everything under control. Have a pleasant trip."

With Bilic's demise, Stryckland had assumed control of the mercenary deployment in the UK. He had delegated Sobieski to manage the detail of the insurgency with the mercenary commanders. Sobieski's first call was to the group commander who had been inserted in a small budget hotel in Birmingham, his troops posing as cleaners and maintenance men were eating lunch in the canteen when Sobieski's call came through.

"... yes, Patron, everything is going to plan. We are ready to go at your signal.... very well, I understand."

The atmosphere amongst the men was muted; they chatted quietly amongst themselves as they ate. A bell rang, signalling the end of the break; most of the men got up and left. At one table, six men stayed behind, when the room finally emptied, one of them stood, the commander. "We have two days until our mission. Our task is to take and hold the TV Mast at Sutton Coldfield. We've trained for this, and I know we're all ready. We'll assemble here on the day at 1400 hours, a van will take us to the target, we'll reconnoitre the surroundings and be in position by 20:00, ready to attack. Everyone clear?"

At another budget hotel just outside Manchester, another group of Bilic's mercenaries were having a similar conversation in the hotel's plant room.

Their team leader was a tall Algerian, "The day after next, we relocate and attack and secure the Ladybower Power Station. You will be ready to move out by 0000 hours, we will take up position at the Station by 0200 hours. Does everyone understand their jobs? Good, dismissed."

Back at his apartment, Stryckland mixed a gin and tonic; he looked out over Hyde Park. He had just finished a call with Gittins and, as usual, was depressed. Increasingly Stryckland found the man draining, tolerating him only because of how he managed to get Stryckland out of a hole. Nevertheless, Stryckland felt it was time for a change. He took a long sip of his drink when the landline rang.

He muttered, "God! What now?" then, "Ah, yes...Countess! How wonderful to hear from you again.... My pleasure, a satisfactory conclusion for us both. You keep your estates, and my rival is eliminated... Not at all; it was thoughtful of you to tell me... You're right; the Old Families must put their differences aside in times of trouble. Don't worry, I'll get your daughter back. Yes, Countess, once the Americans have been dealt with. Europe's Families will regain their rightful position."

Stryckland replaced the handset. He mulled the pros and cons of returning Susie to her Mother; maybe he would, and maybe he wouldn't.

Back at Marsden Green Facility, Gittins leant against his car smoking a cigarette. Chester's latest interrogation had given him a splitting headache and put him in a foul mood. Irrationally, he came out of the interrogation room respecting Chester's bravery as he tried to safeguard his sources, especially the name of the thief who caused Gittins' own deceitful overlords in the Establishment so much alarm. Nature and circumstance had bred in him violence as a means of solving problems, and despite using that routinely for Stryckland, he recognised and respected Chester's intellect and honesty. Stryckland had got under his skin; Gittins had had enough of being used. Just then, his mobile vibrated. Speak of the devil, "Your ears must be burning."

Stryckland was flummoxed, "Sorry?"

Gittins sneered he didn't often get the better of Stryckland, "Nothing, bad line."

Stryckland composed himself, "I see. Did you get anywhere with the River Police?"

Gittins sighed; his headache was rapidly developing into a migraine, "Just a vague description, although it sounds promising, the bugger did a runner and abandoned ship, shots were fired, but nobody found. They're searching for him as we speak."

"What have you got from the journalist?"

"We've bled him dry now - he doesn't know any more… he's given us his run of the mill sources, but the thief is clever: he uses disguises and code names, so we've no concrete description and no sensible name."

Stryckland exploded, "Christ" What are you people doing? I give you a simple job with carte blanche to get the information by whatever means, and you still fail me. Cut him up until he talks!"

Gittins had reached boiling point with Stryckland, "You really don't know what you're talking about, do you? You haven't the faintest clue what it takes to keep digging you out of the shit! Shut up and leave it to me. I'll call you when I know something."

Furiously, Gittins cut the call, then slammed his fist on the car's roof, "Twat!"

As Stryckland was calculating his next move and the search for Marat's hideout was keeping the Chinese hackers busy, a stiff offshore breeze sent clouds scudding across a waning moon. Heavy surf was making life difficult for three RIBs trying to reach a desolate beach on Yorkshire's coastline. Sobieski and de Braganza watched apprehensively from their Range Rover parked on a nearby headland. This was the coup's most important cargo – the legionnaires for the hit squad. They were to be entrusted with assassinating the British Prime Minister.

Sobieski was chain-smoking. He flicked another dog-end out of the half-open window, "Christ! I knew this would be risky; surely to God, we can't lose another cargo? And where the hell is Bilic? He's supposed to be managing this. Why the hell is Stryckland suddenly giving the orders?"

De Braganza puffed on a cheroot, "He went to Budapest… urgent business apparently."

Sobieski grunted, "What the hell could be more important than this? The man's an idiot!"

"That is a fact, my friend. However, there is no need to worry. This is the last batch of legionnaires, so we have contingency if we need it. The squads posing as service workers are in place, according to Stryckland. Everything is going to plan."

"You know Bilic has pissed me off; the Patron should have his balls for this. At least Stryckland stuck to his job, and he can organise."

Chapter 46: Breakthrough

The debilitating tension at St. Jean's Hostel had not diminished. Dark was seated at a workbench scrutinising the contents of the SD card on a laptop screen; they had been at this for over 24 hours. Heinz and Manfred stood behind, looking at the giant wall-mounted screen. Dark was trying various encryption keys from a notebook he had stolen from Vanguard Security. One after another, they failed to unlock the file list summary. Dark flicked over a couple of pages and, in desperation, picked a key at random and began typing. The screen suddenly burst into life.

Manfred shouted, "God! That's it! We're in!"

Dark punched the air as Manfred clasped him in a bear hug.

"Hell, we had a dozen people working on that! Excellent bit of thievery that notebook. It would have taken forever otherwise."

With not a small hint of irony, Dark replied, "No sweat, just genius."

Heinz was impatient to see what the files might hold, "Get on with it; George, scroll down and let's see what's there."

Dark scrolled down through a list of folders, "Nothing unusual so far."

Heinz jabbed a finger at the screen, "What's in the Albion folder?"

A few clicks, and Dark scrolled through another set of folders, but now the contents were much clearer. As each folder was highlighted, a preview of the file contents was displayed in another window. Each file referred to a British Regional administrative unit.

Manfred, "Look, there are entries for Local Councils, Police, Justice, Transport, Utilities and media."

Heinz looked bemused, "Meaning?"

Dark slapped the desk, "Of course, this must be what Rafa was telling me. Each of these bodies is either already under Kalyptra's control, or they are going to be taken over by Kalyptra."

Heinz was still didn't see the point, "Sure, we know Kalyptra controls politicians and civil servants… it's not that surprising they would move further down the food chain and control local services, especially the police and magistrates."

Masquerade

Manfred ventured, "I know they wouldn't want this stuff to become public knowledge, but why kill one of their own to get the card back and protect the information? It's not that revelatory considering some of the stuff they're up to."

Dark nodded, "You're right, but there is more to it than that. And if you consider Rafa and his skills, I think you can begin to piece it together. Rafa was going to be part of a private army controlled by Kalyptra."

The big picture was beginning to dawn on Heinz, "Of course, look at these organisations; they control vital public services. If Kalyptra owns these, they've got the country by the balls."

Now it was Manfred's turn to look confused, "But why bother with junior officials when they already control the executives running the organisations?"

Tersely Dark replied, "Because they need control of the public at street level. Look, put the pieces of the jigsaw together: Gunther's story of people smuggling along the Danube to all parts of Europe, Rafa's story of all these people being ex-military. Then look at the contents of these files. Kalyptra not only want to control the government; they want to be the Government. It's a plan for a coup! And Britain is just the beginning; look at these folders, Holland, Denmark, Austria, and Italy. All of Europe is here. They're going it alone, kicking the American Corporatists out of Europe."

Stunned, Heinz held his head in his hands, "God... out of the frying pan into the fire!"

Dark, "I need to speak to Gunther. If he's carrying cargo, then the coup is going down."

Heinz, "You have a number for him?"

On the English East Coast, Gunther buttoned his black reefer jacket against a stiffening breeze coming in off the North Sea. Spotlights on massive gantries swept backwards and forward, illuminating the huge dockside. Massive cranes shifted sideways like crabs shifting containers between cargo ships and muster yards ready for transportation. Gunther's boat was docked at a small jetty, dwarfed by the massive bulk carriers further along the quay. Even at this late hour, the docks buzzed with the activity of international trade. Now he had unloaded his cargo, Gunther could relax. He lit another cigarette and leant against the guard rail surveying the activity on the dockside. Mechanically, he reached for his mobile as it vibrated against his chest; it was Dark. "Have you unloaded your cargo?"

Gunther took a deep drag, "I wondered when you would call. As we speak, sixty packages are on their way to Manchester."

"The usual?" inquired Dark.

"There was a last-minute change to the manifest... the packages are specialised this time, French North Africa."

Dark sounded nonplussed, "You mean Foreign Legion?"

Gunther was dog tired after a choppy crossing. He wanted to make sure Dark understood that these men were extremely dangerous, natural killers. "Yes, my friend. They are professionals, hard and deadly. Not like the African youngsters, they shipped over before. This lot scared the crap out of me."

Dark cut the call and turned to Manfred and Heinz. Gunther says there is a squad of Foreign Legion soldiers heading towards Manchester. Can you find out what's happening there?

Manfred scoured the internet for upcoming events in Manchester; it didn't take long. Heinz paced.

"The Prime Minister is due to visit in two days' time; that's got to be it. His itinerary includes several local technology firms plus a speech outside the Town Hall."

Heinz stopped pacing, "If we're serious about destroying Kalyptra, we have to prove they are behind the coup and assassination."

Dark looked up, "You're right. I need to visit the man who knows all the details, the Rt. Honourable Giles Stryckland."

"Fine, but first, we need to get Susie back," Heinz insisted.

Chapter 47: Rescue

Dense woodland surrounded Marat's estate, enclosing a vast area of parkland. The night was deathly quiet. A pheasant's call broke the still night air. The frantic beat of its wings marked its flight to safety. Both gamekeepers froze mid-stride. The older keeper turned and scanned the impenetrable murk in a vain attempt to find the cause of the pheasant's alarm. Tonight was a full moon, but little of its spectral glow penetrated the forest canopy. The Estate employed several teams of keepers to deter unwelcome visitors. Most of the keepers were ex-forces, as many would-be poachers could ruefully confirm. A thick layer of mulch covered the ground deep within the forest, deadening the men's footsteps. They were so expert at moving silently they often got close enough to surprise the occasional deer.

The keepers waited for a good five minutes, ears straining for the slightest sound. Then the older keeper signalled to his companion to move off. They turned away from a clump of ancient oaks and walked in single file down a narrow path.

Less than six feet from where the younger keeper had stopped, a pile of leaves rustled. Close to a decaying log, Dark pressed his face deep into the damp earth and waited. He felt more than heard their stealthy footsteps moving away. He waited five minutes more, then tentatively crouched behind the log. Viewed through his night vision scope, the coast was clear. Fifteen minutes later, Dark found himself at the edge of the forest, scrutinising his biggest challenge, eight hundred yards of open ground. There were scattered patches of cover: rhododendron bushes and mature trees dotted the landscape. But there was plenty of open ground where he would be completely exposed. As camouflage, he was wearing a mid-grey linen bodysuit; the colour blended with most backgrounds and the material allowed him to move silently.

Dark crouched as he moved slowly across the immense open space. He knew any sudden movement would attract the attention of the guards. A freshening wind sent clouds scudding over the moon; the night was treacherously bright. He couldn't depend on cloud cover to hide him from sight. A small herd of deer had taken cover in a stand of trees close by. Their occasional sortie from the safety of the trees for forage provided enough cover for Dark to move quietly past them. It took him forty

Masquerade

painstaking minutes to reach the terrace on the southwestern side of the Château.

Marat stared into the darkness of his bedroom. Unable to find sleep, he sat in an easy chair mulling the events of the afternoon. News of Bilic's death had been a shock. Bilic had always seemed indestructible. The question that troubled him was who was responsible? Who would have the nerve to assassinate a senior member of Kalyptra? Possibly a rival Oligarch? No, they wouldn't dare. No individual he knew of had the resources to do it. So if none of these, then who? It didn't make sense. He was too preoccupied to sleep. A sharp analytical mind and detailed planning had helped him outmanoeuvre his enemies for decades. The problem was: he couldn't make sense of this turn of events. He didn't like loose ends; they had a habit of coming back to bite you.

He would need to reassess the plans for the coup. Bilic's mercenaries were central to the success of the plan. Stryckland would still be the titular head of Government. He would get Sobieski to find whoever was responsible for Bilic's death. He could be relied on to get to the bottom of the affair. The Americans would want answers; he needed to have one ready. During their last meeting, Samuel Gardner had expressed a preference for Bilic to succeed Marat.

Marat couldn't shake off a nagging doubt that the assassination was connected to the imminent British coup. He needed to control every European Government to stand a chance of facing off his current employers, the American Corporatists. The UK was the crucial first step, the Americans' door to Europe. By the time that the Americans realised he planned to set up his own Corporatocracy, it would be too late; he would be too strong for them to take down. The UK coup was the lynchpin of his plan.

He decided to call his remaining lieutenant in the morning. Stryckland would have to shoulder some of Bilic's other tasks as well as looking after the legionnaires. His thoughts were interrupted by a knock on the door. One of his aides entered without waiting, showing no concern at seeing Marat awake in the chair.

"Patron. A phone call. It's Mr Gardner. He sounds rather agitated; he would like to speak to you."

Masquerade

Just prior to Marat's butler knocking on the door, Dark had passed through the second screen of guards. These wore more usual dark overalls and were armed with pistols and automatic rifles. The ground floor was heavily patrolled, so Dark had scaled the side of the building to the first floor. A ledge had afforded him a path along the length of the building. Spotlights illuminating the exterior of the house cast exaggerated shadows of shrubs and garden ornaments at this level, providing plenty of cover. He was edging along a ledge when the clouds parted, allowing enough moonlight through for him to discern a figure sitting in a dark room. The figure sat quite still. Curiosity made Dark edge to the open window. The murmur of a voice drifted out to Dark.

"This is Marat." A pause. "Everything is in hand. The loss of Bilic will not affect our plans. I have contingencies in place." Another, longer pause. "Very well, I'll keep you updated as necessary. There are only a few days before we initiate the plan. I am confident we will succeed." There was a click as the call was terminated.

"God! This was Marat, the head of Kalyptra." Dark flattened himself against the building as he heard the soft footfall of guards making their rounds below him. He heard movement in the room, then the soft thud of a closing door. Continuing his search from the ledge, he checked each room; most were unoccupied. In the far wing, he found Susie at last. Tied to a bed. The windows in her room were locked and barred. He made his way back to Marat's bedroom. Once inside, he paused, waiting for his eyes to adjust to the murk, but it was no use; clouds had again eclipsed the moon, and the darkness was total. He'd have to risk a torch. Seconds later, he was heading down a dark corridor towards Susie's room. The door lock delayed him only briefly before he was through. Susie was curled up in a ball, sobbing quietly. She recoiled at Dark's silhouette.

"Susie? It's George." He pulled back his mask.

"Thank God! How did you find me?"

"I'll have to explain later now, shush, or you'll wake the guards."

Susie sat up, indignant, "Don't tell me to shush."

"Just do as you're told, for once."

The squabble continued in hushed tones to the door.

Susie tugged Dark around, "I will not be ordered about!"

Dark scowled at her, "That's exactly why we're in this mess! Now for the last time, shut up!"

Susie was furious but bit her lip.

Dark wanted to find a way out via the ground floor. They were halfway down the grand staircase when a guard silently appeared out of nowhere and crossed the hallway. They both dropped low, hardly daring to breathe; the guard was too busy checking the front door and missed them. They were just about to carry on when another guard appeared from underneath the stairs and crossed the hallway.

Susie was becoming more and more nervous, "This is too dangerous. How did you get in?"

"I had to climb through a window on the first floor."

"OK, let's try that. I don't like this. We are bound to be caught."

"No, this will be fine. Just follow me and keep quiet. It's much better than having to drop from the first floor."

Susie was dubious but followed Dark anyway. "If you say so."

They crept down the stairs and turned into a long dark corridor. Their footsteps were softened by a thick carpet. There wasn't any light, so Dark used his night scope to find the way. After what seemed like an eternity, Dark heard faint voices. He pushed Susie flat against the wall. The voices didn't get louder or fainter; puzzled, he took Susie's arm and walked gingerly towards the sound. The corridor curved away gently. As they rounded the corner, Dark could see a faint slit of light across the floor; a door was slightly ajar. The voices came from within.

Carefully Dark edged closer to the door. He recognised Marat's voice. He risked a glance through the crack. Marat was sat with his back to the door. Before him, mounted high on a wall, a large LCD screen displayed four faces. Marat's most trusted lieutenants. Stryckland, Sobieski, Bennetti and de Braganza.

"Gardner just called. Bilic's assassination has caused a commotion in New York. The Americans need reassurance. They want us to find out who murdered Bilic. More than that, we need to demonstrate the coup will still proceed as planned."

Masquerade

He turned to the Pole, "Jan, use your contacts to find out who killed Bilic. We need to move quickly if we want to keep breathing. Bring the person responsible to me. Alive! Do you understand? I mean it. All our lives depend upon it."

Sobieski nodded respectfully.

"Stryckland, since you have taken on the burden of Bilic's mercenaries, have you uncovered any problem?"

Stryckland's replied laconically, "No, Patron, there is no problem. You may rely on me."

"Bennetti. Have you made any progress finding the Hacker group?"

"Very little, Patron. They are widely dispersed. Impossible to pin down. They are extremely clever. No sooner do we think we have traced the source of their activities than it jumps to the other side of the world. They are defeating the expertise of the British and American Digital Security Agencies. They seemed to be operating from the offices of the GCHQ... maybe they even were!"

"Very well. One day I trust I'll be free of these infuriating bastards. God help them if I ever meet up with them."

Dark tugged Susie's sleeve and pulled her away. "We need to find a way out of here quickly. Remember everything you heard in there. I'll text Heinz and confirm the coup is definitely on."

Fifteen minutes later, they had checked every possible exit from the ground floor and found the doors and windows locked and alarmed. Ordinarily, that wouldn't have worried Dark. But this time, he wanted to make sure Susie would be able to escape. One of them had to confirm news of the coup to Heinz. If he couldn't, then Susie would have to do it. First, she needed to get clear of the Château and the Estate.

"We'll have to go up. Those windows aren't alarmed. There is a ledge we can use to climb down." They crept back upstairs. Dark knew the west side of the Château was closest to the forest. They would find an exit there. They would have to be quick; dawn would be upon them in an hour.

Dark selected a door at the end of the corridor. Cautiously he turned the handle. Someone was fast asleep; soft rhythmic snores drifted over from a large four-poster bed. No matter, they would take their chance here. Quietly they crept over to the window; it was the same as Marat's. Gingerly

Masquerade

Dark pulled it open. He let out a deep breath; it hadn't made a noise. They felt a welcome cool draught on their faces. Dark straddled the window and helped Susie onto the ledge.

"It's quite wide. You won't have any trouble with it. Just put your back to the wall and shuffle along. I'll keep hold of you."

Susie nodded bravely. She was petrified of heights, but she was even more frightened of Marat.

After five minutes of careful manoeuvring, they found themselves above a wall. To one side was a garden; to the other, open parkland and the forest.

Dark whispered to Susie, "We'll climb down onto that wall. Then it's a short drop to the ground. There are plenty of footholds, and I'll guide your feet. Now sit on the ledge, and I'll climb down to the wall."

Susie was nervous, but she gamely agreed to his plan. Dark was helping Susie find her footing as she climbed down to join him when a loud shout came from the bedroom.

"What damn fool's opened the window?" Moments later, a large bald head poked out of the opening, "Bloody nuisance!" The windows were about to close when Susie cried out as she lost her footing and fell heavily on top of Dark, knocking the breath out of him.

"What's that" Who's there? Damnation, we're being robbed." The voice rose into a deafening shout, "Guard! Guard!"

"Let's get out of here!" Dark winced as he swung Susie down to the ground then followed her through the shrubbery at the foot of the wall. He checked for guards; there were none. It would take them a few minutes to find the source of the alarm. They needed to make good use of those precious minutes.

"Come on, we have to run." He grabbed Susie once more and dragged her along, running as fast as they could. She kept up with him easily, "Come on, can't do better than that?" she called. He let go of her arm, and they sprinted towards a large stand of rhododendrons. Dark glanced behind them, no guards as yet, but he knew they wouldn't be long.

Lights began to appear as the Château's residents were roused from sleep by the cacophony. On the edge of the thicket. Dark explained to Susie, "We have another couple of hundred yards of open ground. We'll be most vulnerable there. Once we reach the forest, limited visibility will help us.

//
Masquerade

But they have guards in there already; we'll have to watch out for those. Let's go while we can; we'll be safe in a couple of minutes." Together they sprinted across the park; as they ran, they could hear shouts as Marat's guards organised themselves into groups. Ominously, they heard the howling of guard dogs caught up in the excitement of an impending chase.

"Just keep running; ignore them," Dark called out.

He risked another glance behind; a line of torches began to advance towards them.

The tree line was two hundred yards away when Dark tripped on a tussock of grass and went sprawling. Susie stopped and ran back. "OK?"

"I'm fine, just winded. Come on, we've got to keep going." He checked behind again. The line was closer; four hundred yards separated them. They sprinted to the trees, falling in a heap as they reached the tree line. Dark was in agony; his lungs were burning. He lay flat on his back, desperately trying to suck enough air to stop the pain. Susie, by contrast, was breathing deeply but easily.

"They are getting closer; we ought to move." She remarked. Dark looked astonished and gasped, "How the hell have you got enough breath to speak?"

"Hours in the gym, Darling. We need to go."

"OK. We need to be careful in here. The gamekeepers will have heard the dogs and been told to look out for intruders. They have guns and night vision scopes."

"How far before we reach the wall?"

"It's about half a mile, maybe."

They dodged stray branches as they weaved through the trees. Dark desperately checked in front of them for signs of the keepers. The forest was dense enough to restrict them to a jog. Dark couldn't see any sign of a path; it would probably be patrolled anyway.

The sound of the dogs was getting closer. At this rate, they would be caught well before they reached the wall.

"Do you think they know where we are yet?" Susie asked

"I don't think so. The sound of the dogs seems to be spread out. If they knew our whereabouts, the sound would be concentrated."

Just then, Susie cried out as she fell into a small drainage ditch. Now it was Dark's turn to go back to help. He could see the line of torches winding their way through the trees. The guards were gaining on them. It was going to be touch and go.

"Come on, up you get. Are you all right?"

"I think I've twisted my ankle. How much time have we got?

"Not much."

"Let's go; I'll be fine."

They set off again; Susie was hobbling badly now, though, slowing their pace considerably. The sound of the dogs was getting closer by the second. Dark could clearly hear their menacing, deep-throated growling as they strained at the leash.

Suddenly Susie fell to the ground. Dark rushed to her side, "Is it your leg?"

Susie hissed at him, "Shush. Get down. Look." She pointed. At first, Dark saw nothing, then a grey shadow moved out of the cover of a large oak not fifty yards in front of them. Dark crouched low. The shape gestured to another silent shadow, then a shadow less than twenty yards to their left moved forward, directly towards them. Dark pushed Susie's face down and pulled his mask over his face. He watched as the shadow moved silently towards them. He lay frozen to the spot, hardly daring to breathe. The other shadow was moving parallel to the keeper nearest to them; he would miss them easily. The guy on their left kept coming; this was going to be close. He walked by with three yards to spare.

Dark released Susie's head. He put his finger to his lips and shook his head. She glared at him but said nothing. After a few moments, they silently crouched and made their way forward again. The keepers were out of sight.

"We've got to run again. Can your ankle stand it?"

"I'll try, but what about the noise?"

"We've got to risk it. They're getting too close. When they meet up with the keepers and realise they haven't picked us up, they'll turn back for another sweep. There is no way they will miss us then."

They had just stood to run when there was a deafening crack. A large shower of razor-sharp splinters peppered them both. Instinctively they both ran hell for leather. A second crack rent the night air, covering them with more splinters. Though it wasn't as loud as the first.

"Where the hell did he come from?" Dark swore.

"Don't know... let's get the hell out."

Shouts from the guards suddenly grew louder. Fifty guards were converging on their position, guided by the sharpshooter's radio.

"How much further?" Susie cried out.

Dark noticed there was a lot more bracken around; they were fighting through chest-high clumps of it.

"I think we are close, maybe a hundred yards."

He caught up to her, "Look, take the car keys. It's an old Renault 4. It's parked next to an old tin barn. Rusty grey colour. Drive into Paris and dump the car. Catch a train to Geneva."

He thrust his wallet into her hand. "There's plenty of money in there. I don't want them to find it. You have to tell Heinz what we overheard. He has to stop the coup somehow. I'll help you over the wall."

"But what about you?"

"I'll distract them and catch up with you in Geneva."

Suddenly they saw the boundary to the estate before them, a fifteen-foot stone wall.

"Up you go."

"But I don't know what to do!"

"You'll be fine. Now climb."

Chapter 48: Hedging Bets

In a private dining room at an exclusive London club, Giles Stryckland was entertaining a group of eminent Shanghai businessmen to a lavish dinner. "Mr Lee... Gentlemen... I do hope you all had a pleasant flight?"

Mr Lee, the aide de camp of the select group, bowed to Stryckland, "Thank you, Home Secretary. It was most kind to provide us with a private jet for our visit. It has been a long time since you discussed mutual opportunities with our esteemed Premier."

Stryckland returned the bow, "Indeed, now is a most auspicious time to meet and plan the next phase of our operation."

Mr Lee looked puzzled, "Why is that, Home Secretary?"

Stryckland leaned forward; his look took in everyone around the table, "The leadership challenge we discussed is about to take place. When I assume control of Kalyptra, we'll dismantle the fascist American capitalist system and replace it with a traditional, more... shall we say... paternal arrangement?"

Mr Lee was satisfied with a reply which corresponded with his own values. "I agree, it's time for two older and more sophisticated cultures to depose the uncivilised Americans. China has taken thirty years to attain economic parity with the imperialistic Corporates ruling America. Now is our time; between us, we should assume control of the global economy."

Stryckland smirked, "Very soon, we will destroy the dynastic families that control the American Corporates. We will profit from the Americans' addiction to consumerism, China controlling the West Coast, Kalyptra controlling the East. Then they will be our slaves."

Masquerade

Chapter 49: Ensnared

"Mathilde, is Mother back? Is she all right?"

"So so, Mademoiselle... she is still resting."

Susie rushed past the maid and hurried into the library; she picked up the phone.

"Heinz? It's Susie. They've got George."

Heinz's voice was husky; the call had woken him after a few hours snatched sleep. "Susie? ... Where the hell are you? Slowly now... start at the beginning...."

"After Bilic was shot, we heard police sirens wailing in the distance... his men panicked and bungled me at gunpoint into one of the vans... they took me to a Château outside Paris. A man called Marat owns it, and he runs Kalyptra."

"Hell! Susie, why didn't you stay inside the hostel? I told you to stay in the building...."

"But I'd lost the men that followed me. It couldn't have been them."

Irritated, Heinz snapped, "I suppose it didn't occur to you they may have planted a tracking device? Anyway, we'll discuss that another time... so, it's this Marat who has George?"

"Yes... I guess he must still be at Marat's Château. His guards nearly caught us. Just as we reached the wall at the edge of the estate, they caught up. George pushed me over the wall, but the dogs got him... he'd already told me to go to his car and then drive here to mother's place in Paris straight away and then call you...."

"OK, we think we know where the Château is... we gave the address to George. Can you confirm?"

"Not the name of the place, but I can take you there. As I said, I drove back to Paris... it's about an hour's drive."

"OK, wait for me there; I have Klara's address. I'll get the TGV; it will be quicker than flying. It's about three hours. This time don't move!"

Susie, chastened, replied, "Yes, I'll stay here... I won't go anywhere."

"Good."

Exhaustion overtook Susie; she hadn't slept for two nights. She went up to her room and immediately fell asleep.

Mathilde was just serving mid-morning coffee in the garden when Heinz arrived.

"Morning, would you like a cup?" Susie gestured for Heinz to sit next to her. "How was your journey? You look tired." Susie poured a cup of strong black coffee and passed it to Heinz.

Heinz looked at her speculatively, "I'm fine. More to the point, how are you?"

Susie smiled ruefully, "All right, I suppose. Exhausted... worried about George."

Heinz nodded, "He's not on Europol's most wanted list for nothing."

"Describe Marat for me. What was he like?"

"Small, elderly. Not much over five feet tall. Very intense dark eyes, almost black. His face is set. His expression hardly changed during the time he spent with me. I've never experienced anything like it, but this force seemed to emanate from him... it was tangible. He was the most frightening person I've ever met. I think it would be impossible to deny him anything."

Heinz weighed up the picture Susie had drawn of him for a moment, "What did he questions did he ask you?"

"He was only concerned with Bilic. He wanted to know how he died. Had Bilic said anything about his work? He was a pretty cold-hearted bastard. Then he told me I was to stay at the Château while he decided whether to sell me to the Sheikh. I was taken back to the bedroom. That's where George found me."

Heinz could barely contain his excitement, "Do you know that you are the first person to positively identify a member of Kalyptra? We have been fighting these people for twenty years in a virtual war. We know they exist, but until now, we have never known who the leaders are. This could be the thread that unravels the veil hiding them from the world. How did George get you out?"

"We had to jump from a ledge on the first floor. Problem was, we disturbed someone on the way out. They raised the alarm, and within minutes hundreds of guards were swarming all over the grounds. The worst part was being hounded by the dogs; they hunted us all the way to the edge of the Estate. God, their howling was terrifying."

"Tell me again, what happened to George?"

"He pushed me up to the top of the wall, then he started to climb after me, but the dogs caught him. They were huge ferocious brutes. Even though he was halfway up, probably six or seven feet, they leapt up and dragged him down. He shouted at me to run, to find you and tell you what we had found. The last I saw of him was lying on the ground being mauled by those damned brutes."

Susie broke down as she remembered George desperately trying to fight off the hounds.

"I'm so worried about him. God knows how badly he was hurt when those animals attacked him. They were huge; I've never seen anything like them. He had no chance."

"We'll get him out, don't worry. But before we go, did you find out anything about the coup?"

Susie dried her eyes, "George said he found out more about the Americans and Kalyptra in ten minutes on the ledge than in ten years on a computer. Kalyptra is run by Marat. They are sort of enforcers for the American Corporatists. George overheard Marat talking to an American called Gardner. Kalyptra is orchestrating a coup against the British Government. Someone called Stryckland is going to take over as Prime Minister. He will declare Martial Law as soon as he assumes power, using a terrorist attack as an excuse. They are importing a small army of mercenaries disguised as immigrant workers. They will seize control of strategic infrastructure assets, power stations, water supply, TV and internet infrastructure."

Heinz looked worried, "Sounds like the files are genuine. They were on a memory card George brought back from the UK. He found the card on a murder victim... someone who was trying to steal the coup plans. We were trying to make sense of the files on the stick when you were kidnapped." Heinz couldn't contain his frustration, "Our problem is that the only person who can stop this madness is now being held by the organisation we need to destroy."

Masquerade

Heinz and Susie spent the next hour working out a plan to get into Marat's Château... the path they took to get out last night... what she remembered about the layout of the place... how many guards were there?

Eventually, he was satisfied he had got as much information as Susie was able to remember; he sat back. "We can't start until it's dark. Everyone needs to be in a deep sleep before we go in. Is there somewhere I can rest for a couple of hours?"

Susie showed him to a spare room.

A little after midnight, they set off for Marat's Château. It would take an hour to get there, longer if they were to disguise their final approach.

Heinz and Susie peered over the wall. Ahead of them was the familiar blackness of the forest. Heinz had brought his own night vision scope, which was fine for scanning the overall terrain ahead but useless for working through rough forest.

Quietly they climbed down over the wall using a knotted rope, then warily made their way through the tall bracken at the edge of the wood. After thirty minutes or so, they reached the far end of the wood and looked out over parkland. Before them, beams of light sliced through the darkness. Tonight Marat had his guards patrolling in force.

"How are we going to get through that lot without being caught?" Susie hissed.

"We'll have to get from one cover to another. Do you think they will notice an extra torch?"

"Are you mad? All the lights are over there. We'll stick out like a sore thumb all the way out here."

"We won't use it until we get closer. Trust me."

"Why? Are you as good as George?"

Heinz had no response other than, "Come, let's go."

They had walked quietly for a hundred yards when out of the darkness, before them, came a challenge. "Gaston? Is that you? Switch on your torch before you get shot, you idiot."

Heinz dutifully turned on the torch.

"Good, now move back into position."

Masquerade

Heinz pulled Susie closer to him and walked purposefully forward. As they stumbled through the undergrowth, a voice called out of the darkness.

"Gaston! Not that way! Where are you going? Gaston, answer me!"

Suddenly a bright searchlight blinded them. Heinz swore loudly, "Shit! Time to go!" He grabbed Susie and ran back towards the forest as fast as he could.

Susie cried out, "Oh God, not again."

Behind them, all hell broke loose. A dozen searchlights were trained upon their fleeing backs. Once again, the dread baying of a pack of killer hounds rang out through the night.

Susie's shredded nerves tingled up and down her spine. "Heinz, run faster. Please don't let them catch us."

"They won't; run like the wind."

Shouts rang out – whining angry cracks. Heinz felt the bullets zipping past them like angry bees. They burst into the wood and were showered with flying leaves and wood splinters as the guns concentrated their fire on them.

Heinz grabbed Susie's hand again. "Zig-zag. Come on!" he urged. They moved off at a tangent. Ominously there were shouts to either side. Then the rapid metallic crack of assault rifles raking fire through the trees.

"Where's the rope?" Susie managed to gasp.

"The hell with the rope! We just need to get to the wall."

"Oh God, no! Not again. The dogs will get us. They're going to rip us apart."

"Not if I can help it." Heinz was resolute.

"You fool. You haven't seen them. There's nothing you can do."

"Just run. Run as fast as you can. Run for your life!"

Masquerade

Chapter 50: Extraction

As Heinz was taking the TGV to Paris, Dark came to in blackness. For a moment, he thought he was still in the forest. The overpowering stink of dank decay made him gag. Every part of his body ached. He was lying on a rough, uneven floor. Jagged stones dug into him, and damp earth chilled him to the bone. Painfully he lifted himself onto his hands and knees and began to feel around. He sensed he was in a large dark space. Feeling his way, eventually he felt coarse stone – a wall. He stood unsteadily and groped his way along the wall. He wanted to see how big the space was, so he called out, using his voice to measure the void. The sound was muffled, diluted by the large emptiness. It gave him no clue.

After he had followed the stonework for a few moments, he heard a dull metallic clang. He turned and was dazzled by a bright light. He could just make out two bulky silhouettes framed in a shaft of yellow light. A door was set high in the wall. Dark realised he was in an oubliette, a pit where prisoners were thrown and left to die.

"Attend! Ici!" One of the figures called out. The other beckoned Dark over.

Dark hobbled slowly towards the light; by the time he reached the wall, he was close to collapse. One of the guards threw down a rope and dragged him up to some stone steps hewn into the solid rock. Dark was too weak to climb on his own, so the guards had to pull him to the top. On the next level, they lifted him between them and carried him towards a heavily stained, rough-hewn door. As they approached, the door swung open, revealing a rough-cut stone stairway leading to another door. Flickering lights cast dancing grotesque shadows of other prisoners being led away.

The guards pushed him into a gloomy chamber, whose only light came from a few weak fluorescent tubes sporadically placed along bare rock walls. A dark red concrete floor failed to hide the bloody history of previous interrogations. A stout wooden chair, with heavy leather straps attached to its arms and legs, was placed in the centre of the room. Close by was a large iron bath. Behind these, a gas forge hissed as it radiated heat. Next to it was a large metal cot. A sweating, bare-chested giant appeared from behind the forge. He dragged Dark toward the chair and strapped him in. Dark, who had been drifting in and out of consciousness, was suddenly jerked awake by the acrid stench of the giant's body mixed with the room's pervading stench of piss and vomit. The rough leather straps re-opened the lesions from the dog bites on Dark's arms and legs. The wounds bled freely and began to pool around the chair.

In the shadows close to the forge, three men waited. The smallest, Marat, impatiently gestured for the giant to step back. To his right, Stryckland, with his customary supercilious demeanour, smoked a pungent Turkish cigarette in a futile attempt to ward off the chamber's stench. The third man, Gittins, the least important, stood sullenly behind the other two. He was still smarting after being rebuked by Stryckland during the flight from London. He had had enough; it was time to end the alliance with Stryckland. His treatment had festered and gnawed at him since the row over money. The malicious reprimand on the flight was the last straw. He was going to make the swine pay dearly for that. The question was how?

Gittins was so preoccupied with his thoughts, he didn't notice Stryckland rush at the prisoner with a hammer, his face a rigid mask of hate. A shout from the giant stopped the politician in his tracks. Marat pushed his way over to him,

"Giles!"

Marat continued, "I too have been waiting to meet one of these meddling bastards. I'm going to enjoy watching him suffer. They have interfered with our business too many times. Using this bastard, I'll destroy them."

He picked up a leather-covered cosh and walked behind Dark. Without warning, Marat smashed the cosh against the back of the chair, "Wake up!" Dark jerked upright as he felt the force of the blow jar his spine.

"Now I have your attention, you should listen carefully and make this difficult situation as easy for yourself as possible. First, I want you to tell me about your villainous band of revolutionaries. I want to know everything. Then you will tell me what you know of my organisation. You must tell me everything, leave nothing out. I will decide what is important and what is not. Do you understand?"

Dark turned his face away from Marat and stared at the floor. He didn't say a word.

Marat pursed his lips, "Very well. Bruno! Give him a taste of what's in store."

The giant stepped forward, lifted a massive fist and smashed it into Dark's face. Even though he was strapped in, the blow lifted Dark back into his seat. His head smashed against the seatback, and his nose split into a bloody pulp.

Marat grabbed hold of Dark's hair and forced his head back. Dark's eyes were closed, and his chest palpated with shallow breaths. Marat slapped his face hard.

"Ready to talk?"

Silence.

"Listen to me! Tell me your name?"

Dark turned his head away. More Silence.

Marat barked at a guard, "Bring in the prisoner." He turned back to Dark, "Let's see if this changes your mind. We have been working on this specimen for two days. After a lot of persuasion, his mind is completely broken; he has no willpower."

Dark watched in horror as a mangled corpse was dragged in on a stainless steel trolley. He retched as the body was left before him. His skin had been cut away, leaving raw, bloody flesh. In places, yellow bone protruded from the flesh, thick globules of blood oozed from gaping wounds and dripped onto the floor. Suddenly the body began to shudder, a low guttural moan emanated from lacerated lips.

Marat nodded at the giant. Once more, an iron-hard fist smashed into Dark's face. Dark grunted with pain as blood and gristle dripped from his shattered nose.

Marat repeated his demand for Dark's name. Silence. Marat began to lose patience. He looked at the giant. "With more intensity this time."

The giant fists battered Dark's face and upper body with well-practised ferocity. After three or four minutes, the inquisitor was forced to pause for breath. Marat shouted, "Don't stop until I tell you, idiot!" The giant's chest heaved at the unrelenting effort as he danced around Dark, landing blow after blow. A few minutes later, the exertion was too much for the giant.

"All right, rest for a moment," Marat called out.

The giant collapsed onto a stool, his body drenched with sweat.

Marat regarded Dark for a few moments, then turned to Stryckland, "Let's leave the bastard to stew a while. He might come to his senses."

Stryckland was worried that Dark's evidence might prove embarrassing for him. He would much rather Dark was eliminated without delay.

"Dear God, Patron! Why are you bothering with small fry like this?" Stryckland complained. "He won't know anything. Just kill him. We have more important business to attend to."

"Attention to detail, Giles. It keeps us ahead of the game. Come! Lunch awaits."

Gittins stayed behind as Stryckland followed Marat out to the terrace. He looked carefully at Dark. This young man wasn't as weak as first appearances might suggest. He began to formulate a plan.

On the terrace, Marat and Stryckland sat under a large white canopy. A gentle breeze took the edge off a warm summer sun. Their conversation was desultory; Marat regarded his companion speculatively. He swirled the wine in his glass, "So Giles, it's a shame we have lost a man of Bilic's talents, no?"

Stryckland nodded, "Indeed. His untimely death will be felt most keenly. "

Marat concurred, "Just so. The Americans are becoming anxious. I had another call this morning from Gardner."

"How so?" Stryckland picked at his crab salad.

"They are concerned the British coup will be compromised. These Hacker bastards have been getting uncomfortably close. Then Bilic is murdered. They're wondering if these things are linked. What do you say?"

Stryckland paused momentarily, "They may well be correct. It's rather coincidental, isn't it?"

Marat had a set smile, "You could say that. Although Bilic had made many enemies over the years."

Stryckland placed his knife and fork on his plate. "It's hardly surprising. God knows he wasn't an easy man to deal with."

"It would be unusual for an ordinary businessman to hire a contract killer, though, wouldn't it? Normally they like to take their revenge using money."

"Patron, who knows with Bilic? He infuriated many of his business associates; it could be anyone. He ruined plenty of them. It's hardly surprising if one of them wanted retribution."

Masquerade

Marat didn't look up but casually replied, "You were an associate Giles, did you do it?"

Stryckland didn't miss a beat, "Obviously, we had our difficulties, but that was in the past. I would never harm a Kalyptra member."

"Agreed, that would be most unwise. If you were found out, the penalty would be severe. You know it is impossible to keep a secret from Kalyptra. The young man below will experience Kalyptra's capacity for retribution."

Marat studied Stryckland. He's good, he conceded. Not the slightest sign of tension showed on his face or his body language. Nevertheless, Marat's unfailingly accurate intuition told him Stryckland was responsible for Bilic's murder. On the other side of the Château, Gittins paced along a gravel path puffing furiously on a cigarette. He was still fuming after the browbeating from Stryckland. It gnawed at him. Enough was enough. Requests for promotion had been ignored. His share of sweeteners never materialised. The prospect of a substantial reward forever being offered but never given. It was always, "Just one more job... then everything would be sorted out." Finally, on the plane, the truth hit him. The promises were never going to materialise. Stryckland had strung him along like a fool. Now the 'fool' was going to exact revenge... with interest.

Gittins realised Stryckland badly wanted Dark dead. Gittins also strongly suspected Stryckland was involved with Bilic's murder; it was too convenient for Stryckland. Plus, the man's normal sang-froid had deserted him when he received the call about Dark on his mobile. He had been visibly agitated. Gittins thought the timing was significant. He suspected Stryckland was worried that Dark had known about the connection. It made sense. Stryckland wanted the top job. With Bilic out of the way, he would be a shoo-in... unless they found out who murdered Bilic, of course.

Back on the veranda, Marat dabbed his chin, "Do you think de Braganza can handle the mercenary project?"

"Of course. He has years of experience handling gangs of men."

"Yes, Yes. I know. But he doesn't know the routes through Germany, Holland or Romania. Or the boat captains, for that matter."

"I'm sure he will get to grips with that. He's a natural leader; the gangmasters will respect him.

Masquerade

Marat marvelled at Stryckland's insouciance; perhaps he had underestimated him. "Shall we resume?"

"Of course. But I still think you should just terminate the traitor."

They found Dark had regained consciousness. His face was swollen and bloody. The eyes were completely closed, puffed up bags. Thick gobs of blood caked Dark's face and chest. The giant prodded him; Dark groaned but said nothing.

"Can he answer questions?" Marat asked the giant, who nodded and replied, "He can understand well enough. But who knows if he will talk?" He shrugged. "It's anyone's guess."

Marat fumed, "So, he needs encouragement! Let's see if we can wash that blood away shell we. Strap him on the board."

Marat paced quietly up and down beside a battered, rusty galvanised bath. The giant dragged Dark over to the board and secured the straps. One end of the board was hinged above the bath. The other end could be raised or lowered into the bath using a simple lever. The giant filled the bath with cold water. When the board was lowered, anyone strapped to it would be submerged, apart from their feet. It was a variation of the American's waterboarding technique.

Dark was conscious enough to struggle; he could hear but not see the water filling the bath. Marat stood next to the lever, dispassionately watching the prisoner's futile exertion.

"Now, young man, where did we get to? Ah yes. I want to know who you are. The next few minutes will be extremely unpleasant for you if you don't cooperate. Answer my questions, and you will stay out of the water. Refuse, and I'll submerse you. Every time you fail to answer, you will be held under for longer until I leave you there permanently. Do you understand?"

Dark said nothing.

"Very well." Marat lowered Dark's head into the freezing water. He left him there for a few seconds before lifting him. "Well? What do you think? Is it worth a name?"

Dark gasped and spat out water but said nothing.

Once again, the polite enquiry, "Name?"

No response. Marat submersed Dark completely. He left him there for half a minute before lifting him out. Dark choked and gasped desperately for breath and tried to blow water from his nostrils. But still, he said nothing.

Stryckland interrupted Marat. "For Christ's sake. We're going to be here all day. Why not give him the truth drug then shoot him."

"Giles! You are too impatient. This is an art. You need to appreciate this fact for future reference. Breaking a man down is one of the most satisfying experiences you will ever have. It is a journey, and each step must be walked. When the break finally comes, it is an intimate moment shared between victim and inquisitor. It creates a strong bond between them. Both of you reach altered states of consciousness. It has been this way for thousands of years. To truly own your opponent, you are constrained to do this. Drugs do not facilitate this symbiosis: pain must be experienced and endured in order to break the spirit and alter consciousness. It is not to be rushed."

Gittins nodded. He had noticed a subtle change between the two men since the lunch break. There was a definite undercurrent, an unspoken dialogue between Marat and Stryckland. Gittins knew something was worrying Stryckland, who was uncharacteristically nervous — nothing a stranger would notice, but to someone familiar, the signs were there: small jerky movements, adjusting and readjusting his tie, removing imaginary fluff from his sleeve. What was unsettling him?

Marat was still giving his lecture, "This young man is trying to keep his secrets safe. He understands if he gives me just one piece of information, it is the beginning of an inexorable journey of betrayal. He knows he will give control of his very soul to me. It is not something one relinquishes lightly. Now I am going to break him. It will take some time; I suspect this is a resourceful individual. But it will be worth the wait. He must be one of his organisation's best men. Imagine the secrets he can tell. When he breaks, he will give us the key to destroy his infuriating network. There is the appealing possibility of turning him against his own people. Trust me, Giles, I know what I'm doing!"

Stryckland looked unconvinced. "If you say so. But I still think this is a special situation. We're too near the coup to waste time breaking him. We need to know if anyone knows about our plans straight away. And that means drugging him. But, it's your decision."

Masquerade

Marat glared at Stryckland before turning his attention back to Dark.

Gittins felt a shiver run down his spine; he was a tough, seasoned street fighter. He had stood toe to toe with the most hardened criminals Europe had to offer. But there was a casual brutality to Marat that frightened him. Despite this, he wanted to hear what Dark knew. If Stryckland wasn't going to reward him, there might be a way for him to get it somewhere else, and his meal ticket was the person strapped to the board. Gittins had pieced together enough information over the years to know what Kalyptra was all about. There were people who would pay substantial amounts of money to have that information. Enough for him to retire and disappear. Perhaps even this guy's principals would pay him.

And then Dark's near-death experience resumed: the board submerged, and the victim choked to the point where the lungs started filling with water. The board was lifted and water forcibly expelled by the giant. Dark passed between bare consciousness and total oblivion.

Dark didn't speak, and so the routine continued. Marat timed the immersions perfectly. He watched air bubbles froth from the victim's mouth and nostrils as the lungs fought for air. Once the bubbles stopped, he waited a few seconds before lifting the board clear of the water. The giant leaned on Dark's diaphragm, squeezing water from his saturated lungs. Marat allowed the victim a few moments respite, then submerged him once more, repeating the torture.

For his part, Dark uttered not a word. He choked, passed out and vomited, but never once did he look at Marat. With each episode of non-acquiescence, the arch inquisitor began to lose patience. He had not been presented with this situation before. After ten or so submersions, his victim's resistance normally broke, and the process of extracting the truth began. As his patience disappeared, so he reverted to cruder methods. He beat Dark with a wooden stick. Dark still remained silent. Eventually, Marat's frustration reached boiling point. Inquisitors in Guantanamo broke prisoners after ten immersions. So far, Dark had endured more than twenty.

Gittins looked on quietly. Even with his casual approach to brutality, he was appalled at Dark's treatment. There would be a great deal of money to be made and a score to be settled with Stryckland. Gittins reasoned that if Dark had lived for years without appearing on the government's systems, then he could make Gittins disappear. Who knows how many non-persons there were in the world. Hundreds? Thousands? Tens of Thousands? The germ of an idea began to take shape.

After two hours, the normally immaculate Marat was drenched in sweat and venting his frustration against the wall. In thirty years of vicious inquisition, never before had a prisoner defeated him. He was unable to control his temper any longer. Dark lay unconscious on the board; his body was beginning to break down. He was passing out more frequently. Severe oxygen depletion meant his body took longer to recover after each resuscitation.

Marat shook with rage as he stormed out, "I need a break! Get the damn serum and a recorder. Draw the maximum dose, then wait for me... I'll be thirty minutes. When we've finished, you can kill the bastard and get rid of the body." Marat beckoned Stryckland to follow him. Gittins followed at a distance. At the doorway, he turned and watched as the giant placed Dark on a trolley and wheeled it under a set of spotlights.

"Careless, very careless," Gittins muttered; he waited outside the door for the giant to leave. Now it was payback.

Masquerade

Chapter 51: Improbable Allies

Gittins walked out into the night. He closed the heavy wooden door softly. He needed to think about his next move carefully.

The cosy relationship with Stryckland was dead. He had a substantial nest egg deposited with a Spanish bank. He had always dreamed of retiring to one of the Costas. His mother had been particularly fond of the Costa del Sol – that would suit him nicely. "Stryckland can stick his Machiavellian shenanigans," he mused. "These Whitehall bastards were all the same: obnoxious, arrogant prigs. They think they're better than the rest of us. Well, I'll show them who really pulls the strings."

He took a fresh pack of cigarettes from his pocket and lit one. He stood at the edge of the veranda looking out over Marat's formal gardens, bathed in bright monochromatic moonlight. The night was comfortably cool and calm. Not a sound could be heard apart from the whisper of a light breeze tugging at nearby trees. It was the only reason he heard the quiet crunch of gravel immediately followed by a quiet click. Instinctively Gittins threw himself over the stone parapet into the void beyond the veranda. He felt and heard a hot buzzing as a bullet zinged millimetres away from his head.

"Bastard!" He landed face-first in a large rhododendron bush which scratched and clawed him as he plunged through the foliage. He hit the ground hard and lay dazed and winded. He waited for a few seconds as he caught his breath. The deadly 'phut' of more bullets aimed speculatively in close proximity got him on his feet and moving rapidly. Still struggling for breath, he stumbled through the undergrowth away from danger. Hidden rocks and sharp branches made the going treacherous and frustratingly slow, though thankfully, he was hidden from view by dense foliage. Whoever was shooting at Gittins hadn't heard him run off; the area he had jumped into was still being targeted. He dropped to the ground in a small thicket and tried to get his breathing under control while cursing Stryckland; he must be behind this.

After twenty minutes of painfully crawling to the edge of the shrubbery, he found himself a hundred yards away from the veranda. His next obstacle was a wide limestone path, which to his dismay, shone brightly in the moonlight. "Damn!" If he moved out from the undergrowth, he would be seen clearly from the veranda. Cautiously he peered out at the night sky; the moon was radiant in a cloudless iridescent night sky. He squatted on his haunches, weighing up his options. To his left, the path ran parallel to

Masquerade

the veranda and would take him back towards danger. Beyond the path and in front of him lay the formal gardens, short trimmed hedges, and flower beds. Nothing higher than his knee, no cover there. To the right, the path ran back around the side of the Château. But beyond that lay several acres of thick woodland – plenty of cover. The only problem was the fifty yards of manicured lawn that separated him from safety. Even at a run, it would take him ten seconds at least. If the marksman saw him break cover, he would have a couple of shots at least. Those weren't favourable odds. Everything considered it was the only realistic option he had. Slowly he unbent himself and turned to peer over the top of the rhododendron bushes. He scanned the veranda for signs of life. There were none; whoever was shooting had come down after him, so he'd better move quickly or risk getting caught.

He listened intently for the slightest sound; only a dog fox called for his mate in the middle distance. Gittins cursed it, then concentrated on the silence once more. He waited for an age but heard nothing. He peered cautiously to the left then right. Satisfied there were no untoward movements in the shadows, he stood up straight, keeping well back in the undergrowth. His heart pounded, his breathing was fast and shallow. His shirt was soaked with sweat despite the cool night. He could barely bring himself to take the first step. He knew they were out there waiting for him to make a move. He'd seen at least fifty guards on the way into the Château as he arrived. He had little doubt that most of those would now be around the grounds looking for him. This is Stryckland's doing, bastard! He inhaled deeply, trying to settle his nerves. The pulse at his temples pounded so hard it made him see double. "Bloody Hell! Can't wait here forever."

He took another deep breath and sprinted across the killing zone. As he hit the path, the leg propelling him forward slipped on the gravel, and he half stumbled before regaining his balance, another stride and he was on the grass and found the rhythm of the sprint. He focused on the tree line, measuring the distance with every stride. It took an eternity. Despite playing Sunday football, Gittins was chronically unfit. His lungs felt as if they would burst; snatched breaths seared the back of his throat. But a mixture of terror and adrenaline forced him onward despite the pain. Distant shouts signalled imminent danger. He was only halfway. "Dear God, give me strength." His legs felt like lead; he gritted his teeth and forced them to keep pumping. The angry buzz of hot metal zipped past him. Too close for comfort. Divots of grass kicked up around him. Another ten yards, and he would be safe. Then his legs gave up the fight; he half stumbled but somehow managed to keep going. His burning lungs sucked in jagged breaths. He pumped his arms in a vain effort to keep going. He felt a light tap on his left shoulder as if someone had nudged him. It was enough to send him sprawling onto the grass. But not enough to stop him scrambling on all fours over the last couple of yards to the relative safety of the trees.

Gittins scrabbled through the pine cones and needle-strewn floor of the wood. A concentrated fusillade of bullets tore chunks out of the trees around him, peppering him with razor-sharp splinters. He could hear the shouts of guards directing reinforcements to concentrate more firepower in his direction. Fifty yards in, the hail of lead had diminished enough for him to chance standing. He chose a large oak tree to hide behind. He wiped the sweat from his face and peered through the gloom, looking for a route through the densely packed trees. Nothing! He decided to set off at a tangent to the line of fire, hoping his pursuers would plough straight on. He needed to throw them off his trail. He waited for a moment listening. The fusillade of gunfire had reduced to stuttering speculative shots. The odd shout drifted through the night air. He wasn't fooled by this hiatus. He knew the guards were quiet because they were setting up an organised search for him. He had little doubt there would be dogs chasing him very soon.

Gingerly he examined the wound; it was the size of a euro in his left shoulder. He fished a handkerchief out of his pocket. Unable to see the wound in the dark, Gittins bit down hard on his cigarette lighter, and he poked the handkerchief into the exit wound. He had to stop a couple of times when he thought he was going to pass out. But eventually, he managed to stop the flow of blood.

Where could he run? He had no transport; Stryckland's car had driven them from the airport. He had no idea of the topography of the countryside surrounding the Château. He decided to put more distance between him and his pursuers, then work out a plan of action. He knew it was useless to run blindly onwards, hoping for something to turn up. His eyes had by now become accustomed to the murkiness of the wood. He cut across a large drainage ditch to his left and decided to find a route to the top of a large bank he could just make out about half a mile away.

Masquerade

From the summit of a mound, Gittins crouched low amidst tussocks of rough grass surveying the landscape. To his left in the distance, perhaps a mile away, lay the Château. Lights shining brightly in the night. He noticed there was a lot of activity around the stable yard and outbuildings, which lay to one side of the Château. A large group of men, he estimated around fifty gathered to one side of the yard. On the other side, an assortment of flatbed trucks and four-wheel-drive vehicles were being parked. The hunt for him was extending to the whole estate. They were quite obviously being sent to the remote parts of the estate to look for him. He peered back down to the woods, looking for signs of a search party behind him. If they managed to throw a cordon of men around the perimeter of the estate meant he would soon be trapped. It would be impossible to outrun them. It had taken them half an hour to travel from the main gates to the Château. It would take him at least two hours to walk that distance even when he was fit. Now he was injured, it would take hours – assuming he wasn't caught, which was likely. He decided that option was impractical. He looked for an alternative. He found he was pretty much in the middle of a large wood. Further to the west, away from the Château lay open parkland, beyond that grazing land for cattle. Then arable crop pastures. Most of the land was open, with very few places for concealment. Looking to the south seemed a better option. A river meandered through water meadows with copses scattered along its path. He had noticed cattle grazing there from the terrace. He couldn't see northward beyond the Château nor eastward for the same reason. He didn't seem to have many choices. His shoulder was throbbing. He needed to make a decision quickly. But what should he do? Where could he hide undetected until they gave up searching?

Gittins quietly eased himself into the chill water of the slow-running river. He tugged a loose tree trunk away from the bank until it floated free. He positioned himself so that he was hidden from anyone on the bank, then held on to a branch and let the tree take him downstream towards the Château. He had stumbled and crawled his way to the bottom of the mound and through the trees into the river just before the guards had reached the summit. There were still some guards moving along the bank, but they were all headed west away from their muster point; soon, the bank would be deserted. The rest of the guards were fanning out towards the perimeter of the estate. He was gambling that the only place they wouldn't look would be the Château; he would hide there for a few hours until things quietened down.

Masquerade

He peered over the log and found he had drifted almost beyond the Château. He let go and paddled quietly to the bank. He crouched half in half out of the water, trying to stop his teeth chattering as he shivered in the cold night air. The moon was still bright in the starry, cloudless sky. Cold as he was, he took his time scanning the monochrome surroundings for the slightest sign of movement. After a full five minutes, he was satisfied the coast was clear and carefully pulled himself on top of the grassy bank and lay flat on his stomach, hardly daring to breathe. Ears pricked in anticipation of a shouted warning. Despite the knots in his stomach, he stayed prone on the bank, carefully checking for guards. Slowly he got to his feet. His shoulder throbbed from the cold. He walked quietly to the shadow of a box hedge, following its shadow to the side where he could climb through a rockery up to the veranda he had jumped from earlier that night; from there, he could easily get to the room where the Dark was held.

Once more, he checked the coast was clear before he climbed over the veranda wall. He was aware he stood out like a beacon as he walked across the veranda, silhouetted against the moonlit white walls of the Château. He reached the door to the cellar and gently prised it open a crack. There was no guard beyond; it hadn't even been locked. He slipped through the door and closed it quietly behind him, then slowly crept down the stairs. He heard nothing as he descended into darkness. He panicked momentarily at the thought that they may have moved Dark somewhere else. Abruptly there were no more steps; he had reached the cellar. The place was completely dark apart from a very faint glow in one corner. Gittins remembered the forge. Quietly he sat down on the bottom step and waited. He wanted his eyes to become accustomed to the darkness.

Gittins shivered. He wasn't sure whether it was because of his wet clothes or whether it was nerves. He padded softly across the room to where he thought Dark lay on the rack. He was walking almost blind and held his arms in front of him, feeling his way. He thought he was about halfway when his foot struck something solid; he bent down cautiously, feeling for the obstruction. His hand felt cold skin, he moved his hand some more then he heard a groan. "This must be Dark." He fumbled in his pocket for a lighter. A couple of clicks later, it produced a small dull light. Gittins moved it following the shape of the body until he got to the bloody and swollen head. He needed to look very closely to make sure it was Dark. Both eyes were swollen blue-black and shut tightly. Dried blood crusted around his nose and mouth. His face was a mess. Gittins wasn't even sure he was alive. He bent over, placed his ear close to Dark's mouth, and waited... and waited. At last, he breathed a sigh of relief. He felt the faintest breath on his cheek; Dark was alive – just. His plan to wait for a few hours wasn't feasible now; he needed to find medical help for Dark as soon as he could. If he died, he wouldn't get his revenge. He ripped the straps from the congealed blood on Dark's wrists and ankles. Dark moaned quietly then jerked into consciousness.

"Bastard."

Gittins hissed, "Shut up! I'm getting you out!"

Dark slumped back on the trolley, unconscious once more. Gittins was relieved, "he's got more life in him than I thought. Perhaps we've still got a chance."

Gittins decided he would have to risk turning the lights on. He would need to find something to move Dark. He remembered there was a control panel near the door. Gingerly he walked in the general direction. Using his lighter, he examined the switches carefully until he found the lights then turned them on.

He found an ancient wooden coal cart. It had been left next to a decaying wooden door obscured by the forge. Gittins had not noticed it before. It looked incongruous given the antiseptic neatness of the rest of the room. He turned the door's iron handle and pushed it inwards. The sagging rusty hinges creaked in protest as Gittins heaved and peered into the silent darkness beyond. He let his eyes adjust to the darkness. In the distance, he could make out a faint blue-grey light. Before him, he could just about see roughly hewn stone walls. Was this an old tunnel that led out to the Château grounds? If so, then this was his escape route. Quietly he closed the door then carefully manoeuvred Dark onto the cart. He wasn't sure if Dark could hear him but spoke to him anyway.

"Hold tight I'm going to get you out of here. It might be a bumpy ride. If it gets too much, let me know, but don't shout out; we have to get past a lot of guards."

The trip through the tunnel proved uneventful. The floor was well paved and even. Dark wasn't jostled too much. At the mouth of the tunnel, Gittins paused and quietly checked for signs of movement. He saw nothing. In the grey light cast by the moon, most of the garden was visible. There were no guards, dogs or lights. Nonetheless, Gittins moved cautiously, constantly scanning for any movement. Gravel crunched softly under the iron wheels of the cart. Dark didn't cry out. As Gittins pulled the cart along the path and rounded a corner, he saw three or four service vans parked for the night. He smiled, just the break he needed. For an East End boy, hotwiring a van was as easy as falling off a log. Resisting the urge to hurry and keeping in the shadow of a high box hedge, he soon reached the vehicles. A quick check found one that wasn't even locked. A few moments later, Dark was installed in the back. Gittins pushed the cart into the hedge, hotwired the van and coasted down a service road in a matter of a minute. They were clear. All the guards must be searching for him at the other end of the estate where he had first managed to dodge the bullet. He shook his head in disbelief. These people were too arrogant; they'd had things their own way for far too long. He was going to change that, big time.

Fifteen minutes later, he drove into a small village. There were no lights showing; it was four in the morning. Gittins felt safe enough to pull into the side of the road at the far end of the houses. Gently he shook Dark, "Where can I take you? Where will your friends be?"

Dark looked dully at him. "How can I trust you? You've been hunting me down for years."

Gittins looked perplexed, "I had a fallout with Stryckland on the plane over here, and then while you were out cold, they tried to shoot me – I'm on your side now... and believe me, I know where the bodies are buried. I can help you take these people down."

Gittins controlled his rising anger.

"Look, I'm your only chance right now. You people have been sniping around at the edge of Stryckland and Kalyptra's activities. All you've got is 'smoking guns', but I can give you specific names and tell you where the money goes... put names to places and events. With information like that, you can destroy these people to such an extent it will take them decades to recover. What's more important to me is to teach these bastards a lesson and make enough money to disappear. And to do that, I need you. Think about it; we both get what we want. Be sensible, let me take you to your friends. They can patch you up, and I can give them all the information they want. So where do we go?"

Dark slumped on the van floor. He was quiet for a long time. Gittins looked at him, trying to gauge his reaction, but Dark's face was clothed in shadow. Gittins was about to make another appeal when Dark moaned, "Geneva, take me to Geneva."

As Gittins drove away from the village, he calculated the trip to Geneva would take about eight hours in the service van. Dark would have to give him a specific address once they were there. Dark had settled as best as he could on a pile of rags and appeared to be asleep. Briefly, Gittins considered changing his purpose in taking Dark to Geneva. Once Dark gave him the address, he'd then know where the hacker's secret base was located. He could phone Marat, telling him he had duped Dark into letting him take Dark back to his friends and thereby finding the people who had put Kalyptra in such jeopardy. He knew Stryckland and Bilic had been desperate to put an end to the constant public announcements about Kalyptra by shutting down the hacker network. If he did it, it would certainly put him back at the top table.

However, he couldn't let go of his anger at Stryckland and the Establishment; he needed revenge more than another empty promise. He needed to lance the boil and then move on. Only weak people let insults pass without reprisal, and he was not weak.

Gittins pulled the van over onto a grass verge. His adrenaline levels had dropped, and he felt exhausted. He needed a break. Gittins checked his watch: four-thirty. He glanced over at Dark, still unconscious but breathing.

Gittins picked up Dark's mobile and muttered, "Now, time to even the score, Home Secretary!"

Heinz's phone vibrated insistently, but he didn't dare get it as he needed both hands and all of his concentration to keep his car on the road as he sped along the Boulevard Périphérique after escaping Marat's guards. Eventually, Susie had the presence of mind to get the phone from his jacket.

"It's George."

Heinz muttered through gritted teeth, "Put it on loudspeaker... George? Where the hell are you?"

"I've got Dark; he's hurt but safe."

"Bloody Hell! Is that Marat?"

"No... no names yet. We need to talk; you'll get your friend back, and we will discuss something for our mutual benefit." Gittins had initially considered taking Dark to Geneva, but the journey would be too much for him. "Where are you?"

Heinz hesitated, "Not far from Paris."

"Good... I'll be at the main entrance to the Hippodrome de Longchamps in the Bois de Boulogne six this evening?"

"I'll be there. Just make sure George is safe."

Gittins grimaced, "Just make sure you're there at six..."

Chapter 52: Inside Information

"We're coming in to land; please fasten your seat belts."

The stewardess gently nudged Dark awake. Susie's head rested on his shoulder. She, too, had slept for the whole flight from Paris.

"Wake up; we're nearly there."

"Did I sleep the whole time? How do I look?"

"You look fine."

Susie fastened her seat belt and fussed with her hair. "Are you feeling better? I'm dreading this next bit. I don't know how I'm going to manage to pull it off."

Susie was worried about getting through Passport Control with forged documents and a disguise, despite reassurances from Dark, to whom it was second nature. He tried to persuade Susie that everything would be fine if she acted normally. "Don't look around or look up. Just relax and look ahead, try not to yawn or fake a mood: the officials are trained to look out for unnecessary gestures and ask questions of the people making them."

Susie wasn't convinced it would be so straightforward.

They disembarked last after the other passengers had made their way out. The stewardesses helped Dark into a wheelchair. He was still suffering from Marat's interrogation. Susie dropped her bags in his lap and pushed him to the end of the queue in the crowded arrivals hall. They joined the line for EU Nationals.

Periodically the line shuffled along. "I don't suppose you are used to queuing? I bet you usually step straight off your private jet and get escorted through a VIP entrance, eh?" teased Dark.

"Well, now you mention it, this is a new experience. I wish I could say I'm enjoying it."

"You're doing fine. Just keep chatting about anything you think of. We'll look like any other ordinary boring couple who just want to grab their bags and get on with their holiday."

Gradually they neared the front of the queue; despite his injuries, Dark kept up a flow of inane small talk. Susie managed to maintain the masquerade

Masquerade

by quietly chatting and smiling. Occasionally glancing down at him but never looking around or giving the CCTV cameras a clear picture of her face.

As they waited behind the white line, Dark murmured, "You've done really well. This is actually the easy part. Remember neutral expression. When he checks your passport, look him in the eye for a couple of seconds, then look away. Here we go." Dark handed the passports to an impassive faced official behind the glass.

The Border Control officer dragged their passports toward him. He had been watching these two since they joined his queue. Good looking couple, especially the girl, pity about the bloke in the wheelchair. He scrutinised them carefully whilst he felt for the thick plastic photo page. Without taking his eyes off them, he scanned first one passport then the other, briefly glancing at his computer monitor for the results before inspecting the passports themselves. He looked from face to picture and back, slowly drawing the moment out, frowning slightly. He kept them waiting. What was it with pretty people; life was too easy for them. They never had to fight to survive like normal people. Hearing his supervisor walk up behind him, he quickly closed the passports.

"Anything wrong, Scarman?"

"No, just checking everything is in order."

"And is it?"

"Yes, Sir."

"Then let them through, Scarman. Remember the Department targets. You need to play your part. Understood?"

"Yes, sir!"

Scarman glared at the couple as he shoved their passports back under the glass partition.

Dark leaned back and held Susie's hand as they made their way down a featureless corridor decorated in various insipid shades of blue towards the customs gate and the departure hall.

Susie gasped, "God! I thought he was going to arrest us when the supervisor came over. I'm shaking all over. My legs feel like jelly."

"I think the Supervisor gave him a ticking off for holding up the queue."

They hurried through the departure hall and followed signs for the taxi rank.

Two hours later, the taxi dropped them off in Firborough Road, and Dark directed Susie north to their safe house in Hogarth Road. By now, Susie instinctively mimicked Dark's habit of lowering her face as she walked along. Ten minutes later, they passed unnoticed to the door of their temporary hideout, a small nondescript flat owned by the friend of an activist.

Inside, Susie collapsed onto a small battered sofa, "God, I'm shattered and starving; how do you cope? I'm completely stressed out."

Dark began a thorough examination of the flat, "Oh, you get used to it. You learn to trust your skills. It's not as difficult as you imagine. Come on, let's get settled. I need something to eat as well. There are some microwave meals in the fridge. Then I need to get ready for tomorrow; it's going to be a long day."

Dark roused himself at two o'clock in the morning. He had dozed on the sofa while Susie had gone to bed. He was disguised as a street cleaner so he would fit into the nocturnal urban landscape perfectly. This was the time the workmen from the Council normally carried out maintenance and street cleaning. In his high visibility jacket and overalls, he would pass muster from a casual glance. He closed the door of the flat and made his way down the rear service stairs out of the back door. From a shed at the rear of the property, he retrieved a street cleaner's handcart that had seen better days – another invaluable prop provided by Heinz. Dark steeled his aching body and pushed the cart quietly down the narrow alleyway, careful not to attract neighbourly attention. He didn't want any night owls witnessing his departure. His target was in Holland Park, thirty minutes away. He reached Cromwell Road and glanced left then right. The road was deserted. Orange street lights cast a melancholy glow over the road. Satisfied the coast was clear, Dark trundled the cart down the road, using it as a prop to support his aching limbs until they loosened up.

Meanwhile, twenty thousand feet over the Midlands, ensconced in a Government jet, Stryckland fidgeted in his seat. He was anxious and found it increasingly difficult to hide the fact. The small overheated cabin of the aeroplane made him feel claustrophobic, which didn't help. Why the hell had Prime Minister made the last-minute decision to send him to Edinburgh instead of going himself? It was typical of the bloody man. The PM's erratic behaviour had very nearly scuppered his preparations for the coup. He had relied on the PM habitually following routine in everything he did. A last-minute change of plans was alarming, to say the least. He should have spent all day in the office overseeing last-minute preparations for the coup d'état. Instead, he had been forced to run this menial favour like some bloody errand boy. Anyone in the cabinet could have opened the factory, but it seemed the PM took every opportunity to remind Stryckland of his place in the pecking order. Little did the bastard know how quickly that was going to change!

Stryckland's Private Secretary lurched down the aisle, "We're ten minutes from Northolt, Sir. Would you fasten your seatbelt, please?"

The Right Honourable Giles Stryckland and his entourage were escorted by Special Branch officers from the Bombardier jet across the rain-drenched tarmac to a waiting fleet of Jaguar limousines. North London's RAF Northolt was used frequently by Government officials who valued its privacy and proximity to central London. They would reach Whitehall in thirty minutes under blue lights. Stryckland pressed the intercom, "Driver, fast as you can to the Home Office, please."

He needed to contact his field commanders urgently. It was imperative they were ready. There had been frantic text messages back and forth all day. Where the hell was he? He was supposed to be in London overseeing last-minute preparations for the next day. Eventually, he had placated them all, but he needed to reassert his authority tonight with a phone call to each of them. He pictured the schedule: during the early hours of the next morning, they would move into position close to their targets, ready to strike. All this would happen minutes before the Prime Minister was gunned down along with hundreds of spectators at the Manchester rally. A major terrorist attack would be cited as the reason to declare Martial Law, and Stryckland would seize control of the country, providing the calm leadership needed in a National Emergency. It was imperative his command team trusted his leadership

As the convoy of limousines sped through the rain-soaked night, Stryckland mentally processed the details of his commander's objectives for the next day. He wanted to check everything was in order. His first call would be de Braganza. He had been put in charge of Bilic's mercenaries. They had been assigned infrastructure targets; several large reservoirs feeding major conurbations would have their dams bombed. Two large food distribution warehouses would have their stock contaminated. The oil refinery near Southampton would be bombed. Brigadier Sir Charles Haughton, with squads of paratroopers, would support the Legionnaires at TV and radio stations in London. Bristol, Manchester and Newcastle. The Air Chief Marshall was due to commandeer and block Heathrow, Gatwick, Manchester and Liverpool airports using military transport planes.

There needed to be enough chaos to provide the press with sufficient evidence of widespread acts of terror, but not so much that he could not recover the situation without causing himself too many problems. Last on his list was General Richard Dunham; with a squad of British ex-Forces, Dunham would run the clean-up operation. There would be no inconvenient witnesses to the subterfuge. Bilic's legionnaires and mercenaries would be eradicated after they had completed their assignments. Kalyptra demanded discretion.

Just as Stryckland started his journey home down the Great North Road into London, Dark carefully closed the first-floor window at the rear of the Stryckland's Holland Park apartment. He stood silently for a good five minutes, listening intently for the slightest indication the apartment was occupied. Satisfied he was alone, he switched on his head torch. It cast a narrow beam around the room, which was richly decorated in a late baroque style. Dark had entered one of the bedrooms; quickly, he made his way to the door and cracked it open – the coast was clear. He found himself in a wide hallway. To his right was a large oak door, the main entrance to the apartment. Swiftly he checked three doors on his side of the hall, another two bedrooms and the dining room. An archway led into the lounge. Dark worked his way down the doors on the opposite side of the corridor: a storeroom, then a locked door. Quickly Dark unpicked the lock and slipped inside.

The torch beam picked out wood-panelled walls. One wall contained a floor to ceiling bookcase full of leather-bound volumes. At the far end of the room, beyond a sofa and easy chairs, was a large table that served as a desk; Dark made a beeline for it. The spotlight picked out the usual office stationery accoutrements: blotter, desk lamp, a neat stack of files... but no computer, he noticed. Swiftly he checked the files; nothing of interest, just some personal correspondence and utility bills. Dark checked behind the frames of prints and maps – nothing. He turned his attention to the bookcase and began examining the shelves closest to him.

Masquerade

Meanwhile, Stryckland's convoy sped through the rain-soaked streets towards the city centre. "Fifteen minutes, Sir." The driver's voice interrupted Stryckland's musing. Suddenly he felt exhausted; nervous tension had caught up with him.

"Driver! I've changed my mind. Take me to Holland Park." It had been a long day, and he needed to freshen up before facing tomorrow's challenge. Besides, he had a personal control centre set up in the study at his apartment; he could quite easily control the initial stages of the coup from there.

The driver acknowledged, "We'll be there in two minutes, Sir."

Back in Stryckland's apartment, Dark had drawn a blank in the study and had moved on to the sitting room. After making a circuit of the large room, he had found an expensive-looking leather briefcase propped against the side of a sofa. Dark didn't have to look any further; inside were details of the coup. Quickly Dark flicked through pages of names, times, maps. Stryckland had been meticulous. The plan for the whole coup was here.

Suddenly Dark heard the soft murmur of voices. The front door opened, and lights in the hallway came on. "Damn!" Quickly he grabbed the briefcase and files and dived behind a sofa, listening intently to the voices in the hall. The light in the sitting room was turned on, and he heard a voice say, "I'll just check the rest of the apartment, Sir." Then, footsteps walking along the hallway. There was a clinking of glass near Dark's position. He held his breath. He could smell whiskey. Someone was having a stiff one. Next, the muffled sound of closing doors. Had he shut the window properly? He hoped there wasn't a breeze to disturb the curtains. Then the footsteps returned. "All clear, Sir. Will you be needing security in the morning?"

"No, Hodges, I'll phone if I need someone."

"Very good, Sir. Goodnight."

The front door slammed shut. Dark gave it a few seconds, then peered cautiously around the edge of the sofa. The room was empty. He stuffed the papers back in the briefcase as he moved stealthily towards the hall. His only escape route was the front door. As he reached the hallway, he checked the coast was clear. Softly he tiptoed the few feet to the front door and gently prised it open; there was no one outside. He was safe!

Masquerade

Just as he pulled the door shut behind him, he heard, "Hodges? Is that you?"

Dark dashed towards the stairwell, only to be confronted by a muscular man in an overcoat coming up the stairs. Hodges had forgotten something and was returning to Stryckland's apartment. He was astonished at the sight of a street cleaner running out of an apartment he had just searched carrying an expensive briefcase and for a moment froze. Whoever was the most surprised at the confrontation, Dark was the first to react. Without breaking stride, he gave Hodges a swift blow to the nose with the heel of his hand, sending the Special Branch officer tumbling backwards down the stairs. Dark leapt over him, fervently hoping there wasn't an accomplice waiting at the bottom.

A cool breeze was a welcome relief as he ran down the street into a row of mews cottages where he had left the handcart. He stuffed the briefcase into the rubbish compartment and walked away, trying to disguise his limp.

Hodges came to just as Dark pushed the trolley out of the mews. As he scrambled upstairs, he radioed to the chauffeur waiting outside, "Did you just see a workman running out of the building?"

"No, nothing here; it's all quiet. Why? What's wrong?"

"Hang on, I need to check the Home Secretary."

Hodges banged loudly on Stryckland's door. Moments later, Stryckland opened it half-dressed. "What's wrong, Hodges?"

"Sir, a workman just assaulted me as he ran away from your floor. Did he try to break in?"

"No. I haven't heard anything since I called after you when you slammed the door."

"What? I didn't slam the door, and I didn't hear you call me. I used the key to close the door quietly as usual."

Stryckland reeled as it dawned on him the slammed door must have been the intruder. He dashed into the sitting room to check the briefcase. It had gone! "Oh, Christ!" His voice shook as he shouted to his bodyguard, "Hodges, raise the alarm. Get MI5 here immediately, plus an armed response squad. This is a National Emergency. Hurry, man, every second is vital; that man has stolen classified material! He has to be caught."

Masquerade

As Dark hastened down Abbotsbury Road, the distant wail of sirens began. "Damn, that was quick." Now he knew they knew the briefcase was missing. He needed to put Kensington High Street behind him before the police locked down the area around Holland Park if he was to have any chance of reaching his hideout. They would also monitor the CCTV cameras, so he had better keep to the back streets. He found a narrow gap in a wall used by builders renovating a house. Dark pulled aside the tarpaulin and shoved the cleaning cart inside. He ripped off his hi-viz jacket and pushed it inside the rubbish bin. Then he grabbed the briefcase and stuffed it under his jacket.

At Melbury Road, the sirens were closer. The Police had systematically cordoned off the area street by street. He ran across the road into the wooded garden of a large house. It would provide him with plenty of cover, and Kensington High Street lay just beyond. He broke into an ungainly run. Five minutes later, he crossed the High Street and ran down St Mary Abbot's Place. More sirens wailed as police cars hurtled back and forth, frantically searching for him. Above, he heard the thump of a helicopter flying low. He would need to get a move on, the search was still behind him, but it was getting too close for comfort. Dark was certain once he got past Earl's Court Exhibition Centre, he had a straightforward route to the flat.

That was the theory, at least! Dark reached West Cromwell road without incident. Using the plentiful tree cover, he was able to hide from several Police patrols. He noticed they were all heavily armed and in riot gear. He felt for his taser. Cromwell Road was a significant obstacle – two lanes-wide in each direction, plenty of CCTV, not much cover. His only advantages were the stand of mature trees growing on the traffic island and a row of trees on the far side of the road. More worrying was the armed Police van parked across the carriageway a hundred yards up the road. Cautiously he looked for signs of a patrol. A pair of Policemen were patrolling on the far side of the van facing away from him. He could see the head and shoulders of another copper on the passenger side of the van talking to someone inside. They didn't seem to be paying attention to the road. There was no traffic. The street lighting was good, so he couldn't find any useful shadow. As he watched, a dog patrol van pulled up, and two policemen got out and walked to the back of the van to release the dogs. That made Dark's mind up; if the dogs caught his scent, he was dead. He had to cross now. He hesitated for a second, then crouching low, he ran to the trees in the

Masquerade

middle of the road. Once hidden in the shadows, he paused to catch his breath. There hadn't been any shouts of alarm. Cautiously, he moved to the edge of the tree line and studied this side of the road. To his left, the vans were still in plain sight, although the patrol wasn't visible. To his right, the road was empty, although he could see the reflection of blue lights bouncing off the white-painted buildings lining the road. There were no patrols visible. Okay, he just needed to time his run to the trees on the other side. He crouched low, checked both sides again and was about to run when he felt cold steel shoved into his neck.

"Don't move a bloody muscle, or I'll blow your damn head off!"

Dark froze. Where the hell had this guy come from? It was as black as pitch under the trees. The copper was invisible in his riot gear. But Dark was dressed in black too. Slowly he pulled the taser from his pocket. The copper would be wearing a stab vest; his vulnerable points would be neck and groin. Dark was crouching down. He felt the pressure on his neck relax very slightly, then heard the click on the copper's radio. Abruptly Dark swivelled around and jabbed the taser deep into the man's groin. He heard a strangled gasp then felt the copper's limp body crumple on top of him. He let it fall gently to the ground. The radio buzzed with static. But there was no response. Dark peered back into the gloom under the trees, looking for the copper's mate. It was too dark to see anything. Then he turned his attention to the road. No one was looking his way. He took a deep breath and limped to the other side. Again he waited under the trees expecting a shout or even a shot – but nothing. The strobing flash of Police emergency lights made Dark dizzy, but there was no alarm at his crossing, nothing but silence.

The following morning the first phase of the coup began.

Barton Airfield was a small private flying club on the outskirts of Manchester. It was only six o'clock, but Heinz and Gittins had persuaded the caretaker to open up and make them instant coffee.

The caretaker shuffled into the clubroom, tentatively grappling with two steaming mugs, "Here you go, gentlemen. I'm sure the Committee will have something to say when I tell them about this... not procedure, you know."

Heinz smiled and tried to pacify him, "I know it's unusual, but it's an emergency; DCI Gittins here is on the job and needed to get back to the UK urgently."

Masquerade

The caretaker harrumphed, "Something to do with that Prime Minister do at the Town Hall, is it?"

Gittins smiled, "Something like that, yes."

The caretaker walked away, "I'll let you get on. I might as well open up now you've disturbed my routine."

Gittins turned to Heinz, "Where are your boys?"

"They're flying into Manchester Airport. Thye should be landing anytime now. We'll meet them at the university, we'll borrow one of the IT labs and hack into the Home Office System. That'll give us their schedule."

Gittins calculated the various scenarios, "Are you sure you can block Stryckland's broadcast?"

"Yes, we've got that covered; our guys are experienced hackers. But can we rely on your lads?"

Gittins laughed, "You can always rely on East End lads, mate. Don't you worry, they're on their way."

Chapter 53: Antidote

Susie gunned the Mercedes hard up the slip road and onto the motorway. Early morning traffic was sparse, and in her eagerness to leave London behind, she quickly hit a hundred. In the passenger seat, Dark reviewed Stryckland's plans. As soon as he had reached the safety of the flat, he had shaken Susie awake, "Come on, we need to leave! The Police know Stryckland has been burgled. I've got the plans; we need to make ourselves scarce."

They had found a powerful old Mercedes saloon in the next street to their flat. Dark had cracked the locks and started the engine with practised ease. Susie drove while he ducked down in the back seat keeping out of sight. The Police had saturated the Holland Park area. To avoid them, Susie had driven south, then west, then north. The detour cost them an hour before they picked up the motorway out of London. Only then had Dark felt safe enough to sit up and check through the contents of the briefcase.

It was early morning, and according to Stryckland's notes, the PM was due to speak at two o'clock. They had eight hours to stop a murder and a revolution.

Dark turned to Susie, "Slow down, we're safe now. We don't want to draw attention to ourselves."

Dark fished in his pocket and retrieved a mobile phone, "Heinz! We're on our way... yes, I've got them. The main event is at fourteen hundred. The support acts start fifteen minutes later... not sure; we'll meet you as arranged... say ten? Ciao!"

He turned to Susie, "Can we make Manchester City Centre by ten?"

"I guess. The roads are quiet." Susie was right; the only traffic was a sparse line of juggernauts on the inside lane of the motorway. The heavy traffic was heading towards London on the opposite carriageway. She eased back on the accelerator; George was right. Dark returned to the phone. Soon he would need to direct Heinz's Swiss mercenaries to their precise targets. It was ironic the fate of his country was being decided by two opposing groups of mercenaries. Ordinary people, the ones with the most to lose, were completely unaware of the decades' long power struggle for supremacy that was about to reach its climax. If Kalyptra succeeded, it would mean the possibility of having a humane and free society would be lost for generations.

Masquerade

Meanwhile, at various locations around the country, Bilic's mercenaries were leaving their motels and getting into buses and vans which would transport them to their targets. They all carried heavy canvas holdalls; they were dressed in dark combat overalls with a Vanquish logo on the shoulder. They might have outnumbered Heinz and Gittins' crews, but they were unaware they were being stalked by adversaries who knew their whereabouts.

An hour later, Dark called Heinz with instructions. "These are their main targets: Reservoirs at Elan Valley, Derwent Valley in Derbyshire, the fuel depot at Grangemouth, the oil refinery at Fawley and an oil terminal at Milford Haven. Your soldiers need to prevent the attacks on these."

Heinz exclaimed, "Christ, the scheming bastards! We can't possibly cover all of those!"

Dark retorted, "We must! Pick the ones we can reach first. There isn't time to be selective; we just need to disrupt them, knock them off their stride."

Heinz would just have to get on with it. There would be plenty of time to complain later.

"There are more! Listen," Dark continued. "There is a food distribution depot at Rugby, TV transmitters at Sutton Coldfield, Wenvoe and The Wrekin, plus the Ladybower power station. You should be able to cover those; they are closer to you than some of the other targets. The transmitters may be the most important targets of the lot. It's imperative your mercenaries take those and hold them. You will have the benefit of surprise; the last thing Kalyptra will expect at this late stage is any opposition fighting back. We need those transmitters for Susie's broadcast."

Heinz hadn't finished arguing yet, "Christ, George! This is impossible! We have a few hours to stop a meticulously planned military operation run by God knows how many trained mercenaries. Our people are going to get slaughtered."

"Not if you plan it properly. Don't underestimate the element of surprise. Besides, what other choice do we have? Do nothing? Let the bastards keep on ruining our lives. We have to do something to stop them." Dark paused, "Your soldiers have to be ready by one o'clock at the latest. They are going to have to scout their locations and find the Kalyptra squads. Can they do that?"

Masquerade

Heinz replied quietly, "As you say, we have no choice. We must do it."

Dark calmed down. "OK, let's get to the main event. The Prime Minister. He's giving his speech on the Town Hall steps. The plan is for the assassin to take his shot from the roof of an office building opposite the town hall. He can't miss; for an experienced marksman, it's like hitting a barn door from a couple of yards. I'll take out the assassin. I'll need half a dozen soldiers disguised as Policemen to deal with his support team. You'll need soldiers in the square – that should be Gittins' men. It looks as if they are planning on using an explosion to cover their tracks. We need to make sure no one gets hurt. With any luck, the failed assassination will confuse them enough to completely disrupt their plans. As soon as I've dealt with the sniper, I'll signal you. Now, what's the plan for the broadcast?"

Quickly Heinz summarised a short announcement that Susie would record. If the PM survived, he would make it instead and expose the coup. They would use footage recorded by camera operators accompanying each squad of mercenaries. Heinz was going to run it as a continuous loop through the TV transmitters his mercenaries were guarding. This would at least contradict the propaganda that Stryckland would be broadcasting. With the transmitters in their control, they would cover most of the country apart from London.

It was after twelve by the time Dark had completed a covert reconnaissance of the area around the Town Hall. They rushed to meet Heinz in a side street a quarter of a mile behind Herbert House, the assassin's base. Police had cordoned off most of the streets close to the Town Hall. They estimated only a couple of thousand people would gather in the square to see an unpopular PM.

"Are the teams in place?" Dark asked tersely.

Heinz was still subdued after Dark's earlier reprimand, "Yes. Apart from the Elan Valley team, they were caught up in a traffic accident. I've diverted them to the Runcorn oil refinery. The reservoir was a difficult job for one team anyway: the topography was against them, Runcorn will be manageable."

"OK, that's sensible. Are the TV studios and transmitters squads in place?"

"Yes, I've got teams at each location. We think the mercenaries only carry light arms. They were obviously relying on shock tactics to overcome any security they might encounter. As you say, surprise and disguise will be our most effective weapons. The squad leaders don't see any problems taking them out. Gittins will have his men stationed around the PM guarding the platform."

"How are they going to do it?"

"Tear gas. Every site is an enclosed space; even the transmitters have solid perimeter walls. It's enough to contain the gas long enough to disable anyone inside."

Dark was satisfied. He didn't want a firefight or a bloodbath. He would leave the indiscriminate violence to the Corporatist's 'democracy' crusade in the Middle East.

Heinz held up a hand and put the other to his ear, listening to a message on his radio. "We have just taken the Salford studio; now we can use it for our transmission. No casualties. Stryckland is checking each of his teams by radio every fifteen minutes. We'll stay off-air until you give us the signal."

"Wasn't that dangerous? Jumping the gun?"

"I wanted to make sure we had the studio to record the announcement. If we don't get the message out, all this will be in vain."

"Well, let's hope they don't let the cat out of the bag before the main event. Now, you need to get your team as close to the PM as possible, get to the front of the crowd. If the sniper gets a shot off, they will run for cover into the Town Hall. It's imperative you tell the PM about the coup plans and Kalyptra as soon as you can. You might even have to take out his bodyguard to get to him. He is the only person with the authority to stop Stryckland from taking control of Cobra."

Heinz grimaced, "Don't worry! These men are experienced soldiers. They have worked in black ops all over the world. Outside of the SAS, they are the best there is."

"Let's hope so."

Heinz handed Dark a heavy canvas bag, "Here's your gear. And your weapon. It's a silenced Glock and a modified magazine, fifty rounds. You'll have another five magazines like this on your vest. It should be more than enough to deal with the sniper or anything else you run into."

Dark snapped, "I don't intend to use it if at all possible. I want that sniper alive. It's important a witness swears Kalyptra organised the coup. If we haven't got an evidence trail leading directly from the assassination to the Corporatists, they will worm their way out of it and blame some random terrorist attack."

"Well, we'd better catch them red-handed then! How do you plan to stop the sniper?"

"Stun grenade. It will disorient him long enough for me to handcuff his hands and legs. Besides, the noise will create enough confusion for you to move on the PM. Are the men ready to take out the sniper's support team?"

"They're monitoring them as we speak. We scouted the building earlier. There are two guards at the rear fire escape. One on each side and two at each end of the roof. The sniper will set up his position centrally on the roof. He is using an air conditioning duct for cover. The service door is twenty yards from the sniper's position. It's a clear flat roof with only ducts between the door and the sniper."

A police van drove slowly down a road a hundred yards away. To avoid suspicion, Dark, Heinz and Susie moved into a nearby alley, and Dark began to change into the riot police uniform Heinz had given him.

While Dark changed, Heinz began collecting his own gear: a kit bag full of short wave radios, laptops and ammunition. He gave Susie another bag with spare video cameras, "Your script is in there, by the way, so don't lose it." He turned back to Dark. "When you have finished, Gus and Charlie will be waiting here on motorbikes. Drive around to the Town Hall, and the riders will get the PM and Susie over to the studio in Salford. The team will be waiting and will start the broadcast as soon as they arrive. You and I will follow after we clean up in the square."

Stryckland's plans had highlighted the building the sniper was to use to target the Prime Minister. Dark had been dropped off at a service entrance. It had taken him fifteen minutes to climb the stairwell to the roof.

Sure enough, when Dark opened the door a crack, he saw the sniper in position on the eastern side of the building. A powerful sniper's rifle was mounted on a low wall, the shooter lay prone, making last-minute adjustments to the weapon.

Quietly Dark climbed through the door and crouched down, drawing the Glock. The flat roof was jam-packed with ducting and pipework. A hundred potential hiding places for the assassin's accomplices to ambush an

Masquerade

intruder. One duct, waist-high, ran between Dark and the sniper. He would have to climb over that to get to his target. It would be a huge risk. Furtively he scanned the rest of the roof for the sniper's backup. Nothing visible.

Piped music announced the proceedings below were getting underway.

"Well," Dark thought, "now or never."

He sprinted the twenty yards to the duct and crouched down before checking his surroundings once more, all clear. The cacophony from the square below covered Dark as he negotiated the duct without alerting the sniper. Another thirty yards to the target, he checked his watch; he knew the PM would be approaching the lectern at any time. He needed to silence the sniper without delay. As he stood, one of the sniper's support team, thinking Dark was unarmed, jumped up in full view on an adjoining rooftop, assuming he was safe. Dark took aim, the Glock's laser sight projected a red dot on the guard's right shoulder, Dark squeezed the trigger, and the guard collapsed. Quickly he scanned the rooftops for another guard, nothing. Too late to worry about it now, he checked his watch again, now there were only seconds left before PM was due to speak. Dark grabbed a stun grenade, pulled the pin and threw it towards the prone sniper. Dark curled up in a defensive ball.

The blast deafened Dark despite the ear defenders built into his helmet. He looked up as the smoke drifted over across the rooftop. The cacophony from the square below stopped abruptly; the crowd turned, looking for the cause of the explosion. Office alarms blared as Dark sprinted the last few yards to the sniper, who lay dazed, the rifle discarded. Dark kicked it away and grabbed an arm, ready to pin it behind the sniper's back, when suddenly he was felled by a vicious kick to the back of his knee. He collapsed, lost his grip on the arm and was immediately pinned in a headlock. Choking and caught completely off guard, Dark thrashed around trying to free himself. However hard he tried, the vicelike stranglehold held him secure. Gradually after much desperate heaving, Dark managed to turn his head enough to breathe. Then he manoeuvred his fingers deep into the crook of his assailant's elbow joint and began probing and manipulating the nerves. The sniper's grip weakened slightly. Desperately Dark fumbled for his spare Glock; he was beginning to pass out. At last, he yanked the gun out of his holster and, with as much force as he could muster, smashed it against the ball of bone on the outside of the joint. He felt the arm spasm and immediately release its grip. Dark wriggled free, his chest heaving as he sucked in air. The sniper lay moaning on the floor, cradling the shattered joint. Dark grabbed the sniper's good arm and cuffed it, then pulled the shattered arm back to cuff that. The sniper screamed at the pain but then kicked out again, sending Dark flying backwards. Incensed, Dark scrambled to his feet, bellowing at the sniper to lie still. He yanked off the sniper's hood, only to be confronted by a woman. If Dark had been a fly on the wall at a certain villa in the South of France at a particular time, he would have recognised her as the blond masseuse who entertained Bilic to a night of pleasure, then put a neat hole in his forehead that blew his brains out. She also just happened to be one of Stryckland's lovers and a very secret weapon.

Dark gawped, taken completely by surprise. At which the blond jumped up and turned to run, but her foot caught the edge of the ducting, sending her sprawling; she landed hard on her face and skidded over the edge of the roof. Somehow she managed to grab some cabling with her good arm, but her bodyweight tore the cable away from the wall. She dangled a hundred feet above the pavement, face contorted with pain. To lose her grip meant certain death. Dark rushed over and grabbed her wrist, but the handcuff stopped him from getting a firm hold. He could feel his strength ebbing away; Marat's torture had taken its toll on his body. "Hold on, I've got you," he shouted. Screams came from the pavement below as the crowd noticed the drama above them. "Hold on, just don't let go!" Dark shouted. He needed the woman alive. She looked up at him in despair, knowing her strength was failing. Agonisingly, little by little, her grip loosened, and despite Dark's desperate efforts, she plunged to the pavement. Dark fell back exhausted; he heard the flat thud as her body hit the pavement. "Damn!" A wasted life and no evidence.

Dark's radio crackled into life, Gittins's voice was hoarse with adrenaline, "We've grabbed the PM and his entourage. We're going back to their hotel. Forget the studio; meet us there."

Dark raced back down to the street where Heinz and Susie were waiting next to the Mercedes. The Swiss mercenaries had formed a cordon around the street searching for Kalyptra's Legionnaires.

Heinz grabbed Dark, "Come on, Gittins and his men have got the PM safe. We need to take a squad of mercenaries and meet them."

Masquerade

Dark was covered with dust and shards of brickwork. He had a shallow gash on his forehead. Susie attempted to wipe the blood away, "Not now, let's get to the hotel first, then I'm all yours. Can you set up the broadcast from the hotel?"

Manfred grinned. "Of course not a problem."

Dark was beginning to feel they had the edge over Kalyptra, "Well, they couldn't have expected that little intervention."

Twenty minutes later, their Mercedes roared up the hotel's gravel drive and pulled up at the entrance.

A dozen plainclothes police were stationed before the door, all of them armed with stubby machine pistols. The leader stepped forward, "Identify yourselves."

Heinz slammed the car door shut, "I'm Heinz, take me to Gittins."

Inside the PM's suite, Gittins' men were stationed at the windows and doors. Gittins was talking to the PM and his aides when Heinz, Dark and Susie were shown into the room. The PM was in a state of high anxiety; he was gulping a large whisky.

"What the hell just happened? Gittins, why are you leading the security team, not Palmer from MI5?"

"MI5 have been compromised Prime Minister. You have just survived an assassination attempt planned by Giles Stryckland."

The PM gawped at Gittins, "Are you mad? The Home Secretary planned to murder me?"

Heinz stepped forward, "Prime Minister, if you please, DCI Gittins is correct. Your murder was to be the first step in a coup masterminded in part by Stryckland."

"And who the hell are you?"

Heinz stepped closer, "My name is Heinz Gombricht, a retired diplomat for the Austrian Government. Now I coordinate operations for the Hacker Network."

The PM grimaced, "Christ! You're nothing but a bunch of terrorists playing havoc with the Government. Bloody crooks, the lot of you."

Dark pushed aside one of the PM's aides, "The crooks are closer to you than us if you care to open your eyes and look. The corruption has been happening right under your nose?"

"Who the hell do you think you are?"

Dark's temper got the better of him, "That's easy; we're the people who just saved your life. We're the people who know which members of your Government are puppets for big business swindling millions of pounds from the taxpayers and who want you dead. That's who the hell we are!"

Dark's outburst punctured the PM's bombast.

Heinz stepped forward, "Prime Minister, for some time, our organisation has been collecting evidence of widespread corruption instigated by multi-national corporations. They have been determined to take total control of the British Government and eventually every Government in Europe. You had to be killed and replaced by Stryckland for their plan to work. To prevent any further security threats, you must appear on television and announce to the country that you have survived an assassination attempt and are taking control of the operation to bring those responsible to justice."

The PM slumped onto a sofa, "Why? For god's sake, we bend over backwards for these American corporations as it is. Will their greed never be satisfied?"

While the conversation between the PM and Heinz had been going on, Dark had been thinking deeply. He understood Kalyptra; he was convinced they wouldn't give up until Stryckland was in Number 10. "We need to get the PM to a safe place." He turned to the PM, "Where is the nearest Defence Location?"

The group were gathered near a French window when there was a knock on the door. One of Gittins' men opened it and let in two maids pushing a trolley laden with tea and refreshments. They began handing out tea. Gittins, who was facing the window, looked up and saw the maid's reflection, "Where the hell have I seen that face before?"

The girls continued handing out refreshments, gradually getting closer to the window. Gittins stared at them; they were almost identical – tall, slim, blond hair tied into a ponytail. The nearest girl returned his look and smiled; behind her, the other girl looked determined as she reached down to the trolley.

Masquerade

"Get down! Gun!"

In a blur of movement, the girl drew a Sig automatic and aimed a volley at the group by the window. Instinctively Dark dived at the PM, bundling him to the floor. Behind them, the window shattered, showering them with glass shards.

The other maid pulled an Uzi from the trolley, and as she raised it to fire, Susie leapt over the sofa and kicked her in the small of her back, sending her crashing into the trolley. Now Gittins' men drew their automatics and began shooting back. Seconds later, both girls' bodies lay slumped on the floor, riddled with bloody red holes.

Hurriedly Gittins pulled the PM to his feet and ordered his men to escort him to their cars. Dark rushed over to Susie, "Come on, let's get out of here before they try anything else. Are you alright?"

Whilst the blond assassins were carrying out the second attack, Marat and Sobieski were having a video conference with Stryckland, who sat in his office in Whitehall. The three pored over a large scale map of Europe, absorbed in their plans for the next coup. A large screen displayed the UK installations where Kalyptra needed to seize control. Expectantly, the icons all blinked amber, status unknown.

Marat stood arms folded; he was trying hard to contain his mounting excitement. The culmination of twenty years of meticulous planning was about to come to fruition. With the regrettable exception of Bilic's demise, the plan had been executed perfectly. Stryckland had done well. Marat had nurtured Kalyptra since the end of the Second World War. Using American money, he had quietly schemed, and step by step put into place an organisation capable of wielding total power over its dominion, Europe. But Marat was impatient to dispense with the gauche American Corporatists who had raped Europe and imposed their crude values on the world. It was time for a more sophisticated approach. Lost in thought, he took no notice of Stryckland's mobile ringing.

Stryckland thought the call was from one of his girls. "Hello?"

When he heard the voice of the caller, his face registered disbelief, "Gittins?"

"Stryckland, you bastard! Your girls are dead, and so is your plot. The Prime Minister is alive, and you're screwed!"

Then Stryckland's face contorted with rage, "They told me you were dead! You bastard, this is not over. I'll get you!"

He stopped himself as Marat demanded, "What's the matter?"

"They failed. The Prime Minister is alive."

Marat gawped at Stryckland. He couldn't take it in; he was so confident of success he had been preoccupied with the next phase of the plan. Mercenaries were in place in Germany, the next target; they were just waiting for the order to go. "How could this happen? The plan was working perfectly?"

Sobieski turned on a TV, an all-day news channel. The British Prime Minister appeared on the screen. He spoke to the camera delivering an emergency broadcast, assuring the country that everything was under control after he had survived an assassination attempt. He had convened COBRA to manage the situation. A number of suspects were already in Police custody.

Marat groped for a chair and slumped down, holding his head in his hands, muttering, "My God! We're finished. We've got to get away before the Americans find out. Sobieski, get the jet ready. We'll go to the winery in Mendoza."

He turned to the teleconference screen Stryckland, "Giles, if you know what's good for you, you'll disappear. Lose yourself. I'll contact you all again when it's safe."

Stryckland smiled sardonically but refrained from putting the boot in.

Chapter 54: Volte-Face

The unlikely assembly of Dark, Heinz, Susie, Manfred and Gittins sat in the lobby of the Hotel Metropole, just off Hyde Park in London.

Heinz picked up a coffee, "So, the Prime Minister addressed the nation on TV again. He's spinning yesterday's events as a terrorist plot led by domestic agitators."

Gittins asked, "How are they explaining Stryckland's absence?"

"Apparently, he's been suffering from stress for some time. He's taking leave to convalesce."

"He'll need quite a bit of convalescing after I've finished with him," Gittins retorted.

Susie piped up, "You shouldn't worry about him. He's a marked man. The PM knows what Kalyptra are up to now; they're finished."

Gittins growled, "The bastard still owes me!"

Dark shook his head and turned to Susie, "You're wrong, you know. These people never give up, they'll lie low for a while, but they'll be back. And that being so, the job's not finished. Marat founded Kalyptra; if he is killed, his organisation dies. He won't let that happen."

Heinz chipped in, "On that note, Manfred's checked the private flights out of the UK, France and Italy."

Susie was puzzled, "Why are they running? I thought they were so powerful they didn't worry about breaking the law."

Heinz laughed, "Oh, they're running alright. But not from the law. They're running from the people who have lost hundreds of millions of dollars with the failed coup... the American Corporatists."

Susie didn't understand, "Why? They're supposed to be working together?"

"The Corporatists don't tolerate failure; they view it as weakness and kill those responsible. Marat and Stryckland will be dead very soon if we don't get to them first."

"And the evidence of decades of corporate corruption with them," Dark muttered.

Masquerade

Two days later, Manfred and Gittins were sat in the back of a large van, whose interior was crammed full of surveillance equipment. They were monitoring a large house in the Bund, an exclusive area of Shanghai. A CCTV camera they had attached to a tree opposite the house relayed pictures to screens in the van.

Gittins was chain-smoking, filling the van with a dense fog, "Christ, these Chinese fags are bloody awful!"

He turned to Jimmy, the Hong Kong hacker, "So what have your contacts told you about this new foreigner, this 'gai-gin'?"

Jimmy replied, "There wasn't too much detail: tall, dark-haired, fifties, typical British aristocratic arrogance –it's got to be Stryckland."

Gittins made a face as he took another drag on his fag, "Are your contacts reliable?"

"They saved your bacon in Manchester, didn't they?"

Meanwhile, across the pacific in Argentina, Marat, de Braganza and Sobieski were sprawled on two large sofas in the study of Marat's Bodega. They had spent the night devising their next move. Braganza chain-smoked; he was agitated and constantly fidgeting. The more he fidgeted, the more irritable Marat became.

"Christ! Jan, will you open the window: this smoke is killing me!"

He turned on Braganza, "Stop fidgeting! You're driving me insane!"

Braganza shot back, "Then bloody well call New York! Get us out of this mess."

Marat snorted, "Are you bloody mad? If I do that, we're dead."

Sobieski had opened the windows and leaned out, gulping in early morning fresh air.

Suddenly the agitation drained from Braganza, "I don't see why! It wasn't our fault. It was Stryckland and his mercenaries. I knew Bilic should have run the operation."

Marat shook his head in exasperation, "We can't call Gardner in New York. You know very well the Americans do not tolerate failure, no matter whose fault it was. They will find us and kill us. It is highly likely there are teams looking for us as we speak. I don't intend to make it easy for them."

Masquerade

Defeated by Marat's logic, Braganza reached for another whiskey, took a large slug and stared silently at the glass. Sobieski turned back to the room, "Patron is right. We need to lie low. We're safe here; there are plenty of soldiers to defend the bodega. In time we will get new passports, then we will have our revenge on Stryckland and that bloody thief. If we hold our nerve, we'll be fine."

As Marat and company were discussing their next move, a Gulfstream jet landed at San Juan airport and taxied directly into a secluded hangar. Once inside, two muscled men in business suits and Stetsons climbed briskly out of the jet and into the first of two black Cadillac Escalades. As soon as their baggage was loaded, the convoy sped out of the hangar.

Masquerade

Chapter 55: Pursuit

Dark, Heinz and Susie stepped out of the overheated cabin of the LAN Airlines Airbus 319. Although the flight from Buenos Aires had taken under two hours, they were stiff and tired from their earlier Trans-Atlantic flight from London.

A refreshing breeze blew down from the Andes, helping to clear their heads as they walked to the terminal building. Heinz was grateful for the relief. He'd been sick after prolonged periods of heavy turbulence during the flight. Susie and Dark had been entertained by the spectacular lightning bolts as an electrical storm raced towards them from the majestic peaks of the Andes; Susie said it was a sign the gods were calling them. As they drifted into the arrivals hall, two of Heinz's local agents, Carlos and Juanita, waited for them. They held up a card for the Hernandez family, their contact sign. They were long-time associates of Heinz, having joined the network straight after University in Cordoba five years before. Argentina had become a favoured haunt for Corporatists wanting a quiet break. Its magnificent scenery, the European atmosphere of its capital city and vast empty countryside where one could disappear were big attractions for people obsessed with privacy.

From their modest apartment in the Boedo district of Mendoza, Juanita and Carlos monitored the visits of Corporatists who came from all over the world. Many had established vast estates in the country, especially in the temperate wine-growing region of Mendoza, situated in the foothills of the mighty Andes. The remoteness guaranteed secrecy from prying eyes... or so they thought.

A network of local informants monitored Argentina's many local airports. Travel agents and taxi drivers fed a constant stream of information to Carlos, who relayed the intelligence back to Heinz in Geneva.

Heinz spotted them, "Carlos, Juanita! Good to see you. You know George, and this is a new addition to our ranks, Susie."

Carlos grinned broadly, "Let me help you with your bags. We have a car waiting. Come!"

Juanita took Susie's bag and escorted her to a large battered jeep in the car park.

"You can stay with us; our neighbours are away for a week on holiday. They've let us borrow their apartment so you can come and go as you please."

"Thanks. Any news on Marat?"

"Yes. We tracked a private jet into San Juan three days ago. That's when we contacted you after you broadcast the message to the network. The flight plan stated they flew from Orly to Charleston, then on to San Juan. We know some of the ground staff; they told us a fleet of six black SUVs with blacked-out windows took a party of ten people from the jet. The baggage loaders overheard the drivers talking about the best route to Valle de Uco. It's a wine-growing area. A lot of successful businessmen have bought bodegas out there. We just have to find which one Marat is staying at."

Juanita drove the pickup with verve through the thinning traffic on the outskirts of Mendoza. Evening commuters had long ago reached home and were safely ensconced watching TV with their families.

Eventually, they pulled up outside some low rise apartments. It was a clone to a dozen or more others on the block. Force of habit made everyone disembark quietly, apart from Susie, who slammed the door shut. Everyone turned to glare at her.

"What?" She asked.

Dark shook his head wearily but said nothing. Quietly they walked into the vestibule; if anyone had heard the car door, they hadn't bothered to check.

At the door to their apartment, they bade Carlos good night and arranged to meet at nine o'clock the next morning, after breakfast.

Dark and Susie retired straightaway. Susie set her half-finished coffee on the bedside table, "So what's the plan?"

Dark plumped up his pillows and sat up. "We need to check the people on that jet were Corporatists, and Marat was amongst them. Juanita said they had taken plenty of hi-res photographs of each passenger so we could work on identifying them. Then we need to find this place, Valle de Uco. After that, it's a case of staking out each bodega to see if we can find Marat. Once we find him, we need to plan how we can snatch him and smuggle him across the border to Chile. Heinz has arranged a flight from Santiago back to Amsterdam. He has persuaded the International Court of Justice to review the case and hold the suspects in secure custody until the trial starts. He mentioned that Isabella Ferrucio, the international rights lawyer, would meet us in Amsterdam to plead our case. She plans to use the UK coup as evidence of terrorist activity. There will be a Royal Dutch Air Force transport plane standing by in Santiago, ready to pick us up once we confirm Marat is here."

Susie snuggled up to Dark and put her arms around him, "How long have we got?"

"It's open-ended. The courts have a busy schedule. But I guess three months minimum to review the evidence."

"Shut up, you idiot. I wasn't talking about the Corporatists." Giggling, she pulled him under the duvet.

Later that morning, Heinz looked out over the verdant valley beneath them. Juanita poured him a cup of steaming black coffee from a large thermos flask. She dropped the car window down a couple of inches as the heat from the coffee steamed up the windows. It was early morning, the sun only just rising. They were staking out the first of the bodegas in the valley. Heinz realised this wasn't going to be easy. There weren't too many bodegas or fincas where Marat could stay. The main problem would be remaining hidden in the wide-open spaces of the valley. Heinz was philosophical; all they could do was move quietly and watch.

An hour later, Dark and Susie pulled up behind them.

Heinz got out and walked over to the jeep, "Any luck?"

"Nothing. Usual MO. As we expected, no records of their arrival. The flight was listed as a cargo drop. We checked with the ground staff, and all they could tell us was that some people were ushered quickly into the convoy of new SUVs. So, no records, no trace."

Heinz shrugged, "Maybe. But they weren't invisible. People saw them. We know roughly where they went. We just have to track them down somewhere in this area. That's not too difficult. Carlos has people stationed at every bodega in the valley. We will hear something soon, you'll see."

Heinz finished his coffee and handed the cup back to Juanita. "This place is just waking up. Nothing to see apart from the odd workman going about his business."

Masquerade

Susie piped up, "It's probably taken them a few days to get over jetlag. I don't suppose you'll see much this early in the morning."

"Could be. Why don't you and George take a jeep and check out the San Salvador winery... it's a couple of miles down the road on the left. We'll drive out to Finca Ventura. Don't forget, we are on channel nine on the radio. Keep in touch."

Dark nodded, "OK, see you later. Oh, where is Carlos, by the way?"

"He's back at the apartment. He's getting updates from Geneva. It seems the Met wants to arrest Gittins. Manfred hid him in the hostel when he came back from China."

Dark smiled, "And to think I owe him my life. Strange. I guess the Americans didn't take kindly to his ruing their plans to overthrow an elected Government? Fancy, the Establishment not getting its own way, whatever next? Truthful politicians?"

Heinz laughed, "I can imagine there was hell to pay. Stryckland has gone to ground in China with no sighting for days."

Dark remarked ruefully, "Well, Kalyptra won't be doing anything for a while. But in time, they'll regroup and rebuild. The failure of the coup is just a blip in their schemes. They're too well established for a localised event to undermine them. Besides, they still have people in the British Government. They censored any attempt to mention the plot was planned by them. They've deceived the public yet again."

Heinz's phone buzzed. It was Carlos. "The Swiss Justice Department has just taken two men into custody. They were trying to enter the country without the correct paperwork for their rifles. They couldn't provide a sensible reason why guns needed silencers. They are known hitmen; Manfred thinks they're probably looking for Gittins. It will be a while before they are released... that's if the Police don't find any outstanding warrants for them in the meantime."

Heinz interrupted, "What nationality are they?"

"They aren't exactly talkative, but it looks as if they are English. Ex-special forces, no doubt."

Dark grunted, "Stryckland probably paid them. The nationality fits. I bet Stryckland wishes he gave into Gittins demands now."

Masquerade

Carlos smiled, "He may well have done, Gittins won't say. Manfred said he did make a call to Madrid just after he arrived at the hostel. My guess is it was to his bank."

Juanita's walkie-talkie crackled into life. Her face lit up as a metallic voice delivered a message. "I don't believe it! He's been sighted! It's the bodega at the head of the valley. Guillermo spotted one of Marat's companions from the airport. Let's go!"

Dark and Susie followed Juanita's pickup as it bounced down the dusty, rutted track. After a mile or so, they turned left onto a paved road which they followed for another five miles. As they rounded a bend, a figure jumped up out of the shade of a tree and waved them down. Juanita stopped while the man got in the back seat, then pulled off the road and drove up a steep bank; Dark followed. There was no track, so they had to drive slowly over the rough ground. Eventually, rows of vines came into view as they crested a rise. Juanita followed the edge of the vines for a hundred yards before diverting to the right, up another very steep hill. The crown of the hill was covered by woodland. They drove over the crest and parked in the cool shade of a stand of trees. Off to the left, Dark could see the ground drop away and a panoramic view over the valley as it funnelled into the foothills of the Andes. To the right, four horses were tethered to a tree. They joined Heinz and Juanita as they talked to a group of weather-beaten workmen.

One of the group produced a camera with a huge telephoto lens. Everyone else gathered around and peered at the display. There were dozens of pictures. Most of them were grainy due to the magnification, although the faces were perfectly recognisable.

"There's Marat!" Susie cried.

"That's Sobieski, the giant," Dark exclaimed.

Then a new face. "Who is the tall thin guy?" Susie wondered.

"I think that's de Braganza... the Portuguese guy... one of Marat's inner circle."

Heinz leaned forward and scrolled through the pictures quicker. Abruptly he stopped.

"What's the matter?" Dark asked.

"We've seen that man before; he is in quite a few of Juanita's photos."

Heinz pointed over the man's shoulder, "Not him. Look at these two figures behind him."

Two men stood in the shade of the veranda, deep in conversation. Both wore hats that covered their eyes. However, each man had a distinguishing mark that would be easy to spot. The man on the left had severely pitted skin, the result of chickenpox. The man on the right had a jagged scar running from the corner of his mouth across his cheek to his neck. They would be easy enough to spot in future.

"Who do you think they are?" Susie asked

"Not sure; I haven't seen these two before. What do you think, George?"

"Me neither. Judging by their dress, I'd guess they were European. Quite wealthy. Their facial features are more difficult to judge. They've got the aura of hitmen. But hitmen don't wear jackets in this heat, so they could be Corporatists."

"Could they be American?" Susie asked.

"Possibly. Didn't Marat's jet stopover in Charlotte on its way to Mendoza?"

Heinz interrupted, "OK. We can assume we have the right place. Now we need to get them out of there."

He turned to Juanita, "Can we get a detailed plan of the bodega? We could do with a man on the ground."

From the escarpment, they could see the general layout of the farm buildings and the main house. Rows of vines spread out from the buildings surrounding them on all sides.

"I'll ask Alvaro to go down. He can make out he's looking for work. He'll be able to give us a better description." Juanita declared.

Dark turned to Heinz, "Did you bring the equipment I asked for?"

Heinz nodded, "Yes, back at the apartment."

"Okay. Let's get to it. Susie, you and Juanita stay here and keep an eye on the bodega. Heinz and I will fetch our equipment... be back in a couple of hours. We'll plan to go in tonight in the small hours; everyone should be asleep."

Susie and Juanita took two guides back through the bush to their lookout position. They lay flat on their stomachs, hidden beneath thick gorse bushes and stunted windblown trees that studded the escarpment. The view over the Bodega was spectacular, two hundred feet below them at the base of a steep slope, vineyards spread out to the other side of the wide flat bottomed valley. The winery buildings were at the centre of the estate, with the house a few hundred yards away. Close to the house lay a group of outbuildings; garages, stables and sheds. The vines would give them ample cover to reach the house undiscovered.

Juanita turned to Susie and pointed to the base of the slope. Susie looked closely; surrounding the vines was a grid of darker soil. "They're irrigation ditches. We can use them for cover. Can you see it passes underground just before the outbuildings and then reappears beyond the house? It looks deep enough to keep us hidden from the bunkhouse." She turned back to Susie; her curiosity got the better of her, "How are you finding undercover work?"

Susie shrugged noncommittally. "It's okay so far. But I haven't done very much. How about you?"

Juanita scanned the Bodega through her binoculars, "I've been doing it for three years. Ever since the bank repossessed my father's business. I met Carlos when I went to a protest meeting. The country was being raped by the capitalists. They seized anything of value and sent the money to America. Ordinary people like us were left to pick up the pieces. The protesters all vowed that one day we would take back control of our country. So a few of us set up a group to check on the activities of government ministers. Through that, we eventually made contact with Heinz through the darknet."

"Are you making a difference?"

"A lot of the time, it doesn't feel as if we are. Mostly it's routine, boring work. But every now and again, something happens, just like now. This is when you feel you're making a difference. This is important; this is so the people can regain control of their country."

Susie looked at Juanita. "I'm glad you told me. I was having some doubts about whether we could actually force change on the Corporatists. For most of my life, I've been part of their society. I know how ruthless these people are. We seem so small and powerless in comparison."

Juanita smiled, "I know how you feel. I felt that way, too, when I started. But wait until you achieve just one small victory. Then you understand."

Masquerade

"Understand what?"

"Understand they are frightened to death of us. Our sheer numbers terrify them. They know if we have a mind to, we can overthrow them easily. That's why they have to indoctrinate us, frighten us with scare stories about disasters that will befall us if the system is changed. They try to convince us only they can save us from these terrible events. But if we looked beyond this fabrication, we'd realise we could control our own lives and dispense with their so-called expertise.

Besides, we aren't quite as powerless as you think. Heinz has been fighting these people for years. He's built up an extensive network of people around the world just like us. They are prepared to fight for their freedom. And we have more like Dark, although he is the best agent we have. He is like the Scarlet Pimpernel; he is far too clever for them."

Chapter 56: Rat Run

It was time. A crescent moon gave them enough light to pick their way quietly down the steep face of the escarpment. An iridescent night sky cast an ethereal light onto the distant snow-capped peaks of the Andes. Susie felt she could reach out and touch them even though they were many miles away. As they reached the valley floor, Heinz clicked the transmitter button on his shortwave radio three times. He received an answering click immediately. He gave the thumbs-up sign to his companions, then pointed in the direction of the drainage ditch fifty yards away. No one spoke. They crept slowly and silently to the ditch. Just as Juanita had guessed, it was deep enough to hide them as long as they didn't stand. Dark had brought them the grey linen suits he favoured for covert work. The clicks were part of a series of signals Dark had arranged with their lookouts on the escarpment. One-click meant yes or all clear, two clicks - no, three clicks - danger, four clicks - the lookouts were in danger.

Twice Heinz received three clicks. They squatted in dirty water at the bottom of the ditch until the 'all clear' came. They had half a mile to cover until they reached the drain cover. It was heavy going; the bottoms of the irrigation channels were full of water; by the time they reached the drain, their legs felt like lead.

"Let's take a rest. My legs are killing me." Heinz gasped.

Dark risked another peek over the parapet of the drain; the coast was clear.

"This is a hell of a lot easier than getting into the Château," Heinz said.

"Well, it didn't take a genius to work out someone would come to get me," Dark retorted, "they were expecting you... today they're not."

Suddenly Dark held his hand up. Three clicks. Everyone froze. A few seconds later, another three clicks. Above them, they heard gravel crunching, then silence. They waited for the one-click all clear. Faint snatches of conversation drifted down to them. Susie wrinkled her nose as the sharp tang of tobacco smoke wafted into the drain. Dark shrugged and held up two fingers while he looked quizzically at Heinz. Heinz shook his head and held up three. Juanita gagged as she suppressed a cough, but Carlos pulled her to his chest and muffled the sound. Even so, the faint chatter of guards stopped as they checked around. Eventually, boots scraped on gravel, and three cigarette butts hissed and died in the wet soil at the entrance to the drain.

Masquerade

Silence... they waited for five long minutes before Dark peered cautiously out of the drain. He held his hand up, making his companions wait. Then, "Let's go!" He beckoned them to follow him through the drain.

Fifteen minutes later, Dark peered out of the ditch. A hundred yards away, the house was silhouetted against the night sky. Dark watched the guards patrolling. They completed a circuit of the house, passing just in front of the drain. Thirty seconds later, they disappeared around the corner of the building. Alvaro estimated it took them two minutes to complete the round.

Dark decided to let them complete another circuit, just to make sure. They waited in the cold, cloying mud, nerves jangling, feeling very exposed. Dark in comparison was cool and calm, seemingly unperturbed.

"Carlos, take your team to the field hand's hut. Use nitrous oxide to keep them quiet. Then form a skirmish line in the vines outside the main house, escarpment side. Give me six of your men to carry Marat and the others. We'll meet you in thirty minutes. Come on!" Dark whispered.

Dark's team scrambled out of the ditch and followed him to the nearest corner of the house. They all lay flat in the darkness of the veranda next to a French window Alvaro had noticed. They waited for the guards to pass once more. Then Dark picked the lock; thirty seconds later, they were inside, and the doors shut.

The house was in darkness; grey light from the crescent moon slid across the floor. Dark told Susie and Juanita to check the guards were still making their circuit. Then he ordered the group to put on their night vision goggles. The room turned from grey to green. They found themselves in a large, richly decorated room. Judging from the bookshelves, it was a library and an opulent library at that. Carefully Dark cracked open the double doors. They led into a spacious hallway. To his right lay a grand staircase.

"This way," Dark called softly.

They filed out behind Dark. Then crouched by the stairs while he checked the other rooms for signs of life. After a few tense moments, he returned.

"A guard is asleep in the kitchen, but the other rooms are empty." He whispered. Then he led them upstairs. Cautiously Dark peered over the top step onto a large square landing. No guards. Two corridors, one to the left, the other to the right. Dark turned left. They were presented with four doors. Juanita and Carlos were sent to check the farthest door on the left.

Masquerade

Heinz was sent to the opposite door on the right. Dark watched them listen before cracking open the doors and going inside.

He took Susie to the nearest door on the left.

Susie whispered, "Déjà vu."

"This is becoming a habit!" Dark whispered over his shoulder.

"Well, you are a notorious burglar."

Dark stopped beside a door; he raised a finger to his lips. Impulsively Susie brushed it away and kissed him. Dark murmured, "Be serious!"

Cautiously he opened the door an inch. The room was empty, quiet as a graveyard. The bed was made, and dust sheets covered all the furniture. A few empty cardboard boxes were stacked next to the bed. An open door led to an en-suite bathroom.

They tried the next room. From the doorway, Dark could hear faint sounds. This room was occupied. Gingerly he turned the doorknob and listened for a change in the heavy rhythmic breathing. He crept inside. Thick curtains were drawn against the night. Two figures lay on the bed, both facing away from him. Cautiously he crept towards them.

"Damn!" Dark swore under his breath. Susie touched his arm. One figure was an older, heavyset man – Sobieski, and the other a naked, young Argentinean girl – probably a servant. They were sleeping soundly, dead to the world. "Susie, fetch two men to put these two to sleep with the nitrous. Tell them to bag Sobieski only and take him to the landing and wait."

Susie tip-toed out, followed by Dark. Outside Heinz, Carlos and Juanita met him on the landing. Carlos shook his head, "Nothing."

Dark looked at Heinz, "Sobieski and a girl," then he pointed to the other corridor. As they reached the nearest doors, Dark motioned them to follow the same procedure. As they listened at each of the doors, it was obvious this wing was fully occupied.

Susie returned and sent two men to Sobieski's room; she went with Dark and checked the next two rooms. They were occupied by the two shadowy figures who had stood under the veranda. Each one had a female companion. Dark and Susie returned to the corridor to find Heinz walking stealthily towards them. Suddenly Juanita poked her head around the door, waving her arms vigorously. Doing her best to contain her excitement, she mouthed, "Marat".

Marat was fast asleep. He lay on his back as still as a corpse; he wore a silk sleeping mask. His breathing was shallow and regular. On the far side of the bed, his companion, a servant girl, lay on top of the sheets. Dark motioned for Heinz and Carlos to take care of the girl. He would knock out Marat with the gas. On Dark's signal, Juanita planted a mask over the victim's nose and mouth. Dark vaulted onto the bed and sat astride Marat's chest while Susie grabbed Marat's arms. There was a brief struggle, but Marat's thrashing quickly subsided as the gas rendered him unconscious.

Heinz and Carlos had a much more difficult time with their victim. She fought like a cornered lioness. Carlos was sent flying with a haymaker before he could force the mask over her mouth. Heinz struggled manfully to hold her down, but her arms and legs flailed about with ferocious accuracy; she was giving Heinz a vicious beating. Out of the blue, Susie stepped in and administered a crunching uppercut which knocked her out cold.

Anxiously Juanita hurried to the door to see if the commotion and roused the household. She returned a few moments later as Carlos and Heinz were tying up the servant. "Everyone's still asleep."

Dark breathed a sigh of relief, "Good, let's get Marat into the body bag. It's going to be light soon. We'll need to be well away from the house by then. Heinz, can you bag him? Don't forget to gag him. Juanita, go to the top of the stairs and keep a lookout. Use the radio to warn us. Susie, you can help me sort out the weapons."

Ten minutes later, they regrouped on the landing with Sobieski, Braganza, and Marat completely unconscious in their body bags.

"Any movement?" Dark asked.

"The guard went to get something from the kitchen a few minutes ago. But he's back in his room now. He was half asleep anyway."

"Okay, let's get the hell out of Dodge."

Dark led them out while Carlos' men carried the three body bags. Light grey streaks on the Eastern skyline gave notice of the onset of daybreak. They would need to move quickly. With their heavy baggage, it would take them half an hour to get back to the bottom of the escarpment.

Masquerade

Carefully Dark opened the French windows. There was no sign of the guards.

"End of the watch?" Dark thought no more of it.

Marat weighed no more than a teenage child. But the two men carrying Sobieski and de Braganza cursed fluently as they heaved their bulky cargo over uneven ground. Hastily they dropped into the irrigation ditch and hurried along the drain. So far, so good. The sides of the drain were low, so they had to drag the body bags along. Their captives would have sore heads when they woke up.

Halfway back, Dark peeked out of the drain once more. Grey streaks in the east had grown into large gashes of light. Visibility was much better; Dark could see clearly into the distance. Looking back at the house, he could make out the detail of the doors and windows. They didn't have much time to get to safety. The house was still in darkness. Quietly they shuffled back along the irrigation ditch. They did not get more than fifty yards when they heard a growing clamour behind them.

"Down!" Dark ordered.

He scrambled out of the ditch and risked a look through the vines. Back at the house, the servant girl stood on the veranda swaying unsteadily. She was still naked apart from a sheet draped loosely around her shoulders. Two guards stood on either side, supporting her. One of the heavy-set men, in a dressing gown, stood next to them shouting orders to a group of sleep sodden farmhands who began stumbling out of the bunkhouse, still feeling the effects of the nitrous. Another man, probably a foreman, thrust a gun at each workman as they gathered in the yard.

The man on the veranda shouted, "Shoot on sight. But God help you if you shoot Le Patron."

Another man handed out torches and organised the men into a foraging line. They were going to work down the rows. Straight towards them. Dark estimated there must be at least a hundred men. Not the best odds.

He jumped back into the ditch. "They're coming straight for us, although we should be at the edge of their search line, so we've still got the advantage. They're all feeling the effects of the gas, and there are so many of them, with a bit of luck, they will start shooting at each other. Follow me; we need to move before they wake up properly. Come on! Get out of the ditch. Hurry!"

Masquerade

Rows of vines provided cover as they scurried towards the escarpment. Dark realised the low rising Sun would dazzle the searchers; they would be looking directly eastward as they stalked the intruders. When you are blinded by the glare from the sun, all you see are shades of black. It would be impossible to look directly in front of them. As long as Dark's group stayed on their current course, they should be invisible to the pursuers. They reached the edge of the vineyard without incident when suddenly Dark saw a slight movement at the foot of the escarpment. The slowly rising Sun that had hidden them now turned its glare on them. Dark couldn't see his lookouts. He clicked the radio, but there was no answer. Instead, shouts followed by a fusillade of bullets kicked up the dirt at their feet.

"Back! Hide in the vines. Guards on the escarpment. Thank God they can't shoot straight!"

"We walked straight into that!" complained Heinz. "Where are the lookouts? They are supposed to warn us."

Carlos retorted, "If they didn't, it's because they're dead. Those guys wouldn't have given up without a fight. They aren't cowards!"

Heinz replied, "Sorry, I didn't mean anything."

More shouts from behind them, the main search party had heard the commotion. They were probably in radio contact. The roar of 4x4 engines reached them.

"This is no time for small talk. We need to get out of here fast," Dark butted in. "Juanita, how far away are we from our trucks?"

"We're almost directly below them, but we'll have to take a detour to get around the guards. There's a path a few hundred yards down that way." She pointed to their right. "The climb will be easier, but we will have less cover. It will take twenty minutes to reach the cars. I just hope they haven't left any guards up there."

Dark pushed Susie toward Juanita, "Right off you go."

"What about you?" Susie looked anxious.

"You need a diversion. Something to draw these guys away from you. I'll go that way and meet you back at the trucks. Don't wait for me for more than ten minutes." He looked at Heinz, "Go straight to the rendezvous at San Juan. If I don't meet you on the road, I'll catch up with you there."

Masquerade

"I'm coming with you!" Susie cried.

"No, you're not! Heinz needs you!" Dark ordered. "Now go! Quickly!"

The shouts and commotion from the search party were getting very close now. Less than a hundred yards away.

Heinz took charge, "George is right. We must get Marat out of here. We need to move." He turned around and waved at Dark, "See you later!"

Dark waited momentarily until the others were out of sight. Then stood up straight and fired a burst in the direction of the guards near the escarpment. They responded with a wild fusillade of shots, totally inaccurate. Dark moved to his left, away from Heinz's party. He crashed through the vines letting off another volley in the direction of the guards. They tracked him with the odd speculative potshot. Behind him, the search party had picked up the commotion and joined the pursuit, confident they would outnumber the thieves.

Dark picked up the pace as they closed in on him; their volleys became more accurate. Bullets kicked up dirt at his feet and shredded rows of vines splattering Dark with juicy dark red flesh. In the half-light, his pursuers looked like giant rats racing through the early morning mist. Two bands of pursuers joined together and formed a crescent, forcing him to run before them. Dark kept firing random shots making sure they didn't lose track of him. He managed to keep the distance between them constant, and they seemed content to drive him onwards.

Battering a path through the vines was heavy going; Dark was beginning to flag. He had to duck between the wires strung along each row to support the branches as they became weighed down with grapes. He tried to veer towards the escarpment but was driven back. Suddenly he could see why. Before him, a cordon of men stood waiting at the edge of the vineyard. Two huge American pickup trucks were parked in front of the men. Each vehicle was kitted out with searchlights and, more worryingly, a heavy machine gun mounted on the flatbed behind the cab. The searchlights and machine guns moved menacingly from side to side, trying to pick him out in the gloomy dawn light.

Immediately Dark dropped to the ground and scrambled to his right. He needed to get as close to the escarpment as possible. He scrambled back towards the line of pursuers on his hands and knees. His sudden disappearance caused consternation amongst his pursuers. Alarmed shouts rang out, becoming more frantic the longer Dark stayed out of sight. Furious volleys of shots were fired into the darkness between the two groups. Careful not to disturb the vines Dark eased his way back through one row and waited. The rear phalanx was getting closer. Suddenly he felt the hot the stabbing sensation in his calf. A bullet had nicked him. He squeezed into a thick row of vines that seemed to offer more coverage than the rest, then curled up, making himself as small as possible. It was a risk, letting his pursuers walk right past him. But there was so much confusion he had to take the chance. They came upon him in a rush. Shouting, randomly firing their guns. In an instant, they had rushed by.

None of his pursuers noticed the grey phantom slip away up the escarpment before melting into the tree line. However, from a bunkhouse window, a tall thin, balding American followed Dark's progress through powerful night vision binoculars. As Dark crept up the escarpment, the American dialled a number on his mobile. "The target is climbing the escarpment to the east of the Bodega, fifty yards south of the storage barn. Track him until he meets his companions, then kill them all, including Marat. Keep me informed. I'll call Gardner."

Chapter 57: Cordillera de la Ramada

The rag-tag group of refugees huddled together in the corner of a small cave, desperately trying to find some warmth. At such a high altitude, the air was thin and freezing. It seeped into their bones. They used any and every means of retaining what little warmth they had. Even Marat was used by his guards, trying to eke out some body heat. Susie wrapped her arms around Dark, her fingers burrowing deep into his jacket. Every bone in her body ached from the penetrating chill of the Andean night. Plaintively she called out, "Please can we have a fire?" The leader of the rescue squad, Nelson, had forbidden them from lighting a fire when Susie made the suggestion earlier. Not that there was much wood around to start one. He turned and glared at her, dismissing the suggestion with a shake of the head.

Heinz grumbled, "How in God's name did we get out of that unscathed? Those weren't your average farm hands."

Susie replied, "Didn't Chester's mercenary contact say they were recruiting Foreign Legion guys? Maybe they shipped some over here?"

Nelson's radio crackled into life, abnormally loud in the heavy silence of the night. He listened intently to the static laden transmission, then turned to Heinz, "Aircraft ETA sixty minutes." Stiffly, he got to his feet, rubbing his arms in a vain attempt to get warm, then walked to the mouth of the cave, contemplating the rough dirt landing strip half a mile below them down a treacherously steep scree slope. Absentmindedly he checked a large canvas rucksack for flares. The Hercules would need them to locate the landing spot. He decided to give his men more time before sending them down to mark the strip. They were exhausted and needed rest. He turned and watched them, each one quietly making their preparations for the next stage of the job. Periodically one of them would hold a clear plastic mask over their nose and mouth and greedily suck in a deep lung full of oxygen. They weren't as badly affected by altitude sickness as the rest of the group – they had only taken their tablets fifteen minutes before; it was yet too soon for them to be effective.

Thirty thousand feet over the Argentinian-Chile border, Captain Jan Wynkoop switched on his mike. "Okay, guys, I've confirmed our ETA. We've got sixty minutes. We're looking for a rough disused airstrip, so it might be a bit bumpy. I want a ten minute turnaround time to allow embarkation before we begin take-off. We are expecting twenty passengers. They can sit in the forward area of the cargo bay. Gijs, make sure there are blankets for them."

Although only twenty-five years old and looking more like a teenager, Wynkoop was an old hand at running hazardous black ops missions. He and his crew had flown thousands of hours running humanitarian missions in Asia and South America on behalf of the Netherlands government, many of them under hostile gunfire. Equally, he was familiar with the variable flying conditions around the Andes Mountains. They had delivered dozens of water storage tanks to Bolivia and Peru only six months before, so his navigator Pete was guiding him down a familiar route. "Seb," Wynkoop turned to his co-pilot, "keep an eye on the radar. I want to know if any high-pressure areas are developing over Chile. This is going to be interesting!"

Seb grinned, "Piece of cake compared to Tripoli, skip!"

Back at the cave, Nelson was still studying the landing strip. He was concerned that the runway would not be long enough for the Dutch Air Force Hercules to land, turn around and take off again. This was an old disused Chilean airbase, used to patrol the border with Argentina. It was never meant to take heavy military transport planes.

They had caused quite a bit of damage at the Bodega. There had been a fierce firefight at the top of the escarpment between the rescue squad and Marat's bodyguards. They had almost got to the top of the ridge unnoticed when a radio had burst into life, alerting the guards. Then they had had four hundred yards of open ground to cover before they reached the trucks. The cost had been severe. Nelson had lost six of his men, all of them involved in the rear-guard defence, but they had given their comrades enough time to escape. It grieved him to have had to leave the bodies of his men behind, but he had little choice if he wanted to save the lives of the others.

In fact, the Hercules needed a surprisingly short runway to take off. Nelson knew Heinz had managed to call in a big favour with contacts in the Dutch Military. He had persuaded them to send an aircraft from their base in the Caribbean island of St. Maarten down to Argentina. Dark's plan was to fly back to a military airbase outside Rotterdam via Ascension Island. Then take the prisoner to the high-security prison close to The Hague, ready for his trial.

Masquerade

Nelson picked at a stray thread on his webbing holster, a nervous habit he could never quite kick. He paced back and forth at the mouth of the cave; he was getting worried. He had sent a squad of men to lay a false trail from the Bodega. In the opposite direction to their intended escape route. After twenty miles or so, they should have looped back around and met up with the main party at the cave, leaving plenty of time to catch the flight. By his reckoning, they should have arrived half an hour ago; they were cutting it too fine for comfort. He had been determined not to break radio silence, but then again, he was determined not to leave anyone else behind. He turned to his radio operator, "Fernando, call Jorge, find out where he is and his ETA. Tell him to get a move on."

The radio operator gave a curt nod and began to unpack the short wave radio. Nelson knew how risky any communication would be; the message had to be brief. The whole area was probably swarming with Kalyptra patrols; they would be desperate to stop Marat talking. Kalyptra considered itself above the law, and he knew they could act with impunity to eliminate anyone they considered a nuisance. Nelson had had several skirmishes with Kalyptra's assassins. In their shadowy world, they were the most feared, ruthless and efficient killers in the business. And right now, he was certain they would be hunting him and his crew. The Hackers only viable escape route was the Hercules. He hoped to God it would arrive on time. If Kalyptra caught them first, that would be the end of them.

"But where the hell is Jorge?" Fernando shook his head as Nelson fretted. The last thing he needed was to hang around for him. He paced at the mouth of the cave, abruptly he turned to his men and ordered, "One of you climb up to a vantage point; see if you can see Jorge. Keep an eye out for Kalyptra patrols while you're up there. Take the infrared scope. Report back in twenty minutes."

Dark was worried; he turned to Heinz, "Are you sure Nelson's guys are up to this?"

Heinz, "Listen, these guys know their stuff; this is bread and butter to them."

Dark shifted his weight around on the cold floor. His legs were causing him a great deal of pain, now that the morphine was wearing off. "So, what do you think our chances are of getting a conviction?"

Masquerade

Heinz scratched his chin, "We're in new territory. The International Court of Justice at The Hague has never been used to try a case of Government connected extortion and fraud before. And certainly not against powerful people like him." He nodded at Marat. "However, we do have testimony from Gittins. Plus, your first-hand evidence from him must count for something no matter how immoral he was. As for Marat, he was the leader of the European organisation; he knows all of their secrets. Plus, there is the attempted coup; we have their plans, names, places, the evidence you stole."

Dark grimaced, his leg throbbed like hell. "Any idea who will sit on the judge's panel?"

Heinz shrugged his shoulders, "Well, in theory, they are able to choose from any senior judge from Europe or America. Traditionally they have appointed European judges to sit on the panel. In this case, they may decide to look further afield in view of the European and American domiciles of most of the organisations that are accused. I guess they could choose from Mr Fudosan from Japan, Mr Jong from South Korea, Mr Tao from Hong Kong, Mr Lim from Singapore or Mr Barrat from Australia. Unfortunately, we don't have too many judges versed in commercial and international law that are not based in Europe or America."

Dark watched Nelson pacing back and forth, "What is happening with Gittins?"

Heinz's face lit up, "He is giving us chapter and verse on Kalyptra's activities in the UK. He seems to know a great deal; I suspect in readiness for a time like this. He has been given immunity from prosecution. They have video cameras recording his interviews as well as stenographers documenting his testimony. He's giving the prosecution lawyers everything. Names, places, deals, bank accounts, the works. The prosecution team think they will need months to gather all the evidence. The only question is: can they get it before Kalyptra destroys it?"

Dark looked quizzical, "Can't the Hackers get that data rather than the prosecution team?"

Heinz winked, "Strictly speaking, that would compromise the impartial nature of evidence gathering. However, we have several of our specialists downloading data from several private banks in Shanghai and Zürich just in case the evidence disappears before the prosecution lawyers present their writs."

Dark was thoughtful. "You know there will come a time when they will try to get to the judges? This is the most high-profile international criminal court case since the Nuremberg Trials. The Corporatists won't just sit back and wait for the case to come to court. They will try to stop it. And we know they consider themselves to be above the law. They will target the judges, the court officials, the police, the court security as well as witnesses. It will be a mammoth task to insulate these people from any possible contact with Kalyptra."

Heinz nodded in agreement, "That's true, but consider this. We have torn the veil of secrecy they use to shield their deals and secrets from public scrutiny. That is a victory in itself. Now the whole world knows how these people have been manipulating Governments for profit and power, deceiving us all with fake news for decades. Already we have exposed something that the elite spend a great deal of time and effort concealing. Make no mistake, this has hurt them badly. And if I have learned anything fighting these people, it's this: the court case will start an internal war. They will accuse each other of the crisis. Marat is in custody, so Kalyptra, the organisation they use as a buffer between them and the outside world, will be dysfunctional. Because one thing is certain, they are too arrogant to think they will lose this battle. They'll think when the initial anger has died down, they will be able to manipulate the court process in their favour."

Dark, "It's dispiriting, isn't it? We have all suffered in an effort to show ordinary people how badly their governments and large corporations treat them. Yet, the reports in the media and videos on the internet are met with indifference and apathy. It makes you despair. What will it take to wake people up from this fantasy that people holding high office are to be trusted? What can we do to open their eyes?"

Heinz took a drag on his cigarette, "I don't think we're going to get a flash of enlightenment with this. It will happen gradually. Hopefully, this will be a significant step in turning public opinion against their corrupt leaders."

The radio burst into life, and the operator grabbed his headphones and listened intently for a second. He looked up to Nelson. "Boss! Jorge's team have been spotted. They're heading our way, fifteen minutes ETA."

Masquerade

Nelson breathed a massive sigh of relief. Then he noticed the look on the radio operator's face, "But?"

"There is a problem, a big one. They're being followed. A large plume of dust a couple of minutes behind them... looks like a big team. Also from the North East, another plume of dust. Ten minutes ETA. Looks like we're going to have a party."

Nelson thought, "This was getting out of control." They were going to be hemmed in and outnumbered in a firefight, and their only means of escape was thirty minutes away. Boarding the plane was going to be interesting... that's if it wasn't shot out of the sky trying to land.

Quickly Nelson calculated the odds. Abort the pickup and escape into Chile. Or take their chances with the plane and hope they could all get on board under heavy fire. "Fernando, get me the pilot! Quickly." The radio operator punched in the channel numbers and called the plane; he handed the mike back to Nelson. "Flight Sixty-Six, what is your ETA at the landing zone? We have approaching hostile forces from north-east and east, numbers unknown. ETA fifteen minutes, expect hostile fire. Over."

Twenty thousand feet up, Captain Wynkoop looked across the dimly lit cabin to his co-pilot, "Looks like another Djibouti – all hell breaking loose and everyone in the shit. Get in and out and pray we don't take a big hit. Don't you just love this job!" He picked up the mike. "Nelson, touchdown fifteen minutes. Understand hostile reception awaits! Prepare to board at the southern end of the airstrip; I won't stop, but you can embark as we turn the plane around. Then we'll get out of there like the devil himself is after us."

Nelson listened to the message, hardly believing their luck. He turned; everyone else had heard the message too. "Okay, you heard what the man said; let's get down to the airfield. Ferdy, get Jorge to drive down to the southern end of the airstrip PDQ." He clapped his hands and shouted, "Let's go, get a move on!"

Galvanised by his bellowed encouragement, everyone jumped up, rubbing frozen limbs whilst moving out of the cave.

Nelson guided them down one at a time as if he were sending parachutists out of a plane: "Steady there... Stay on your feet... look where you are going...." He gave Susie an encouraging pat on the shoulder, "Don't look down the slope; keep your eye on the guy in front of you, and if you lose

Masquerade

your balance, try to fall backwards. You'll be okay, don't panic." He watched her for a moment or two that she made her first faltering steps down the steep scree slope. Satisfied she was coping, he turned his attention back to the remaining passengers.

Two more went, then Marat came with a guard on either side. As he reached Nelson, he held his hands up as if to say, "Untie me." Nelson shook his head, "The guards will support you. But remember, there will still be a gun on you, so no tricks." He stared at Marat, who stared back arrogantly.

Nelson left Marat to the guards and turned his attention to the remaining four people in the queue, the last two being Dark and Heinz. He gave them an encouraging nod as he watched them step over the edge and slither down the steep slope. He knew Dark was in a great deal of pain... the sooner he was on the plane, the better.

He waited a moment until he could see the lookout crew clambering down the steep rocky path just above the cave mouth; they would be with him in a minute or so.

At that moment, he heard a shout below and whirled around just in time to see Marat darting off from the column, doing his best to run down the slope away from his guards. One guard slid on his stomach down the slope knocking people over as he fell. Without hesitation, Nelson bounded down the slope in pursuit. He shouted to the guards to fire warning shots over Marat's head. The short crack of the shots did nothing to deter Marat's escape. Two of the guards veered away from the column in pursuit. "Get back in line!" Nelson shouted at them as he powered down the slope, trying to close the hundred-yard gap to Marat. From the corner of his eye, he was amazed to see Heinz and Dark were also racing to catch Marat and that Dark had managed to close the gap to sixty yards; he was likely to catch Marat before him.

With lungs burning from the effort of running and keeping his footing on the treacherous slope, Nelson was beginning to run out of steam; he just about maintained the gap to Marat, who was nearly at the bottom of the slope. If he reached the smoother, level ground, it would be almost impossible to catch him before he was able to hide amongst the bushes and large boulders scattered about. That would certainly give the chasing soldier's time to engage them in a firefight and stop them from boarding the plane. They had to stop him somehow. His brain was whirring with

Masquerade

possible strategies when Dark closed to within ten yards of Marat. Nelson heard Dark shout at Marat to stop, or he would shoot. He saw Marat's headlong dash slow as he chanced a glance over his shoulder; he hadn't seen Nelson. Nelson immediately made his decision. He unslung his rifle and dropped to one knee, brought the gun up to his shoulder and took aim in one smooth movement.

Marat had almost come to a standstill; he wavered indecisively, certain Dark was going to shoot him. But he hadn't seen Dark carrying a gun. Then suddenly, he heard a crack - a split second later, his thigh exploded with pain. He collapsed backwards onto the smooth earth at the bottom of the slope. He clasped his thigh, blood seeped through his fingers. "Oh my God!" He rolled around on the ground. The pain was unbearable. It felt as if someone had plunged a red hot knife into his thigh. He screamed loudly; he had to get away. It was the only way Kalyptra would allow him to live. Before he could gather his wits to make good his escape, rough hands grabbed him and dragged him behind a huge boulder.

"Another move like that, and I'll blow your kneecap off. Comprendez!" Dark shoved Marat back against a rock. A sharp edge jabbed painfully into Marat's spine.

Nelson turned to Fernando, the radio operator. "Put a dressing on that quickly." He looked up, eyes scanning the northern sky as he heard the low rumble of high-powered turbo-prop engines being throttled back as the Hercules prepared to land.

The rest of the group had gathered around Marat, leaving him in no doubt that he wasn't going to be able to run off again. Nelson gave them their instructions, "Everyone needs to get to the southern end of the landing strip; we have to board the plane there. Hurry! There isn't much time. José and Manny, when you get there, take a man and cover each side of the landing strip. Put up a green flare for Jorge to follow. Move! Things are going to happen very quickly; we have no time to waste.

Dark and Heinz scrambled over to Marat. Dark smiled mercilessly at him, "You're with me from now on, time to face the music." He grabbed Marat's arm and pulled him up, ignoring Marat's pain ravaged expression. He looked pointedly at Marat's bloody leg, "Don't worry, you'll live." Fernando pulled out a morphine jab stick, ready to give Marat a shot. Dark stopped him and shook his head. "Don't worry about that; a bit of discomfort will stop him from getting bright ideas and running off again."

Masquerade

The group moved off at a fast trot, the injured were half carried, and half dragged along. Nelson called out to them as they ran, "The plane isn't going to stop; we'll have to jump on board as it turns. Don't forget, Kalyptra's thugs will be right behind Jorge, and they will have heard the plane by now. So they will be firing everything they've got to stop it taking off, we can't hang about, or we'll all be dead meat."

Heinz watched Dark take charge of Marat and the two soldiers guarding him. He smiled grimly. He had known Dark for quite a few years now; he had come through a tremendous ordeal during the last ten days and survived. It had been a baptism of fire.

Jorge was driving the leading pickup truck like a madman. Dodging football-sized rocks, crashing through tumbleweed bushes, he kept his foot flat to the floor. His backup squad in another pickup kept pace with him slightly behind and off to one side. Two soldiers were doing their best to brace themselves upright against the heavy roll bars in the back of each vehicle whilst spraying their pursuers with staccato bursts of machine gunfire. Although completely inaccurate, it had the desired effect of keeping them a hundred yards back. The problem was, they were running short of ammunition after twenty minutes of constant fire. Somehow, they had reached the landing strip unharmed and were minutes away from safety. Jorge could see the green flares showing them the way.

Abruptly, they were deafened by the roar of four massive Rolls Royce engines as the plane passed a few feet over their heads on its final approach. A second roar nearly blew the pickups over as the pilot throttled back the engines and stood on the brakes. The men in the back of the nearest truck were thrown to the floor, nearly falling out as the pickup bucked and bounced in the jet's turbulence. Jorge steered the truck away from the choking dust cloud thrown up by the plane's huge wheels. He could hear and feel bullets zipping through the air inches from him. They pinged off the jeep's bodywork and sent up spurts of dust around the vehicle. Suddenly the windscreen shattered, and razor-sharp shards of glass scratched his face and hands. "This is too close to call," he thought; "We've cut it too fine this time."

Up ahead, he could see the plane had slowed to a walking pace as it reached the end of the runway and began to manoeuvre, ready to take off again. They were three hundred yards away from safety. Suddenly he was thumped hard in the back and thrown forward into the steering wheel, which jerked out of his hands. One of the men in the back had been thrown out of the pickup as it had been flung from side to side. Jorge wondered what had hit him; he looked behind and saw the remains of the other soldier's body slumped against him, cut to ribbons by machine-gun fire. Instinctively he stamped on the brakes and threw the four-wheel-drive around to go back for his fallen comrade.

"Damn! We were so close! They'll reach us in a couple of seconds. Hell, we almost made it." The slight chance of escape having disappeared, his only thought was to rescue his fallen comrade. Frantically he waved the other driver on towards the plane, but he was ignored, and they stopped with him. Four men jumped out of the vehicle and began laying down covering fire as Jorge ran over to the motionless body of his buddy. He grabbed one of his webbing belts and dragged him back to the cover of the four-wheel drives. Peering over the bonnet of the truck, he could see the headlights of six vehicles driving towards them at high speed. Flashes of red tracer accompanied the ping and crack bullets flying around them. He took a deep breath and snatched a grenade from his belt. He pulled the pin and threw it as hard as he could towards the charging vehicles. A huge explosion showered them with dirt and debris, swiftly followed by the screech of tortured metal as trucks crashed into one another. Nonplussed, he peered over the bonnet again; he hadn't expected that big an explosion. Two of the pursuing vehicles lay mangled on their sides, bodies flung around on the ground beside them. Another explosion showered them with more dirt. He was facing the plane this time and realised someone near it was firing a mortar at their pursuers. With the explosion ringing in his ears, he grabbed his comrades and, holding their still unconscious comrade, ran as fast as they could towards the Hercules.

Back at the plane, Nelson had supervised the embarkation of the hackers and their prisoners into the Hercules' massive cargo hold. His voice was drowned out by the whine of the engines, so he motioned to his squad, and they followed him off the loading platform at the back of the plane. Four of them ran to help the Hercules' cargo crew firing the mortar and heavy machine gun. Nelson and another three sprinted through the dust and dirt and grabbed Jorge and his crew, who by now had slowed to an exhausted crawl through the rough brush at the edge of the clearing. Nelson nearly lost his bearings with the noise and the dust raised by the screaming engines. But just in time, caught sight of the mortar crew retreating towards the rear of the plane, laying down covering fire with their machine guns at Kalyptra's remaining mercenaries, who stubbornly refused to give up the chase. The howl from the engines increased as it powered up, ready for take-off. Just in time, they flung themselves onto the loading platform and crawled exhausted into the hold. The deck master counted his crew. He walked over to Nelson and shouted, "Have you got everyone?" Nelson clambered to his feet and counted off his party. Two were missing. Jorge shook his head, "We lost two, boss."

Nelson looked back at the deck master, nodded and gave him the thumbs up. The deck master spoke into his mike and closed the loading platform. They could hear the rattle of bullets ricocheting off the fuselage, but nothing came through the hull. Wearily Nelson lurched over to an empty seat next to Jorge and slumped down. All strength drained from his body now the surge of adrenaline had dissolved. "I hope to Christ, it was worth it," he said to no one in particular, then closed his eyes to rest.

In the cockpit, Wynkoop gunned the engines; the four powerful turbines filled the bare cargo deck with a high pitched whine.

The huge plane surged forward. Somehow they had succeeded; they had rendered Marat and company. "Talk about playing the Corporatists at their own game and winning. Result!" mused Heinz, looking over to Dark. He needed to get to a hospital quickly. He had endured his injuries without complaint since Gittins had pulled him out of Marat's torture chamber. Dark lay flat on his back in a thick sleeping bag. The crew had rigged a makeshift bed for him; he was exhausted, lying down was the only position where the pain was bearable. There was a military doctor at Ascension Island; Dark could be examined there.

Susie gently nudged Dark awake "Time for your next dose." She stabbed him with a morphine stick. "Try to get some sleep; it's a long flight." Dark dropped his head back on the bed and closed his eyes. Satisfied Dark would settle, Heinz clambered up a short flight of stairs to the cockpit.

"Hey, skipper. That was some landing! The reception was a bit hot, though! I thought they had us cornered. The prompt turnaround was much appreciated."

Wynkoop swivelled around his seat, "No problem, glad to be of service. It's been a while since we've had some excitement, eh, Seb?" He grinned at his co-pilot. He held his hand out to Heinz, "Dirk Wynkoop."

Masquerade

Heinz grasped his hand with a firm shake, "Heinz Gombricht, I'm very pleased to meet you. I'm glad our friends in Amsterdam were able to get hold of you so quickly; it was literally a lifesaver."

Wynkoop grinned, "Sure, no problem. Angela Distel from The Hague called the boss. Told him she had an emergency situation on her hands and needed an extraction at short notice. You were lucky, another couple of hours, and we would have left St. Maarten for Amsterdam."

Heinz wiped the sweat from his brow, "Hell, that was close. Thanks anyway. I'm sorry to have put your guys in such a dangerous situation. We didn't think they would catch up with us so quickly. The firefight started just as you landed; we had a patrol just in front of Kalyptra's mercenaries taking a lot of fire. We didn't think they were going to make it, but thanks to that nifty landing, they're safe."

Wynkoop waved his hand, making light of the rescue.

Heinz ventured, "What's our arrival time at Ascension? One of our guys is beaten up pretty bad. He'll need medical attention when we land."

Wynkoop checked his watch, "It's 01:30 hours now, and we're carrying a slight tailwind, so we should reach Ascension by 1200 hours. Is he okay until then? We have a medic onboard; if he needs anything, ask for Gijs."

Heinz nodded, "Thanks, appreciate it. I'll let you guys get on."

He turned and slid down the gangway back to the cargo deck. The crew had turned the lights down, and the cabin was in semi-darkness. Heinz could see his crew spread out, falling into exhausted sleep. He found an empty row of seats and sat.

Marat was being attended to by the Dutch medic; he leaned forward, "Do you really think this is going to change anything?"

Exhausted Heinz, "God, I hope so! Putting you bastards away can only be a good thing for ordinary people. Imagine being free from having your private affairs being snooped on by Corporatists."

Marat laughed out loud, "You're so naive! The genie is out of the bottle! Pandora's Box is flung wide open! You can't put this technology back. It's got too far! And if it isn't us using it, it will be the next group of corporatists. That could even be you one day."

Heinz bristled, "We just want people to get their privacy back, free speech, free from every tin-pot company circulating personal details of people's lives with their crony companies."

Marat sneered, "Do you think people really want their freedom? That means being responsible for their own choices. You're worse than naïve; you're a fool. People just want an easy life. Bread and circuses... feed and entertain them, keep them docile. They won't admit it, but they want to be told what to do and think."

"People aren't as gullible as you think. Once the Court shows how your Corporatists have lied and manipulated them, they'll think differently."

"You're deluded! Do you actually believe the Americans will allow us to be taken to Court? Understand this, idiot. We're all dead! As of now, you've forfeited your life for a lie. Democracy is a lie!"

Marat eventually shut up, and Heinz fell asleep plotting Corporatist's downfall at The Hague. The Hackers were compiling a thick dossier of damning evidence which would expose the full extent of the Corporatists' immoral empire to an unsuspecting world. He hoped they would suffer the full consequences the justice system could offer.

Back at Marat's bodega, the two heavy-set men who had arrived in the private jet were supervising the destruction of the estate, along with the shadowy man who had called in the hit on Dark. They were Gardner's enforcers whose task was to send a message to Kalyptra's remaining members. A thick tower of pungent billowing smoke rose and merged with thunderous grey clouds. Mutilated bodies lay scattered on the ground: men, women, horses and dogs. Thugs with machetes scoured the compound. A tractor ran in crazy circles crushing row upon row of vines, its lifeless driver slumped over the steering wheel.

One of the Americans made a call, "The mercenaries failed, they got away with Marat... yes, it's burning – the place will be ashes in a few hours, and all the workers are dead... confirmed: nothing will be left of it."

Chapter 58: Justitia

Dark awoke as the Hercules touched down in Ascension. He winced as he tried to sit up, forgetting his injuries for a moment. He slumped back onto his makeshift bed. Instead, he listened to the roar of the plane's engines as the pilot throttled back the engines to slow the giant aircraft as it hurtled down the runway. He looked around the hold for Susie and Heinz. But all he could see was the bare grey aluminium airframe, the various straps and buckles used to secure cargo, but not much else. Gradually as the engines' roar died to a low-pitched whine, he could hear the sounds of people stirring in their seats, getting ready to disembark. As the engines stopped, he heard disembodied voices chattering somewhere back in the hold. He strained to see what was happening. He wanted to know that Marat was securely locked up. He wanted to be sure the snatch squad had made it to the plane unharmed. And most of all, he needed to be sure that his friends Heinz and Susie were safe.

He felt a hand stroke his head. He looked up to see Susie smiling. "You're awake at last. You've slept for ages. I was beginning to think we'd given you too much morphine!"

Dark was still groggy but returned her smile. "Where are we? Ascension?"

Heinz walked over to them. His face was lined and grey. He looked exhausted. "So the patient wakes at last! Yes, we are going to refuel here, then in another twelve hours or so, we should land at Schiphol. Do you want to sit up?"

Gingerly Heinz and Susie manoeuvred Dark into a sitting position, legs dangling over the side of the bed. Dark looked down the enormous metal cargo hold as the snatch squad stood stretching and yawning as they stowed their gear in cargo nets hung from the sides of the fuselage before disembarking into the cool morning air of the mid-Atlantic.

"They did an amazing job, didn't they?" Dark nodded towards the group.

Heinz nodded, "Yes, they're pretty good company when you're in a tight spot."

The whine of the engines died completely. The noise in the cargo hold seemed inordinately loud as Dark's ears popped. From behind them, the co-pilot shouted out, "It'll take an hour or so for us to refuel so you can have that time to get some air and freshen up. We'll be taking off again at 0700 local."

Masquerade

The leader of the snatch squad, Nelson, looked up at the announcement and saw Dark sitting. He waved in recognition before turning and walking down the ramp at the back of the cargo hold with the rest of his group into the cool early morning air.

"Coffee, anyone?" A young Dutch air force private held a tray with mugs of steaming black coffee. They all took one.

Dark took small sips, "I'm absolutely knackered. I feel as if I have been trampled on by a herd of elephants."

This was the first time they had been able to talk freely since Gittins had rescued Dark. Heinz regarded Dark with a great deal of concern. "You've been through a hell of a lot. The way they tortured you was particularly sadistic. I'm not sure many people would have been able to keep silent whilst enduring the appalling pain. It's to Gittins credit that he untied you when he did. If you had remained in that position for the rest of the night, you would have been permanently crippled."

Dark nodded in agreement, "Who put my shoulder back in?"

Susie winced as she replied, "Gittins did. Apparently, he has some experience with this type of injury. He played football for a number of years... seen his fair share of broken bones, apparently. He said you screamed like a pig then passed out.

Dark muttered, "I wonder what made him turn on Stryckland in the end? Can we trust him, do you think."

Heinz looked non-committal. "We'll see; he's spilling his guts as we speak. We're treating everything he says with caution until we can verify it. As for the reasons he betrayed Kalyptra? Well, only he will ever know the real reason. These people always end up fighting each other; greed and paranoia are in their nature, they can't help it.

Dark winced at a stab of pain in his shoulder. "Where is Gittins now?"

He's at the hostel with the Europol Intel guys. So far, everything he has given us is verifiable. He certainly knows the whereabouts of a lot of skeletons... it seems he kept a journal over the years. It's paying dividends now. Our own sources have substantiated everything he has given us, and there have been one or two gems, I have to say. Did you know the Chairman of Danillo Foods International Inc. paid Kalyptra ten million dollars to get legislation repealed in the UK? In return, Kalyptra got the

Masquerade

British Government to lift import quotas which had prevented them from selling their products in Europe. We knew there was something suspicious about that, but we couldn't prove anything."

Dark looked pensive, "The sixty-four thousand dollar question is whether he will give evidence on oath when the time comes. That's when he will be under the most pressure and when our case will be most vulnerable. Unless we can convince the judges that the Corporatists and Oligarchs have almost completely taken over the British and European establishment, the public will never believe us. Gittins will be a key witness, and Kalyptra will do anything to stop him from testifying. As an insider, his testimony will carry more weight. I hope to God they haven't got to the Judges."

Heinz leaned back in his chair and scratched his leg with a pencil, "We are taking the precaution of videoing his evidence in the presence of two notaries. Even if they do get to Gittins, we have verifiable evidence that's as good as personal testimony."

Susie interrupted them impatiently, "Come on, you need to see the doctor. He's expecting you. Can you manage to get into the wheelchair?"

"With some help from a beautiful assistant, I could."

Heinz wheeled Dark out into the blue-black sky of early morning light. The chill air hit Dark like a knockout punch. He was breathless and light-headed, unable to focus as they made their way across the tarmac towards a wooden hut. Susie chattered, but Dark didn't hear a word. As they neared the hut, the heady aroma of freshly brewed coffee hit Dark like a dose of smelling salts; his head cleared instantly.

Forty minutes later, Susie wheeled Dark out of the Base Doctor's Surgery across the tarmac towards the Hercules.

"Hold up!" Heinz shouted out as he ran to catch them.

Susie looked over her shoulder, "Something on your mind."

Heinz, "I have actually. We've just had word the Korean police narrowly missed Stryckland crossing the border into North Korea. They got there a matter of minutes after he cleared the border control. We have notified the Chinese authorities, but they have asked for a warrant before they begin to search for him. The paperwork will take at least twenty-four hours. He could be out of the country again by then. Still, looking on the bright side, it didn't take us too long to track him down this time. He won't be so lucky next time."

Dark winced as the Hercules' take-off thrust him back in his seat, "Do you think it was luck? Or was he warned, I wonder? How long before we land at Schiphol?"

Heinz checked his watch, "I'd say we've got another twelve hours before we enter Dutch airspace."

Susie, "What's the plan when we land?"

Heinz, "A team from the Justice Department will meet us in The Hague. They have arranged for a squad of the Justice Department's guards to take Marat and company into custody in their high-security remand unit. It's amazing, actually; you've never seen anything like it. They have a High-Security Building attached to the Courts. Apart from the Court Rooms, there is the remand unit and secure accommodation for vulnerable witnesses and court officials. They also have fully staffed medical facilities.

Once we hand Marat over to the authorities, we'll be taken to the hospital to get Dark examined and let him recuperate. As a precaution, we'll stay in a private suite of rooms in the secure block for the next few days. In the meantime, I'll organise the search for the members Gittins identifies. We don't know how far Kalyptra's tentacles reach into Europe's establishment at the moment, so our position is still extremely vulnerable. There are very few organisations we can trust to fight the Corporatists. The Hague is one of the few organisations Kalyptra has not been able to infiltrate.

The plane bucked and bounced alarmingly as it hit a pocket of turbulence. One of the crew made their way up the cargo bay, stopping every now and then to advise passengers to buckle up. When he got to Dark, he told him to lie down and helped fasten his safety straps. It was going to be a bit of a rough ride for the next hour or so.

As the plane continued north, Seb put away his checklist then radioed Military Air Traffic Control at Schiphol. "Schiphol MAT, this is Netherlands Royal Air Force Transport, Quebec Tango Charlie 490. ETA 01:30 hours CET. Requesting secure landing arrangements. We are expecting an ECP escort on arrival. Please confirm landing reservation and security arrangements."

"Quebec Tango Charlie 490 this is Schiphol MAT. Message received, 01:30 hours landing slot confirmed. On touchdown follow a courier vehicle from Runway 18 Charlie 36 Romeo to Secure Hanger Number Two."

Masquerade

Seb was satisfied he had the landing procedure organised according to Heinz's instructions. "Roger Schiphol. See you in ninety minutes."

He turned in his seat and gestured to the navigator, "Tell Heinz that Schiphol is ready for us. All arrangements are confirmed."

As one door in Argentina closed, another opened in Asia. In the lobby of the Shanghai Mandarin Oriental Hotel, Stryckland was meeting Xuang Zhouzin, a Senior Member of the Chinese Oligarchs Council. Stryckland reclined on an oxblood chesterfield; his scheme to run Kalyptra and replace the American Corporatists and divide America with China was proceeding satisfactorily. He had been negotiating with the Chinese for over twelve months before the UK coup was planned. Cautious, yet a risk-taker, the UK coup was a feint for this, his real objective. He was determined to run Kalyptra and open up the American markets to British control. Marat was too subservient to the Americans. Stryckland had the blood of the 16th-century British merchant venturers: bold, cunning and ruthless. Moreover, there were still untold riches in Asia. That was where he would do business; America's jingoistic attempt to build a lasting empire was doomed to fail with its instant gratification mentality. The Chinese, on the other hand, thought in terms of millennia, and the British were always savvy enough to adopt local customs from their subjects.

"I can facilitate a coup in America; I have an excellent team. We can secure control of Wall Street with six strategic assassinations, then replace the Dollar with the Yuan."

Xuang was interested but wasn't about to jump into bed with Stryckland just yet, "Is that so? I heard several were killed in the failed attempt on the British PM's life."

Stryckland smiled as he lied, "Those were Kalyptra's; mine don't miss."

Xuang, "If our negotiations proceed, we are agreed you will control of the American Eastern Seaboard. But, we expect full co-operation with trade tariff talks."

Stryckland looked impassive, "Agreed. Now, the American Corporatists are trying to destroy Kalyptra's European structure; I assume I can rely on your assistance to repulse them?"

"Of course, we will step up our fleet exercises in the Pacific as well as provoking the Japanese confrontation."

"And you're agreeable to stop your petroleum trades in Dollars and use British Pounds?"

"It suits our purpose for the time being. What has become of Marat?"

Stryckland looked grim, "Bad news, the insurgents got to him before the Americans. They are taking him to Holland to stand trial."

"And how do you know this?"

"I have an informer in their group."

Susie had been dozing whilst the plane bucked and jolted its way through turbulence. She was awoken as the Hercules dropped the last few feet onto the runway at Schipol. Rubbing her eyes, she glanced around the cargo bay before concentrating her gaze on Dark. He was still sleeping. They had given him a slightly higher dose of morphine to get him through the turbulence and the landing. It seemed to have worked.

Susie turned to watch the security convoy draw up to the ramp at the rear of the gigantic cargo plane. The snatch squad had already collected their gear and disembarked.

Various people from the security convoy walked into the cargo bay, a group of six heavily armed guards walked over to Marat's cage. They locked themselves in the holding pen as they began to process the three prisoners. Marat watched impassively as they shackled his feet, then secured another chain above his knees. They clamped his hands behind his back and finally linked all the chains together with a length of chain that ran from his feet to his knees and up to his neck, where a titanium collar was locked in place. Thus bound, he could only shuffle with half a stride. Escape would be impossible without someone picking him up. Sobieski and de Braganza were chained in exactly the same manner.

A group of medical staff wheeled a gurney stacked high with hard-cased medical bags. They headed straight for Susie and Dark. Susie put a finger to her lips, the lead medic nodded and motioned his colleagues to take a corner each of Dark's bed. They quickly transferred Dark onto the gurney without disturbing him. The medic turned to Susie and Heinz, "Would you like to travel in the ambulance? We're taking everyone to the Hague Medical Centre for check-ups."

Susie replied, "I'll go with George." Heinz nodded, "Me too." They wheeled Dark through the now crowded cargo bay, which swarmed with ground crew unloading kit. As Susie walked down the ramp, she could see black-uniformed soldiers had formed a perimeter around the giant Hercules aircraft. The Terminal buildings used by ordinary passengers were far off in the distance. Susie could see only squat dark grey concrete buildings beyond the guards; there were no other buildings in the vicinity. She turned to Heinz, "They aren't taking any chances with Marat, are they?"

Heinz smiled grimly, "We can't afford to, Susie. We have to assume Kalyptra will try to snatch Marat or even assassinate him. They will be determined to stop him from standing trial. The only people we can take on trust at the moment is The Hague, and even then, we can't be completely sure they haven't been infiltrated. Come, let's make sure George is comfortable." He took her arm and guided her to a seat in the back of the ambulance. Two orderlies pushed the gurney onto its cradle and locked it in place. Their ambulance would have a military escort. Another orderly closed the back doors, pulled out a folding seat and sat facing the gurney. Immediately the ambulance moved off and took its place in the convoy formation.

The convoy travelled at some speed, and Susie swayed from side to side as the ambulance raced toward The Hague. She tried to imagine what would happen next. Since she had left her mother's house in Paris, her life had taken one unexpected turn after another. She had been kidnapped by her would-be stepfather, shot at, beaten, found a soul mate. More importantly, she now had a purpose and self-respect that filled the void in her life. Now she felt normal, not a parasite.

A heavy jolt broke her musings. Heinz was busy tapping away at his smartphone. The paramedic was leaning over Dark checking his blood pressure.

Noticing Susie was awake, the medic said, "Five minutes, and we'll be at the Medical Centre." Then turned his attention back to Dark.

Susie was concerned, "How is he?"

The paramedic undid the monitor's Velcro strap from Dark's arm. "He's okay, considering his injuries. BP is holding up 140/89. Pulse is a constant 65. Once we get him into ICU, we'll have a much better idea."

The ambulance suddenly slowed to a walking pace. The paramedic sat up, "We're here; that was the perimeter gate. If you collect your things, the guards won't be hanging around."

Masquerade

Susie picked up her bag as Heinz came back to life and put his phone away. "That's a relief; I wasn't looking forward to that journey. It was an ideal opportunity to ambush us."

They sat quietly as the Ambulance drove through the compound at a walking pace; eventually, it came to a gentle halt. They heard the slamming of doors and shouts as the rest of the convoy disembarked from their vehicles. "Are we getting out?" Heinz asked the paramedic. "Why are we waiting?"

"It won't be long; they're checking it's safe for us to get out. We were briefed this morning; we are operating on Protocol Level 3, which means we have to assume the base perimeter fence has been breached and we may have hostiles in the compound. That means you are escorted everywhere unless you are inside a building."

A knock on the door, which then swung open revealing a dozen guards, dressed in black overalls, black helmets and boots, each one was carrying a short-barrelled machine gun. What made them seem altogether sinister and alien to Susie were the gas masks they wore. No part of their faces was visible. They were looked like anonymous, robotic killers.

Chapter 59: Tribulation

Steel-grey rainclouds had been saturating the Dutch countryside, causing chaos during the week before the trial. TV news programmes were either about the weather or the trial. Everything else was forgotten. A month ago, Dark and the hackers had hijacked the Corporatist's most potent weapon, the TV set. One evening at peak viewing time, every television network across Europe had been commandeered by the hackers. Susie had hosted a TV programme that exposed how Global Corporations had stealthily infiltrated every major western Political Party and civil service until they were able to control Governments.

The exposé had galvanised Europe's public, who were heartily sick of avaricious and reckless bankers, lawyers, bureaucrats, politicians and everyone else who relentlessly browbeat them. Their simmering anger had finally reached boiling point at this latest catalogue of deception and manipulation. The public had finally been woken from their trance, and now they wanted a reckoning.

Dark stood in his dressing gown and peered anxiously out of the rain-streaked window at a glowering sky. He wondered if it was an omen of things to come. After weeks of legal wrangling, The Hague's fifteen judges agreed they had jurisdiction and would proceed with the trial. Nevertheless, Dark was apprehensive; proceedings were due to start today. He knew very well that Marat, Sobieski and de Braganza came from countries under the control of the Corporatists. As members of NATO, each country held the power of veto, meaning the trial might not even start. America had frequently exercised this right whenever its interests had been threatened. If that happened, he wasn't sure how the Hackers were going to get the authorities to jail the guilty corporatists. Dark barely suppressed a guttural snort of disgust as unbidden, a grainy black and white image of an old 1960s TV newsreel flashed into his memory. The earnest-looking reporter describing refugees fleeing from East Germany to the West naively referred to Western Europe as the "Free World". What a sick joke that seemed now. He prayed no one exercised the veto before the trial had at least started. The judges decided a televised trial was in the public interest and gave permission for an impartial Swiss TV channel to record and broadcast proceedings. Dark looked at his watch, 7:00. Time for his breakfast rendezvous with Susie and Heinz.

Masquerade

Susie drained the last drop of coffee into Heinz's china cup. "Do you need more?"

Heinz, mouth full of brioche, nodded. Susie gestured to the waiter.

"Did you sleep well?" She asked. "I couldn't settle." She had slept fitfully. Her stomach churned. She felt nauseous and exhausted; she continually yawned – it was nerves. She made feeble attempts at conversation with Heinz. He didn't respond, too preoccupied with his own problems to take much notice.

"Where is George?" she complained. "Aren't you nervous?" she demanded, glaring at Heinz. "How can you be so calm? " Susie looked around the restaurant for Dark.

Heinz gave in, put his paper down, and gently clasped her hand. "Susie! It's perfectly natural to be nervous today. But you must think positively. Your own Father gathered much evidence before he disappeared. As did George's Father. It all makes a very compelling case for us."

Dark pulled out the chair next to Susie. "Hi. What's up?"

Heinz looked up, "Morning, George. Susie has pre-match nerves... understandable, I suppose. I'm just telling her that we have a cast-iron case. We have done everything humanly possible to show the world what these scumbags are really like. Now it's up to the world to take notice and do something about it. We've played our part. The next step is up to the judges."

Dark smiled reassuringly at Susie. "I didn't sleep well either, but it's out of our hands now. We have to trust the authorities will do the right thing."

Susie was mollified for a moment. "What if they have got to one of the Judges? Does it have to be a unanimous decision before he is found guilty?"

Heinz smiled, "No, Susie: it has to be a majority, by two clear votes. Now can I please finish my breakfast?"

Susie fiddled nervously with her napkin but kept quiet.

Everyone in the minibus was silent as the driver gingerly picked his way through the sauntering crowds. As the bus pulled into the porte-cochere, a concierge in an immaculate dark green greatcoat stepped out of the foyer

Masquerade

and opened the door. He ushered them towards the Reception area. "Well," Dark thought. "This is it."

As they stood waiting in line for the security check, an elegant woman dressed completely in black joined them: Isabella Ferruccio, their lead advocate.

"Buongiorno," she smiled, greeting them. "How are you feeling? Looking forward to today's proceedings? It should be very interesting, no? You must be extremely proud to have brought this organisation to court?"

Heinz replied, "Morning, Isabella. I think we are all rather nervous, to be honest. None of us knows what to expect. We are well and truly out of our comfort zone here."

"Oh, don't worry too much. For a few days, there will be the usual wrangling between the legal teams. Not much of interest will happen until Friday when the arguments start. "

Dark's ears pricked up. He hated any sort of bureaucracy. He looked at Heinz, "Does that mean we don't have to be here until Friday?"

Heinz looked sternly at Dark and Susie. "I think it would be a good idea for you two lovebirds to show your faces to the court for a few days at least!"

Isabella's team gathered around them as they were speaking, loaded with heavy bundles of documents bound by colourful wax-sealed ribbons. "Well, we all seem to be here. Shall we go through? Let battle commence!"

As they walked through the security checkpoint, they were carefully frisked by burly armed guards in the same green uniforms as the guard at the door. Each of them was checked carefully by three different guards. Only when Susie, the last of the group, had been searched did they walk into the courtroom together. The lawyers took their places at their table to the left of the judge's bench. Their clerks sat in the row directly behind them, with Dark, Susie and Heinz alongside.

Dark was visibly edgy. He had handed over Marat and his henchmen to a bunch of bureaucrats, the type of people he distrusted most. He wasn't at all sure they were up to the job of running the trial. What would the Corporatists do to sabotage the proceedings? They were unlikely to let the accused divulge any secrets; there was too much at stake. At least any disruption would show the world how dangerous the Corporatists were.

Susie noticed Dark was lost in thought; she leaned over, "Penny for them?"

Masquerade

Dark had been so preoccupied, he realised he hadn't taken the time to look around the courtroom. Aware that the murmur of chattering voices had grown much louder since he arrived, he turned to look back at the public gallery, already full to capacity. To his left, the three rows of seats for the press were similarly full. He looked to his right to see a raised bench where the accused would be prominently displayed. It was protected at the front and sides by thick panes of polycarbonate glass, bound by a metal frame. Heinz nudged Dark and nodded towards the dock. "In case someone decides to become judge and jury?"

Dark nodded distractedly. He turned and scanned the courtroom for anything that looked out of place: anyone acting nervously, trying to look inconspicuous perhaps.

Heinz noticed, "They would have to get through a hell of a lot of security before they could even get a shot off. But maybe someone has tried it; you can never tell these days. God knows, there are plenty of lunatics out there."

There was a loud bang as a steel door opened off to their right and announced the arrival of the accused. Dark suddenly felt Susie gripping his hand tighter as they waited for the first prisoner to appear in the dock. It was Marat, who, like a General leading his men into battle, came out first. He paused at the top of the stairs and looked calmly around the courtroom. He took his time surveying the assembled crowd. "Fools," he thought. "If they think they can stop me with this petty charade, they are mistaken." He caught sight of Dark, Heinz and Susie sat behind the Advocates and gave them a lingering malicious stare. Then abruptly, he looked away, his expression changing as he recognised someone in the public gallery. He gave a curt nod before he turned and led his co-accused to their seats.

A concealed side door opened to one side of the judges' dais, and a procession of black gowned court officials walked slowly into the main chamber. As they reached their allotted stations, they peeled away from the line and stood behind their seats. The door opened once more, and three more Officials marched solemnly into the chamber. These were obviously a more senior rank. Their robes signified their higher status, and the symbol of Justitia, blindfolded with her scales and sword, was embroidered in rich Red and Gold upon their left breasts. They marched in step to a large ornate bench below and before the judges' dais, where they too waited.

Masquerade

Several moments elapsed before large double doors swung open beside the judges' dais. A large, florid faced man in a burgundy gown walked through, gilded ceremonial staff in hand. This was the Court Superintendent; he stood in front of the dais facing the courtroom and instructed the courtroom to stand. The noisy chatter suddenly died. Then on cue, the twelve judges entered the Chamber in single file. Each wore a deep red velvet gown over their business suits with black velvet Renaissance caps. Judges were elected to sit for fifteen years, with one Judge nominated as the senior member. They were selected from countries allied to NATO. This almost caused Heinz and Dark to pull out of the trial and take their case somewhere else. They had considered the European Court, but Dark argued with some conviction that it was more easily influenced than The Hague.

The judges made their way slowly to their seats. Then they turned to face the courtroom and waited for the Superintendent, who on cue struck the ground three times with his staff. "The court is now in session. Their Excellences and Judge Marion de Bellefort presiding". The Judges sat. A moment passed, then the Superintendent instructed, "The Court will be seated." Dark dropped to his seat with a thud. "God! This is going to be nerve-wracking: extreme tedium mixed with fear of assassination."

Heinz looked over Isabella's shoulder as she rechecked her papers. He recognised the document as their opening remarks, which would be directed to the judges.

The Superintendent called out, "The accused will stand to enter a plea to the Court." Slowly, the three accused stood up. Each of them stared contemptuously at the court.

The Senior Clerk addressed the accused. "Louis Marat, Januslav Sobieski, Fabian de Braganza ….. You are collectively charged with murder in the first degree, accessory to murder, extortion, human trafficking, and bribery of government officials. How do you plead?"

One by one, the accused stridently replied, "Not Guilty!"

The Senior Clerk ordered them to sit and called on the Chief Prosecutor to outline her case. Isabella gathered her papers and stood. She began reciting her brief, which summarised the evidence Dark and Heinz had painstakingly gathered over the last ten years. It had come at great personal cost for many people in the group, many of whom had taken huge risks gaining evidence of Corporatist's wicked activities. Some had lost their lives, many had been imprisoned and tortured using the blanket legislation of Anti-Terrorism – allowing authorities to secretly detain people indefinitely without access to lawyers and without any evidence of guilt.

Dark listened closely for the first few minutes of Isabella's speech. Then something bizarre grabbed his attention. A small pinprick of iridescent red light danced upon Isabella's head. Jumping and moving amidst her hair as she read from her notes. Dark gazed mesmerised, uncomprehending. Abruptly his bewilderment turned to horror as he realised the red dot was the laser beam from a telescopic sight. Isabella was about to be murdered.

Dark jumped to his feet and screamed, "Get down!" He launched himself at Isabella. Too late. At the very moment, he lunged forward, a large scarlet hole appeared where the light had rested. There was no sound nor sharp crack of gunshot; Isabella slumped gently forward onto the table, as if resting, her life snatched away. As Dark tumbled to the floor, there was a stunned silence. A prosecution clerk let out a long, harrowing scream as she saw the bloody gore of Isabella's pulverised face turn the pile of documents crimson. Her scream was cut short by the sound of a heavy, dull whump.

Lying beneath the advocate's table, Dark saw the outside wall expand and bulge inward as if a giant fist was trying to push through. At the same time, he felt a searing stabbing pain in his ears. A bomb! He threw his hands up to protect his ears whilst desperately trying to scramble back to Susie and Heinz. He needed to get them under cover of the table. The steel and glass structure of the wall gave up its futile resistance to the deadly explosive force of C4. A blinding flash and a cyclone of scorching hot air sucked a deadly mixture of glass and steel splinters like a scythe through the room, vaporising everything in its path.

The bomb had been placed to one side of the dock so that the blast bypassed the accused. It was expertly done. The blast pulverised the judges' dais into millions of lethal splinters, which, combined with the glass and steel shrapnel, were driven directly across the courtroom into the press desk opposite. In an instant, the twelve Judges, their Clerks and over fifty journalists were mutilated; their bodies shredded into a bloody mess of gore and bone, which coated the rubble and walls of the chamber with a gelatinous film. Within the blast zone, there was not a recognisable body part in sight. The prosecutor and defence desks were at the periphery of the blast zone, partly protected by the dock, and so sustained relatively

Masquerade

light damage. Even so, the defence team took the force of the blast. Two of the advocates lost limbs while their clerks and two other advocates were riddled with steel and glass fragments.

In contrast and by dint of careful planning, the six-inch polycarbonate armoured glass partition had protected Marat and his associates, who now sat calmly in the midst of the carnage and chaos. Six men dressed entirely in black, their faces covered by gas masks, appeared in the smoke-filled void left by the explosion. Dark's ears were still ringing, but he could still make out the loud, heavy whump of helicopter blades, sending spirals of hot air and smoke into the courtroom.

Heinz mouthed something at Dark. Then he was gone. Dark, still disoriented, grasped the overturned table for support and, fighting the pain from his injured shoulder, stumbled after Heinz. Ten yards away on the far side of the blast zone, two wounded guards struggled free of rubble. Heinz pulled an assault rifle from the nearest guard and began firing at the two soldiers guarding the hole. Dark fell beside him and grabbed a Sig automatic from the guard's holster, then began firing at the side of the dock where a snatch squad had killed two prison guards. More masked gunmen appeared through the smoke and formed a skirmish line to protect the escape route. One of the masked men used a set of bolt cutters on the chains tethering Marat, Sobieski and de Braganza to the dock. Another grabbed them and dragged them through the gaping hole in the wall. Dark was incandescent; he knew the Corporatists would attempt to stop the Trial, but not so murderously. Their arrogance was breathtaking. The thick swirling smoke prevented Dark or Heinz from shooting with any accuracy; they just fired into the black billowing haze. Suddenly the skirmish line fell back, and the attack was over as quickly as it had begun. It had taken less than five minutes to snatch the three most wanted men in the world from the grasp of Justice.

Dark fell back on the floor, "God no! Not now! We were so close!"

Chapter 60: Reformation

Three days after the Corporatist's breakout at The Hague, Dark, Susie, Chester and Heinz had escaped from the interminable police interrogation and travelled to Switzerland. Heinz rented an out-of-the-way villa nestled amongst the steep wooded slopes above Lake Maggiore in Ticino.

It was early morning; breakfast had been served on the veranda which overlooked the lake. Susie, who had nursed Dark since Gittins brought him out of Marat's Château, attended to his shoulder. Dark winced as Susie removed an old morphine patch on his arm. Although his shoulder had been successfully relocated after Bilic dislocated it, the joint was still extremely tender and bruised even after a month.

"Sorry, darling! I'm not as good as the physios, am I?"

"Don't worry, it's just a relief to get the damn thing off. Stick it on the other arm, will you?"

Chester had lost a lot of weight in the rendition facility. He had bought new clothes which were way too big, so big they shrouded his gaunt frame. He peered over his newspaper. "What's the plan for today, lovebirds?"

Nursing done for the moment, Susie sat back and began to munch a croissant. "I think Heinz has booked a boat trip over to Ascona for lunch. Ecco, I think."

Chester whistled, suitably impressed, "Count me in!"

The strong early morning sun glinted off the gently lapping waves of the lake. Dark tried to settle himself once the new patch had been applied. He had to squint as he took in the view. Sailing yachts tacked into the breeze as they made their way to a favourite anchorage. Eventually, he let his head fall back; a refreshing breeze cooled the warm sun on his face. He was tired. But he felt able to relax. For the first time in five years, he didn't feel the nervous stress of being hunted. For the moment, at least he could relax in the company of trusted friends.

The Swiss authorities had guaranteed them protection from any attempts to extradite them to Europe or America. Belatedly the Swiss government was taking its neutrality more seriously after The Hague revelations of corruption involving American and European corporations and governments. In 2014 they were forced to reveal details of private Bank accounts to the SEC. This had steeled Swiss resolve not to be coerced again by tyrannical American bureaucrats.

Dark smiled as he felt Suzie stroke his hand. He turned to Chester, "Is there any more news about the casualties in the courtroom?"

Susie took her coffee to the veranda's balustrade, her features clouded with concern. "That was so awful. Thank goodness no more of the prosecution team were killed. Poor Isabella, she was so vivacious. They were so lucky considering, they were the closest to the blast. I think two of their clerks lost limbs, though."

Chester exhaled a stream of smoke, "Fortunately, some had already thrown themselves to the floor when George shouted."

"Morning, everyone. Have you heard the total casualty figures yet?" Heinz walked onto the balcony and took a seat next to Susie.

Chester shook his head, "No, nothing since the update last night. It still stands at forty dead and another fifty injured. Anything on Marat and company?"

Heinz pulled a face as he poured a coffee. "Nothing, I'm afraid. I've just been talking to Manfred in Geneva. We've asked our network guys in Toronto and Japan to get their teams to run a sweep on the latest flight plans and shipping movements out of the main European ports and airports. They won't be stupid enough to use the obvious escape routes. But you never know, they might have made a small mistake. We have to cover all eventualities. We are trying to trace the identity of Marat's boss in America. The Corporatists will want to replace Marat as soon as possible. The obvious place to look would be to some homegrown American talent, somebody they can keep an eye on."

Chester leaned forward stubbed out his cigarette, "What about the helicopter pilots and the snatch squad? Have they been found?"

Heinz looked grim, "Executed. Shot in the head and left with the helicopters at a remote site in the middle of the Ardennes Forest. They were a smoking pile of ashes by the time we found them. Marat's prison uniforms and handcuffs were found at the site as well. They were obviously picked up by another team, destroyed anything that connected them with The Hague and disappeared to God knows where. The Belgian authorities have a forensic team there now. But we're not sure if they can be trusted.

Masquerade

We'll have to see. Having said that, we have the master of disappearing without a trace in our midst. What would you do, George?"

Dark shrugged, "It's obvious: you lie low, avoid as much contact with people as possible, look for the safest way of getting to sanctuary, then go off-grid."

They all looked dejected at the news. The three most senior figures in the Corporatist European paramilitary force had disappeared into thin air, just as Dark had done. So now the boot is on the other foot. The breakout had obviously been extremely well-planned by professionals, probably a Special Forces unit. Nothing had been left to chance, and they had covered their tracks efficiently, leaving no clues. To make so much progress at breaking the Corporatist's monopoly on the media only to fail at the last hurdle was hard to stomach.

Susie looked around at their downcast faces, "Come on. Let's not be too despondent. We did manage to expose the Corporatist's devious scheming to the public. At least now, the public realises these people have been exploiting them for decades. Chester has been belittled for years because he dared to publish the truth about the corrupt British Establishment. Now it's been proved he was right all along. That's something surely?"

Chester smiled thinly, "I know Susie. But we have won one battle. There is a war to win before we can say we have defeated these bastards. Don't forget, the public have short memories. We need to keep reminding them that the Corporatists exploit them constantly. Every day we need to tell the public they are being oppressed. With constant publicity, maybe we can keep the revolutionary bonfires burning."

Heinz agreed, "Chester is right. Our work isn't finished. But we have made a start, we have exposed the Corporatists, and there has been a massive outcry. We have been vindicated. Dark has fought this battle for five years. The network and I have been fighting for longer. Now I can say that two of my dearest friends didn't die in vain. We will need to keep reminding people that their politicians constantly lie to them and that multinational corporations regard them as nothing more than cash-generating automatons. We will need to counter the seductive propaganda of the ironically named *free press*. But my friends, we have taken the first steps on a long road to destroying the Corporatists' corrupt and cruel system."

Masquerade

Dark stood and walked slowly to the balcony. He paused for a moment gazing absentmindedly at a flotilla of yachts keeling over in the wind. He turned to face the group. "In that case, we need to plan our next move. Now that Marat and his cronies have gone to ground let's tempt them back into the open. Let's hit them where it hurts. Money. They do what they do for power and money. Let's disrupt their money supply."

Chester's eyes lit up. "Christ, you're right! We have attacked the way they wield power by exposing the way they use the media to subdue the public. After the attack on The Hague, we are credible commentators. Our version of events will be believed now."

Susie interrupted, "So if we use the free media to expose the connections between corporations and politicians, we can show money is changing hands. They will have to find an alternative."

Dark gave them the next step, "And the best way to expose the money trail is to expose the crooked bankers that help keep the Corporatists in power. If you think about it, the bankers funded the whole corrupt system."

Heinz looked around, "Well? What do you think? Sounds like a plan? Now, what we need is a man on the inside." He looked at Dark.

"Oh no! Not me again? Can't you find some other idiot to do your dirty work?"

"Not with your skills, we can't!"

THE END

Printed in Great Britain
by Amazon